T0088933

KING OF THE JUNGLE

FICTION

Kraftgriots

Also in the series (FICTION)

Funmilayo Adegbite: *Bonds of Destiny*
Frank U. Mowah: *Eating by the Flesh*
David Adenaike: *The Mystery Child*
Olu Obafemi: *Wheels*
Babatunde Omobowale: *Seasons of Rage*
Florence Attamah: *Melodies of a Dashed Dream*
Ifeoma Nwoye: *Death by Instalments*
Uche Nwabunike: *Forever She Cried*
Clement Idegwu: *Broken Dreams* (2000)
Vincent Egbuson: *Moniseks Country* (2001)
Vincent Egbuson: *A Poet is a Man* (2001)
Benedict Ibitokun: *Sopaisan: Westing Oodua* (2002)
Vincent Egbuson: *Love is not Dead* (2002)
Tayo Olafioye: *Grandma's Sun* (2004)
Ikechukwu Kalikwu: *The Voice from the Grave* (2005)
Wale Okediran: *The Weaving Looms* (2005)
Richard Maduku: *Arigo Again!* (2006)
Vincent Egbuson: *Womandela* (2006), *winner 2006 ANA/NDDC Ken Saro-Wiwa prose prize*
Abubakar Gimba: *Trail of Sacrifice* (2006)
Abubakar Gimba: *Innocent Victims* (2006)
Richard Ovuorho: *My Grandfather* (2007)
Abubakar Gimba: *Witnesses to Tears* (2007)
Abraham Nnadi: *Not by Justtification* (2008)
Majovo Amarie: *Suspended Destiny* (2008)
Abimbola Adelakun: *Under the Brown Rusted Roofs* (2008)
Richard Masagbor: *Labyrinths of a Beauty* (2008)
Kayode Animasaun: *A Gift for the Corper* (2008)
Liwhu Betiang: *Beneath the Rubble* (2009)
Vincent Egbuson: *Love My Planet* (2009), *winner 2008 ANA/NDDC Ken Saro-Wiwa prose prize*
Richard Maduku: *Kokoro Compound* (2009)
Ted Elemeforo: *Child of Destiny* (2009)
Yahaya Dangana: *Blow of Fate* (2009)
Jonathan E. Ifeanyi: *The Campus Genius* (2009)
Kayode Animasaun: *Perambulators* (2010)
Ozioma Izuora: *Dreams Deferred* (2010), *winner 2009 ANA/NDDC Ken Saro-Wiwa Prose Prize*
Victor Akande: *A Palace for the Slave* (2010)
E.L. Agukwe: *A Tale of Trioubaz* (2011)
Chris Okonta: *Trampled Rose* (2011)
Bolade Bamidele: *Wits Battle of Awareness* (2011)
Sam Omatseye: *The Crocodile Girl* (2011)
Ozioma Izuora: *Scavengers' Orgy* (2011)
Ozioma Izuora: *Merchants of Flesh* (2011)

KING OF THE JUNGLE

FICTION

Bizuum Yadok

kraftgriots

Published by

Kraft Books Limited
6A Polytechnic Road, Sango, Ibadan
Box 22084, University of Ibadan Post Office
Ibadan, Oyo State, Nigeria
✆ +234(0)803 348 2474, +234(0)805 129 1191
E-mail: kraftbooks@yahoo.com
Website: www.kraftbookslimited.com

First published 2014

ISBN 978–978–918–209–1

= KRAFTGRIOTS =
(A literary imprint of Kraft Books Limited)

First printing, November 2014

This book is for the woman who has been there from the very start – Hannatu Tercin Iliya

Acknowledgement

I couldn't have done this without the consent of the Divine, who also gave me the enablement. My parents, Mr & Mrs G.D Iliya, have constantly encouraged me in very many ways to write. Longtong, Zenret, Nandak, Dangsen, and Makrop gave me the push to finish the work when I almost gave up. They represent a small fraction of the entire Koduwam and Dukup families that supported me in no small ways.

Douglas Kaze would have flung the first draft to my face if he were me, but he patiently and assiduously read the draft. He made more useful suggestions than any other person who had gone through the manuscript. Biplang Yadok's critical thoughts gave birth to better ideas, and Manta Adamu noted errors that would have marred the work catastrophically. Emmanuel Shaiyen was there to lift me up when critics weighed me down, he literally forced me to the press. Niri Pam Shut added an invaluable touch to this work. Chalya Dul, Sabarka Aliyu, and Tongret David made useful observations for which I am grateful. My brother and friend, Ignatiaus Usar, has also been very supportive, morally and financially.

Kenneth Boniface, Longrin Wetten, Gideon Dashe, Samuel Wakdok, Yiro Abari, Dr.(Mrs) Anthonia Chukwu, Santos Larab, Smart Bako, Mrs Peace Longdet, Mr. Deme, and Lengshak Gomwalk have inspired me in many ways.

Dr. Dul Johnson treated the work as if it were his own. He remains a source of inspiration and a great mentor. Prof. Kanchana Ugbabe offered a motherly helping hand which could only be given by her alone. Prof. Isaac Lar, Mr. Godfrey Fwangs, Dr. (Mrs) Z.P Duguryil, Mr. Sati Lubis and Prof. (Mrs) O. M Ogunkeye have indirectly affected the work positively.

My friends: Zenret Gwankat, Tongshishak Danjuma, Samson Gotom, Sly, Jake, Gideon Dada, Rufina Tuamyil, Joey Tush, Henry Frank, Jerry Cole, Kim Choji, James Jimwan, Gwom Shut, strivers, Nanribet Ezra, Machizmo, the list is very long. They have helped in many little ways.

GOSA members, staff and students of BSS Gindiri, staff and students of FCE Pankshin, particularly the departments of English and Chemistry, have been immensely helpful.

One

The assembly hall of Plateau High School, also known as the J.D. Gomwalk Hall, was filled with students, parents and invited guests. Balloons of different colours hung on the four corners of the ceiling. At the centre of the ceiling, light-coloured satin ribbons connected the balloons in an X shape. Giwa gazed at the ceiling for a while appreciating its aesthetic composition. As if to compare, he turned to the wall on his left. Above each of the seven large windows were jumbo-sized photographs of past principals including that of the incumbent — Mr. Dodo.

While all the six past principals wore smiling faces in their photos, Mr. Dodo maintained an indifferent face in his; whether he was happy or sad, only God could tell. The first three photographs from the front had faces of white men. The others were pictures of natives from various parts of the country. The wall on the right was densely covered at the top by framed pictures of past headboys. The picture of the present headboy wasn't there, Mr. Dodo promised it would be hung by the next term — if a space could be created.

The guest speaker was delivering a long speech. Giwa had read his copy of the speech twice already, but the speaker was still reading his speech, pausing at intervals to illustrate with anecdotes, and sometimes in Pidgin or Hausa. More than half of the students in the hall buried their heads in their papers while they dozed. Giwa glanced at his wristwatch. It was 2:00pm and the speaker was still not through. Turning backward and looking at photographs of different sets of final year students, he observed the tall muscular SS3 boys of the early 80s as well as the motherly girls of their sets. In one of the pictures, Mr. Dodo was sandwiched between two fat girls. Evidently, he never grew taller after his secondary school. Among the girls of 1996 set was Amina Zubairu, Giwa's school-mother. Giwa reminisced about the good times he had with her. She was known as B & B by most students because she was beautiful and brilliant. She never dated a fellow schoolmate unlike other senior girls who were socially compelled to have a relationship with their classmates, seniors, and, occasionally but secretly, with their juniors. The "hard girls" went for NYSC members because that made them to feel superior to their mates.

Amina Zubairu won all prizes in the science class during their speech and prize-giving day. She was also the best student in English and Economics. She became the cynosure of all eyes and everyone, but Mr. Dodo, was dying to pose for a picture with her. Her prizes were rather too heavy for her to carry, so her darling son, Giwa, helped out with some of the books. Her female friends had a myriad of reasons to envy her, but Giwa could not blame them because he would have done the same, or even worse, if he were in their shoes.

Amina and Giwa had something more than a blood relationship. She was the older sister he never had. She probably was drawn to him when she discovered his remarkable performance in class, and being a brilliant person; it was only natural for their kind to attract each other although they had a lot of differences. Amina was a Muslim, an extrovert and a lover of sports; Giwa was a Christian and an introvert who tolerated sports because of Amina. However, the mutual love they had for each other was boundless. Sometimes, she was called Mamman Giwa and she was proud to bear that name.

An Achilles heel for Amina would lie in her religious obligation. She hardly cared about covering her hair or even saying the morning and evening prayers. During the holy month of Ramadan, Amina would sneak out to eat, and still pretend to be fasting. These and other acts of impiety invoked dislike from her Muslim sisters but she wasn't bothered.

There she was in the picture smiling at Giwa. He longed to see her again.

"Thank you all for listening." The guest speaker finally finished his speech in a tedium that enwrapped the hall, then the students clapped their hands more out of boredom than appreciation. The tone of the clap conveyed tonnes of ingratitude. Giwa's attention was drawn to the stage. Chief Dr. Thomas Bello, as he loved to be called, wore a frown as he made for his seat. He must have decoded the unsaid words of the students.

Why won't he restrategize his type of speech, Giwa wondered.

The high table was sufficiently supplied with soft drinks, bottled water and snacks wrapped in foil. Two SS2 girls stood, one at each end of the stage with an opener to serve any of the guests who wanted a drink. A guest, a fat man, had already finished the drinks on his table and saved the bottled water for the last.

The stage backdrop had a large mural of a figure, silhouetted against the white background, broadcasting grains on a field with a calabash in his hands. Above the man's head was a bold inscription, "WHATEVER A MAN SOWS, THAT HE MUST REAP". Mr. Dodo read this over and over during assembly, especially when defaulting students were about to be lashed, suspended or expelled, depending on the magnitude of their misdemeanor.

After this moment, we shall all be free, free to do whatever we want to do and whenever we want to do it. Giwa thought. While the final year students were ready to launch vigorously into the "wider world", Giwa was ambitious and determined to make money with the speed of lightning. He hated arrogant children who prided themselves on their parents' wealth, those ones with closed ears and wide-open mouths. They were never willing to learn yet ever willing to teach what they do not know. Yanga was one of such prima donnas. Yanga was at it again this afternoon, sniggering at the guest speaker when everyone pretended to be sober after the Principal motioned them to stop their prolonged rude clap. He sat in the row before Giwa.

"And now, the moment we all have been waiting for, particularly you students and, of course, parents. We shall start from the bottom to the top, that is from JSS1, JSS 2...."

Mr. Samson, the English teacher for the senior classes, taught with obvious ostentation. It was said that he sat for his WAEC SSCE six times before making it into the university to study English where he graduated with a third-class degree. He was always careful to pronounce English words properly and sometimes, though rarely, he spoke pidgin with a crude British accent. For most school programmes, Mr. Samson was privileged to be the MC for lack of resources to hire a renowned MC. Usually, when teaching a class, he sauntered with his hands in his pocket while his notes lay on the table. He maintained a straight posture with his head hanging in the air. Nothing has changed about him today; he still wore the same attitude, resplendent in a white caftan and black sandals.

The village head of Vom was invited to give out the prizes to the best students of JSS1. He shook hands with the students after giving them their prizes while the photographers took pictures. A roar of thunderous applauses was heard whenever students were called to receive their prizes

Everyone was excited during this session of the programme. Some students whistled to cheer their friends while others stood up to clap. It was quite easier to identify with success.

As the MC approached the top of the list, Giwa became apprehensive; a drop of sweat trickled down from his hair and rolled onto his cheek. Mock SSCE results determined who emerged as the best student in every subject. The SS3 students had taken their WAEC SSCE and were on the verge of finishing their NECO. Giwa had put in his best, he promised Amina he was going to bag at least an award too, eventhough she was not there, he knew his promise must be kept.

"Now the champions in every subject..." Mr. Samson's sonorous voice echoed in the hall and made Giwa's heart beat two times faster. His lips twitched as his legs quivered. From nowhere, the phrase "What a man sows..." entered his head, of course in Mr. Dodo's voice. Giwa knew that ten more minutes in his present apprehensive mood would render him a dead man, but he could not control a reflex.

Abigail tapped him from behind. "Don't worry you are going home with five prizes."

"How did you know?" Giwa responded in a low tone amidst the mumbling of students.

"Just trust me na!" She squeezed her face innocuously and beamed a smile.

"Thanks anyway," Giwa replied as he turned to face the stage, holding back the "*Ameboh*" he readily would say on a normal day because of her soothing words which could be true, or false, or somewhere in-between. Anyone who believes that there is an iota of truth in every rumour would definitely believe the words of Abigail. Abigail Akinwumi, also known as 'Ameboh', was the primary source of almost every rumour in the school community. Mr. Dodo was very fond of her because she always supplied him with news of secret hostel activities. Clever students got acquainted with Abigail in order to know Mr. Dodo's intention, what happened in every staff briefing and domestic vices within the staff. Some staff members also relied on her to know what was happening in the principal's office.

Giwa paid attention to her whenever she spoke; she was his major source of information in the school, and she could even pay one to listen to her. Her company was most desirable in the afternoons because aside from the free information, she bought him lunch just to listen to her. Giwa was always careful not to comment on any story she told him because he was sure to hear the same story elsewhere with his comment inclusive. Most probably, Mr. Dodo employed the same "no comment" tactic to hide his intentions from Abigail.

"Can we please have some quiet in the hall? Parents and students, please be patient, the programme is coming to an end but not without your co-operation." Mr. Samson's voice emanated from the speakers positioned at the four corners of the hall. Everyone was eager to leave the hall so a level of silence was attained. "Thank you for understanding. Without much ado we shall proceed to dish out awards to SS3 students that have distinguished themselves in various subjects. Once, I aspired to receive an award too but now I have the privilege of calling out the names of the awardees which is as good as receiving the award. Afterall, it is more blessed to give than to receive hahaha..." Mr. Samson had a good sense of humour which he used whenever he wanted to ease tension in the hall.

"To the award recipients, we shall also add an award to the best science student, best social science student and best arts student. To him who has, more shall be added unto him, no be so?"

In unison, students and parents alike responded with a loud "Na so!" This was one of the rare occasions when Mr. Samson would let out a few words in Pidgin in order to hold the attention of the audience.

"We would like to invite Mrs. Keziah Nyam, the Special Assistant to the Governor's wife, to present these awards to the students that have excelled academically."

Mr. Samson had bowed about three times as he spoke facing her before she stood up. "Let's give her a round of applause as she walks to the centre of the stage: Mrs. Keziah Nyam, looking very gorgeous, elegant, adorable...." The sheepish smile, of a flattered person, pulled the ends of her lips to the shores of her cheeks as she walked to the centre. She was well adorned with beads on her neck, wrists and ears. Standing at the centre of the stage, her lips spasmodically tried to conceal her dazzling teeth, she released dozens of smiles.

"For the best student in Economics, we have ... Giwa Bako!" Electrified, at that instant he felt like his ears were not attached to his head.

"Oh! Giwa, my Giwa," Ameboh resounded his name.

Your Giwa? Since when? Not even Jemimah, the girl who had turned down his well-rehearsed wooing words with a blatant "No!" could call him her own. But Abigail was calling him her own. Giwa stood up and began walking to the stage to receive his prize with his heart palpitating. He suddenly became conscious of his steps and walked a bit majestically. Uncle Harry's voice came clearly as though he was there himself saying "Miracles happen when you least expect them."

"Well done, Senior Giwa," Manji whispered and touched Giwa's trousers as he passed by his side. He believed that by merely touching his mentor he would absorb some of Giwa's intellect. Giwa simply winked at Manji in response. Manji was Giwa's roommate. He had great admiration for Giwa; he wanted to be like Giwa in all spheres. Giwa's eyes caught Mr. Dodo looking at him and he tried to avoid looking through those transparent pair of glasses as a sign of respect. He bent his head downwards as though he was shy but was actually ensuring that his shirt was neatly tucked into his trousers. When he was sure of that, he fixed his gaze on the prizes on the large table. Mr. Dodo had warned them the previous day that he would not tolerate any form of disobedience on this glorious day. He threatened that he would send anyone who was not properly dressed out of the hall even if the person was about to receive a prize. Giwa wouldn't want to dare Mr. Dodo, at least not on this happy day. He tripped and almost fell when climbing the stage.

"Yes! This is Giwa, please keep on clapping." The English teacher scrutinized Giwa with his eyes, as if he was looking for a blemish that would deter Giwa from receiving his prize. Giwa felt like a national award winner, as he politely bowed to receive his prize, a few camera flash lights pounced on him and Mrs. Nyam. She shook him warmly with a loud smile on her face, her hands felt like soft cotton wool, the skin on her arms and neck was darker than her fair-complexioned face. Miss. Renault, the French teacher, was in charge of sorting out the prizes according to the names of the recipients. All the prizes were either textbooks or books congruous with one's area of distinction, or inspirational books neatly wrapped in a silver-coloured pattern sheet.

"Ladies and gentlemen, Giwa has also distinguished himself as the best English student, best Government student, best Commerce student, and best Geography student in addition to being the best Economics student." Mr. Samson kept talking as Miss Renault quickly sorted out the prizes, five of them in all, and handed them to Mrs. Keziah Nyam for a ceremonial handshake with Giwa.

Mrs. Nyam squeezed his hand before giving each prize and kept saying, amidst loud cheers, and thunderous clapping, "I wish you were my son, your mother must be very proud of you."

Giwa simply replied, "Thank you ma."

It all looked like heaven with thousands of angels shouting "Giwa! Giwa! Giwa!" He couldn't believe that even some of the staff were shouting his name. Tears of joy rolled down his cheek. He wished that his mother, uncle, sister or any of his blood was there to share in his glory. Armed with his prizes, he took two steps off but heard: "Giwa, please come back, we are yet to finish with you." It was Mr. Samson again. "This boy is also the best Social Science student." Miss Renault swiftly handed Giwa a small gold-coloured shield with an inscription, boldly written: GIWA BAKO, BEST SOCIAL SCIENCE STUDENT, 2000 SET. She then realized that the shield should have followed a chain from her to Mrs. K. Nyam and then to the recipient. Mrs. Keziah Nyam looked at Miss Renault with eyes that seemed to say, "What is wrong with you?" An apologetic smile was given in response. Having comprehended the unspoken words, Mrs. Keziah Nyam nodded her head and turned to face the increasingly cheerful fans of Giwa as he went down the stage.

Perplexed and feeling so nervous, all that could come out of Giwa's mouth was "Thank you Lord," facing the ceiling, "we have made it to the beginning of this journey." Giwa stole the day. He did. When he finally sat down, the hall was in disarray; some junior students used the opportunity to sneak out and felicitate with their friends who were already taking snapshots with their prizes. In vain, Mr. Samson tried to call the attention of everyone. Seeing that he failed with the majority, he called out the names of other distinguished students amidst the noise.

"Ladies and gentlemen, we are about to round off." There was silence in the hall. Nobody wanted to miss the last minutes. "Now, for the best overall student who has distinguished himself, academically and in character, I present Giwa Bako!"

Giwa received a Gold medal and before he went down again,

Dauda, the strongest student, lifted Giwa on his shoulders and went out of the hall. Many students followed, chanting "Giwa! Giwa! Giwa!"

Two

Silence was adequately saturated in the whole of Tambes village. That was the first time that anything of its kind had occurred. Under the shade of the gigantic African olive tree, the elders of Tambes village convened for an emergency meeting.

Bakka, and Ladi, the chief's third wife, stood at the centre of the circle formed by the elders. Bakka faced the earth wishing it would open up and swallow him. He felt so ashamed that he was caught in an adulterous act with Ladi who was not just a woman but a married woman, and the chief's favourite wife at that. Even the birds and other animals understood that a heinous crime had been committed, the goats went foraging around without bleating unnecessarily, he-goats grazed along, they too did not disturb. The village came to a standstill, it seemed.

Ladi posed contumaciously beside Bakka. She hummed to herself and cared less about the consequences of her action; she had just been caught sleeping with a local farmer. It was her third time at the illicit act and she was caught for the first time. She was ready to die having satisfied her long desire. Da Powan, her father, had forced her into marrying the chief against her wish. The chief picked interest in her as a child and insisted on having her as his third wife when she blossomed into maturity. Da Powan quickly seized the opportunity to demand for a large piece of fertile land which belonged to the chief. They happily exchanged possessions oblivious of the fact that a hideous day like this might come. Da Powan buried his head in shame. He did not raise it up until the Chief cleared his throat to speak.

"My elders, you have now heard the disgraceful thing that happened between my wife and this infidel," he pointed at Bakka with his staff. "I want you to suggest what is to be done immediately. But before then, I want Da Kupshak to tell us whether such evil has ever happened in this village and if it did, what was the punishment for the offenders." The chief motioned Da Kupshak to speak as he sat down.

Da Kupshak stood up with the help of his third leg. He shuffled a few steps forward and eased his weight on the stick, then he cleared his throat to speak.

"Live long my chief, elders of the village. It is true that an act, almost of this magnitude, has once occurred in this village about seventy years ago between an unmarried man and another man's wife. Both of them were banished from this land and have never returned since then." He looked up to the sky then he redirected his gaze downwards, he raised his head and continued. "However, this case is different, they are both married and she is the chief's wife..."

Ladi cut in, "Can't I love the man I want because I am the chief's wife?"

"Will you shut up that impudent mouth before I shut it up for you?" Her father almost pounced on her but for the timely intervention of the other elders. He continued raining curses on her until the chief called for order.

The chief stood up once again. He waved his staff at Da Kupshak imploring him to take his seat. "Da Powan, I want to remind you that the woman you were about to lay your hands on is my wife even though she is your daughter, she is my burden to bear. Bakka!" pointing at him with his staff, "you will leave this village before dawn tomorrow. You may take your wife and children if you wish. As for you Ladi; you will remain permanently in the compound." He searched the faces of the elders for approval of his biased judgment. Many of them consented with nods, Da Powan shook his head while the oldest man in the village, Da Kupshak, remained indifferent. Seeing that he had earned majority of the votes he dismissed the elders and headed for his hut.

Ladi eyed the elders contemptuously as each one of them took his leave. At last, only two of them remained. She became glum when she looked at Bakka knowing she was the cause of the fate that had befallen him. She raised her hand to console him but he violently shoved her away and walked towards the direction of his house with his eyes fixed on the path till he reached home.

Bakka was among the skillful hunters of Tambes village. He was also a sedulous farmer though he ploughed a small piece of land as his own apart from the commercial farming he did for other people in the village. Farming was his source of livelihood. Bakka faced many challenges growing up as an orphan. His parents were victims of a deadly cholera outbreak that nearly wiped out his clan. His nephew, Haruna, was his only surviving relative. They were treated as outcasts because it was believed that most of their clan members who died were witches and wizards. It was widely speculated that the gods sent the disease to purify the village. Bakka and Haruna lived at the outskirts of the village, across the stream that flowed between the village and its farmlands. Bakka became, more or less, the village farmer, tilling and ploughing the land for paltry sums of money. Most of the money he earned was used to send Haruna to a primary school. On countless occasions, he was hired by Da Powan to plough his land. It was there that Ladi fell for him. She nursed the thought of marrying him in her heart but her dreams were shattered when her father declared that she would become the chief's next bride.

Bakka believed in no gods, he viewed every event as a product of chance or circumstance. He believed firmly in doing good. Nanlep, his wife, was also an orphan; that was why it was easy for him to marry her, though he paid what seemed to him a fortune for her bride price. Her uncle was more in a hurry to dispose of her probably in order to buy himself enough beer for a month since he was an alcoholic.

At twilight, just as Bakka reached his door-step, he halted. He had betrayed his family, his one-year-old marriage and two-months-old son. Haruna would not be happy about it too. He couldn't go back now; he could not forfeit his house. He summoned courage and stepped inside.

Nanlep stared at the lantern but she wasn't looking at it; her mind was far away. Tears trickled down from her eyes uncontrollably. From the look on her face, she had wept all day. The baby sucked her much exposed breast voraciously yet she seemed unmindful of that. She was motionless.

Dead silence enveloped the room as Bakka entered and saw the demented figure of his wife. He was dumb for some minutes. His wife decided to help him out.

"What did the elders say?" She said, still gazing at the lantern.

Bakka inched closer. "Sorry about what happened... I did not do it intentionally... I am..." Before he finished speaking, she cut in.

"What did the elders say?" She asked again amidst sobs.

"I was sentenced appropriately, I leave this village before dawn. The better for me, where else would I hide my shame?" He sat down on the bench. He didn't ask for food or water. Guilt was enough to satisfy him.

Bakka searched for words that would lighten her mood but found none. Telling Haruna and watching his reaction would be another cumbersome task but he was caught between the devil and the deep blue sea; either way, he was doomed. The young man also fixed his gaze at the lantern for some minutes. He gathered courage and asked,

"How is our son?"

"As you can see." She examined the baby's head and balanced him on her back with the help of her wrapper. "I am going with you, I can't stay here alone," she said, now looking at her husband's face. Bakka couldn't believe the words that came out of her mouth but they were real, she was not the kind of person that would joke with tears on her face. He didn't know when tears flowed from his own eyes. He stood up and embraced his wife and they both cried hard.

Haruna returned from the stream just as Bakka dried his eyes.

"We are leaving this village as early as possible tomorrow morning," he declared to Haruna.

"Okay." Haruna knew better than to ask any questions in view of the prevailing circumstances. The whole village had learnt of Bakka's banishment even before he reached home. Haruna was told at the stream.

Bakka sold all his landed property that night, including his five goats, for a worthless sum that would hardly last him and his wife a month. He dug open a hole where he buried some precious stones given him by his father before he died and loaded them into his goat-skin bag. They ate to their fill that night and set out at the first cockcrow. They bid farewell to the village that showed them little love and respect, the place they had called home.

The banished family trekked for days, settling in different places until their food was finished. They stopped at a place called Zonkwa. With the help of Haruna who could speak little English and Hausa, they were able to secure a room at a missionary's boys' quarters for the night.

The next day, Bakka was employed as a gardener, Ladi as a housemaid, and Haruna was guaranteed completion of his primary school education. In a short while, Bakka and his family became

Christians. His little son was named David by Pastor Derek, one of the last breed of missionaries of the Sudan United Mission, who was also Bakka's host. For some preposterous reason, Bakka chose to call his son Giwa, which in Hausa means 'an elephant'. Pastor Derek's wife, Mildred, preferred to call Haruna 'Harry'. Haruna was always pleased whenever he was addressed as Harry. He wasted no time in adopting the name Harry even on his notebooks and textbooks.

Bakka did not hesitate to show his farming abilities to the village. Here again, he was gainfully employed by many people to the extent that earned more than he could spend. Haruna brought up the idea of land acquisition and before long Bakka owned large hectres of land in a land that knew him not. The people of Zonkwa, unable to pronounce his name correctly, referred to him as Bako, 'guest'. He became popular with the name and it gradually came to replace the original name, Bakka.

After three years, Bakka, or Bako, sent Harry to a secondary school, Plateau High School, in Vom, a growing town about thirty kilometers from Jos. During Harry's second year, Pastor Derek was retired from the missionary work and called back home in England. He handed over his house and almost everything he owned to Bakka and his family. In exchange for Derek's kind gesture, Bakka brought out his goat-skin bag, from it, he gave Derek a handful of glittering precious stones. They sparkled under the sunlight. Derek's eyes blinked, his mouth hung open and his face shone like the sun. Pastor Derek was more appreciative of the precious stones than Bakka was of the house. Nanlep could not be consoled as she wept when Derek and his family were leaving. They were the only people that appreciated them and showed them love in a way they had never experienced before. Indeed, Derek's family was the only true family Bakka and his wife knew.

Giwa grew speedily in stature and wisdom, his father's son. Soon afterward, Nanlep gave birth to a girl. They called her Kyauta but Bakka fondly called her Maama for two reasons: firstly, mama was her very first word and she called it for months before inculcating other words into her fragile brain. And secondly, she was a carbon copy of her mother.

Things moved well for the family, Giwa had started primary school, Bakka acquired more lands and Harry excelled in his academics. They were living in peace until tragedy struck; Bakka was infected with cerebrospinal meningitis, he refused to go to the hospital thinking that it was just a pain in the neck that it would disappear like any other. Finally, when he couldn't endure the pain, he willed over his possessions to Harry on his death bed. Harry was given the mantle of headship of the family. Bakka gave up the ghost and was buried in Zonkwa. The whole village mourned his death; it was as if the chief was dead. At such a tender age Giwa was confused but he kept asking about his father. Since Harry was not such a farmer himself, he began to sell Bakka's lands one by one in order to pay his fees at the university as well as Giwa's, and also to provide for the family's basic needs.

At the time Harry graduated from the university as a medical doctor, Giwa was due to commence secondary school. Harry had sold all the farmlands Bakka had acquired in order to cater for the family's needs, and of course his wants too, save for one large piece of land which Nanlep cultivated annually.

Giwa passed the entrance examination of Plateau High School as well as the interview. News about Giwa's success in the exams spread round the town like wild fire, being the only pupil to gain admission into the prestigious Plateau High School among other pupils that sat for the exams. Many elders congratulated him, often with a handshake followed by some naira coins. Usually when Giwa was sighted, fingers pointed at him. "This is the only boy, in the whole of Zonkwa that passed the common entrance examination of PHS," was one of such comments that ensued. Many mothers wished he was their son. His fame in the town rapidly increased and in no distant time he became a celebrated local champion.

Harry was overjoyed when he heard of Giwa's success, he promised to pay for his education and any other thing he may need. He kept to his word. Giwa moved to Harry's place even before he started secondary school. Harry took care of his only family as if he was their father, ensuring that they were not lacking anything. Giwa eventually started schooling and things began to take shape for the family until Harry got married when Giwa was in JSS 3.

Regular packages of foodstuff and provisions which Harry usually sent ceased. He devoted less time to visiting his foster mother until he stopped completely. Two 'Ws' occupied Harry's mind - his 'wife' and his 'work'. To Giwa, Harry became practically insane, remote-controlled by his one and only wife whom he loved dearly and thought the feeling was mutual.

* * * * *

Giwa was not pleased with the fact that he was going home, particularly because this was not a normal break; he was not going to come back to school again, at least not as a student. The thought of that alone bruised his emotion but not more than the thought of meeting his mortal torturer - Aunty Mercy.

Giwa wore his saddest mood as he journeyed home. He recaptured his last moments in school: Jemimah's last hug amidst tears with a vow to keep in touch, her love came too late, he hoped it could be reciprocated if space brought them closer in the future. He thought about the hilarious Duff and the stubborn Gasko, his former room-mates who taught him how to drink alcohol outside the school's boundary. Thankfully, they were expelled shortly after they began teaching him so he dropped the habit. Giwa would never forget his last meal with his juniors. Tears brimmed in his eyes, feeling that he would never meet some of them again. Jemimah's note was still in the grip of his fingers. He unfolded it and read it for the twentieth time:

Time and space may pass away
but I cannot forget you
You mean a lot to me
I love you with all my heart
Jemm

Could this be love? Away from school, he gawked at the trees and shrubs which appeared to be running against the car. Giwa leaned back, then he wound down the glass beside him so that the breeze would caress him and maybe make him feel better.

"Eureka," he shouted unconsciously, which drew the attention of other passengers in the in the taxi who until that moment were mute. An idea struck his mind. He would spend a few days at Harry's place then go to Zonkwa to see his mother and his sister. Giwa had agreed with himself that he was going to stay there till he got admission. That was the only possible way for him to have peace of mind.

The car began to jerk and slowly decelerated, but the driver was able to manouvre the car to the pedestrian lane before it stopped. He got out of the car, went straight to the bonnet and opened it. The passengers began to complain amidst issues, some were blaming the government while others blamed the drivers. Giwa blamed it on both; it was the same thing to him. After a quick look, the driver shut the bonnet and returned to announce that the fuel was exhausted. The voices grew louder this time, the angry passengers began to curse both the driver and the country but they lowered their voices when the driver brought out a gallon of petrol which he would use to siphon the fuel into his car. The car came alive again and it didn't stop till Giwa reached home. He looked at the gate and he shook his head.

Giwa struggled under the weight of his box and his mattress, the load in his heart made it worse for him. Whisky barked at Giwa from a distance but he scurried forward, wiggling his tail when he recognized Giwa. "Whisky! Whisky! My boy!" Giwa said as Whisky hurriedly came and pounced on him. His first and warmest welcome home was given to him by Whisky. It wagged its tail profusely. Whisky did everything but literally said 'welcome' to show Giwa how happy he was to see him. "I would rather live in a house full of Whiskys than live in a house with one Aunty Mercy," Giwa would often say. The only reason Whisky was content staying outside the house was because of Aunty Mercy. It avoided her at all times and she too detested it with every fibre of her nerves.

Kauna sat under the huge mango tree which stood a few metres away from the house. Aunty Mercy's sister; the last child in their family. Kauna rose to her feet to welcome Giwa. She was reluctant to usher him in and spoke in a low tone. He was too tired to decode the signals she was making and hurriedly walked into the house, he didn't know when Kauna stayed back. Whisky happily followed Giwa until he was about to enter the house, the dog backed away. Apparently, Aunty Mercy was inside the house.

The door to the sitting room was ajar, Giwa went straight into the sitting room and he was stunned by what he saw. Utterly confused, he did not know when he said, "Good morning... Uncle...eh!...uh... Good evening Aunty Mercy..." This time he knew how Moses in the Bible felt when he saw the burning bush. He dropped his mattress and box, anticipating anything including death as his punishment for witnessing a secret affair.

At the time Giwa arrived, Aunty Mercy was deep in the throes of passion: She was ensconced in the arms of her lover, who was pawing and kissing her on the three-sitter sofa. She was moaning in wild ecstasy until Giwa's voice came through. She opened her eyes and before her was a dumbfounded Giwa, too astounded to say anything further. They weren't making love yet, but if he didn't appear, they would have peaked their foreplay.

Her lover turned out to be Mr. Zakary, Uncle Harry's best friend; he was also working in the hospital, a father of three and a deacon in the church. He also heard Giwa's voice then he came to himself. He couldn't say a word; he stood up and paced a little, scratching his head and grunting. Aunty Mercy was shocked too but being the kind of person she was, she simply adjusted her creased dress, which had ridden up her thighs. She instantly assumed a ferocious countenance, her shaggy hair made her look more ferocious as she approached Giwa.

"So you have the guts, the audacity to enter my house without knocking the door! *Eh*! What did you think the door was meant for eh?" Her eyes were wide and her venomous tongue unleashed thunder on Giwa as she yelled.

"I'm sorry ... the door..." He swallowed a growing ball in his throat. "The door was wide open and I didn't know you were arou—" A hot sweaty palm landed on his cheek before he could finish speaking.

"Lies! Wretched liar! You knew I was busy inside and you still came in. You have just pronounced your death sentence, from today onward it's going to be me and you, you hear?" she gave him a knock on the head. "What did I say?" squeezing his right ear as he repeated after her and saying it together "me and you."

Mr. Zakary was still staring at the floor, probably wishing that he could disappear into the air. His hand wandered through his hair looking for something that was not there. He cursed himself under his breath.

Giwa waited for the worst but it seemed she had done her worst. "What are you still waiting for? Will you get your things inside your room? Nonsense!" Without a tinge of hesitation Giwa trudged to his bedroom.

He locked the room as he entered. Giwa did not feel sorry for himself as much as he felt for Uncle Harry who had a whore as a wife and a backstabber as a friend. From his room he could hear Mr. Zakary barking at Aunty Mercy. "It is not the poor boy's fault, you were supposed to coax him so that he won't tell Harry, I'm ruined now, all thanks to you! See what you have caused now."

"Zaky!" She called in a pleading tone. "Sorry it turned out this way. I promise it won't happen again." She came closer as if to embrace him but he pushed her away.

"Don't even try anything funny!" He warned sternly with an accusing finger directly pointed at her face. "No games until you follow the rules! My rules!" He jerked his suitcase and stormed out of the house. She wanted to say goodbye but he slammed the door to her face. It was enough to show how mad he was.

Aunty Mercy hissed and turned backwards. She went to Giwa's room and knocked hard before he answered. Giwa put on sleepy eyes and yawned loudly when he opened the door. She stood at the door, still looking scary but not as she was a few minutes before.

"Listen," she said, "nothing will happen to you as long as you keep your dirty mouth shut concerning what happened this afternoon. If you dare mention as much as a word about what happened, I will make sure you lie beside your father's grave the next morning. You hear me? Say nothing!" she turned and headed for the sitting room, without looking at Giwa she said, "you can fetch your food in the kitchen but take nothing more than a piece of meat from my pot of soup."

That was one of Aunty Mercy's ways of saying "welcome."

Three

Uncle Harry arrived at about 7:30pm. Kauna informed him that Giwa had arrived. Uncle Harry dropped his coat and bag on the sofa in the sitting room; he called Giwa while walking towards his room. Giwa opened his door just as Uncle Harry was about to knock.

"Hey my son, come and give me a hug." He threw his arms around Giwa and gave him a warm embrace. That was the second time Uncle Harry embraced Giwa, the first time was when Giwa got admission to Plateau High School. "I am really proud of you," Uncle Harry declared. "Where are the prizes? Bring them out let me see!"

"He didn't tell me he won any prizes o!" Aunty Mercy intruded, she briskly walked up to her husband and hugged him.

"Welcome honey. Hope you had a wonderful day?" She gently rubbed Giwa's hair and picked a strand of wool from it. "The boy came in and locked himself inside until this moment, I think he misses school a lot." She winked at Giwa menacingly to remind him of their deal.

Giwa simply hung his head down as though he was shy but he decoded the message. *Witch! Bitch! Slut! Whore! You are everything but a faithful wife.* Looking up to Uncle Harry's face, he smiled, *Shine your eyes!* Giwa yelled loudly in his mind but the smile on his face veneered his thoughts. Then he spoke up, "the prizes are inside my bag, should I get them?"

"Yes please," Uncle Harry replied.

"The boy works so hard in school, I believe he will definitely take after you," Aunty Mercy remarked. Uncle Harry caressed his beard in a way that showed he was thinking critically.

"I am just an understatement of what this boy will be; I can see a rising star in that boy. He reminds me so much of his father who was a very hardworking man."

The young boy came out with a pile of books in his hands, "These are the prizes — what I have worked hard for." Giwa proudly stated hoping it would invoke Aunty Mercy's envy. The prizes included a dictionary and a Holy Bible.

"Wow! These books are expensive, I am very proud of you son." Harry looked into Giwa's eyes. His eyes confirmed what he said. "I should have paid more fees then," he examined each of the books while skimming the notes on the back covers. "We will go for lunch tomorrow, I will take you shopping and I will ..."

"It's okay! Remember you have not finished payment for the piece of land at Rayfield," Aunty Mercy interrupted Uncle Harry. It was deliberate, she knew he would have made more promises and that was what she would not condone. Uncle Harry's characteristic way of being generous largely depended on his mood; the more excited he was, the more he was likely going to give.

"Your dinner is on the table honey! I am sure you don't want to eat Giwa's prizes for your dinner, I won't allow you to waste my food o!"

"Giwa, let me go and eat before your Aunty crucifies me for not eating her food."

"No stay now! You may as well feed on his books" pointing at Giwa's books which fell on the floor, "and I will bring you some water to push it down." Aunty Mercy said, and all three of them laughed as Harry made for the dinning table.

Aunty Mercy watched him go until she was sure that Uncle Harry was out of earshot. She turned to Giwa who had already finished arranging his books and was about to enter his room, her smile immediately constricted. She inched closer to Giwa and whispered. "As we agreed earlier, not one word from your smelling mouth or else..." She snapped her finger and hurriedly left. Giwa watched her disappear behind the curtain then he shook his head and went into his bedroom.

Uncle Harry had always counted Aunty Mercy as a blessing to his life. Unknown to him, she was a curse in disguise, she had been married to Uncle Harry for four years without a single child, although she took in every year — so she made them to believe.

Aunty Mercy was a second child in a family of eight children of which the last was Kauna. Her father was a peasant farmer and her mother a petty trader. Although Aunty Mercy was undeniably the prettiest lady in her family, she had the worst character in her immediate as well as her extended family. She had been eclipsed by her ego right from her tender age. She tried to please herself alone in everything that she did at the detriment of her siblings. Being the most beautiful girl in the family, Aunty Mercy believed that every good thing should come to her first before any other member of the house, preferably the one she had chosen.

Harry first met her at a friend's party, a bachelor's eve. Aunty Mercy was among the girls hired to keep the men company. Harry had a flair for beautiful ladies but he never knew that Mercy was going to be the last of the beautiful girls in his diary. She was his date for the night and the next morning, she insisted on following him home. At that time, Uncle Harry was living with Giwa, just the two of them in a large and well furnished apartment. When she came into the house, she didn't want to go out.

A large fish had been caught in her hook, she mustered all her gimmicks to ensure that the fish eventually fell into her basket. She inquired about his small family and before long, a strong relationship followed. Aunty Mercy would take out time to personally visit Giwa in school, buy him provisions and give him some money. Sometimes she visited Giwa's mother, who readily pronounced her as her daughter-in-law. Aunty Mercy often came to spend the weekend with Harry and Giwa. On such weekends, Giwa only had to eat and the table would be cleared by her.

After three months, Aunty Mercy came in one morning to say that she was pregnant. Harry became confused so he proposed an abortion to her but she refused and wept bitterly until he married her and she became their tormentor. Giwa was among those that encouraged Harry to marry Aunty Mercy, his mother too. For their reward, they got a halt in the supply of their foodstuff and household items. As for Giwa, he became the house-boy. That was a costly mistake that Giwa wouldn't want to repeat, given the same option in another world.

The next morning, Aunty Mercy sent Giwa on different errands not allowing him to talk to Harry for at least five minutes, she already knew what the outcome would be — Uncle Harry would set up an appointment with Giwa in order to fulfil the promises he made to Giwa the previous night. Somehow Harry understood her pranks. As he was about to enter his car, he called Giwa outside but Aunty Mercy followed him, she didn't leave a leaking hole.

"Unhm...uh..Giwa!" Harry stammered when he saw Aunty Mercy trailing a few steps behind his boy. "Your room...tidy it up and carefully arrange those books eh! I will see you when I come back." Facing his wife, he said; "Prepare my favourite dish for dinner tonight." It doesn't take more than two days after meeting Harry to know that his most cherished delicacy was yam and beans porridge with spinach and dry fish. He switched on the ignition, the engine was quietly roaring.

"You are my own patient, I take care of you and you take care of many patients, so more or less, I am the real doctor, doctor of the doctor. Heh! Hehe!" Aunty Mercy's humour was always alive whenever she wanted to avoid any suspicion. She smiled broadly, pronouncing her dimples which unarguably made her look more beautiful to her husband or any other person she deluded but not Giwa.

Harry zoomed off and left Giwa and Kauna at the mercy of Aunty Mercy. She turned to face Giwa, "What are you still doing here? The bathrooms and toilets are waiting for you, make sure they are clean before you enter your cockroach-infested room!" She walked in ahead of Giwa in her typical way of enticing young men before she married Harry, and Mr. Zakary after she married Harry. Her seductive body made no more sense to Giwa than a bag of cement.

No one had ever told Giwa to tidy his room because he picked it up as a habit from the time he was very young. Every morning, he would lay his bed before going out of his room. He still went inside his room to ascertain that everything was in order. He saw his books scattered on the table. Giwa hissed and began to re-arranage them again until he saw a thick envelope stuck in the centre of his Bible. He quickly opened it and saw a wad of five hundred naira notes. Still in the envelope was a brief note that read;

This will cover up for all promises. Keep it strictly between me and you, don't be eager to spend it. Harry.

Now Giwa understood the import of Uncle Harry's "carefully arrange those books". He counted the money and found it was seven thousand naira, enough to get him some new clothes and even transport him to Zonkwa. He sighed and whispered a short prayer, "Thank God for Uncle Harry and for the money."

Aunty Mercy sat on the sofa and was watching a series of Nigerian films which Giwa rented for her earlier, that was likely how she intended to spend the entire day. If there was any other job for Aunty Mercy, it was to instruct Giwa and Kauna to do the house chores, and go on errands for her. She was actually a bag of lazy bones. Kauna handled everything in the kitchen; only Kauna could tell which food item was lacking and which food item was abundant. Kauna was the real brain behind every delicious meal in the house but the glory always went to Aunty Mercy. Giwa was in charge of every other thing but the kitchen, sometimes both Kauna and he joined hands to perform all the chores.

Kauna came into the house a month after Harry got married to Mercy. Aunty Mercy complained that the chores were too much for her and Harry allowed her to bring Kauna to help her, little did he know that Kauna was brought to take over the household chores including his meals.

Initially, Aunty Mercy had to convince her parents that Kauna was coming to school, that she would sponsor her education, or, at worst, sponsor her to acquire a vocational skill. The parents released Kauna to a life of perpetual enslavement in the hands of her own sister. Aunty Mercy reneged on their agreement and therefore did not allow Kauna to go for any holiday for fear of being exposed. At home, Aunty Mercy did not oblige when Harry declared his intention of sponsoring Kauna's education. She said Kauna was too dull to learn anything. Mercy herself was complacent with a WAEC Senior Secondary School Certificate that contained only one Credit, two Passes amidst several Fails. She had the highest certificate in her house, and so she didn't want others to go further.

Kauna, at thirteen, was also beautiful. Her breast began to protrude from a flat chest. Underneath the drap and oversized hand-me-down dresses which Aunty Mercy always insisted she wore, were hints of a curvy figure. She managed to read with great difficulty, although she understood English a little but was barely able to speak it. Sometimes, Giwa would teach her how to read and do some simple arithmetic. Aunty Mercy disliked it whenever Kauna was being taught and always referred to Kauna as "coconut head" and Giwa as "block head". She had to find another name for Giwa because he proved he was more than a 'block head' with the prizes he won in school. She would only be exposing her ignorance if she dared to call him a 'block head' again. Kauna and Giwa had mutual respect for each other seeing that they had one thing in common: They were domestic slaves of the same mistress. The only thing Kauna lacked was formal education, otherwise, she had the potential of being an ideal woman. She was beautiful, sedulous, obedient, assiduous and a skilled cook.

By the time Giwa finished his chores, it was noon. He ate his lunch and went to his room. From the corridor, on his way to the bedroom he heard Aunty Mercy at her favourite hobby, snoring loudly. Aunty Mercy loved sleeping; sleeping with someone or sleeping alone. She must have slept for three-quarters of her life.

Giwa read a novel until he fell asleep. He woke up at a quarter past four in the afternoon. Aunty Mercy was still sleeping. Quietly, he went out of the house and took a stroll around the Doctors Quarters in Dogon Dutse. The streets had much peace to offer that under the roof where Aunty Mercy stayed. Directly opposite the gate of the Doctors quarters were several shops, bars and a motel. It was a place where the young doctors hung out and engaged in acts of debauchery.

The atmosphere opposite the gate did not seem to welcome Giwa much so he made a U-turn towards home.

"*Kai*, you no know elders again ko?"

Giwa turned and recognized the speaker as Abdul. His first friend in Jos, Abdul, had changed; red eyes, dark lips, stained teeth plus he bore an offensive odour of gin mixed with marijuana. Giwa needed no ghost to tell him that Abdul was emerging from the hill behind those shops.

* * * * *

"When will you come back?"

"I will come back in less than a month, I need to see Mama and Kyauta, they said she is becoming a woman like you," Giwa teased and Kauna chuckled. She avoided laughing because she was sure that Aunty Mercy was eavesdropping.

"Broda, dis no too heavy for you to carry? Who go help you wit am?"

"I go manage am," Giwa replied. "God go bless Uncle Harry and Aunty Mercy for this provision dem. No be small tin o! I sure say Mama go dey happy." He was also certain that Madam Terrorist was listening even though she pretended she was just watching the television. Her ears were stuck to the ground. That was why Giwa sugar-coated his words.

Two weeks had passed since Giwa came back from school. He pleaded with Uncle Harry to allow him go home to see his mother and sister. At first, Uncle Harry didn't like the idea, it pricked his conscience; he had not visited Giwa's mother in two years. After much persuasion, he yielded to Giwa's request. He also bought provisions and gave Giwa ten thousand naira to give his mother, then he told Giwa to inform them that he would be at home for Christmas.

Aunty Mercy was losing one labourer, she didn't like it that house work may be too much for Kauna so she would have to help out where necessary. She told Giwa that she used her money to buy most of the provisions but Giwa couldn't believe her, he knew that all the money she had was given to her by Harry. She couldn't boast of a kobo from her sweat.

"Greet your mother for me, and don't forget to tell her that I bought the provisions *ko*," Aunty Mercy grinned as she spoke. Giwa had read her like most of the subjects he scored 'A' in. He knew that behind that smile was acrimonious hatred she had nursed for him from the time her colour changed. That was exactly two weeks after she got married to Harry.

"I will," he said, "I won't forget. Kauna! Take care of Uncle Harry o!" he said as he mounted the bike that was warming up to go. He meant what he said. Only Kauna could take care of both Uncle Harry and Aunty Mercy. The motorcyclist launched the first gear to set the bike in motion and they zoomed off.

Kauna was still waving him goodbye from a distance. Her eyes were wet as Giwa took off. Aunty Mercy immediately went back into the house and left Kauna and Whiskey waving bye-bye. Kauna cried bitterly. Giwa was the only one that understood and knew her pains because he wore her shoes, naturally, he knew where it pinched.

* * * * *

Home was calling, Giwa could even smell it. The vehicle going to Zonkwa was in motion. *Home is always the best; your own na your own*. He sat in the front seat beside the driver who cruised at a hundred and forty kilometres per hour, but Giwa did not mind the suicidal speed. He feared that Aunty Mercy may change her mind and come back for him.

The wings of the night were falling on Zonkwa at the time Giwa arrived. So many things had changed. Light bulbs shone from every building. The town had greatly developed. The hard ground he was marching on was a tarred road. Some magnificent buildings were sparsely distributed within the town. Giwa observed some young girls in mini skirts and spaghetti tops chattering in Hausa. They also chewed gum in an obnoxious manner.

Giwa flagged down an *okada* and was almost at a loss for the name of his abode. “Ehm! Em! Do you know where ECWA church is?”

“Mission,” the rider said.

“Ah! Yes! Take me there. How much is it?”

“We will talk about the cost on the way, just climb and bring your load. As you can see, it is getting dark.”

They talked about the changes that had occurred as they sped to the interior part of Zonkwa. “Do you know Mamman Giwa?” Giwa chipped in.

“Yes I know her very well… Wait,” things clicked to the boy, “are you Giwa?” he asked, to be sure that he was not merely guessing.

“I am Giwa,” but I don’t really remember you.”

“*Kai*! *Kai*! *Kai*!” the okada boy screamed, “you don change *wallahi tallahi*.”

“Na God oh!” Giwa replied. They soon reached Giwa’s house. The boy alighted from the *okada* immediately and parked it. He shouted Giwa’s name as he hugged him.

“You don’t remember me? Samson now!”

“Oh! Wait... Which Samson? Samson the strongest?” Samson nodded. “The guy I fought with in primary six?”

“Yes oh! Na me be dis.” The boy declared posing in a typical American gangster way. He wore a loose-fitting black jacket and baseball hat with NY bodly crested on it. Samson was the oldest boy in class then but here he was of the same height with Giwa.

Many people came out to know what the hullabaloo was about. They were surprised to see that the young visitor was no stranger at all — he was Giwa, their son. More and more people trooped into the compound to welcome Giwa, many of whom he could hardly remember. A girl of Kauna’s stature embraced Giwa. He was shocked to find out that the young girl was Kyauta, his one and only sister. He hugged her tightly again.

“Where is Mama?”

Kyauta pointed at the house, but Giwa couldn’t see anyone, just the desperate voice of his mother calling out.

“*Yaro na*! *Yaro na*!”

The crowd made way for her. Giwa threw his weight on her as

soon as he saw her, "Mama, Mama, Mama *na*!"

"*Yaro na*! *Yaro na*!" was all she said. For a long time, they remained in each other's arms sobbing hard. Many people were driven to tears at the sight of a mother and son's reunion after six years. Others simply shook their heads and said "*eiya…eiya…*" as they departed from the scene one after the other.

Very few people remained after the long welcome. Samson marched the kick-starting pedal of his bike, he promised to call the next day then he dashed off. "*Sanu da zuwa yaro na*, you are welcome my son," Mama kept saying as she dragged Giwa inside the house. She stopped to adjust her wrapper which almost fell off her waist.

"Kauna! Get his belongings inside!"

Giwa was extremely happy to be back home where he was greatly celebrated and not tolerated like in Uncle Harry's house. Here, Giwa was the king, he could decide what to do and what not to do, what to eat and where to go.

"Six years is a long period," he told himself as he entered the old house his father inherited many years ago. The area where they lived was now counted as one of the remote areas of Zonkwa. The place was now inhabited by Burkutu drinkers, it became their rendezvous even though the neighbourhood was still referred to as 'Mission' by most people in Zonkwa because it was occupied by European missionaries for a long time. So much for one night, Giwa slept soundly for the first time in two weeks.

Four

"*Yaya! Yaya*!" Kyauta called softly.

"Mmnn..eh! What is it?"

"Mama said you should come out for prayers," she replied in her soft morning tone. Morning prayer was a tradition that was alien to Giwa, thanks to Aunty Mercy's abhorence of early morning starters.

"I'm coming," he yawned like a hungry cat. Nothing had changed about his room. Nanlep took time to clean Giwa's room every week lest he came back to find the place inhabitable. She had hoped for what seemed like eternity that her son would come back. She had never taken anything out from the room nor brought anything into the room. The room was intact except that it smelled of mice faeces.

His mattress was just three times thicker than a floor mat and it was poised on a bamboo frame, a six-spring mattress at the time it was bought. Although it had shrunk almost to the thickness of a mat, it was the kind of mattress which was known as 'sleep and die' by PHS students. Giwa got up, stretched his body, and yawned again as he walked to the sitting room. The trio sang a hymn after which Kyauta struggled unsuccessfully to read a passage from a Hausa Bible. Giwa came to her rescue; he took the Bible from her and read it expressly. Mama could not read but she determined which passages were to be read after which she would explain in detail stressing the moral lessons therein. Long years of experience with the missionaries and pastors had taught her that much. That morning, Giwa read from the book of Genesis, about Abraham and how he was patient with God until God gave him a son. Nanlep admonished her children to be patient with God so as to achieve their ambition at God's appointed time. She made an incongruous example of herself as she patiently waited for God to bring Giwa to her, and he did.

When morning devotion was over, Mama asked of Harry and

Aunty Mercy.

"They are both fine, they send their warmest greetings. Ehm…er Maama!" he referred to Kyauta, "go and bring the two Bagco bags I brought yesterday." Giwa relaxed on his father's favourite armchair while his mother examined her son.

"Is that moustache on your face? Your voice has changed; it sounds just like your father's. Oh! I am so happy to have you at home. *Yaro na kenan*!" She nodded proudly as she spoke to her most treasured possession sitting before her.

Kyauta brought the bags that were filled with provision and foodstuff for the family. She laid them before Giwa then she pushed it forward for Mama to have a closer look. Mama began picking the items from the bags one by one. A large tin of milk, chocolate beverage, a packet of Maggie seasoning cubes, then she paused when Giwa opened his mouth.

"Aunty Mercy said I should tell you that she bought the provisions but I saw when Uncle Harry gave her money to buy all these at the market," Giwa remarked.

"We thank God and we thank them, they tried. Remember the Bible says we should be thankful at all times." This was the kind of humility that annoyed Giwa. He believed that they deserved more than the token from Uncle Harry, having taken over his father's possessions and sold their lands to pay for his fees in the university. He blamed Aunty Mercy for being a barrier to Uncle Harry's generous intention for the family. As if Mama didn't notice the frown on her son's face, she asked if Aunty Mercy had given birth.

"That woman can never give birth. Mama, that woman is a prostitute!" Immediately, Mama looked round to be sure no one else was listening at the same time she squeezed her face like someone who heard an abominable word and stuck her palm on her mouth, her eyes wide.

"Shh! Shh! Enough! That girl is my daughter-in-law, don't use such a word on her again!"

"But Mama!" Giwa protested.

"No, no, don't Mama me anything!" she was waving her hand, refusing to tolerate one more word against Aunty Mercy.

"Allow me to finish speaking now?"

"I won't, I don't want to hear any story, leave everything to God. Besides, time will reveal everything to us." With that she silenced Giwa permanently about Aunty Mercy. She refused to listen to anything he had to say against her.

Giwa told her about the prizes he won in school during their annual speech and prize-giving day as well as the graduation ceremony of SS3 students. He brought out pictures for her to see. Even before he explained the activities and the people in the pictures, Mama rushed out broadcasting to the neighours that her son emerged as the best student in Plateau High School. She boasted and danced gracefully to the admiration, or envy, of her neighbours. Many of them came into the house and shook hands with him, praying for more blessings upon him. One particular woman brought a cockerel for Giwa.

Many people from the nooks of Zonkwa came to see the only boy in Zonkwa that was admitted into PHS in his time and who eventually became the best student. The height of the visits was when the chief, also known as the Mai Angwa, came into the house with his entourage. He reminded Giwa that Zonkwa was still his home. He told him that he could settle and build his house in Zonkwa when the time comes. Somehow, Giwa became a measuring standard for the young boys in the area. Many parents cited Giwa as a model whenever they scolded their children.

Samson surfaced at noon and took Giwa out, the duo visited places that were almost erased from Giwa's memory. He vaguely recalled the market and the clinic although both places had been transformed tremendously, almost beyond recognition. The market was meticulously redesigned with bold writing on each lane which indicated the commodities sold. Unfortunately, it wasn't a market day for him to see how the traders coped with the development which was new to Giwa.

"So many things have changed since I left this town."

"Well, that is the only permanent thing in life…change. What do you expect?" Samson replied without looking at Giwa, he spoke with an aura of pride. "Whether from good to bad or bad to good, change must occur."

"I know, but in such a short time?" he asked naively.

"The difference between life and death is but a breath, between a bachelor and married man is less than an hour of solemnization and…"

Giwa broke in, "I see you have learnt so much on the streets. Did you have a tutor or were you just a disciple of every corner of the street?"

"All I have acquired was given to me by God."

"You mean He came down upon you from heaven?" Giwa teased menacingly, eyeing Samson in a ridiculous manner which elicited laughter from both boys.

Ten metres away from the boys stood a nicely designed bar, a rendezvous for young boys and men which temporarily disengaged them from the challenges, sorrows and mysteries that the world offers.

"How about we have a drink here?" intoned Samson.

"Why not if not?" the intelligent boy obliged.

The Black Pride, in the recent past, had received kudos from most, if not all drinkers and smokers in Zonkwa. It boasted of different brands of bottled booze and also the locally brewed burkutu which they bought, refrigerated and sold in tumblers. Packs of cigarette were also displayed on a shelf like books in a bookstore. Connoisseurs from all around recommended brands of beer and cigarettes from the Black Pride.

A young Igbo woman took advantage of the teeming patrons of Black Pride, she sold pepper soup of fish, goat head — also called *Isi-ewu*, and cow's intestines. Outside, a middle aged man and his apprentice were sticking tiny chunks of suya. Giwa and Samson stepped into Black Pride in the morning of Black Pride time. She ran a different time; night was as good as day time in Black Pride. Those interested in night business found a haven in her, she starts selling from 4pm till 6am.

They found themselves a seat in a choice corner, from where they could clearly see and not be easily visible. Two other people were also in the spacious room, a boy and a girl. Giwa knew that the boy was wooing her. The boy flaunted his money with the meat and the bottles before them, he tried to impress her for a while, at least till he scored a goal.

"This joint is rather too large," remarked Giwa, who had never sat in a bar of that magnitude before.

"At nine o'clock, you may be standing with your bottle in your hand praying for someone to leave."

Giwa's mouth widened astonishingly, "You mean all these seats will be occupied?"

"Certainly, and even those ones piled to the ceiling. Behind this wall are a lot of makeshift tables which will be used at the outer arena" Samson responded adding an emphatic nod.

"Oga Henry, how now?"

"I dey, na you be oga, two of una." Henry, the bartender, approached their table to take their order.

"Give us one jug of chilled palm wine," Samson said. "Fresh one o!" Samson shouted as Henry made for the bar. Samson proved himself as a regular customer with the cordial salutation he posed.

"Samson the strongest, Samson, Samson, the strongest man in the whole world," the young Igbo woman appeared, hailing one of her esteemed customers.

"Mama Chidi, you have started again, please leave me alone," he said as though he didn't enjoy her flattery. "Two plates of isi-ewu for me and my friend, hot one o!"

"Don't worry, na you go first taste am today, I just cook am finish be dat." Turning to Giwa, she looked sober, "Welcome *nwamooo*, how your family?" Without waiting for an answer, she continued, "You know say friend of strong pesin na strong pesin too... ha ha ha."

She adjusted her wrapper and ran back to the kitchen just in time to avoid Samson's roaring reminder of "two plates!"

"She got married about five years ago and she already has four children, rumour has it that the fifth one is within," he rubbed his stomach, "but time will tell."

"Where does her husband work?"

"He is an attendant at the hospital."

"Oga, the palm wine is very fresh and sweet," Henry announced his arrival with a gleaming smile. The boy was handsome, light-skinned, and of average height. Giwa wondered if the workers at Black Pride had undergone a course in hospitality. Perhaps the regular customers and new ones always come back because of them. Mama Chidi's isi-ewu supported the jug of palm wine on their table. Before long, the boys were lost savouring the isi-ewu and palm wine.

"Eh heh! Do you remember Talatu?" Samson asked when he found his senses.

"Talatu, Ta-la-tu... Yes!" Giwa replied when he got rid of the meet that impeded his thought. "The girl that caused us to fight in primary six."

"Exactly!"

"What about her?"

"Jesus Christ!" Samson exclaimed as he looked through the

window at a young woman with a baby strapped to her back. She also carried a twenty litre keg of water. Her clothes were shabby, she wore a pair of rotten slippers which held her feet from touching the ground. The young woman hummed a familiar Hausa hymn. "Talk of the devil!"

Giwa was shaking his head, "I'm sure you don't mean it," a doubting Giwa put in.

"Are you blind? This is her, the girl we both had affection for, the one that made you challenge the strongest man," he thrust his chest with his middle finger, "to a duel."

Giwa dodged from the facts of the past, he didn't want to recall how he was severely beaten in his first fight, how he earned himself an indelible mark at the back of his neck.

"But she was adorable then, *kai*! How could she have turned into something pitiable, detestable? It's hard to believe."

"Change!" Samson almost screamed, "change, my brother, change!" Samson collected his nerves, he looked at his half-filled glass of palm wine as if he was speaking to it. He drew a copious gulp and let the tumbler come down on the table with soft thud.

"She was expelled from school in J.S.S.3 because she was pregnant for a certain rascal who rides a motorcycle like me. She was forced to marry, you know…live with him. The baby you saw on her back is her second one. You see! That is the change we are talking about. I broaden her smile sometimes with some money."

"That is..." Giwa slurped. "That is very kind of you, I suppose you do it often," he stated, more affirmatively than interrogatively.

"See, I don't want to blow my trumpet but I help as often as I can since it's not mandatory."

"Who do you spend your money on? I mean, which girl benefits from your sweat?"

"You mean my girlfriend?"

"They say an average Nigerian answers a question with another." The newest customer of Black Pride grimaced, and then his lips creased a smile. "Of course I mean your girl or should I say girlfriend?" He wore a clowny face that first demanded laughter before any reasonable reply.

"Zaitun, she is my one and only. I always think of her." His hand reached to his hip then and he brought out a wallet-sized image of his girl and handed it to Giwa. The wallet looked old but it served its purpose, including safe-guarding a cherished picture. The upper half of Zaitun was nicely captured in the portrait. She was veiled but deliberately omitted the frontal part of her hair, her right palm hosted her cheek and a melancholic smile exposed a small portion of her teeth. Her arms were also embellished with a washable tattoo. "Na my last card be dat o!" Samson chipped in as Giwa perused the photograph.

"Is she a Muslim?"

"She said she will become a Christian if we eventually marry, but I don't care whether she is a Muslim or Christian, we both believe in a superior being who created love." He snapped in self defence from a judgemental pair of eyes that pried into his relationship compatibility. "What about you? Who is your..."

"Can we have another jug of palm wine?" Giwa shouted tipsily while trying to avoid an imminent question which he didn't want to answer.

"No, we won't have another jug, we are going home," Samson declared.

* * * * *

Days turned into weeks, weeks turned into months, and Giwa was still basking in the freedom of Zonkwa. He had promised Uncle Harry that he would return in two weeks but Uncle Harry would have to wait till he gained admission into the university or better still, till thy kingdom come. Mama too made it impossible for Giwa to ponder about returning, she deified him as the Lord of the house; every meal was decided by Giwa. Often, one would hear her saying, "I like...but Giwa prefers...so I bought it" or "Giwa says..." Her son's opinion reigned over her own opinion. Women in the neighbourhood soon adopted the code, 'Giwa says' for Nanlep when they talked about her. They frequently used the code when she became the subject of their gossip.

Mama's obsession with her only son infuriated her only daughter. Kyauta wasn't annoyed only because Mama spoke too much about the intelligent boy but also because she was reduced to Giwa's messenger. Her feet were set in motion whenever he snapped his fingers, even before completing his command.

He sure felt like a miniature male version of Aunty Mercy. Giwa only bothered himself with two things: Leading the family's morning devotion, being the most educated person among them and making the choice of what would be consumed and how it should be prepared.

Kyauta also made use of Giwa in her own way, in a few months she learnt many topics that she had struggled with for years. Her performance in class soon drew the attention of teachers and students towards her. Classmates who often despised her ensured they saluted her in cool camaraderie. She had just attained puberty and the signs were beginning to manifest on her, she was blossoming into a pretty lady with a pretty sharp brain growing simultaneously with her feminine features.

Samson, the erstwhile enemy of Giwa, became his best friend in Zonkwa. They visited each other habitually, they were mutually beneficial to each other. Samson worked less and spent more time with his best friend. He taught Giwa how to ride a motor cycle and also how to swim in Kwer, a tributary of the legendary River Kaduna which was widely speculated as a harbor for crocodiles. Giwa encouraged Samson to go back to school and work hard for an O level certificate so that he could alteast secure admission into any tertiary institution of his choice. Giwa's admonishment fell on deaf ears.

Harsh harmattan winds began to blow; the whole town looked very dry and dusty. They were in the month of December and Christmas was around the corner, and that was supposed to be Giwa's first Christmas in the town in more than five years.

It was barely two weeks before Christmas, a Saturday morning, Samson came to wake Giwa from his after-prayer sleep. Giwa usually slept for at least one or two hours after morning devotion in order to cover up for the hour he used for prayer.

"Samson!" Giwa grunted as he staggered to the sitting room, his eyes were bloodshot. "You are here so early, hope you slept at home?"

"No, I slept in the bush. Where else was I supposed to sleep?"

"Okay, okay, its enough, I brought about the whole trouble." Giwa admitted, envisaging that what he kindled may result into battle of innuendoes.

"I hope you slept well?" Samson asked.

"I did." He leaned back on the old faded cushion. "So, what will happen today?"

"I will be seeing Zaitun later in the evening today, she came back from Zaria yesterday, and I would like you to meet her. I asked her to bring her friend along for my naughty friend," he teased.

Giwa gave a long hiss. "You are not serious!"

"I had to figure out other means of passing time for a friend who is fast becoming an ardent *palmwinoholic*."

"All thanks to you — the initiator," Giwa snapped.

"Shh! Don't be loud, else your mother will find out that her beloved home pastor has signed up with Black Pride."

"Did you have to come so early, Mr. Romeo?" Giwa suddenly opted to change the topic in case Kyauta's eardrums were picking soundwaves from the sitting room.

"I know you wouldn't like to miss a refreshing session at the ultra-natural stream, Kwer."

"Now you are talking. Give me some minutes, let me get us some breakfast and a tuber of yam so that we won't lose all the energy on our way back home."

Giwa stepped into their kitchen, a round hut made of mud and thatch. The kitchen was laced on the inside with a thin black layer of smoke, the cobwebs were also blackened by the same smoke. His eyes searched for the pot.

"*Yaya*!" Kyauta beckoned him to come closer, he understood that she had something confidential to say so he didn't object. She spoke almost in a whisper. "I heard you talking about Kwer, please don't go there again *o*!" She held her right ear, resounding the warning to her brother as a mother would to her son. "They say the river takes one life as a sacrifice at the end of the year. As you know, we are in the month of December, I hope you want to see Christmas day," she concluded and watched Giwa hoping that her words had sunk deeply into his heart.

"Forget it," Giwa hissed. "I've learnt about this myth even before you could pronounce the word 'Mama' and I can cite three consecutive years that a life was not lost in that river. Moreover, it is only God," pointing upwards, " that protects." He dismissed her fear and marched out of the kitchen.

"I have told you my own," she shouted at his back as he disappeared into his room.

The stream had three main points of activities, the first point was used for washing and other domestic activities, the second part served as a bathing spot for the girls and the third part, the deeper side, was where the boys swam and hunted fish. Neither the males nor the females were allowed to trespass to each other's boundaries.

First things first; the yam was instantly set under hot coals as soon as they arrived. No time was wasted in pulling off and diving into the river. Samson tested Giwa at deeper sides, he nearly recommended Giwa as an expert but something happened. A small plastic ball was thrown for Giwa to catch and swim back with. He caught the ball, but soon disappeared under the water and the ball was left afloat. Few seconds later, his hands stretched out and grabbed the air, his head snapped out for a second and he disappeared under the water releasing strong turbulent bubbles. From intuition, Samson knew that a ton of water was finding its way into his friend's stomach. In a desperate effort to rescue his dying friend, Samson went under the water, below Giwa, and lifted him up with his back. Samson was almost drowned by Giwa in the process. Giwa was eventually rescued with the help of an onlooker. He lay unconsciously on the bank of Kwer as he vomited litres of water. After a long rest, Giwa was fed with a morsel of yam and he coughed profusely bringing back the laughter and cheer that eluded them minutes ago. Others who witnessed the encounter from the start began to mimick Giwa, and Samson in his panic-striken imbroglio. The boys devoured the roasted yam and set out for home. Both boys hardly remembered that they had an appointment, the near-tragic event of the day was enough. If something was left undone, it was the thanksgiving they had to offer to God in church the following Sunday morning.

A great surprise awaited Giwa as he opened the door of his house. A man in a clean white Kaftan sat in the sitting room, it was Uncle Harry.

Five

It was almost a year since Bakka was controversially banished from Tambes village. A week ago, Ladi, who until now remained the chief's favourite in spite of her scandal, gave birth. She delivered a bouncing baby boy. The chief was very affectionate towards his new son. He fervently tried to draw similar features between himself and the boy, most of which remained obscure to many members of the royalty. Only Ladi knew the real father of the baby and she was certain that it was not her husband. The naming ceremony was a beehive of activities. A lot of jollof rice was served, supported with plenty kunu. The 'men' perched at a corner. Before them, a large clay pot with a capacity of a hundred litres was set. Each one of them held a calabash, and they used a smaller calabash tossed about by ripples of the Burkutu to serve themselves. A deafening hubbub emanated from their area and measured up to more than half of the total excitement in the chief's yard.

The chief himelf was restless, he pranced about, almost without direction. If he tried to conceal his excitement, his teeth would be the first to betray him accompanied by a spasmodic smile. That was his second male child and a promising handsomeness lurked conspicuously around him. Already, the first son manifested signs of cowardice and profound ineptitude to retain the remains of the splendor of the Tam dynasty.The chief of Tambes who was also known as Da Mwen settled for a few calabashes of Burkutu, then he rose to proclaim the name of his new son. The drummers were asked to stop beating the drums, and the dancer's steps simultaneously decreased to a stop with the beats. Womens' voices muted, 'the men', as they referred to themselves, forbade more sips of the Burkutu until the chief had announced the name of his new son.

"Thank you all for being part of history today. I am very happy today for the obvious reason which all of you are aware of; another son has been added to my wealth of children." He spoke with an almost palpable pride as though the child was a product of his power or might. Da Mwen held a fluffy end of a cow's tail which signified his leadership over the Tambes people. On his left hand, he held a calabash of Burkutu, he gulped a mouthful and swallowed in an instant. He poured some on the ground and chanted an incantation believing that something was happening in the ancestral realm.

"Tambes was the first person to set his foot on this land. Tambes, our forefather, was a daring hero, that is why we named our land after him. I therefore name my son Tambes. Thank you all." The partying resumed as dancers, invigorated by the new name, perfomed at their peak. More Burkutu went in circulation while women and children settled for kunu and maasa.

The villagers trooped in, one after another, to see the new prince who was called Tambes. Others took time saying wishes to the child and in a way buying time to ascertain whether what the previous visitors said was true —- that the baby boy in no way resembled his father. The math could be easily done; if the mother had an affair nine months ago with another man, then that man, is most probably the boy's father since the supposed father, her husband, shared no physical features with the boy. It was that easy to discern but no one was bold enough to share this logic in a group of three. As much as everyone tried to conceal his or her little observation, the news spread faster than wildfire that the much celebrated new prince was not Da Mwen's offspring. It was tacitly established almost without an atom of doubt that the boy belonged to Bakka, the poor farmer who was unjustly banished from Tambes land. Thus, Ladi's treasured hidden fact became a public secret.

At sunset, most of the villagers had returned, very few of them stayed behind unlike other similar occasions when the whole day would be spent and more than half of the night too. The spirit of the excitement died together with the day. Da Powan held his grandchild in his arms. He gave a long scrutinizing look at the boy swathed in wool hoping his vision may counter his fears but it did not.

"Nothing is hidden under the sun. You have just started paying the price of your adultery. The corn you planted months ago is now ripe." His words felt like a double-edged sword piercing Ladi's heart right through her soul as he spoke. He handed the baby over to his mother and said, "If anything happens, you are still my daughter and you have a home." With that, he left the room. Ladi was at a loss for words for a long moment, tears blurred her sight and a lump was formed in her throat.

Outside, the chief shared a joke to which other men laughed, more to please their superciliously excited chief than the humour which the joke evoked. Da Powan came out to announce his departure. Da Mwen saw him off to the far end of the compound.

"My son-in-law, I am happy for you but you need to work hard for your own son. It's a pity you have named him already."

"Ehm...Da Powan, I don't really understand what you mean..."

"My chief, you are a man, not everything must be broken in edible pieces for you. Go home and rest." Da Powan strode swiftly along the path that led to his home.

For the first time throughout the felicitations, the chief smelt a rat, though his superficial mind wouldn't allow him to reason logically enough to land him at a conclusion.

The chief changed his happy countenance. As he entered the compound, he lightened up to conceal the puzzle that nagged at his mind. He excused himself once more from the crowd in order to see his "newest pride" as he put it.

Lengnen, his eldest wife, stayed in the room with Ladi and rendered assistance to her. About three other women in the room pretentiously showered accolades on the prince of Tambes. Da Mwen stepped inside and observed the boy, with a hyprocritical smile.

"He looks every bit like me, I think I looked like Tambes when I was eight days old." He glanced at the women who grinned widely. Ladi laughed loudly and Lengnen gave a prolonged hiss. Lengnen grabbed the chief's arm motioning him to follow her, implying she had something confidential to tell him. As soon as they were out of earshot, she spoke.

"Are you deaf? Are you blind? Open your eyes and your ears. Don't you hear what people are saying? That baby is not yours, or have you forgotten that your 'favourite wife' was caught in the act with a miserable farmer who you passed biased judgement on?" Lengnen was the only person with enough guts to confront the chief. She gave him advice as a friend would and she never hesitated to scold him as a mother would. She was his first wife.

"That boy is my son, I don't care what you and other people say, he looks every bit like me for all I know." He protested in a rising voice.

"Old fool!" She looked around to be sure no one was watching before she continued: "We need a big mirror in this house because it seems you have forgotten what you look like, or you have a problem with comparing two things. If I were you, I would start thinking of a way to get rid of that farmer's son." She eyed him from head to toe hastily in a few seconds, gave a long hiss and left him wallowing in a confused state.

Da Mwen grew pale and sick for several months. He often was ill at ease to perform his official duties like settling land disputes and some domestic misdemeanour. The sight of the boy he named Tambes sent drops of fever down his spine. He despised the boy more than he ever loved him and on many different occasions he contemplated killing him but he knew it would only cause him more regrets.

When Tambes was seven years old, Ladi took him to Pankshin, a town about fifteen kilometres from Tambes. She believed the boy would find solace there even as a houseboy. Tambes became a houseboy to Reverend Father Thomas Brown, an Irish priest who was accustomed to the culture of the people. He spoke Ngas and Hausa fluently, and his English was still superb.

Reverend Brown saw the brilliant potential of Tambes, he enrolled him into the primary school owned by the local church but not before he changed his name to Solomon. Tambes became widely known as Solomon or 'Solo' for short. His mother had insisted that his surname should be Bakka. On the cover of his books, he wrote his name as Solomon T. Bakka. He became a pet to Reverend Brown and another houseboy was recruited to handle the chores of the house to enable Solomon have more time to study.

A few times in a year, his mother would visit him for a few hours and then sneak back home. She willingly ostracized him from his people. He was believed to have been stolen as his mother came back and reported; that was the same day she placed him under the tutelage of Reverend Father Thomas Brown. Many people believed her story especially because she brooded over the missing child for months. Da Mwen had two more sons by her, those ones were carbon copies of their father. Happy days returned to him. Meanwhile, Ladi's regular visits to her first son declined until she stopped visiting completely. Unknown to Solomon, his mother had passed away on the day he completed his primary school.

As much as Father Brown was fond of Solomon, he did not spare the rod when Solomon misbehaved. On two occasions he had to use his *koboko* on Solomon without mercy: The first time was when the reverend sisters of the Holy Cross Convent caught Solomon invading the cashew tree which was at the centre of their compound. They tongue-lashed him, wishing they had used their hands on him but for the reason that Solomon was Father's boy, his favourite. The cashew tree, more or less, was sacred because it sheltered a life-size statue of the Blessed Virgin. Except for the sisters in the convent, plucking a cashew fruit would require express permission from the Mother of the convent.

Stealing was Solo's first major offence that brought about the full wrath of Father Brown, it provided the first event that he had to launch his *koboko* on Solomon. The whip was actually meant for stubborn children who were roaming about the church during confession hours.

News of the crime may never have reached the ears of Father Brown but for the mouth-leaking Sister Vero, as if the scolding wasn't enough, she held him by the ear and brought him to Father Brown.

"This boy was caught stealing the cashew in our compound. I'm very sure that it is not his first time because the ripe cashews disappear before we pluck them. We blamed the birds that perched on the tree not knowing that this," she complemented her words with a knock on Solo's head, "is the big bird."

"But Sister Vero, I only climbed it once!" Solo tried to offer a weak protest.

"Shut that mouth before more lies find their way out and by so doing you continue to offend the Lord and Virgin Mary. That's how armed robbers start, and before long they are on the highway..."

Father Brown interrupted her in his usual calm way, portraying a sense of maturity in handling issues.

"Sister Vero, thank you very much! You did well. Please allow me to carry on from here. I hope you don't mind."

As soon as she left, Father Brown asked Solomon to pull off his shirt and lie down flat on his stomach with his head under a dining chair. Fifteen strokes fell on Solomon's bare back, each with the same momentum as the former. It seemed to Solomon like long hours of torture. Father Brown didn't care whether he stole for the first time, or whether he had been stealing, or even whether he stole one or one thousand cashews. Solomon was beaten for the mere fact that he stole; a vice father Brown utterly detested. Naturally,

Sister Vero became Solomon's sworn enemy.

The second beating was more serious than the first one. A girl was sent to deliver a crate of eggs to Father Brown, she delivered them to Solomon since Father Brown wasn't around. Solomon cajoled her to stay and join him in watching a hilarious comedy. They laughed and shared views as they watched. Solo hoped he could muster some courage to tell her how much he admired her, his hopes fell apart when Father Brown returned impromptu, a day before his scheduled arrival date. Solomon became ice-cold. The house was in shambles, the boy had thought he could tidy up the house after watching the film.

The girl stood to greet father Brown respectfully, Solomon did the same. Guilt was written all over him as he held both hands on his head and felt sorry for himself. The girl was clever enough to vindicate herself by explaining her mission to the house and how Solomon cajoled her to stay, she also begged to leave immediately.

"My warmest wishes to your mother, tell her that I will personally thank her after Sunday Mass. And don't forget to greet your father too!" He shouted as she hurriedly found her way home.

He turned to face a trembling Solomon, "You have guts don't you? If I was asked what you were doing at the moment, I would confidently reply that you have finished your chores and you are studying. I would fearlessly bet with my last breath on that. Little did I know that if I had done that, I would have been a dead man by now. Go get me my *koboko*! Those scars were meant to remind you that I don't tolerate nonchalance. Since they weren't enough, I'll add more for you and I can go on and on until I see your spinal cord."

Without being told, Solomon pulled off his shirt and got his head under the chair, enduring some twenty strokes of the *koboko*. After the exercise, Father Brown warned him to stay away from women and start considering the seminary. After that incident, Solo never dared to as much as involve himself in a three-minutes conversation with a girl. He always felt Father Brown's eyes around him wherever he went. Some of his classmates often called him a misogynist but he cared less as long as it kept the *koboko* from revisiting this back.

Father Brown was more than a father and a mother combined to Solomon. He nurtured deep affection for Solomon especially because of his academic exploits and the virtue of hard work which became an inextricable part of Solomon. He reciprocated the affection shown him by Father Brown. Unfortunately, Father Brown left Pankshin. He was transferred to Lagos diocese and was replaced by Father Kut, an indigene of Kaduna State. He ensured that Solomon was on the payroll of the church before he left. Father Kut and Solomon became cat and dog within a short while. He always found fault with whatever the boy did. Solomon's patience was running out in large quantity.

* * * * *

Giwa's eyes brightened as he caught the sight of Uncle Harry. His eyes, subconsciously, within a flash of lightning, scanned the room for Aunty Mercy and to his relief, she didn't come along. He flew into Uncle Harry's arms and embraced him warmly. Uncle Harry patted him on the back.

"See how big you have grown in these few months, have you been sucking your mother's breast again?"

"No no! The kind of nourishment I get in Jos is better than the one I get here," Giwa managed to chip in a lie. "How are Aunty Mercy and Kauna?" Without waiting for a response, he added, "I really miss them!" Again, he fibbed.

"Your aunty is pregnant so she doesn't like travelling these days though she sends her regards and even bought a Christmas wrapper for Mama." Mama appeared in the sitting room just in time to hear Harry say "wrapper for mama."

"Wrapper for Mama? Oh my daughter! She is at it again, she's never tired of sending gifts to me. May God bless her with the fruit of the womb..." Nanlep was a good actress too, but would never admit that, even to her own son.

Harry laughed confidently, almost arrogantly, and then he declared to Mama that his wife was pregnant and he hoped that it would be a boy.

Giwa thought about the overbearing Aunty Mercy. *Lousy woman, why does she think she can always get away with her tales.* His anger shifted from Aunty Mercy to Uncle Harry, then he pitied Uncle Harry and almost expressed it verbally.

"Is something wrong with you? You seem to be thinking about something, is it worth sharing?" Uncle Harry searched Giwa's eyes attempting to read his mind.

"Actually... I was thinking about what you will possibly name the baby, you know… if it turns out to be a boy as we all hope."

"That is my headache so allow me to take my Panadol."

"Thank you Harry! Let him face his own business," Mama supported Uncle Harry and turned to Giwa, "you had better concern yourself with your studies and the forthcoming naming ceremony." She raised her eyebrows, it had just occurred to her that she had not brought any food to entertain Harry. "We mothers can be very forgetful at times, Kyauta? Hurry up with the food, do you want to starve your uncle?"

Harry attempted to decline, rubbing a protruded stomach and belched prematurely. "Don't tell me anything, if it's about not eating my food, I don't want to hear it." Harry's mouth was already opened then he realized it would be useless to protest further, knowing Nanlep hardly ever accepted a 'no' when it came to her food. She adjusted her wrapper and made for the kitchen as she spoke. "Home food may be bitter but it's always better!" Harry faced Giwa, he shook his head, sighed, smiled and shrugged. He sat down. Kyauta brought tuwo and miyan kuka of which the aroma entangled the atmosphere in the room. She placed the food on the centre table before Uncle Harry. Mama followed closely with a bowl of water. In the other hand, she held an aluminum dish containing her own tuwo that stood like an island amidst the soup. She dropped in on a stool before Giwa. The whole room burned into a frenzy of eating and finger-licking. Mama motioned Kyauta to bring the next course which had a pleasant aroma too, a large plate of isi-ewu. Without a break, Harry devoured the pepper soup to the last bone, sweating and cleaning his nose as he struggled with the last bone.

"I would have missed this sumptuous meal had I said 'no' to your offer. Home sweet home, Mama's food is always the best," he acclaimed while washing his hands after eating.

"Haruna, stop being ridiculous, save the flattery for your next visit," Nanlep pretentiously replied.

"Giwa, please tell Mama that I mean what I just said."

"It's true Mama, Uncle Harry never lies on petty issues as this." Giwa offered his support, he always did that even when Uncle Harry was overtly spinning a make-believe.

"Men will always be men, your words would have moved me had I not heard them before. Besides, Kyauta was very generous with the pepper in the pepper soup."

"Ah ah! That is why it is called 'pepper soup' — because of the pepper in it. Don't forget that she's still learning. If I were to grade her, she would fall within the 'A' and 'B' range. She is definitely taking after her mother, it is a clear indication that a stream of world-class cooks unborn will have their roots in you. Kyauta well done!" He raised his thumb up for her.

Mama smiled at Kyauta, "I can see your head has swollen to more than double its size but don't be carried away by your uncle's praise because he can say that to any woman who appeases the gods of his bowels." They all laughed for a while, then Harry spoke;

"I came here with good news for all of you, especially for Giwa."

"Has he passed his exams again?" Kyauta pried.

"Not only that, he has made all of us proud, his name appeared on the first list of newly admitted students of the University of Jos. That list is also called the Merit list which means his name was there by virtue of his intellectual capability. He is admitted to study Economics, that is the main reason why I came here," facing Mama, "but your delicacy hijacked the news for a while."

Harry's news shocked Mama, she froze with a morsel of tuwo in her hand and her mouth agape. Undoubtedly, she could not believe what she was hearing, Mama dropped the morsel back to her dish, she screamed and danced around the room singing praises to God. Giwa himself could not believe his ears at first, he was convinced when he realized Uncle Harry was in the mood for no jokes. He sat back and whispered a short thank you prayer. Kyauta was already stepping with Mama. Uncle Harry dipped his hand into the pocket of his Kaftan and produced a page from the *Vanguard* newspaper. He carefully unfolded the paper which contained the list of new intakes into the university. They spotted Giwa's name without effort because Harry had earlier underlined it with a red pen. At this point, Giwa's blood was boiling, he could hardly contain the excitement that was rising from within. He didn't know when he hugged each of them twice, including Uncle Harry.

The yellow sun was sending last minutes signals for birds to return to their nests and for people to return home, at the same time it invited a host of nocturnal animals to their day, already, the bats were warming up around a huge mango tree. The celebration in Bako's house was just reaching its peak when Uncle Harry mentioned that he was leaving. Mama suddenly turned pale, she knew better than to ask him to spend the night as Uncle Harry had not passed a night in the house for more that seven years. Harry said he would visit a friend then pass the night there. However, he promised to stop by the next day for lunch before he departed. He also gave them the provisions he brought and Christmas clothes for Giwa and Kyauta. That was another long evening of celebration Giwa would never forget.

Christmas under the Zonkwa sky was terrific. In the morning Giwa was saddled with the irksome task of distributing and receiving different Christmas delicacies from neighbours while Mama and Kyauta prepared an unending variety of food and drinks: Zobo, kunu, jollof rice, moi-moi, doughnuts, pepper soup (goat and chicken separately), fried beef, maasa and tuwon acha. Giwa was careful not to cause a riot in his stomach by eating a little of everything, previous Christmases had taught him better.

Church service was a colourful display of clothes for women and children. The children of the town used the church as an avenue to compare and intimidate one another with the new clothes which were bought for them. Christmas day service was more lively and scintillating than normal Sunday services. The sermon was the normal brief, apt and straight-to-the-point story about Christ's birth and the meaning of Christmas.

The whole town was in a festive mood. A group of women in uniform wrapper danced around from house to house, little children scattered around them like houseflies. Giwa stood in front of his house and observed people moving helter skelter in the spirit of the season.

Samson visited Giwa in the the late afternoon, in company of two beautiful girls, one of whom Giwa intuitively identified as Zhaitun while the other one remained a puzzle to him.

"Merry Christmas Giwa!" Samson initiated the Christmas greeting.

"Same to you, Zhaitun, and her friend," Giwa replied confidently.

"I am not celebrating Christmas, and how did you know my name?" Zhaitun posed, somewhat startled.

"I just guessed, you know am good at guessing," he managed to give an illogical answer which attracted an incredulous look from Zhaitun.

"Don't mind my friend, I showed him your picture." He turned to Giwa, "Since you claim you already know Zhaitun, let me introduce you to Zainab, her friend."

Zainab was tremendously beautiful but Giwa found her repulsive for two reasons: She had a rich Hausa accent which was superimposed on her English, it irked him; secondly, she had a breath-killing body odour that repelled Giwa. She, on the other hand, fell for Giwa hook, line and sinker. She tried to engage Giwa in personal conversation but Giwa gave definite statements without a hint of emotion.

"Hey! Why don't we all go to the Black Pride and cool off with some palm wine. I think it is very boring staying here in the house," Giwa suggested, believing it would pave a way for him to escape his newest acquaintance.

"Now you are talking man," Samson rose to his feet and straightened his shirt. "I am with you."

"We don't want to be seen around beer parlours." Zhaitun said in an ignominious tone.

Within thirty minutes they found themselves seated around a table in Black Pride. The table hosted two jugs of palm wine and also two bottles of malt. Black Pride was unusually filled with people, mostly young boys, showcasing their drinking prowess. At a corner of the bar, some young boys were arguing vehemently about the English Premier League. The words 'Chelsea', 'Manchester' and 'Arsenal' towered over other things they said. The tempo of the argument rose until it became a fist fight. A boy in red T-shirt pounced on another who was wearing a white cotton short-sleeved shirt. It took a while before the boys were separated. The boy in red was injured on his forehead; blood trickled down between his eyes and rolled on his nose. He fumed and ranted and then he cooled down as if all was alright. Then suddenly, he appeared with a big bottle of dry gin and smashed it on the other boy's head. The boy in white short sleeve slumped and his gang of friends agitatedly took over the fight. In a matter of seconds the whole bar became a battle ground for the rivals and it continued on the street. Giwa ran for his dear life, forgetting his friends. He did not stop until he got home. He was happy to have escaped the fight and happier that he got rid of the self-imposing Zainab.

The next day, news went round that the boy who was hit on the head with the bottle of gin eventually died in the hospital. And the boy in red, who committed the atrocious act, was arrested and locked up in the police station. Samson referred to victims of Christmas violence as 'Christmas goats'. He said that violence was a regular occurence at Christmas in Zonkwa in the last three years.

New Year's celebration wasn't much different but it sure was a lot better in terms of violence and vices that accompanied the celebration as compared to that of Christmas. Giwa became obsessed with the thought of being in the university. Tired of the long holiday in Zonkwa, he wanted to experience all those things which he was told about; demonstrations, road shows, matriculation, convocation, campus parties, he could hardly wait. Since Uncle Harry's last visit, Giwa introduced himself and status to new acquaintances as "Giwa Bako, a 100 level student of the prestigious University of Jos." It was deliberately meant to intimidate. The self-acclaimed 100 level student was eventually humbled when he came across a 400 level student of the University of Jos studying Economics. The senior student came visiting from a neighbouring town during the break. He could not identify Giwa's face as a student until Giwa specified that he just got admitted.

"You should have said so earlier, that doesn't make you a student yet, until you have been screened and not found wanting. You will go through the tedium of registration before you are matriculated then you become a student like me. For now you are just at the shore, you have no idea what the hinterland is like." The boy reduced Giwa to a little more than nothing. Giwa would not have felt the effect much if there were not more than a dozen people at the scene.

The celebrations were over, Giwa prepared for his departure. Mama became sick in the week of his departure and lost some weight. Kyauta busied herself with her never-tiring tongue that could talk for more than seventeen hours a day. To her credit, the whole neighbourhood learnt of Giwa's admission the next day after Uncle Harry's visit. More people visited to wish Giwa safe journey, others sent gifts in cash and otherwise. Giwa didn't bother himself with a question such as "How did many people know that I was leaving soon?" He knew the extent of Kyauta's tongue work. He was glad that he didn't tell her a word about Aunty Mercy's terror. Mama mourned his departure as though he was going to die.

The road back to Jos was filled with potholes and police checkpoints. At each checkpoint, the driver squeezed a ₦20 note in his palm, he then plastered the ₦20 note on the policeman's palm and it would stick like some adhesive, the officer would then instruct his colleagues to allow the vehicle to pass unchecked. They passed through seven checkpoints using the same routine. Any driver who wished to bring up an excuse would be asked to 'park well' and would be thoroughly checked, and needlessly delayed for hours. At one checkpoint, Giwa said, “If we continue like this our country will never get better.” The whole lot of the passengers in the Peugeot 504 wagon unanimously agreed, even the driver voiced his agreement.

“My son, you are very right but if we don’t drop something, we will be delayed, which means you won’t reach home in time. It also spells bad business for us.”

As they cruised through the outskirts of Jos making for the heart of the city, Giwa smiled to himself but the smile disappeared as he remembered that Aunty Mercy would be one of the first people he would meet. Nevertheless, he made a firm resolve to throw back his arrows at her. *This time it is going to be fire for fire.*

Six

For the first time in his life, Giwa walked through the main gate of the university, he could hardly contain himself. As much as he gawked at the tastefully designed buildings, well trimmed flowers and the endless stream of fashionable girls and boys, Giwa admired himself the most; a young boy of eighteen, approaching nineteen years of age and a prospective graduate of the University of Jos.

A normal session begins every October but this very session started in January, owing to the prolonged strike embarked upon by the Academic Staff Union of Universities, ASUU.

The students never cared to know what the demands were, nor how many demands had been met, or are being met by the government. Majority of them just wanted to graduate while a smaller fraction of them wanted to learn indeed. In whichever case, all the students craved resumption. The strike was not called off without peaceful demonstrations led by students around the country. The school was full of people; staff and students who have longed to breathe the academic environment after a very long while, and new students who could hardly wait to be in the university.

The dry season unleashed torrents of cold harmattan winds on the rocky city of Jos, the students of the University were not spared from the cold. Almost everyone was clothed from head to foot.

Giwa, like many other new students, or Jambites, or JJC (Johny Just Come), as they were commonly referred to by 200 level, 300 level and 400 level students, read every signboard, every banner, every poster, every handbill, anything readable to be sure of where he was going. He later found out that reading most of those handbills and posters was irrelevant to his mission in school, and that was when he realized half of the day had passed. He lurched forward with a few steps going somewhere he did not know but felt he was on the right track.

"Hey! Great Jossite! Great Jossite!" Giwa turned and noticed two boys walking up to him, he faced his front and saw no one close enough. Convinced he was the one being addressed as "Great Jossite", Giwa turned and faced the boys who were now standing before him.

"Good morning and happy new year sir."

"Are you talking to me?" Giwa was perplexed. He stood stiff like a rock peering at the young boys, asking the unspoken question, *why me?*

"Yes sir, I am Jerry Dalu, a 300 level student of Mass Communications department. With me here is Clifford Gyang also known as Clinton." Jerry appeared to be perfectly dressed, more eloquent, and he had more charisma than Clinton who was later disclosed to be a presidential aspirant in the forthcoming Students' Union Government elections.

Without any iota of doubt, after a shallow persuasion, Clinton and his forerunner left with Giwa's assurance of unalloyed support. Satisfied they had added a potential voter to their list, they moved ahead after explaining the geography of the university to Giwa laying emphasis on the key places he would have to go for one registration or the other.

"I hope you will remember me when you become the SUG President!" He shouted at the boys who were about ten metres away. Clinton was the first to respond, his suit looked old and too big on him, his eye balls too were large and yearned to drop off from their sockets.

"Most assuredly, you will be among my panel of advisers," Clinton was getting acquainted with the language of politicians. The boys hurried to fish out more potential voters.

Giwa felt fingers covering his eyes, he knew someone wanted to surprise him and he would not start guessing without a clue; he inhaled deeply to catch the smell of the hands. It smelt of cigarette. "Abdul!" Giwa mentioned, wondering what could possibly bring a secondary school drop-out to the university.

"Try again."

Giwa could not mistake his former roomate's voice. This time, he didn't guess. He called out the name and the odour on his palm was the check. "Gasko!"

"Bright boy, you are smart." He removed his fingers from Giwa's face. "How did you know I was the one?"

"You know I will never mistake your voice for someone else's." Giwa turned and they hugged each other warmly.

Giwa was not really surprised when he saw his long-lost friend because he knew Gasko resided close by. Gasko was more familiar with the university environment because he practically grew up in the area close the university known to the students as offcamp.

After all the hustle and bustle of the day, Giwa realized that he had taken only one step of the whole registration exercise, and that was the screening exercise.

* * * * *

Three weeks had passed before Giwa was almost done with the registration process. It was a good time to be away from the sight of Aunty Mercy. Sometimes when he was sure that he had nothing to do in school, he would rather still go and watch the day ebb away. He thought of accommodation in the hostel in his search for flying-bird freedom, to stay alone for the first time in his life, and do whatever he decided. Uncle Harry had stocked him with more than enough money for the whole registration process.

About sixty students were admitted into the department of Economics and the departmental registration availed them an opportunity to know themselves better. New friends were won and enemies sworn. One thing new students had in common was that they carried large brown files about. It was that easy for political unionists, Christian students, Muslim students, and cultists to identify the targets they wanted to woo to their sides. Different religions, ethnic and social groups flaunted their invitation banners or handbills to new students. None of all these groups attracted Giwa because he made up his mind to live a triangular student life —- classroom, hostel and church.

On the Friday morning that Giwa completed his hectic registration, he had two unpleasant encounters; first was a dark shabby guy who approached and spoke to him amicably, telling him about a brotherhood of handsome fellows and asked if Giwa would like to join them. The obnoxious guy also promised him protection on the campus. Giwa had a clue about what the boy implied so he bluntly declared that he was not interested and promptly disappeared before the shabby guy found more seducing words. The queue in front of the department was unusually long but Giwa joined in from behind. Giwa fumed and cursed the dirty boy whose wooing made him lose a valuable space at the front of the line. Suddenly, he felt the urge to ease himself and when he came back, a young girl had occupied his space with two other girls at her back. Giwa tried to be as polite as possible.

"Good morning ladies." Without waiting for a response he continued, "This is my space, if you don't mind, I would like to enter. I just went to ease myself." He gently tried to push his way in front of the fair-skinned girl. He didn't anticipate that the girl could muster enough strength to shove him away and leave him staggering to gain balance. His nerves automatically charged when he got his balance, his eyes boiled with fire only to meet her raging hazel eyes.

"You dey craze? Do you think you can succeed with your *wayo wayo*?" The girl ranted.

"Ask the boy in front of you whether I was not standing at his back before I left to ease myself." Giwa snapped hoping to be vindicated soon but his hope disappeared like smoke in the air when the boy in front replied that he didn't know who was standing behind him. Giwa felt embarrassed, not only because of the boy's reply, but also because the boy's reply was accompanied by jeering and provocative laughter from the girls. Having completed his registration exercise, Giwa retired home in a defeated mood. He wished he was sick.

* * * * *

Lectures commenced immediately after registration. On the second day of the lectures, the class was filled to capacity. It was a course which other students from the same faculty borrowed. Giwa, not unlike other attentive students, sat in the first row with a little room for one person to squeeze in but that small space was overlooked by many students. A fair-skinned lady briskly walked in five minutes into the lecture and whispered pleadingly to Giwa to adjust a little. The attentive boy had no time to even look at who was asking. Being carried away by the lecture, he shifted without taking note of who the person was.

At the end of the lecture, the lecturer, Mr. Adegoke, also known as Adam Smith, began to recite a long list of dos and don'ts in his class. That was the point when the class became rowdy, shuffling feet, squeaking chairs and desks, faint noise here and there, and that was the moment Giwa recognized the girl sitting next to him as the same girl he had a quarrel with last Friday morning. Unfortunately, the girl didn't recognize him, with a broad smile on her face she expressed her appreciation.

"My brother, thank you very much for the space, I don't know how I would have attended this lecture without your kindness, God bless you."

She even calls me brother, he thought. "No problem, it's a pity you don't recognize me again. You know this world is a small place."

"Really! Where? Have we met before?" she raised a quizzical eyebrow curiously wanting to know how popular she had become in so little a time.

He patiently recounted their last Friday's ordeal in front of department not forgetting to add the embarassment he suffered. The girl went cold after he finished talking. She kept mute for half a minute and heaved a sigh.

"I am really sorry, those girls behind me incited me to fight for my right and that *mumu* boy didn't..."

"It's okay!" Giwa cut her short, "let bygones be bygones! It wasn't your fault, you thought you were right. Sometimes we feel all right with ourselves even when we do the wrong things."

"I know, I am really feeling bad for what I did, I will..." Giwa didn't allow her to continue offloading dozens of apology. He cleverly averted the issue.

"My name is Giwa Bako and you are?" The girl was shocked at how amiable Giwa was.

"Hannah, Hannah Musa is my name. I'm pleased to meet you on a friendly ground."

Hannah became his favourite acquaintance. But he didn't extend the warm handshake for nothing, he realized that Hannah was exceptionally beautiful, she had large eyeballs and long dark hair marooned at the end. Had he realized her excessive beauty last Friday, he wouldn't have argued with her even for a moment but he had another chance and he thanked his stars that he didn't blow it.

Giwa made it a habit to locate Hannah every morning before or after their first lecture, she too did the same. That routine continued throughout the remaining days of the week. She was gradually becoming an obsession for Giwa and he liked it that way. Everyday, after the day's lessons, the two of them would hang around the social centre or park and talk for long hours in which Giwa would sit and gaze at her for hours as she spoke. Occasionally, the two would face each other without uttering a word but saying more than they could employ their speech articulators. The 100 level class was *au fait* with the sight of Giwa and Hannah, their friendship was so strong that even some lecturers would not see one of them without inquring about the whereabout of the other. Many students hastily assumed they were dating. Giwa wished it was so.

His feelings for Hannah grew stronger and stronger by the day, Giwa resolved to let the cat out of the bag but on that fateful day, an episode occurred which compelled him to sheathe his sword, his premiere sortie never saw daylight. Lectures were terminated at twelve noon on that Friday of the fourth week. Hannah or Hanny, as he preferred to call her informed him that she was going to Bauchi for the weekend. He thought he could give her company to the bus park and, in the course, express his overwhelming passion to her.

As they strolled towards the park, he cleared his throat to speak but the words just wouldn't come out. Finally, as he made to speak, a white Mercedez Benz C230 pulled up in front of them and a well-built dark guy in black sunglasses emerged from the driver's seat. His teeth were dazzling under the brightness of the sun, he spread his muscular arms open.

Hannah's hazel eyes glittered, "Oh my God, I can't believe this! Sam, it's a lie!" she shouted astonishingly and flew into his arms.

"You had better believe it, I'm back." Sam hugged her tightly for a few seconds, released her, planted a few kisses on her cheeks and forehead then he hugged her again and held her by his side. For that brief moment, she was oblivious of Giwa until Sam demanded who 'that boy' was.

"Oh! Giwa?" She almost forgot about him. "I am so sorry, this is my boyfriend Sam."

"Samuel, Samson, or Sam what? Giwa sneeringly asked, not really interested in knowing him. The guy seemed offended but pretended not to be although he had no inkling what bolting rage had welled up inside Giwa.

"The name is Samuel," he stated. "But my darling here," Samuel wrapped his left arm around her, "calls me Sammy." He tried to intimidate Giwa with his I-own-this-chick posture. Sammy brought forward his hand, "And you are Giwa, right?" Giwa shook him affirmatively.

"Sammy, Giwa is my coursemate and also a very good friend of mine." She turned to Giwa, "Remember the Sam I told you about?"

"Yes of course, you did mention one Sam casually in one of your stories." *But not in the way you mean it now*. Giwa shielded his thought with a smile. "You people will make a wonderful couple, Hanny & Sammy." He teased. "Romeo and Juliet will have to excuse me now because I intend to move into the hostel this weekend and there are a lot of things that I have yet to do." Giwa wisely opted out before he could think anything suicidal.

"I will see you on Monday, have a lovely weekend." She hopped into the passenger's seat as Sam drove away. Depressed, Giwa went home straight and was almost hit twice by two different vehicles because he was lost in the maze of his thoughts.

Hannah was the last child in a family of four and her three older siblings were already working. The first, Naomi, a medical doctor, worked with the Jos University Teaching Hospital JUTH and was married to an alcoholic lawyer. The man was an indigene of the state and both of them resided in Jos. Hannah was putting up with them for the time being but she hoped to get a self-contained apartment.

Hannah's father headed an engineering firm in Bauchi which undertook road, bridge and building constructions. Her other two siblings were bankers, both residing in Bauchi state capital. Her mother was a pretty Fulani woman who was not really educated but she understood English. Apparently, Hannah lacked nothing, at least nothing that money could buy or solve. Moreover, she had the beauty that could earn her any amount she demanded, but she was down to earth, her austere manner of fashion spoke little of her father's opulence. Initially, her father wanted her to attend university abroad but her mother declined on the ground that Hannah was not mature enough to stay wholly on her own because many of those wealthy men's children came back as either drug addicts or deportees. Out of her ingenuity, Hannah's mother suggested that she should school in the country and then she could study for her Masters degree abroad.

The things Hannah hated most were unfaithfulness, cheating and dishonesty. Ironically, those were the apt attributes that described her Sammy, though he played his cards so well that he left no traces behind. Trying to identify those faults in Sam through Hannah's eyes was like looking for a needle in a haysack. He was way too smart for her intellect.

Giwa also became the object of her fantasy but she was in a dilemma because she was already in a relationship with someone who she thought loved her dearly. Besides, traditionally, the onus was on the male to initiate a relationship. Giwa had not yet declared his feelings so she was buying time to set the right response in place.

* * * * *

"How dare you enter my house at this hour! Have you now become my husband that I will cook and clean up the house for? Are you the first person to gain admission into the university?" Certainly, Aunty Mercy was at it again. This time, she was furious and could not hide her exasperation. She didn't know he had resolved she wasn't going to be part of his problems. It was clear that Giwa's potential degree constituted a threat to her.

The young boy stared at her as she ranted, a million responses formed within his head none of which he used. Instead, he let out an unconnected one which was equally provoking.

"I am moving to the hostel this weekend." Though his response was very brief, it had more meaning than Aunty Mercy could decipher. He didn't wait for her to continue, she was left standing there by herself shouting at a walking Giwa. He went straight into his room, locked the door, and dived into his bed covering his head with a pillow. *I have just this weekend to bear*.

Aunty Mercy had no reason to be mad at Giwa since all the cooking and house chores were done by Kauna, except if she was concerned about his safety which was most improbable. She was fussy because Giwa went out and came back at will, and she had no control over his movements.

Uncle Harry arrived thirty minutes later and was given a cold welcome by his wife. From what she said, he understood that Giwa was the cause of her unhappy mood. Harry went straight to Giwa's room and met him half asleep. He gently inquired about the cause of the problem. Giwa narrated their small encounter, not forgetting to add that the hectic and cumbersome loads of assignments kept him so late in school. Giwa seized the opportunity to talk Uncle Harry into allowing him to move to the hostel, promising to come home on weekends. Without any second thought, Uncle Harry hastily approved his request.

"I had that in mind too. I think it will be good for you to move into the hostel in order to stay with your peers. Let me have the list of things you will require first thing in the morning."

Checking into the hostel with the porters was one of the easiest, queueless and stress-free registrations one could possibly do in the university. Uncle Harry dashed back as soon as he dropped Giwa and confirmed his room number was B24, Abacha hostel. Giwa paid his hostel levy; the accommodation fee was paid together with his school tuition.

Abacha hostel accommodated more students than any other hostel in the University. It comprised six blocks lettered A to F. The male students shared three blocks and the females shared the other three. In front of the hostel a large signpost read;

WELCOME TO ABACHA HOSTEL
(ALUTA CRADLE)

Motto: The denial of a right is an invitation to fight for it

Giwa had heard of that particular hostel from the time he was in secondary school courtesy of Duff's incredible stories. He knew it as the birthplace of all demonstrations on campus from the school's inception. Between the male and female blocks was an open space with a flag flown at half mast and a short concrete pillar known as the 'Throne of Declaration'. The open space was known as the Aluta ground. There, all students' activism begin and end.

The ground floors of all the blocks were reserved for new students only, though very limited, because of the craze for hostels since about two years earlier when many students became victims of a religious crisis that engulfed certain areas in the city of Jos. Each block consisted of about two hundred rooms with five bedspaces in each of the rooms. Usually, the first member of each room to pay his hostel dues gets the most confortable space, known as the 'inner space', while the last person to clear his space gets the least comfortable bedspace otherwise known as the 'receptionist's space'. The owner of the receptionist's space opens the door to all visitors and also supplies answers to inquiries on the particular room. Sometimes, the receptionist is asked to check whether a certain member of the room is in or not.

Giwa struggled under the weight of his luggage to his room. Fortunately, he was the first person to clear his bedspace in the room so the inner space became his. It took him an hour to clean up the space and unpack his load. No sooner had he unpacked his belongings than trouble ensued – a young lady arrived and commanded Giwa to vacate the space for her younger brother who was too timid and too shy, he stood a few paces behind her.

"This room was empty when I came in this evening and I was the first to clear this bedspace. It belongs to me." Being a 300 level student, the girl was accustomed to bullying and oppressing new students. It was a common characteristic of most of the older Abacha Hostel residents. Giwa had heard of their type and he readied himself for her. He held on until she could prove the space belonged to her brother beyond any reasonable doubt.

"My brother and I reserved this space on Friday and we couldn't find time to come in until today. Who are you by the way? Do you know me? Go and ask around this hostel and you will know!"

"See, I don't know you and I don't want to know you! Who the hell you are is your own business. As far as I am concerned, I can only discuss this issue with your brother! Hey you! Come here!" He motioned the boy to come closer. "Are you are not the owner of this space? Why did you allow her to speak on your behalf? Is she your lawyer or your god?" Giwa spoke to him as a father would to his son, "Bros! You be guy like me, come make we tok man-to-man." He moved his concentration on the poor timid boy who became limp like cooked spinach. The boy was trembling before Giwa.

"If you know what is good for you, better pack out of this space for my brother," the girl continued arrogantly.

A mature student from the next room, obviously disturbed by the heated argument, intervened with a suggestion that both parties should go back to the porter's office in order to resolve the issue amicably instead of creating a scene. Without any hesitation, both parties agreed and made for the porter's office.

The porter's office became, more or less, a courtroom as different parties trooped in to make one confirmation or the other about a space, or a room, as the case may be. Some accommodation disputes ended as mere quarrels while others translated into fist fights. At that stage, such a case was handled by the security officers of the hostel at the porter's office.

When Giwa and the quarrelsome girl reached the office, they were almost immediately ushered in by one of the porters who seemed to be familiar with the girl. After hearing from both sides, the chief porter verified their hostel dues receipt which was dated the same day but the file in his possession confirmed Giwa's was two hours earlier so the space was his. The chief porter ruled in favour of Giwa.

The girl, already disappointed, faced the officer who ushered them in, "But sir, I gave you something now, why didn't you reserve the space for my brother on Friday?" The girl was almost in tears seeing that she had lost the battle. The man simply shrugged as if it was not his fault for collecting the bribe.

"I told you to pay immediately but you said the money wasn't enough." The officer sought to justify himself. Since she had no receipt to that effect, she couldn't demand for her money back.

The girl apologized profusely when they came back into the room. Her brother too joined her in apologizing to Giwa. "It's one of those things that happen, besides it is good to stand for something." The girl later introduced herself as Jane popularly known as 'De chick' and her brother as Joshua. Joshua looked calm and easy-going contrary to his sister, De chick, who from her seductive fashion spoke volumes about herself. Giwa wondered if both of them were truly born of the same mother as Jane claimed. Hunger followed afterwards and Giwa couldn't help it.

* * * * *

Matriculation ceremony was held exactly a week after Giwa moved into the hostel. Hannah's whole family was there for her, including her Sammy. Giwa on the other hand, had no special guest. The school was full of students and visitors. Music blared from different corners as people were in groups for refreshment under canopies or shades of trees. Photographers took pictures till their films finished. Hannah found Giwa accidentally in the crowd and she dragged him to where her family was gathered. Her meeting him was timely because he was really hungry and the quantity of food given to him was generous; the quality too was good. The food was appetizing, so well that it could entice the most jaded appetite. Assorted drinks flowed like a stream of water. The only thing that spoilt his day was the intimidating presence of Sam who craved for more of Hannah around him to Giwa's chagrin. Engineer Musa, Hannah's father, was extremely pleased to meet Giwa largely because Hanny introduced him to her father as her closest friend in school and also her classmate. He showered words of advice on Giwa, her mother spoke a little, admonishing them to take care of themselves as God would bless them. Her older siblings were interested in the Giwa that Hannah spoke so much about even more than Sam.

Loaded from the stomach to his pocket, Giwa left the Musas celebrating their daughter's matriculation. He would have stayed longer if Sam was not around. Sam's presence made him grow mad with jealousy. Giwa's best option was to leave before he lost control of his nerves. Good food in the belly and good money in the pocket, what more could he possibly ask for from such a kind and wonderful family?

Uncle Harry had informed him earlier that he would not be able to come for his matriculation because he was on an unavoidable call in the hospital. Aunty Mercy must have made up a reasonable excuse to disallow her from attending Giwa's matriculation. Whatever those excuses were, he was pleased that she didn't witness his matriculation ceremony. He pictured himself posing for a shot with Aunty Mercy, it irked him, he grimaced and hissed. His one regret was that neither Mama nor Kyauta were there to witness his initiation into the university.

Among those who were being matriculated on that day were Gasko and Duff. Somehow, they manoeuvred their way into the university through the third list otherwise known as the VC's list. The first list or merit list bore names like that of Giwa, the second list or supplementary list bore names like that of Hannah. The third list came out barely a fortnight before the matriculation ceremony.

Directly opposite the main gate of the University stood a large beer joint with small thatched open huts around but not unaffiliated with the main bar itself, on the gates were large unavoidable writings of concrete readable from half a kilometre away. It read;

THE SHARK'S BAR

The words were more visible than that of the University itself or any other institution located anywhere within a five kilometre radius of the bar. Underneath the concrete name, a slogan in much smaller fonts in italics read.

You can't lack water in the ocean!!

They were very right on that one because they never run out of beer, although they seldom run out of malt drinks, soft drinks, wines and cigarettes but never out of beer. It was said that the owner of the beer parlour once proclaimed that he would rather die than witness a day without beer being sold at his joint. At night, the neon cables on the concrete writings gleamed, guiding alcoholics to their rendezvous.

The excitement of the matriculation ceremony was ebbing away, parents and guardians admonished their wards in their valedictions. Other new students had just begun initiation into different groups. At Sharks Bar, cult groups gathered in different huts waiting for prospective members. Gasko and Duff had been drinking at the bar from morning but took time off to enter the school compound, borrow academic gowns and take what would serve as pictorial evidence that they had been to the University.

Giwa stood at the front of the University gate idly gazing at the Shark's Bar, his thoughts were far away, precisely on strategies on how to outwit his competitor – Sam. Suddenly, he felt a soft poke from behind, he quickly came back to himself and turned around, Duff was standing behind him.

"Wetin you dey do for hia sef? De matriculation dull you? Duff's red eyes and stinking breath told Giwa he had been drinking for hours.

"Oh boy! Na you be dis? I am okay, I'm just at a loss where to go because I think it's too early for me to get back to the hostel."

"You fit come relax wit us for Shark now!" Duff cajoled Giwa. For a moment, Giwa contemplated and then he gave in. He believed some liquor could do the magic of helping him forget the Sam-Hannah trauma.

"Am in, but nothing more than two bottles of stout, Guiness!"

"Ha! ha! ha! Damn! I thought you were totally out of the game. As for me, I'll be drinking and smoking till the day I die! Notin dey happen!" He dragged Giwa across the main road into Shark's Bar. In such a short period, Duff had acquired so much popularity than Giwa could imagine. The name 'Duff' boomed from different corners of the bar. A young girl in dreadlocks entertained some boys in a round hut, smoking a cigarette in her left hand as she spoke, she too saluted Duff as he passed by. Giwa noticed a paw-like tattoo on her overexposed left breast. At a far end of the bar, a round hut housed a bunch of girls also drinking and smoking – it was an all-girls affair.

A standing ovation awaited Duff as he neared the hut where his boys, including Gasko, were relaxing. They all hailed him as a "confirmed Jossite". Gasko took his time to introduce his fellows one after the other to Giwa.

"Gentlemen, this is Giwa, king of the jungle!" They all roared with laughter and he continued when the roar quietened. He stood energetically as though he was delivering a speech.

Duff took over the speech, "Since I have been confirmed as a student today… We are going to drink till I run out of money or…"

"Till they run out of beer!" they chorused amidst thunderous laughter.

The bar man appeared with another round of beer for everyone and, of course, the stout Giwa demanded for. A lot of foul talk filled the air, Giwa wasn't accustomed to it but he endured it anyway, *that may be the price for free booze.*

Giwa barely started drinking his second bottle when a guy in black beret, known as Cheifo, announced that they were running late for the after-matricluation party. In a few minutes, Duff settled for all the drinks with no less than sixteen thousand naira.

A fair handsome boy emerged and took his seat across Giwa. He wore a green T-shirt, black jeans trousers and a pair of sneakers which had patches of black and white evenly distributed on it. His hair was artificially relaxed in a way that made him look like a biracial and his lips were dark, obviously from the cigarette he smoked.

"Your friends are leaving, ain't you goin with 'em?" The guy tried to speak in a poorly disguised American accent.

"I am not yet done with my bottle." Giwa pointed at the bottle whose content had gone halfway as if that was his excuse for not leaving along with his friends. "Besides they are not all my friends, I met most of them here, just like you."

"What about Duff? I saw him leading you here."

"Gasko, Duff and myself have come a long way but we are not tight like before."

"Did they tell you where they were going to?"

"An after-matriculation party," Giwa swiftly responded.

The guy looked at the gate, around, and then at Giwa. "Those boys have bitten more than they can chew, I hope they know what they are staking their lives for!"

"What? What are you saying?" He was reading many different negative meanings from what the boy in green said.

"Never mind, they call me KC."

"How do you spell it?"

"The letters K and C but my full name is Kelechi, only my parents still call me that."

Seven

For the first time, Solomon contemplated going to Tambes, his birthplace, but the thought of being treated like an outcast forced him to have a rethink. He had just finished his last paper and was not willing to spend another week with Father Kut, his number one critic. He endured staying because he had no other building that could shelter him. The food he ate too was free and most importantly, his salary as a church worker flowed constantly as long as he remained in the house. The salary stopped flowing as soon as he reached his final year in secondary school. *There comes a time when all that you have means nothing to you since no one loves you.* His mind was made up about leaving the house.

The Obis came to Solomon as an option, they had always shown concern for him ever since Father Brown left the Parish. The only family that sent him Christmas presents every yuletide season, the only family that followed and celebrated his academic achievements, and that was the only family that provided succour to him in time of need. *They cannot sponsor me for free but I must do all it takes to pursue higher education, that has always been Father Brown's dream for me and I can't afford to disappoint him, not in this life.* He watched a housefly entangled in a spider's web. The spider furiously tied more strings around the buzzing fly. It seemed the housefly was determined to live longer, it escaped from the woven net leaving the spider disappointed. Solomon wondered why the fly would escape in view of the fact that houseflies don't live for more than a week. He heaved a sigh and made for his room. The Obis had to be his last resort and he must have a word with Mr. Obi.

Mr. Obi's house doubled as his office too. The building was a huge one with five shops at the front of which two were his warehouse, one was restaurant owned by a neighbour, another was a provision store owned by his wife and the last was his office where samples of his wares were displayed. The house generally smelt of cement and paint. Mr. Obi was unarguably the biggest distributor of cement in the whole of Pankshin Local Government Area. He also sold paint and other building materials. He was often referred to as the only honest Igbo man in Pankshin, yet he was also the biggest donor in the parish.

He had a bald head and a big fat nose that made him look like a clown in Solomon's eyes, but it was all to his advantage as he was always jovial and easy-going. He had a sugar-coated tongue, which he used to coax people to become his customers and friends. Father Brown once remarked that Mr. Obi had the kind of tongue that can make someone to buy a thick jacket in Lagos despite the heat. Many people were not surprised when he came back from the East with a very beautiful young girl as his wife, they knew that his tongue did the work.

"Good afternoon sir."

"Ah! my son, how are you?" Mr. Obi answered without looking up; he concentrated on counting a huge wad of ₦500 notes. After a minute, he was done with the counting. He looked up and recognized Solomon. "Ewoo Solo! How are you? I didn't know you were the one greeting now! Biko no vex, sit down now! What do you want to drink?" Mr. Obi venerated Solomon just half as much as he would Father Brown. Somehow, he saw Solomon as an extension of his most cherished spiritual father.

"Sir, I'm sorry to disturb you at this hour. I..."

"No! No! No! There is no problem at all my son, you know this is your home too. Feel free son."

I wish he knew I was looking for a home, and that he could help. After a long exchange of pleasantaries, Solomon decided to disclose the purpose of his visit. He started just after Adaku, Mr Obi's first daughter, had opened his bottle of Coke, in case his words were trapped within his throat, the drink would wash them down, that was his belief.

"Hmmn! Eh hem!" Mr. Obi cleared his voice after listening patiently to Solomon for about half an hour, the half an hour that seemed to Solomon as an eternity of persuasive speech. "I have heard you Solomon, I am happy that, as you said, I am the only one that knows about your predicament, which means that you have bestowed a high level of trust and confidence upon me. For that, I'm very grateful. Left for me, I would have just allowed you to pack in immediately but you know I have a wife and six daughters... Do you get my point?"

"I'm afraid I still haven't got it sir," Solomon frankly admitted.

"Solo, my point is, adopting you as a child would greatly infuriate my wife, and you know that we do not have a son. She may consider it as my selfish attempt of bringing an heir that would deprive them of having access to my wealth or whatever when I am no more." Mr. Obi's face reflected the degree of honesty in his heart as he spoke.

"Say no more sir, I understand. I would not have dared to ask if I wasn't living in... in hell." Solo blurted.

"No! No! No! My son, please don't talk like that..."

"But that is the truth sir." A lump had formed in Solomon's throat blocking others words from flowing out and instead, tears flowed from his eyes. He felt helpless like a baby; he buried his face in his palms and sobbed louder. He felt Mr. Obi's hands rubbing his back. His mouth tasted salty when he tried to talk. "Father Kut is never pleased with what I do. He treats me like a piece of rag. Papa Ada, I can't stand it anymore; I don't want to live there anymore." This time, Mr. Obi wrapped him in his arms. Solo felt a bit of what it was like to have a father.

"It's okay. *Ndo, Ndo,* you will be fine, clean your tears and sit down."

"Thank you sir, thank you for hearing me out." He wiped his tears in time to see Baby Nnenna watching her father and the 'church boy' in warm embrace, probably wondering why her father was doing that. Solomon's face brightened up, his lips relaxed into a broad smile, "Nnenna, come here!" The toddler stared at him incredulously and ran for her mother. "That girl is growing like a bamboo stick," he said as he watched the girl disappear through the huge black gate.

"Her physical growth does not bother me as much as her mental growth. She is a little King Solomon in the making, maybe I should have named her Solomia hahaha." They broke into a mild laugh. Once more, Mr. Obi's mirth had resumed to lighten the atmosphere.

"Should I make her my wife then?" Solo teased.

"*Kai, Meshonnu gi,*" Mr. Obi barked amusingly as his eyes almost jumped out of their sockets. They broke into another round of laughter. "They are my boys and girls, they are all I have," he stared into space as he spoke soberly.

Alas! Everyone has a burden to bear, I need a home, he needs a son.

"Are they not human beings? Children are children."

"You are such a good chap, I'll offer you a deal now; feel free to take it or decline."

"Who am I to decline? Anything you say is good Oga, I'll take it." Solomon began to see the silver lining on a dark cloud, it lightened his mood.

Papa Ada cleared his throat. He looked like a septuagenarian about to tell a long proverb; he gazed into the floor and raised up his head as if he had just communed with his dead ancestors. "My son, you will come here as one of my trade apprentices. I'll give you a room but you will help me in my business and since you are reasonably educated, I'll elevate you to the status of Senior Apprentice or Personal Assistant." Mr. Obi tapped Solomon on the shoulder, "I know that all you need from me is sponsorship, of course you will get it. You will be entitled to a monthly allowance at the end of every month, but, like I tell my boys here, you must not have an intimate relationship with any of my daughters; if you do, you will regret ever knowing me. Besides that, I can tolerate any other misbehaviour."

Solomon could hardly contain his excitement, his face glittered. "Frankly, I don't know how to appreciate your kindness sir but God will bless you. I am very grateful sir." Another lump formed in his throat. Solomon knelt before his new master, held his hands and shed tears, only this time it was tears of joy.

* * * * *

"Have you finished your SSCE exams? I just hope the examiners will be lenient enough to give you pass marks."

Father Kut had just returned from the annual seven-day fathers' conference. His response to Solomon's greeting had just given Solomon more impetus to leave. He didn't even answer his greeting. "Must I remind you to set the table for me again? *Mumu*, I don't even know why that *Oyibo* decided to waste the church's money on a fool like you in the name of school. Thank God the school is now over, at least I can now have some peace." He continued shouting until Solomon announced that the table had been set.

As usual, Solomon anticipated negative comments. Solomon's food, to Father Kut, was always too salty, too cold, too hot, too coloured or too anything that can be overlooked. Today the food was too spicy, he blamed Solomon for being extravagant with the spices.

There was a knock on the door, Solomon opened it for Martha, a divorcee who had recently become a nocturnal visitor. She came for Father Kut to help pray for her husband to return to her. The prayers were more effective in Father Kut's room. Solomon understood the procedure but he preferred to mind his own business. They didn't waste time exchanging pleasantaries, she led the way. Solomon knew that he would not see Father Kut again till the next morning so he decided to inform him before the next day.

"Father, I would like to have a word with you." Solomon wore his most polite face as he pleaded.

"Can't it wait?" Father Kut was rather too much in a hurry to get inside.

"But father it is private, could you..." Solomon pleaded again.

"Shut up *mumu*, either you say it now or never. Can't you see that you are wasting my time?" Father Kut was getting incredibly bitter. Solomon observed a protrusion at the front of father Kut's cassock, he then understood what he meant by 'wasting my time,' and the need for him to be as brief as possible so he hit the nail hard on the head.

"I'm leaving tomorrow by His special grace. I have found a home." He stared at both of them as they froze, dumbfounded.

* * * * *

Two seasons had passed, Giwa was in his second year in the university, yet so many tragic events had occurred within the previous year. Uncle Harry had been robbed of a large sum of money; the amount which he never disclosed, but Giwa believed it was worth a fortune. In that year, Aunty Mercy had another bout of her self-orchestrated miscarriage. In the same year, Giwa's mother was bitten by a black cobra and the doctor said she would have survived if the case was reported on time.

Giwa's 100 level results were released along with those of other students and he found out that his performance wasn't really impressive, it was merely on the average. He blamed his inability to perform excellently on the nauseating events of the previous year and Hannah's estrangement from him. Hannah's bossy lover, Sam, had hired a mole who reported Giwa's every contact with her: Every hug and every handshake was reported to Sam. Sam would call Hannah and threaten to quit each time he received a report from his mole. For no justifiable reason, Hannah stayed miles away from Giwa, or any other male student at all. She was slavishly misled into thinking that Sammy would eventually marry her since he was the person who broke her honey pot. Her mum used to tell her that "the first person to have carnal knowledge of you must be your husband."

The school system began to bore him as much as Uncle Harry's home, his heart's desire would dare not smile at him because she believed Sammy's spy could be lurking anywhere within the vicinity, probably with a pair of binoculars to ascertain the broadness of the smile.

Out of boredom, and pressure from Christian brothers, he decided to join the Fellowship of Christian Students (FCS). He was not fully at ease, however, he felt he was carrying out his mother's last wish on her death bed — as he was told — that he should seek the face of God in all his endeavours. The same words in different combinations and different languages fell into his ears during Mama's funeral. Many people encouraged him with such words, including Aunty Mercy, whose sympathy he hoped was genuine. At the graveside, she wept and held the casket persistently as if it was her own mother.

At first, he enjoyed attending the fellowship services of the FCS but it was not for long. The new leadership of the FCS came up with strict rules, some of which included; compulsory prayer and fasting every Monday of the week, ban on use of expensive jewellery and sunshades for members at all times, compulsory joining of a ministeration group and compulsory speaking in tongues for all members. Giwa tried to adhere to the new rules but he had a great deal of difficulty abstaining from food on all Mondays because Monday's lectures were unusually longer than all others. He couldn't endure it. He didn't fancy jewellery and he didn't care about sunshades either; that one was fine by him. He tried to join a ministration group —- the drama group, but failed the interview on the grounds that he was not born again in the spirit, which meant he couldn't speak in tongues and which also meant he was not qualified to be a member of the fellowship.

On one of the fellowship days, an invited speaker called all non-speakers of the heavenly language (speaking in tongues) to the front; Giwa was among them. The speaker promised that they would speak in tongues after he had laid his hand on their heads. Giwa noticed some students falling backward, some fell forward and others just stood still, chanting some incomprehensible words which the speaker might have understood as the heavenly language so he left them and moved to the next person. As he moved closer, Giwa silently hoped that he would not fall anyhow. Instantly, he decided to stand firm.

As the man of God laid his hands on Giwa, he chanted the heavenly language squirting tiny drops of saliva on Giwa's face. His breath stank of garlic, or some obnoxious spice, and then he said "I command you to loose your tongue and let the Holy Spirit have his way in you, loose it, *ebababarich talamaya sakorica*!" He yanked Giwa's head forward with his strong fingers and pushed it backwards repeatedly as he spoke, but Giwa's feet on the ground was firm. The man of God pushed harder and spoke louder, Giwa couldn't endure it any longer.

He heard the FCS president, now acting as the speaker's assistant, saying "Brother, open your mouth and speak in a new tongue, don't disgrace the man of God, brother..." Suddenly, Giwa remembered a sentence his mother used to say in Rom language, so he began to utter it slowly, solemnly, then quickly and loudly as he gyrated. Seeing that he had triumphed, the man of God moved over to the next person until he was through. The man's lace was soaked in his sweat. He therefore declared that they had acquired a new heavenly language and they shall continue to speak it.

"Amen!" they all agreed.

"That is a disgraceful and ungrateful 'amen'. Shout it like you mean it!" The man of God dabbed his handkerchief on his forehead as he breathed into the microphone.

"Amen!" the congregation shouted in unison.

As they walked back to the hostel, a brother was speaking in tongues. He was speaking English and tongues at the same time as though he was translating it into English. Giwa was marvelled, he moved closer and asked the brother how he acquired it. "It's quite easy, just how you learn your ABC, but here you will have to start with *rarara, kakaka, bababa* and before you know it, you will be fluent in the heavenly language just like Papa who spoke today. I learnt he sometimes communicates with his family using the heavenly language," the boy said. "Oh *rashika-parapaya*! Hey!" he hit his head violently as if he had just received a divine revelation. It was the same boy whom Giwa would later learn was involved in examination malpractice and was rusticated.

He was mute, he kept his thoughts to himself. It was at that point that he finally made up his mind to quietly withdraw from the FCS since his personal dispositions were parallel with the teachings of the FCS, but he still respected the members of the fellowship including the Exco, who seldom responded to his greetings for whatever reasons best known to them.

* * * * *

In spite of how determined he was to live right, things didn't work out well at all for Giwa. His condition perpetually plummeted from bad to worse. He was easily angered by anything. In fact, everything made him miserable and he thought he was running insane. Uncle Harry had stopped visiting him. Harry too had become oblivious of him. Giwa's academic activities also were becoming more boring. He became so broke that he would boil beans, add palm oil and salt then make meals out of it for days. At this point he made up his mind to face his worst nightmare. He had avoided Uncle Harry's house for two straight months and was now going for a weekend, although he wished he could stay away forever. Giwa's problems had grown so big that he saw Aunty Mercy as just part of it, a hurdle that needed to be crossed, and permanently, he hoped. He thought of his darling mother, now resting in her grave, or rejoicing with the angels in heaven, or languishing in... "No!" he said. He looked around and found he was sitting beside himself with an empty Ghana-must-go bag. Grains of rice, beans, and garri fell to the bottom of the bag measuring not up to a small container of a tin of milk; that was all the food that belonged to Giwa. He pitied himself but he pitied Kyauta more. He imagined how she would be coping all alone in Zonkwa. The thought of Kyauta made his eyes brim with tears. He vowed to make her life better as soon as he graduated and got a good job.

It was 3pm when he checked his watch; which meant he had been sitting on his bed for about two hours doing nothing but just thinking of how he was going to face the ever-belligerent lioness. A decision had to be made between starving in school and surviving with hot coals of fire on the head.

* * * * *

Kauna was seated under the shade of a guava tree. She held an old newspaper, desperately trying to comprehend the words there or probably just staring at the pictures when Giwa arrived. She didn't notice him. Giwa walked up behind her and peeped into the newspaper Kauna was staring at, the caption read:

HOUSE OF REPS IN A TUSSLE OVER POSSESSION OF MACE

"Mmmh Mmmh!" Giwa cleared his voice, more because of what he had read than announcing his presence. Kauna leaped forward, frightened by Giwa's unannounced presence.

"*Kai*, Brother!" She exclaimed, pleasantly surprised when she saw him. She rushed and gave him a warm embrace. She was so excited to see Giwa again. At the age of fifteen, Kauna behaved like a four year old after she embraced him. She twittered like a canary that has just met its kind.

"Uncle Harry has bought another car, he sold that other one... Do you like Egusi soup? I cooked it yesterday.... Mamman Ngozi, that fair woman behind our house, has given birth to a very cute baby; his name is Ifeanyi. Ifeanyi is the seventh child of the house and the only boy o..." she continued rapidly and disjointedly like a parrot, picking different topics and discussing all at the same time. Kauna was however cautious when she spoke of Aunty Mercy. She had to look around twice and lowered her voice to a whisper when she told him of Aunty Mercy's fight with one of her boyfriends and later claimed it was a domestic accident. She continued talking without a pause. He observed something they shared in common; both of them were starving. He was starving of food to eat while she was starving of someone to talk to, someone who would listen to her.

"Do you have anything for me to eat? Please give me because your stories will not fill my stomach." Giwa dipped morsels of tuwon semo into the egusi soup which Kauna had cooked and swallowed them hungrily as he listened to her endless stories. She explained why she could not give him a piece of meat; not because it was finished, but because Aunty Mercy had counted the pieces of meat for herself and her husband. Kauna ate meat only when there was excess of it, or when Uncle Harry is unable to finish his food with pieces of meat given him.

Aunty Mercy appeared from her bedroom as Giwa was about to swallow his last morsel. He paused for a moment. His heart skipped a few beats.

"Good evening Aunty." He vainly tried to add a fake smile.

"Mmn hmm! What brought you home? I thought you won't be coming back home again." She wore a very stiff face as she spoke.

He was prepared for her but decided to swallow his last morsel before taking any course of action. Aunty Mercy went straight into the kitchen. He washed his hands carefully, slowly, waiting for her next move and calculating his most probable response. Kauna was already trembling at the kitchen's door.

".... and who told you to serve this boy," pointing to Giwa, "meat from my pot soup eh?" She roared as she stormed out of the kitchen. Without waiting for an answer, she pounced on Kauna and gave her a slap. Giwa felt a current run into his ears and pass through his spine, and felt it landing at the sole of his feet. Immediately, he stood up with a bold look on his face.

"She did not give me any piece of meat." He watched as a lump slowly deflated in Kauna's throat. Her eyes were flled with tears but she seemed relaxed as Aunty Mercy turned to face Giwa.

"What did you just say?" She inched towards him hoping her intimidating countenance would compel Giwa to swallow his words or mumble something else, but she was wrong.

"I said, she did not give me any piece of meat!" He declared with an emphatic voice that resonated in the house.

"Till the time your mother died, she could not afford the quantity of meat in my pot of soup and you stand to talk to me like that? Who are you? Poor wretched rat!" She barked confronting Giwa.

"Yes, she may not have had that but at least she had fruits of the womb; something you don't have and will not have till you die, bitch!" He took on her weakest point. He had hit the nail hard on the exact point of torture. She was glaringly exasperated by those words especially the 'bitch' part. Kauna was bewildered; her eyes oscillated rings of surprises as Giwa spoke, and when he mentioned 'bitch', she practically had a nervous breakdown; her lips flung wide apart, her hair was straightened. She simply couldn't believe that Giwa was saying things that even Aunty Mercy's father wouldn't dare tell her.

Aunty Mercy couldn't contain it any longer, she rushed to give

Giwa a sound slap but her right hand was caught in the air, she looked, and saw it was no other person but Giwa, holding it with a firm grip. His eyes were boiling with the rage of a thousand suns. He knew that preventing her alone would not satisfy him.

Within a few seconds, she felt her intended slap land on her left cheek. Giwa must have added momentum as his right palm raced to her face because she came crashing on the floor with a loud thud. He stood facing Aunty Mercy on the floor, panting profusely like a wild tiger about to pounce on its prey having dealt the first blow.

At first, Kauna was neither a referee nor a spectator in the live wrestling match. She was simply stunned, unable to move an inch until Aunty Mercy fell in front of her. She shuffled backwards and she became conscious again. She blinked her eyes in a way that gave Giwa an encouraging pat on the back.

"This is for my mother, for the woman who lies peacefully in the grave. You dare not insult the woman who raised me," he moved closer.

"Giwa, you slapped me! You God-forsaken, poverty stricken chicken shit!" She tried to gather herself from the floor but a quick punch found its way to her jaw before she could stand upright.

"I'll show you what a chicken shit can do." He pounced on her, kicking, blowing, slapping and hurting her in all directions. He too got some scratches but Aunty Mercy was vanquished. She was weeping and insulting him, calling Uncle Harry's name, and later, Kauna's.

Kauna came to her rescue after the deed was done. Aunty Mercy was lying helplessly on the floor, and when Kauna was sure Aunty Mercy was not seeing, she raised both thumbs up for Giwa. For the first time in a year, Giwa felt like an achiever. He knew he couldn't stand the consequences of his fatal action but for the time being, he felt a sense of accomplishment.

"Sorry Aunty Mercy, sorry aunty, sorry..." Kauna consoled her.

"I swear you will regret what you have done. You have just given yourself a ticket to join your mother in the grave," the exhausted lioness yelled as she tried to sit up on the floor.

He didn't need a prophet to tell him that it was checkmate. He went to his room and gathered his most useful belongings. In the sitting room, he saw Aunty Mercy crying helplessly on the sofa while Kauna was being pushed away. Aunty Mercy paused; she stared wildly, probably in an attempt to conceal her state of ignominy.

"If anything happens to my baby, you will wish you were buried yesterday!" She continued sobbing.

Giwa smiled the achiever's smile, then he walked out. Kauna unwillingly cursed Giwa to Aunty Mercy's hearing, hoping it may woo Aunty Mercy to believe that she was on her side. She rushed to her room and came out, pretentiously fuming and ranting "Brother Giwa you are very wicked. God will not forgive you..." she cursed and followed Giwa outside.

"Kauna, please just come back, I don't want him to kill you." Aunty Mercy pleaded.

"No...Aunty...let me go and finish him!"

Kauna barged out of the room, convinced that Aunty Mercy had acknowledged her effort. Giwa heard her cursing behind him but cared less. He knew she was merely acting. If he was in her position, he would have done same too.

"Giwa! Wait... Please..." Her tone informed him that they were out of Aunty Mercy's earshot. He turned, she rushed and hugged him tightly. Tears filled her eyes when she released him.

"In case I don't see you again, I just want to thank you for teaching that witch a lesson. Please have this." She gave Giwa a huge wad of money. He was bewildered and was about to ask, but she motioned him to keep quiet with her index finger across her lips. "I got it on the night Uncle Harry was robbed. The robbers threw the wad at me in my room. I was so scared to tell Aunty Mercy because..."

"She may end up accusing you as an accomplice, right?" Giwa helped her with the story. He had stayed with Aunty Mercy long enough to predict her pattern of thought with near precision.

She wasn't surprised. "Thank God you know Aunty Mercy. I kept the money with the intention of disappearing some day but with what happened today, I guess I will not need it anymore."

Giwa gave her another hug. She turned back and headed for her nightmare. Giwa quickly counted the money, twenty thousand naira. He thanked his stars, blessed Kauna and headed for somewhere to ease off his stress.

* * * * *

Shark's Bar was flooded with neon lights at every hut and every spot. Giwa could hear Tupac's voice in a frenzied hip-hop beat blaring from two gigantic speakers positioned at two corners of the bar. 'Hit 'em up' was the song on replay in the bar. Giwa needed to drink and think. He chose a table which was occupied by one person, and that was the best he could get for an empty table. He checked his watch, it was just seven o'clock but the night had fully overtaken the day. It was dawn for the children of the night. A bar man came and stood before Giwa.

"Guiness, big stout *abeg*!"

"Ok, Sir!"

The boy humbly went to bring Giwa a bottle. This was Giwa's first visit to the Shark's Bar after his matriculation. He was totally oblivious of the boy who was sitting next to him. The bar man arrived with a cold bottle of Guiness stout and a tumbler that was customised for Rock Lager beer. The glass was crested with the logo of Rock Lager.

"I thought I would never see you, here we meet again." The guy spoke as Giwa gently poured his cold stout into his tumbler.

Giwa turned to the wall behind and then towards the boy. He saw no one but himself and was convinced that the boy was talking to him. "Pardon? Me?" He was surprised that the stranger was referring to him.

"Yes, you! Were you not here on matriculation day last year in the evening?" He posed the question like some police interogator; he lighted a cigarette held between his lips. He puffed, inhaled some air and blew out smoke. "Can't you remember?" He stared squarely at Giwa.

For a while, Giwa was nervous but braced himself when he remembered his achievement earlier. "I was… I think I was here…" He fixed the last piece of the puzzle, "Wait a minute! you are the guy I saw in green shirt, right?" The guy nodded as he blew out another long chain of circles of smoke. "Your name is K—something…?" Giwa gently demanded.

"KC, that is my name." He affirmed with a bright smile that revealed his small white teeth. "It's been a long time bro," KC tapped the stick on an ashtray.

"Yes, more than a year and here we are again, sitting at the same table." Giwa's face was now bright.

"Didn't think I will ever see you again but here you are, what is your problem now?" He asked as if he knew Giwa was in trouble.

Giwa gawked at him. He suddenly realized he didn't need to drink; he needed someone who would just listen to him.

Eight

Solomon was fully aware that his forfeiture included his monthly salary which had stopped coming as soon as he finished secondary school. He also stopped attending service at the Pankshin Parish for fear of having an eye-to-eye contact with father Kut, He wasn't sure of the consequences but didn't want to try.

He quickly adjusted himself with the routine of waking up early — that wasn't a problem, loading and offloading cement, buckets of paint, iron rods, and other building materials as they were bought or sold. He also got used to being in charge whenever Mr. Obi was not around, being the most educated among other apprentices; and to something which he didn't like but couldn't help. It was inadvertently growing in him; it was his desire for Adaku, Mr. obi's first daughter — the forbidden fruit.

Solomon had worked for five months already and had acclimatized himself to all the conditions of working for Mr. Obi. He had earned Mr. Obi's trust so much that he became an extended member of the family. Mr. Obi took an extra step by asking Solomon to teach Adaku Mathematics and English language in the evenings. Solomon obliged, lessons commenced immediately, and that marked the genesis of their secret admiration for each other. Adaku would often reluctantly go to school but was always looking forward to the lesson session with Solomon. At first, to Solomon, he was just Adaku's home teacher until she asked him a question that troubled his mind for a whole weekend. It was during a Friday lesson. They met thrice a week; Mondays, Wednesdays and Fridays. On that Friday, in the course of a Mathematics lesson, Solomon observed that Adaku was looking at him and not the mini blackboard in the sitting room, or the figures in her books. She carried a blank expression on her face.

"Adaku! Do you now understand?"

"Ehm, Uncle… I don't understand o! Can you come again?" she replied as she came to herself.

"Okay, come again from which point?"

"Ehm, em… Uncle," she cleared her voice again and looked intently into Solomon's eyes. "Do you have a girlfriend?" She asked like an interviewer on a panel.

Solomon had never been more confused since he stepped into Mr. Obi's house than that particular moment. He froze, his mouth agape for a few seconds in which he saw Father Brown's *koboko* descending on his bare back, his poking finger on his forehead, and his eyes peering through his back. Solomon shook this head in utmost disbelief. *Where did Adaku get the audacity to ask me such a question?*

"Okay, that is not part of our lesson." He pretended he was not perturbed by her question. "As I was saying, the subsets of A and B are…"

"But you have not answered my question, Uncle!" She pleaded puerilely with the tone of a toddler about to throw tantrums.

"Yes, I have not answered, and I will not answer your useless question that has nothing to do with this lesson." He snorted and stamped his feet to drive home his point though he did not mean what he said. She had just softened his heart.

"But Uncle…."

"Shh! Shh! We have finished our lesson for today, go and do the remaining five exercises on your own. We will meet on Monday."

Throughout that weekend, Adaku's single out-of-the-lesson question occupied his mind. *Adaku is only fifteen and Father Brown is not around.* From nowhere, Mr. Obi's restrictive warning about his daughters resonated in Solomon's ears. He quickly snapped out of his thoughts and dwelled on other things until he fell asleep on Sunday night. Monday, after the lesson, he asked Adaku to repeat that Friday's question again. She did and he responded.

From then onwards, after every lesson, they talked about matters of the heart. The lessons were becoming more and more exciting for both Solomon and Adaku. Mr. Obi became suspicious but when he confided in his wife, she pushed away the notion and told him that he was just being overprotective; moreover, results had shown that Adaku had improved remarkably in her class performance, thanks to Solomon. Mr. Obi knew better than to underestimate his business partners, he employed the same business principle in almost everything, and that largely informed his suspicions towards

Solomon and Adaku. He noticed that Adaku was always eager to attend lessons, that lesson periods stretched longer than usual, and that Adaku was never tired of taking messages to Solomon.

On the day he caught her, Mr. Obi sent Adaku to ask Solomon if there was a torn cement bag in the store, he waited for five minutes then he crept up on her and Solomon. He found them entangled in an embrace. He wasn't surprised, it only proved his hypothesis was correct.

"Adaku, your mother needs you in the kitchen!" They disentangled instantly but they had been caught hugging each other, and that was their very first hug. Adaku trembled as she made for the door, wishing there was another exit. Mr. Obi's eyes scanned her for from the tip of her hair to the nails on her toes. He further watched her until she disappeared into the main house. He turned and saw Solomon already on his knees with tears in his eyes. He hissed and slammed the door at Solomon's face. Solomon heard his footsteps as he walked away. Later in the night, Solomon heard Adaku's voice in a wild scream pleading for mercy.

"I am finished." Solomon said to himself.

* * * * *

"Your lesson has been terminated from today." That was the first sentence that Solomon heard from Mr. Obi the following morning, and that was also his response to Solomon's greeting.

Mr. Obi proceeded with many other commandments that included not spending up to two minutes with his daughter anywhere in the world, and no more watching television in Mr. Obi's sitting room. Solomon understood that the summary of all these commandments was that he was to asbtain from any sort of contact or communication with Adaku. "Next time, if you try that again, you will find yourself in a huge parcel in front of Father Kut's door."

"Thank you sir, I'm very sorry sir..."

"No, don't thank me yet, thank Father Brown, for whose sake you are still here. I would have kicked you out since last night."

He avoided Adaku as much as he could for another month. It was in that same month that Father Kut was transferred to another Parish, somewhere in Kaduna State. It was that same month that WAEC results were released and Solomon passed with five distinctions and three credits. Mr. Obi hugged him affectionately when he saw the result. His elation compelled Solomon to wish he was his biological son. Their cordial relationship had resumed in full swing. A bigger surprise came; Solomon was admitted into the Univeristy of Jos to study Psychology, Mr. Obi was more excited about the admission than the candidate himself. This was certainly a December Solomon would never forget but his biggest surprise was yet to arrive. It came on the eve of Christmas. Solomon had gone to collect meat for himself and other apprentices. He came back and saw a black Mercedez with tinted glasses parked in front of the house. He recognized the car as belonging to the new parish priest, Father Chollom Gyang. Then the door of the passenger's seat was opened, a frail and old white man alighted from the car, Solomon couldn't believe his eyes, the man standing before him was Father Thomas Brown.

"I will be going to the monastery son." Fa ther Brown heaved after a sip from the bottle of Coke in front of him. Mr. Obi and his family had gone away for the Christmas holiday and Solomon was left in charge of the house although the main house was locked, Solomon still controlled other buildings.

"For what Father? I thought you said you will live and die in Nigeria," Solomon inquired naively and also fibbed.

"Really? When did I say so? Please don't put words into my mouth. In any case, my main reason of coming here is to tell you goodbye and that you will hardly be hearing from me because I will be in the monastery. *Ka ji ko yaro*?" Father Brown replied in a more emphatic tone. His Hausa was still fluent like that of the natives. He lifted his bottle and gulped some more Coke.

Solomon could no longer say anything; he let tears flow freely from his eyes. Father Gyang moved closer to console him. He gave him a white handkerchief.

"Be a man Solomon and stop acting like Father Brown has just pronounced his death sentence. You should know that the monastery is a place of constant prayer and devotion; he will be interceding along with Jesus and His Holy Mother, Mary, for your fallible soul. Be brave son!"

"Father you don't understand, I am who I am today because of Father Brown. He cared for me and taught me..." Solomon sobbed as he tried to justify the stream of tears rolling down his cheeks.

"I know... It's okay, don't worry." Father Gyang flung his weighty right arm around Solomon. A whiff of garlic hit Solomon's nose, his breath stank of the same odour too. Solomon had a reason to end his fit. Father Gyang released Solomon when dried his eyes.

In his usual characteristic manner, he was impassive almost apathetic, he didn't believe in beating around the bush in order to avoid stirring of emotions. Someone had once said that, had Father Brown been a medical doctor, more people would have been dead; because he would avoid all euphemisms, "Your son is dead, sorry" or "prepare for his funeral, he won't make it" was what Father Brown would likely say. He was looking around like an officer on inspection. His gaze fell back on Solomon. The young boy looked grave.

"So how have you fared academically son, I believe you have completed your secondary school."

"The Lord has been merciful sir, His grace has enabled me to be admitted into the University of Jos to study Psychology and we are to start in January." Solomon cheerfully replied.

Whoever said Father Brown doesn't express emotions at all must be a liar. At that moment, Father Brown was very excited. Solomon had never seen more excitement written on his face before. "Holy Mary, Mother of Jesus!" He exclaimed. He reached out for Solomon, mustering all his strength, and lifted the young boy, "Wonderful!" He let him down and guzzled his remaining Coke. "My coming here to say goodbye is indeed timely. You have made me proud." In a more serious tone he added, "This is an opportunity for you to come closer to the Lord." Father Gyang affirmed with a gentle nod. Father Brown continued, "The Lord will be your helper, only if you allow Him. He has seen you this far, and will surely see you to the end. I understand that the university these days is more of a decaying ground but many people have made good out of it. Do not allow yourself to be distracted by drugs, women or cultism." Father Brown paused and looked at Father Gyang, Father Gyang motioned in a nod which told him to carry on. "It is a pity that I shall not be around to monitor your academic, moral and spiritual progress, or even be there for your graduation but I am sure that the good Lord will see you through to the end."

Solomon told him of all that transpired between himself and Father Kut, and how he had become a personal assistant/head apprentice to Mr. Obi. He didn't forget to mention that his salary as a church worker had been cut off and he remembered to conceal his little relationship with Adaku before he was caught. He was sure that Father Brown would not take it lightly. He had told him everything before they entered the house, after the tumultuous excitement of seeing each other again in many years.

Father Gyang chipped in his words of advice too. Solomon gazed at the floor as he listened to them. "And how do you intend to pay for your tuition and accommodation?" Father Brown said.

"Hmm... ehm... when Oga, Papa Adaku settles me, I will pay for my first year and then work harder in the remaining years, during holidays, to pay for other sessions." Solomon managed to say. It then occurred to him that he had not made any plans for his needs, tuition, accommodation, books, clothes, and food.

Father Brown gauged Solomon with his eyes. "Tomorrow, I will be celebrating my last Christmas Mass in Nigeria. I hope to be in Lagos on the 28th and board the next flight to Heathrow on the 30th of December." Solomon was becoming emotional again. "Speaking of Lagos, I just remembered that I was given a gift, the sum of five hundred thousand naira in cash by some politician who intends to contest for the seat of the Lagos State Governor. Can you believe it?" His eyebrows shifted backwards. "I couldn't decline the offer because he gave it to me amidst his friends after service last week. I didn't know what to do with the money because frankly, I don't need it. I thought of donating it to my church in Lagos but they were in the peak of a financial scandal. So I came here with the money, I was thinking of some useful place to donate the money, I didn't know that I would be bringing it to you." Solomon's eyes widened.

"Sir, I am sorry, I don't understand what you mean." Solomon had been swept off his feet. He couldn't believe his ears were functioning properly. *At last, the Lord has heard my cry, Thank you Jesus, thank you Mary.* He prayed in his heart, hoping that what he had just heard was true. It was true.

"Son, it is the Lord's doing and it is marvelous in our sight. Father Gyang, behold your son; son, behold your father." Solomon recalled where he had read something similar to this in his Bible. "I will instruct Gyang to take you to the bank and open an account in your name. Then the money will be deposited into the account. You, Solomon, will give him a detailed account of how you spend every kobo periodically until you graduate." By the time he finished, another stream of tears was running down from Solomon's eyes.

On Christmas day, Solomon was the first to be in church, he kept Father Brown within his sight until midnight. He stayed around, knowing that would probably be the last time they would be together.

Two days later, when he finally saw Father Brown off, he cried relentlessly like a baby as Father Gyang sped off with Solomon's only true father to the airport. Solomon felt feverish as he made for the shop. The other apprentices were watching, derisively laughing, they curiously wanted to know why Solomon would shed tears for a white man. Solomon did not mention a word to them, he was not sure they would understand the degree of their relationship even if he explained it to them. He sealed his lips, and business continued as usual.

* * * * *

Uncle Harry spoke in a tone which Giwa had never heard before. He warned Giwa never to come back to the house again. It was all about Aunty Mercy. She told her husband a story which exonerated her completely. In her words, Giwa came in already drunk and started beating the hell out of her until she lay down unconscious. She also added that Kauna sprinkled cold water on her and fanned her till she came around.

Giwa secretly believed that Uncle Harry was under a spell or something close to that. So far, she claimed she had had several miscarriages and that Giwa's severe beating was responsible for the umpteenth miscarriage. This acclaimed miscarriage, particularly, drove Uncle Harry mad. It made him feel as if he had lost his last chance of ever having a child.

"From today, I don't want to ever see your foot in my house again," he reiterated, "Now my poor wife is in the hospital because of you and your foolishness. An ingrate is just what you are..." Uncle Harry fumed.

"Brother, please listen to me. It's not true; let me tell you my side of the story..."

"Just shut up! Close that deceptive mouth or I will help you shut it up with a slap. You almost killed my wife, then you have the guts to tell me it's not true? Where did you get the temerity to address me as 'brother'? Am I your brother or your uncle? Uncle Harry barked like a bulldog, like the toothless bulldog he was to Aunty Mercy. In the heat of his anger, Giwa saw his veins clearly mapped across his forehead and neck, he splattered tiny droplets of saliva at Giwa's face. They sat in Uncle Harry's car at the far end of the hostel. Giwa was greatly annoyed but only sighed and let it go. He didn't mention any word again. He only listened to Uncle Harry's haranguing. When he finished, he threw Giwa a huge bundle of two hundred naira notes. "Take this; I don't want to ever see you in my house again. Forget that we are related, No relation of mine would want to kill my child. In the boot are the rest of your belongings. Pack them and never come back."

For some minutes Giwa was mute. He knew Uncle Harry expected a prodigious apology but he swore he would not give it. He had heard of men being bewitched by their wives, seen some in films, and read about some in books but he was experiencing it for the very first time. He thought of collecting his belongings and the money, but a second thought informed him better.

"Thank you for the generous offer, and for sponsoring me all along, thank you for the belongings in your boot, they are actually yours anyway, because I bought them with your money. Sincerely, I don't need them. Keep your money and the things in your boot. All I needed was a listening ear, but it appears you have been deaf since you got married, and even blind as well. Your wife is a scarlet woman who sleeps with even some of your friends." *I hope she dies in the hospital.* Giwa didn't mention his wish. "I tried to keep this from you but I realized there is no need keeping it since we have come to the end of the road." With that, Giwa slammed the door of the car and made for his room. He heard Uncle Harry shouting his name until he stopped and his voice was replaced by the screeching of tyres. Giwa turned and saw Uncle Harry speeding off. He thought about a doctor who wouldn't check his wife simply because he was an ophthalmologist, he would rather refer her to a gynaecologist who connived with her to give false reports. He barged into his room and threw himself on his bed. Supinely, he closed his eyes, and exhaled profusely, certain that the worst had happened.

Later that evening, he was at the Shark's Bar, the same place he was the day before, on the same seat, and with the same guy that heard him, now listening to him again.

"Now my only problem is how to get my degree, find a job, and fend for myself and my poor sister. God! I'm in a hot soup."

"Must you graduate now? Aren't you schooling for the money? With a lot of money, I can guarantee you will buy a degree. I have seen people who have graduated with a Second Class Upper Division, yet are unknown to their classmates. It's all about the money, man.

Money makes the world go round. Even the Bible says 'money answereth all things', sharpen up guy!" KC lifted his chilled bottle of Guiness, he took a sip and inhaled smoke from his cigarette, then he puffed out long rings of smoke. He carefully shook off the burnt tobacco leaves on the ashtray. He paused and focused on Giwa, hoping his words of 'finanical wisdom' were being absorbed.

"Look KC, I won't subscribe to your make-money-at-all-cost Igbotic mentality. Right now, all I want is to see myself as a graduate," Giwa rebelled.

"Ah great! I have another idea." KC was smiling now.

"And what could that be?"

"Just go to your Aunty Mercy, get down on your knees and ask her for forgiveness in the presence of Uncle Harry and the neighbours who must have heard of your ordeal. I know Aunty Mercy will talk her husband into forgiving you."

Giwa became furious. "How can you utter such a statement? You must be out of your mind. I will not, will never, ever be so stupid as to apologize. For what? You must be kidding me KC. E be like say you no know your man again, abi?"

"Okay, then why were you angry when I brought the first suggestion?"

"Because it didn't make sense to me."

"Does the second one make more sense to you?" KC was grinning widely now.

"Naah! The second idea is worse."

"That is it my brother." KC remarked. "Sometimes life throws us onto its precipice and we are usually left in-between two devils. Normally, it is better to choose the lesser devil. What do you think?"

"KC, which department are you in?" Giwa was becoming apprehensive now.

"Good question. I thought you would never ask; my classmates are already in 400 level and where am I? Sitting here and chatting with my new found friend Giwa. Sounds stupid, doesn't it? But before you crucify me, let me inform you that you are sitting with a potential millionaire in the next few months, at most, two years. Isn't that all you are schooling for? Listen my brother, we all seek to make life better for ourselves, and we are not stopping until we use every means necessary. You have a choice man. You either make it or break it!"

"So that means that you are among those non-academic students littering our campus." Giwa said, amazed.

KC nodded and stuck another cigarette in his mouth. He lighted it and said. "Yep! Call it whatever you like. It's not gonna change my status as a hustler and yours as a broke ass."

"This is crazy, gosh! I feel so terrible..."

"That is the way it is when you are about to take an important decision. I will be here to show you 'the way' when you make up your mind by tomorrow."

* * * * *

La Modillo hotel stood a few yards behind Shark's Bar. Giwa had heard of the place before but had never been there. The hotel was infamously reputed to shelter robbers, cultists, and prostitutes. Giwa never thought he would ever see the reception hall of that hotel but here he was, trailing behind KC like a docile ox heading to the abattoir.

A little walk through the gates of La Modillo confirmed that it was another red-light district of Jos. He had to push himself through thick tobacco smoke to get to the reception hall, which doubled as a bar, in order to climb the stairs. KC was not a newcomer here. He waded through the smoke and people, occasionally saying "hi" here and there, without stopping and without turning back. He urged Giwa to quicken his steps. They climbed the stairs and stopped at the second floor, in front of room 101. Giwa panted as KC performed a rhythmic knock twice, then the door was opened. Directly facing room 101 was room 102, its door was opened too, a guy stuck out his head. Giwa recognized him as the one Duff and Gasko referred to as Cheifo. His eyes were red. The combined smell of gin and marijuana oozed from his room. He quickly bolted his door. KC dragged Giwa into the room which was opened for them. Giwa staggered into room 101 but he regained his balance when he saw a crop of fine-looking boys, they were casually but neatly dressed. Five of them in all. Two of them sat on the sofa, the third one leaned on the table close to the window with his right leg on the chair. The fourth sat on the other end of the bed and was a very dark and handsome guy. The fifth one, the odd one in the room, rested his back on a pillow, his legs formed a V shape on the bed. He held the remote control to the small colour TV in his palms, and wore a faded blue jeans and white singlet. A silver chain necklace hung around his neck with a small crucifix in place of a pendant. KC scanned the room in a flash and his eyes met with Da Don.

The guy wearing the singlet was called Da Don, or simply, Don. If only handsomeness was the yardstick for the selection of the boys in that room, Don would have been out of that room, but here, Da Don was the most respected person in the room.

Da Don's head lacked a definite shape. It looked like it was roughly panel-beaten to make it look a bit like that of a human being. The plenty hair around his face suggested that his barber was doing a good job of having it carved always. He stared at KC, then at Giwa, KC again, and then stared at both of them at the same time but addressed KC.

"You are late!"

"Sorry, Don, I had to make a delivery before bringing my friend to the party," KC pleaded.

Giwa heard the word 'party' but the scenario in the room didn't look like any party to him.

Da Don jerked himself up and wore a blue and white horizontally striped T-Shirt. His crucifix still sparkled. He asked Giwa his name and he was told. The Don preferred to address Giwa as G. He offered a handshake to Giwa. Giwa was not pleased to meet him but he put up a weak smile. An alarm rang in the room. The sound came from the wall clock. The clock's shorter hand was steadied at 8:00pm.

"Gentlemen, let's be seated," he motioned KC and Giwa to sit on the bed. The guy leaning against the table now found himself on the sofa. The only chair left was dusted and reserved for Da Don. He didn't sit on it. He stood in front of the chair.

Da Don signaled Nosky. Nosky stood up, bolted the door properly, and switched off the TV. He came back to sit on the bed. Three of them sat on the bed, the other three were balanced on the sofa. They faced one another while Da Don was standing. He clapped his hands and brought their attention to him.

"You are all welcome to this party, a little gathering of extraordinary businessmen, a careful selection of the finest boys on campus, and a diligent set of people that are ordained to make it in life. We are a non-violent group of people that are guided by this one philosophy; get rich or die trying. There are a million ways to make money just as there are a million ways to die." He stared into their faces as he spoke. "In this world, two groups of people exist; the rich and the poor. Some call it, the 'haves' and 'have nots', 'bourgeoisie' and 'proletariat', 'literates' and 'illiterates', and so on. Our coming here is a means of saying goodbye to the poor and squalid life, and also a means of saying welcome to the 'good life'."

Giwa saw KC and four others nodding simultaneously as Da Don spoke. He and the other guy at the extreme were motionless. Giwa soon learnt that the other motionless guy was also a new member, just like him.

"We are known to ourselves as the Smart Boys' Crew, and that is SBC. Being a member of the SBC is more than a privilege, it is an honour. Currently, we operate in over twenty tertiary institutions across the country. We are part of a larger cartel that has its headquarters in Mexico. Guys, if you ever make it to Mexico, then you are a billionaire. If you stop at Lagos then you are a millionaire. In less than five years of being a member, I have risen to the rank of Da Don and if you noticed, a blue Honda civic was parked outside, that should be my first car." At this point, he spoke with an aura of humble pride as politicians would often do. "Boys, this is just the beginning. Some of our ex-members are now business moguls, senators, governors and even CEOs of multinational companies. Work hard boys!"

Having said that and more, he went ahead to introduce the members of the SBC starting from himself; Da Don, or just Don, nothing more. Real names were carefully avoided. KC was second in command, then Willie I and Willie II better known as Willie & Willie. They came third and fourth respectively. Nosky was the fifth. The other new boy was called C4 by Da Don and Giwa was simply introduced as G.

Da Don continued, "Our products are in different categories, they are coded and expensive." G will be mentored by KC, while C4 will be mentored by Willie & Willie. They will fill you in on the rules, codes, customers, marketing skills, our police contacts and NDLEA agents in case of anything. We are connected to the top echelons of this country so there is nothing to fear. In case of any squabbles on campus, Chiefo is next door in room 102." Da Don clenched his right fist and punched it into his curved left palm as he mentioned Chiefo. "He is the head of Black Mamba, he will take care of it only when I inform him. In any case, you have to report to me first."

He brought out a form. It contained seven names already. There was red ink against each name. Giwa wrote down his name and his new name, and C4 did the same. Don brought out a new needle and pricked his new members with it on their thumbs. The first blood that came out was pressed on the paper against their names. He urged them to suck back the remaining blood until it clotted. He switched off the light and lighted a candle. He held the paper before the candle and said:

"By this commitment, you have been absorbed as full blown members of the SBC. All rights and privileges of members of SBC will be accorded to you from this very day. However, if any of you decides to reveal our identity and what we do, we shall, through his blood, call upon his instant death from the shrine of our protector." He pried into their faces to see if they got his message.

Giwa couldn't believe that he had just joined a fraternity.

Nine

“Look what you got me into!” Giwa said as soon as they were clear of La Modillo hotel.

“Is that supposed to be my fault? I thought I was giving you a helping hand? Abeg! If you don’t have anything to say, keep quiet and let me be.” Apparently, KC was in no mood to talk. A lot was going through his mind too. He had the guilt of bringing someone down with him, and the challenge of making it work for them.

“Liar, I hate you… You have killed my heart… Why didn’t you tell me that I was going to be initiated into cultism?” Giwa ranted like a woman that had just lost her first child in the hospital. He cried. He cursed. It was actually the feeling of a young girl who had just been raped.

KC was mute, almost oblivious of Giwa’s yelling, until he felt his shirt yanked backwards. In an instant, he turned and disengaged Giwa’s hands from its grip. He stopped walking and faced Giwa squarely. He combed the quiet shortcut to his house with his eyes until they fell on Giwa. With a finger to Giwa’s face, he stated matter-of-factly, “Now listen to me, I thought I was doing you a favour but it seems as if you have just lost part of your senses. You had the opportunity to back out at every instance, from the very second we found ourselves in La Modillo to the time you said ‘I agree’ to Da Don. Why didn’t you seize those moments? This should be the last time I will hear a nagging word from you. I have the good life ahead of me to think about and I will urge you to do the same.” He turned and continued on the path. The duo became quiet for the rest of the night as they walked to KC’s place. It was a night Giwa would never forget, just as he would not forget his birthday. He would never forget his birthnight; the night he traded his soul for the ‘good life’. KC heard Giwa sobbing before he slept off.

Giwa was awake for a long time before KC woke up. He leaned

backwards on a pillow vertically resting against the wall. He was staring into space. KC opened his eyes slightly, seeing Giwa was awake, he felt a tinge of guilt. He closed his eyes again and pretended he was still asleep for a moment, then searched for a box of cigarette under his bed, took one and lit it.

"Good morning." KC said, at the same time he puffed out smoke that spiralled and diffused into the atmosphere. He checked the time, it was seven o'clock.

Giwa eyed him annoyingly, he felt like hitting KC in that instant. "We need to talk!"

"No, no, no! I need to talk to you. Let me put it rightly; I need to give you a long lecture. This is no time to hear your views about the SBC. It is my time to instruct you from now on. However, I will hear everything else you have to say, but no comments on the SBC. Just questions." KC spoke in the tone that Da Don used the previous night.

"Oh yeah! Since I have only questions to ask about this bullshit, then tell me when I'm gonna get out of it?" Giwa sprang from the bed and flung the blanket at KC.

KC smiled charmingly, "Relax boy, it's probably not going to be as long as you think. With the plans I have on ground, it will take only three years for me, I mean us, to retire. We will settle and do something legit, that is, if our stuff has not been decriminalized yet."

"Good, I can't wait to get out of this mess, although a part of me is liking it now. But hey, what happens to my degree?" Giwa spoke with a mixed feeling of confusion and uncertainty.

"Look man, your lectures will have to be on hold. I mean your academic lectures. However, your Smart Boys' lectures will commence now, after breakfast. So what shall we eat? I am famished already."

* * * * *

Giwa spent most of the day moving out of the hostel. According to KC, the hostel was not a good abode for him. Being a member of SBC, they won't have their members living in the hostel which could be ransacked at any moment and also for the fact that the goods SBC dealt with were delicate goods which should not be seen everywhere. KC helped Giwa to move into his place until he could find him another house. They were done with the work by evening, and they were settled at the Shark's Bar by dusk.

The Shark's Bar was becoming a familiar place for Giwa. He quickly became accustomed to the environment. At this stage he could tell, just by looking at faces, the newcomers and regular customers too. He also knew half of the boys of the bar by name and partially became acquainted to their shifts. KC was quite impressed when he heard Giwa call one of the boys by name and place an order for two without consulting him.

"Aha! That's how a smart boy should be —- coded" KC remarked after the boy made for the drinks. His yellowish face was gleaming with a smile.

"Ha! And what's that about?" Giwa raised a quizzical eyebrow.

"You called the barman by name and even placed an order for me. It means you are getting used to things really fast, those guys at the bar want to be respected too, they love it when you call them by name. In fact, they ignore other customers in order to attend to their acquaintances first..."

"Hey! that is enough! I guess this barman-respect thing isn't part of our supposed lecture!"

"Hell no!... It's not, we haven't touched the tip of the iceberg yet."

Innocent, the barman, or barboy as KC would rather call him, because he looked so young, arrived with two bottles of Guiness for the Smart boys and opened them. Giwa spoke after Innocent opened the second drink as if he uncorked his own mouth.

"Do they really use our blood to call for our instant death peradventure we disclose things about the SBC in the future?"

"Oh! You mean the blood you used as stamp and signature at the party?" KC replied rhetorically.

"Yes, I mean the blood we used at the initiation." Giwa hated that word 'party' because he was deluded by it. He preferred to call it by its name. KC didn't like it. He wrapped his mouth with his left palm, motioning Giwa to avoid using such a word in public. Giwa was unperturbed.

"It's just procedure, you know... It's nothing," KC strugged. "It hardly gets anywhere. It was just meant to scare you, please don't tell me that that was what made you to cry last night."

"Part of it," Giwa said as he raised his glass for a sip. He dropped his half-filled glass on the table as his eyes touched down on a pretty young girl and her supposed date as they settled on an unoccupied table. KC's eyes followed Giwa's eyes until he caught a glimpse of what Giwa was blatantly admiring, then he turned to face Giwa.

"Rule No. 2: Always put business before pleasure; the meaning of our 'pleasure' primarily includes women and other things that spend your money but don't add any to you. The sooner you avoid them, for now, the sooner you prosper." KC had already commenced his lecture without prior notice.

"How about starting with rule No. 1?" he said. Giwa was embarrassed that he had been caught admiring someone else's girl. He cast his eyes on another man's table, the man belched as he drank his seventh bottle. There were six other empty bottles on the man's table. KC followed Giwa's eyes again. "What about rule No 1?" Giwa repeated his question.

"Never get high on your own supply, Rule 1. That is the ultimate rule."

"Isn't that a line from a movie?" Giwa raised a curious eyebrow.

"Yes, 'Scarface', starring Al Pacino, but what matters to us is that it is working for us right?"

"Okay, okay." Giwa finished his glass and poured himself another glass. "I see… So what are the other rules?"

"Easy man! Take it easy. Progress is a gradual process. We have enough time for you to learn by the inch, ain't no need hurrying about it. The good news is, there will be no examination of any sort but when on the field proper, it is either you make it or break it."

"You know what KC? I have a thousand other questions to ask you about this whole SBC brotherhood or whatever it is."

"I was expecting two thousand questions but I feel better since it's just a thousand questions, hahaha!"

"How did the SBC come about here on this campus?" Giwa almost forgot he was drinking something. His whole attention was fixed on KC.

"Well…uhm.." KC lit his first cigarette for the evening, he puffed out some smoke. "My cousin, Donald, was the person who introduced the SBC to this campus. He was recruited in Lagos by a certain businessman whose name Donald withheld until he died but I suspect it is Chief Femi Otunba. That takes us to rule No. 3: Never disclose the name of your supplier, even to your customers. Either they buy your merchandize or no deal." KC digressed a little bit but he came back to his story. "Donald was solo on the business for the first two years. Then he recruited two boys when his supplies and the size of his market increased. Those boys were Oche and Kola, known to us as O2 and K2 respectively. I was recruited about three years ago, after me was Nosky. Nosky was the seventh person. Donald, or Da Don as he came to be addressed later, maintained that we restrict the number of our members to just seven people. He stressed that Da Don should be the official title of anyone occupying his seat when he moves away or attains a higher level. About a year and half ago, Donald's body was found on the streets of Armsterdam. It was all over the newspapers and magazines. Donald ingested some unknown drug which he assumed was cocaine. He died before he could trace the house he was sent to. Later, I became more convinced that someone — probably his business partner, or supplier, wanted to get rid of him, and he did."

KC took a long drink. He paused. He stared into space, then he continued. "Donald was such a good chap. He introduced me into this business and guided me well. I was linked up with some of his partners, the big ones. Before he flew out finally, he warned me to be careful in this business. This leads us to rule No 4: Never assume you know anyone or anything — assumption is the mother of all fuck-ups. Never assume." Another digression, but KC came back on track. "Donald died before he could lay hands on the six million naira that awaited him after the delivery of the merchandise. A year and half ago, K2 took some supplies to a ghetto in Abuja, he never came back and we never heard of him again. That was how Oche or O2 became Da Don and asked that we recruit two more people to make us seven, God's own number. Now here we are." He motioned Giwa to drink on and ordered for their second round. They sipped quietly and slowly as soft music blared from the speakers at the corners of the bar. Giwa's mind was circled on the risky nature of the business.

* * * * *

For the fifth day in a row, Giwa and KC sat on the same table at the same joint with different people; somehow, they became part of Shark's Bar. In less than five minutes since they settled down, Innocent arrived with two chilled bottles of their favourite stout along with two glasses. He carefully placed them on the table.

"Una welcome ogas." He looked at both of them alternately with a broad smile hanging on his face.

"How you dey na?" KC greeted.

"I dey fine sir." He turned and was headed for the store.

"Innocent," Giwa called. He turned and came back. "How did you know what we wanted?"

"Oga na today? Every time una dey siddon for the same seat na him I come tink say una go drink the same drink. Abi I no try?" Innocent spoke happily. It pleased Giwa very much.

"Abeg go do your thing joor, no mind my friend for here," KC commented and the three of them broke into a mirthful laughter. They opened their drinks themselves and the lecture continued.

"Listen Giwa, I know that by now you know we sell stuff, I mean hard stuff, isn't it?"

"Yes, you are on point," Giwa replied.

"Among the drugs we sell, Mary J is the cheapest and commonest." KC noticed Giwa was a bit confused. "I know your next question, don't even ask it! Mary J is also known as igbo, dope, wiwi, ganja, Indian hemp, kush, cannabis or marijuana. I believe by now I must have answered your unasked questions." KC heaved a sigh of relief and leaned back on his chair.

"Yes, you have but there are more questions."

"Ask and you shall be given, knock and the door shall be opened, seek and you shall find."

"That is in Mathew chapter 7:7." Giwa completed the quotation from the Bible.

"I am glad my friend knows the Bible too."

"I should be the one to be glad because my money-minded friend can quote as much as one verse from the Bible."

"See, Giwa, we need God all the time and everywhere, even in this business and who doesn't need money?"

"I do," Giwa said, raising his one hand up.

"Go away joor!" They burst into another round of laughter. They ordered for their second bottle each and KC resumed. "We also have Henny."

"Is that a short form for Henessy or Heineken?" Giwa asked.

"Nooo! Henny is a code name for Heroin. It can be sniffed, but it's more potent when injected into the body. It is highly addictive. Never use it, just supply it to those who need it. Collect your money and..." he snapped his fingers "zoom off." Giwa's eyes widened. He couldn't believe there were drugs like that. Henny is in high demand by traffickers, and in strip clubs. They are also used in some brothels.

It fetches good money and it's very portable. I will show you all these tomorrow at my warehouse."

"I like the Henny."

"Then you have not sold Cocoa yet."

"Which Cocoa? That common beverage? How much would one get from that?"

KC laughed loudly for a long time. Then he paused and looked at Giwa, "Please stop displaying your ignorance. Our Cocoa is not a beverage. It is coke." He moved closer to Giwa in a tete-a-tete and spoke almost in a whisper, "Cocoa is another name for cocaine, Smart boy!" Giwa's eye widened. He felt as if the strands of his hair were being pulled by some mystical powers. He couldn't believe that he could come this close to the cocaine that he had been seeing only on TV.

* * * * *

First thing on Wednesday morning, KC did something Giwa found very absurd. Giwa had no inkling that KC was Catholic. Giwa woke up to find KC saying his Rosary. It took him some minutes to be convinced that KC and his rosary were not part of his dream. After the prayer, KC said "good morning" before Giwa could find his speech.

"Where has the rosary been all along?"

"How about a 'good morning' for a start Smart boy?"

"Okay, good morning. Now where did you pick that rosary from?"

"If you must know, this Rosary has inside my pillow before you ever dreamt of being admitted into this university." KC spoke with an air of finality.

"Fine, now I know you are a Catholic. At first I thought you were an atheist. KC do you have a Bible?"

"I no know who send you dis morning," he stood up from the bed and walked towards his box. "Yes! I do have a Bible, contrary to what you think." KC opened his bag and brought out a clean copy of the New King James Version (NKJV) of the Bible which had 'KC' boldly written on the sides but it looked like it had never been read up to five times before, like it was just bought from a bookshop. Giwa saw it and counselled himself about enquiring any further.

"I intend to pursue a deferment for my studies. I don't think I can handle books and business at the same time." Giwa looked down as he spoke.

"That's it man, now you are talking." KC patted him on the back. "We'll get up and get dressed, eat breakfast and move straight to your damn department."

Oh KC again! Always serious about things that don't really matter. KC was cheerful, even excited about Giwa's decision to defer his studies. He applauded the idea, though he couldn't get a deferment for himself, he simply dropped out.

"And G, we will be going to see the warehouse, I mean my warehouse, as soon as we leave school before we come back home."

For a few seconds, Giwa wondered who 'G' was, or what 'G' meant, then he remembered he had been christened 'G', being his code name for the SBC. "Please drop the 'G' thing; it makes me feel like a gangster."

"But you are my homey, my brother, you are a 'G', man!" KC blurted in his typical idiosyncratic American manner, a trait he exhibited only when he was excited about something.

"Whatever!" Giwa said, to end the mild debate which KC would readily wish to prolong. "Let's get some water from the well."

In a matter of minutes, the boys were walking through the pedestrian lane of the University's main road. As usual, posters of young student political aspirants littered everywhere. There were posters for programmes or activities of departmental, tribal, social or religious groups as well as notices for their meetings. The sophomore Giwa had learnt to ignore everything that could eat up his time. As they walked further, a car with SUG 001 boldly engraved on its number plate slowly passed in front of them. Its windows were lowered as a deafening afro hip-hop beat emanated from the car. Two boys reclined on the front seats. They had an air that made them seem on top of the world. Giwa could hardly believe that he was seeing the refined faces of Jerry Dalu and Clifford Gyang. Clifford a.k.a Clinton was the same guy that met Giwa a year ago, when Giwa was a Jambite, soliciting Giwa's support. Giwa had not followed the elections but from evidence before him, Clinton had won the election and had become used to the 'big boy' life. Giwa recalled how Clinton walked in an old oversized brown suit and wondered how the suit had been transformed into a black shiny elegantly fitted suit. He waved at them smiling gleefully like an acquaintance. They simply smiled back like some sort of superstars who casually acknowledged their fans. Only Jerry Dalu attempted to raise some few fingers in an attempt to reciprocate the gesture.

The car passed, Giwa read the words on the tinted rear glass of the car;

ALUTA CONTINUA...VICTORIA ACERTA

Giwa still couldn't fathom the meaning of those words in Latin, not that he didn't understand the meaning; he was just unable to relate it to the people in the car. He was deflated. The car had almost vanished when KC tapped to remind him that he was walking with someone.

"Forget those boys abeg! Where do you know them?"

"I ... I first met them..."

"It doesn't matter," KC snapped. "You met them on foot, now they are in a car. Levels don change! That is the same thing that our secular politicians do to us. We vote them as we see them but when they are in power, you will hear that 'so so' person was in that black tinted jeep that just passed. You don't get to see them or even wave them," KC stated with a high sense of conviction.

"Hahaha. You are very correct sir!" Giwa laughed again as they moved closer to the Faculty of Social Sciences.

"Hey Smart boy, look at this guy..." KC pulled Giwa's hands to get his attention. He used his mouth to point at a gentle boy with a large brown envelope that was coming towards their direction.

"Oh my goodness!" Giwa felt like he was looking into a mirror.

"You should have asked your mother if you had a twin brother somewhere before she died."

Giwa poked KC on the head. "Don't be sarcastic, dull boy, you are not smart." Giwa was looking at the boy until he passed by them. The boy couldn't get his eyes off Giwa too. Giwa felt a mysterious wave between them, almost like a striking electric current.

"It's a small world Smart boy, shit can happen at any time." KC pulled Giwa whose eyes were now glued to the backside of his replica.

KC found a seat outside Economics department, and allowed Giwa to enter the HOD's office.

"Good morning sir."

"Good morning... How may I help you?" a familiar voice responded. The man was sitting on a chair whose back was facing Giwa. He was watching CNN on a small TV. Giwa was alien to the new HOD as much as the HOD too was aware that there was a nameless student at the door of his office. He spun his chair to face Giwa before he could utter another word.

Giwa was amazed to see that Mr. Adegoke, better known to the students as Adam Smith, had become the HOD of Economics department. The man seemed to recognize his face in a moment.

"Don't I know you young man?"

"You probably do sir, I am a student of this department."

"Good." He nodded and removed his glasses as if to see Giwa properly. "So, what is your problem?"

"Ehm sir...I would like to defer my studies..."

"For a semester, or for the session?" Adam Smith asked calmly as he rested his arms on his table.

"For three years sir," he feebly replied.

"What? Are you mad? On what grounds?" Mr. Adegoke exploded in his usual eccentric manner, asking several questions at the same time "Are you sick?"

"No."

"Is your CGPA below 1.0?"

"No, Sir."

"Are you going abroad?"

"No...no sir." Giwa was perplexed.

"Then what the hell do you need a deferment for? Get out of my office now!" He used his fist as a gavel on the table, and then he turned back and continued watching Christiane Amanpour on CNN as she was saying something about Israel and Palestine that didn't make sense to Giwa. He came out of the office looking like a battered soldier.

"O boy! Wetin happen na?"

"Adam Smith sent me out."

"But Adam Smith..."

Giwa knew what KC was about to ask, "He is the new HOD."

"Cheer up man. You still have your school I.D card. That should give you the licence to operate within the school. They should go to hell with their deferment. You will make it man, by hook or crook. Isn't he working for money too? Let's move on to the warehouse man."

"You are a funny dude, man."

"I'll take it as a compliment. By the way, your mysterious twin brother passed by again." KC sauntered as he spoke. "I stopped him and asked him a few questions."

"For what now?"

KC shrugged. "Nothing personal, just to clear the air and ensure that you are not related."

"And what did you find out?" He couldn't conceal his anxiety.

"First of all, his name is Solomon T. Bakka, from Pankshin Local Government Area of Plateau State, and also a Jambite."

"Is that all?"

"Yes, and he is a Catholic like me." KC raised his shoulders.

"Whatever KC, I'm not in for your superficial religious bigotry."

While in the taxi, they said no word to each other. They alighted at the gate of the senior staff quarters of the university, KC led Giwa to a Boys' quarters located at lane D. He tried to unlock the door which had a sticker. **'THIS HOUSE IS COVERED BY THE BLOOD OF JESUS'** bodly written on it, and before he opened the door, a lanky girl appeared from the other room; she had a few scars. She brightened up when she saw KC. The girl wore a bum short and a short strapless top.

"My neighbour by proxy, you come to visit?"

"Yes o! how una dey now?" KC replied while pushing the door without looking at her.

"I am fine, welcome!"

"Thank you, how is Azi?" KC merely asked to prolong the greeting.

"I am fine sir." A male answered as he emerged from the room behind the girl. KC turned and looked at both of them and smiled. KC beckoned Giwa to come inside. The lanky lady and her lover went back inside her room.

KC shut the door and switched on the light. The room suddenly became blue, then Giwa noticed the bulb was coated blue and that accounted for the blueness of the room. He unlocked a metal box while Giwa fed his eyes on the well decorated room. There were pictures of Jesus and Biblical quotations on the walls but they were neat.

"A good camouflage will drive suspicious eyes away from this room," he said, as though he was reading Giwa's mind.

"True!" Giwa affirmed.

"Now let's do some practical." KC brought out four large and thick brown envelopes labelled with letters 'C', 'H', 'M' and 'DC'. He switched off the blue light and switched on a white fluorescent bulb. He sorted out the envelopes carefully with 'DC' at the bottom, 'C' was next then 'H' and 'M' were at the top. From the box, he brought out a small machine and fixed two big cylindrical dry cell batteries underneath. The envelope labelled 'M' was opened first.

"Wait a minute, I thought you said we were coming to your warehouse," Giwa asked, he was afraid that KC would start some form of ritual.

"Yes, we are in the warehouse," he pointed at the stack of fat envelopes, "and these are the wares. Just relax, believe me, the worst was what you experienced on Sunday night, relax Smart boy, this is smart business." KC spoke like some technologist giving instructions before the practical commenced.

From the M-labelled envelope, he produced a white transparent polythene bag which contained a greenish-brown substance, like dry grounded leaves of a cassia tree.

"Is this tobacco leaves?"

KC shook his head while observing the contents of the bag. "No," he turned and looked at Giwa in the eye. "Smell it! This is Mary-J," he grinned, "It's very good for your appetite and it increases your performance on anything. I have been warned, and I'm warning you as a smart business man; never smoke it even if you smoke tobacco. Allow your buyers to smoke their lives out with it. Compared to the other stuff here, Mary-J is the commonest. However, this one is a rare Jamaican species but it was grown here in Nigeria." KC went back to the small machine. "This is called the perfect wrapper." He used a tea spoon and fetched a full dose of the Mary-J, and meticulously poured it on a well cut out paper. It was a newspaper but was cut out according to some specifications. There were hundreds of such papers in the metal box. KC turned on the perfect wrapper, he placed the paper containing the tea spoonful of Mary-J and it was instantly turned into a cigar stick. KC held it in his fingers and turned towards Giwa again. "Now this is two hundred naira in my hands if I sell it on the street, but it is five hundred naira if I sell it in the club. Normally, I sell an average of ten wraps at the club. If you get too greedy you may end up in a cell, so it is better to be contented sometimes." He quickly moulded nine other sticks of Mary-J. In less than ten minutes, Giwa saw ten sticks carefully arranged on the table before him. He couldn't move or say a word. He was just astounded.

KC put back the polythene into the 'M' envelope. He carefully placed the 'M' envelope into the box. Then he opened the envelope labelled 'H'. "Henny... henny, my honey..." KC said as he observed the bag. It was a white salt-like powder. He faced Giwa, "This is the Vietnamese heroin produced under stricter specifications than the Afghan heroin. Donald told me that South Vietnamese soldiers used this to whack the asses of those fucking Americans out of their country. Henny could be sniffed, ingested orally, or injected into one's blood. It's gotten from the opium poppy; a control plant around the Middle East and Southeast Asia," KC spoke with the aura of a renowned professor of narcotics. "Again don't use henny, it is highly addictive. Allow the users to use their thing."

"But how do I know if it's original, if it's not just some fake powder?" Giwa asked for the first time like an unknowledgeable student.

"Very good question," KC remarked. "If you hadn't asked this question, I would have assumed I was speaking to myself." He smiled, "Henny is soluble in water; which means it can dissolve in water. It should be stored always in a dry place." KC fetched a little of the henny in a teaspoon and poured it into glass and added water to it. He stirred it for two minutes and the water looked like it had nothing in it. The henny had completely dissolved into it.

"That is wonderful!" Giwa couldn't hide his amazement.

"Hahaha, this is just a simple test for heroin. To prove it's the Vietnamese variety, simply add a shot of colourless dry gin to it." He pulled out a small bottle of gin and poured a little quantity into the glass cup. Immediately, the water became pale yellow.

"Wow!"

"Giwa, I tell you, Donald was a genius. He taught me all these, and for the test of Mary-J, simply smell it." He gave Giwa a wrap to perceive the strong smell. No other plant smells like it. When in doubt, give a small portion to a guinea pig and watch it sommersault in its cage."

"How much does a teaspoon..."

"A teaspoon equals five grammes," KC chipped in.

"Yes, how much does it cost?" Giwa asked again.

"It's anything from five thousand naira and above."

"Chai! We are about to make it," Giwa squealed.

Ten

Mr. Obi and his family arrived on the 2nd of January in the morning. They boarded a night bus. That was their first smooth night journey in many years; at no point were they held up by congested traffic, no experience or story of armed robbers on the road, or even ahead them. They didn't stop to address any malfunction in the engine or even change any of the tyres. Mama Adaku insisted that their journey back home was a miracle because she had prayed and asked God for it during the cross-over night prayers they had in church to usher them into the new year. She said that the smooth journey was just a sign of the good tiding that would come their way.

Solomon would occasionally inject a "Thank God!" or "Praise the Lord!" or "Holy Mary!" as Mama Adaku recounted the events of their journey. Her husband and all the children had taken their bath, eaten, and were ready to take a nap by the time Mrs. Obi finished feeding Solomon with all the details of their Christmas break. Mr. Obi had to beg his wife to take some rest before she left Solomon. Papa Adaku intuitively knew that Solomon had been adequately updated, knowing that his wife was incapable of leaving out any part of the story. He inquired about the progress of the business during the break. Thankfully, Solomon had prepared a summary of all items sold and made an inventory of all remaining stock. He also provided a list of equipments and materials to be bought based on the demand. He brought out the summary sheet: It was neat and concise. Mr. Obi was highly impressed but tried to conceal his feeling. In his entire business career, he had never summarized his transaction in the manner in which Solomon did. By experience, he knew profit in his kind business was usually at its lowest ebb in the yuletide season, however, he was glad that the profit Solomon made beat his expectation. Mr. Obi gave Solomon a warm handshake for a job well done. He told Solomon to instruct the boys to lock up the shops and take the whole day off to rest too.

Solomon went into his room, then he suddenly remembered something; he came back to the sitting room.

"Sir, I almost forgot to tell you that Father Thomas Brown was around for Christmas."

"You mean he was here in Pankshin?" Mr. Obi was astonished.

"Yes Sir, he was here in this compound, in my room." Solomon stated elatedly as if he hosted the Pope himself.

"Ooooh God!" Mr. Obi was biting his index finger regretfully.

"Why didn't you tell me *na*?"

"I was surprised when he came with Rev. Father Chollom Gyang." Then Solomon produced a box and two bottles of anointing oil.

Mr. Obi opened the box, in it were a dozen rosaries of different colours and materials. He held the rosaries as someone holding gold coins on his palms. He caressed the bottles mildly then he closed his eyes and whispered a quick thank-you-Jesus prayer. He also thanked Solomon profusely as though Solomon was the Father Brown himself. He packed all the gifts and shouted "Mama Adaku!" as he walked into his room.

Solomon went back into his room, he was bewildered. He couldn't sleep, read, or think about anything. His door was ajar but it was surreptitiously widened and closed almost at the same time. A figure stood before him, a human being. He used his palms to rub his eyes properly. Adaku was standing before him.

"You! What are you doing here?" Solomon was instantly perplexed.

"Shhhh" She motioned him to be quiet. She walked closer to him, "I just want you to know that I was thinking of you all the while during the Christmas break and I want you to know that I still care." She brought out a beautiful polythene bag that she had been hiding at her back when she entered the room. She dropped the bag on his bed and made for the door, not wanting to hear any word or even a "thank you." She peeped outside. When she felt it was safe, she rushed out, straight to her room.

Solomon was baffled. He sat watching the embellished polythene bag for a few minutes. He studied the bold symbol of love on both sides of the bag. Inside it were two romance novels and a box that contained a sheen wrist watch. The novels also had the love symbol on them so he didn't need to read them to be sure they were romance novels. All the same, he hoped to read them sometime soon. The wristwatch was, however, something else. He was certain that Adaku spent a fortune on it. *Where did she get that money?* At that point, Solomon decided not to wear the watch until he resumed at the university. He pulled out the watch to try on his wrist and saw a short note that was placed under the watch.

My love
Rivers may run dry
Rain may stop at the sky
But our love will never die
You are mine from above
Gentle and sweet as a dove

N.B: Forget about what my father thinks. We can keep this love discreetly between us for the time being.

Oh not again! Solomon was helpless. He couldn't believe that a girl who wasn't even seventeen years old yet was steering him into a relationship. He neatly hid the novels under his box, and the wrist watch too, but he held the brief note and read it over and over to himself until he fell asleep.

Solomon woke up from a long siesta and found the note in his hands. He must have forgotten to tuck it in somewhere before he slept. The bout of confusion and restlessness came upon him again. This time, his love note couldn't calm him down. He heard the sound of a car pulling up in front of the house. He peeped through the window. It was Father Gyang's car. The passenger's door was opened, he was hoping Father Brown would emerge but was a little disappointed to see Sister Vero slip out of the car. Two other reverend sisters emerged from the back of the car as Father Gyang led them to the main house. Sister Vero wore a very solemn face as if she had just undergone a compulsory confession. The two other sisters trailed behind her in the same gloomy fashion. Solomon considered going to greet them but decided to delay his greeting until they were almost gone.

He heard Mr. Obi euphorically welcoming his guest but his excitement died down as they exchanged pleasantries. Solomon didn't hear any more words again, though he tried to convince himself that he wasn't eavesdropping. He closed his eyes for some seconds then he heard a loud scream. He recognized Mrs. Obi's voice but he couldn't understand why she was screaming. Her voice was muted in no time. Instinctively, he knew something was wrong somewhere but he couldn't tell. Adaku appeared again, this time without a smile. She told him that he was needed in the sitting room. Solomon sprang from his bed and followed her straightaway. He was greeted by the sad faces, and the teary eyes of Mrs. Obi. Sister Vero pointed at a vacant seat. He obeyed without hesitation. He searched Papa Adaku's face for a clue but on seeing Solomon's face, Mr. Obi dropped his gaze on the floor. They room was dead silent after Father Gyang cleared his troat speak.

"Solomon, I am sure you have heard about the Nada aeroplane that crashed into the Altantic Ocean shortly after departing Murtala Mohammed Airport yesterday in Lagos."

"Yes, yes what about it? It was on radio and on TV yesterday. I even saw a newspaper headline this morning that was captioned 'Black New Year'. He fidgeted and his lips twitched. "I hope no relative of this family was involved," he added, perplexed.

"I am afraid so Solomon; a relative of someone in this family was involved," Father Gyang shook his head as he wistfully declared.

"Whose?" He looked at Mama Adaku, more tears flowed freely from her eyes, she shook her head, Mr. Obi's head was already buried in his hands as he stared on the floor. Tiny drops of liquid fell on the floor between his legs.

Sister Vero said just a word, "Yours."

Solomon poked his own chest questioningly, looking at Father Chollom. Father Chollom nodded. "Who is it then?" Solomon was already feeling a surge of goose pimples instantly protruding under his skin like some instant chickenpox.

"It is Father Thomas Brown," Mr. Obi managed to say without raising his head.

"No!" Solomon shook his head. "It can't be Father Brown, he said he was leaving on the 30th of December, yesterday was the 1st of January. How is it possible?" he argued.

"His flight was delayed for two days due to the poor weather. They finally took off yesterday, and then he went to be with the Lord Almighty."

Solomon stood from his chair, he couldn't believe what he was doing; he was jerking Father Gyang by the collar, "Tell me it is a lie, tell me you are lying?" he demanded.

Father Gyang calmly held Solomon's shoulders "We confirmed it from the list of passengers that took off on that plane." He held a page of the *Nation* newspaper that contained the full list of the deceased passengers with Father Thomas Brown's name underlined.

Solomon freed Father Gyang's collar, He held the page of the newspaper, his body trembled as he perspired profusely. He felt hands on his shoulders gently persuading him to sit down. Whether in rebellion to their coaxing or in sheer disbelief, he screamed. The room was darkened in his eyes. Solomon fainted.

* * * * *

Solomon thought he was already in heaven, the light was bright, and everywhere was white. He saw faces in white robes but couldn't see Father Thomas Brown.

"Solomon!" he heard Mr. Obi's voice. He opened his eyes properly and discovered he was supinely lying in a hospital ward. The people in white clothes were the nurses, a doctor, reverend sisters and Father Gyang also in a white cassock. Mr. Obi was in a white shirt and the white walls of the hospital didn't help either. Solomon didn't like it that he was not dead, that he was not in heaven, that he couldn't see Father Brown, and that he was admitted in a hospital ward that stank of antiseptics. He closed his eyes and opened them again. The same people were there, nothing had changed. He heaved again.

"Papa Adaku," he called, Mr. Obi came and bent his head. "Is it true?"

"Yes," Papa Adaku replied.

"May Father Brown's gentle soul rest in peace," Solomon weakly prayed.

All the people in the ward chorused "Amen." They were discharged from the hospital after another hour. The three reverend sisters stayed with the family till midnight.

Solomon was numb, he could not cry, didn't know what food tasted like. He could not sleep for the next two days.

* * * * *

A week after he heard the most devastating news of his life, Father Gyang came over; a routine he had started for the past week — to pray with Solomon and also to console him. Many other people came and encouraged him to be strong. Father Brown's death resonated throughout Pankshin town like a plague that took away at least a member of each family. For a week since its occurrence, it dominated the discussions of market women and idle people on the streets.

Father Gyang led the prayers as they said the decades of the rosary. The room was silent for some minutes after the prayers.

"I see you have convalesced well. It's hightime you considered going to school. I heard it over the radio that your registration will start on Monday next week. I think it is better you commence schooling early so that the school work will consume you and enable you to forget about your sorrows." He paused for a moment.

"Yes Father, you are right. I was thinking about discussing it with you too. Fortunately, it appears we are on the same page."

"Well, that makes it easy for us. Have you discussed it with Mr. Obi yet?"

"Yes," he nodded. "But I have not told him about the five hundred thousand late Father Brown gave me." Solomon was sober, "May his soul rest in peace"

"Amen," Father Gyang answered. "Okay, I will tell him all about it. All he has to do is just to support you in any area that you may need assistance."

"God bless you Father, I am very grateful." Solomon was about to go down on his knees when Father Gyang held him back.

"I haven't done anything. Father Brown — bless his soul — did everything."

They went to meet Papa Adaku in the office. In a closed door session, Father Gyang explained how Solomon had been divinely sponsored upfront for his degree and the need for Solomon to resume school immediately. Mr. Obi understood, and welcomed the idea. He was even more grateful that his money would be spared. Nevertheless, he resolved within himself to always give Solomon some cash no matter how little it may be.

The whole family welcomed the idea of Solomon commencing school immediately except Adaku; she couldn't bear not seeing Solomon for a whole semester. It seemed to her like they had been parted for ages already. The news of Father Brown's death rocked Solomon and the family so much that she couldn't afford to talk about love to Solomon and she was careful to avoid spoiling his mood. Even at that moment, she knew it would be rash to drag him into any romantic issue.

* * * * *

Monday arrived as if they talked about yesterday. Solomon had spent the remaining part of the previous week getting prepared for school. He shopped for all his needs with the help of Papa Adaku. He bade farewell to all his friends and neighbours, and everything was set on Monday morning. Papa Adaku and Father Gyang offered to drive him to the university and ensure he settled down before they leave. On that same morning, Adaku refused to go to school, her father scolded her but she was adamant. She just wanted to wave Solomon goodbye before she went to school.

Solomon had rightly pre-empted Adaku, on the night before his departure, he composed a long letter, telling her all the lovely things she would like to hear, most of which he picked from one of the novels that she gave him. On seeing that she refused to go to school, Solomon drew her aside and handed her the long letter with a strict instruction to read it only in school. He succeeded in convincing Adaku to go to school.

* * * * *

"You have not seen money yet, my guy. Cocoa has the money you need." KC fetched some of the henny, a spoonful of each in separate papers specifically designed for the henny. He carried the large envelope with letter 'C' on it.

"Now this is the sheep with the golden fleece, Peruvian cocoa." It was taken out of the envelope.

Giwa's lower jaw dropped when KC stated that the white powder was worth hundreds of thousands of naira. He couldn't utter a single word.

KC fetched a very little quantity and poured it in a test tube. "Surprised?" He looked at Giwa. "Donald taught me how to acquire, maintain and use my equipments well." He poured some water into the test tube and shook it hard. The water instantly looked like milk.

"You see, cocoa, or cocaine — if you like — is insoluble in water. Someone could pass it for face powder or even fine garri, but if you want to be sure, look for some carbonated soda." He brought out a bottle of Schweppes soda drink. He opened it and poured in the same quantity as that of the water. He shook it for about a minute or two then he showed Giwa the change that had occurred.

"Ha! Where did you get the green colour?" Giwa was shocked.

"Titration my friend! Titration is what we call it. When you shake the mixture in this proportion, the result will always be the same." KC held the test tube and posed as though he was some authority in Chemistry - Giwa was only surprised at the changes he was seeing as the substances were combined, but KC, to him, at that moment, looked like a quack chemistry teacher in a remote school lab where almost all equipments were improvised. KC continued. "No other substance can change from white to green when carbonated soda is added to it." He lighted a candle and held the test tube in the flame of the candle using a handkerchief to hold the tip of the tube. He heated it for a few seconds and the colour of the liquid changed to dark-green. He put the fire out and held the test tube for Giwa to see. "Now! Only the original Peruvian cocoa can behave like this."

"What about the 'DC' envelope?"

"Relax! One step at a time boy." KC, the teacher, was on top of his game. "Before we proceed; any questions on the last experiment?"

Giwa shook his head. He had thousands of questions rolling in his mind but he preferred not to ask.

"Good. Lastly," he brought out the last envelope, "this is called Daddy's Cocoa, or 'DC', if you like. "Sometimes I call it the Diamond fleece." Five grammes of this cocoa costs ten thousand naira but five grammes of Daddy's Cocoa costs twenty thousand naira. It is very much in high demand and I happen to be the only person who still sells it. For security reasons, I supply only one man with 25 grammes each month — General Hamza."

"General Hamza...the name rings a bell..."

"Yeah, sure it does. He was a member of the Provincial Ruling Council before the last military regime that led to this fourth republic that we are now in."

Giwa nodded in agreement. He recalled General Hamza's face vividly. But there was something more about General Hamza that was still ringing a bell about him.

General Hamza was one of the clients Donald connected me with. Donald gave me this particular supply of Daddy's Cocoa in five parcels; that is five large envelopes. I have been supplying General Hamza since my first month in the SBC. Now I am on the last parcel with less than 300 grammes to go. When this one is exhausted, I can't get any other but hope is on the way."

"How do you intend to get more of the DC?"

"Giwa, that will be for another day. For now, I will just use a very little quantity to show you how to test for DC." KC repeated the last experiment though this time, the liquid changed to black instead of dark-green. "Hahaha!" KC held the tube and observed the colour change himself. "That is Daddy's Cocoa for you, Black is beautiful."

"Is Daddy's Cocoa Bolivian, Mexican or Columbian?" Giwa wanted to know if 'DC' was a different kind of cocaine.

"Nahee!" KC responded using the only Indian word in his vocabulary. "It is a hybrid. Okay, not really a hybrid, but it's a mixture of cocaine and extracts from a native African plant called Zakami."

"Zakami?"

"Yeah right!" KC confirmed. "Zakami is also a plant that is highly intoxicating, an overdose of it could lead to madness. Believe me, you don't want to try Zakami in any of its forms. Here," he said, pointing to the DC envelope, "Zakami is carefully extracted through some very scientific methods, not crude methods of testing like mine o! And it is blended with the cocaine. The result is a more potent drug that gives you a euphoric feeling for up to five, six days, or a week." KC measured 30 grammes of Daddy's Cocoa and poured it in a paper. He also had 30 grammes of cocoa stuffed in different papers of 5 grammes each. They were neatly sealed and contained in a bigger sheet of paper. All the equipments were cleaned up. They cleaned up the room. On their way out, they heard a loud scream. It was KC's neighbour in the other room. Giwa made for her door but was pulled back by KC.

"Hey, Smart boy, don't get yourself involved in this. Allow them to kill themselves."

Giwa became angry, he made another attempt but he was pulled back again.

"What are you? Superman, Spiderman, or the last action hero? Don't involve yourself in this. They have been fighting since I knew them, they get along very well after their fights, and you, Superman, will be scorned at when they reconcile. If you are not careful, they may accuse you of wanting to break their relationship. Let's go get some food man. I am hungry."

* * * * *

They ate lunch at a shabby restaurant. It was made of zinc, and the zinc itself was overused; layers of carbon from the smoke of the firewood formed a black skin to the interior side of the zinc. Cobwebs hung at the corners as if they were part of the decoration. The place didn't look clean but the food was good. Giwa had never been to the restaurant before but KC was already a regular customer. Even the children of the woman who owned the restaurant knew KC by name. The woman was called Hajara. Sometimes, Hajara was referred to as Hajia but the restaurant was called 'Hajo's Kitchen.' Posh cars pulled over as men in fashionable Jilabias and Kaftans alighted to visit Hajo's Kitchen. KC took Giwa through another route in Angwan Rogo that led to his house.

"KC, I am just thinking, what if something happens here? Will we ever get out alive?"

"You mean something like religious crisis or what?"

"Exactly," Giwa confirmed.

"Well, the truth is that I will hardly get out alive but hey! No matter how careful you are with this life, you will never get out of it alive, so every risk is worth taking," KC shrugged. "Actually, I have my boys in this hood, you know, those young Kauri boys. Sometimes I give them up to twenty wraps of Mary-J, not my original Jamaican brand o! I buy the cheap one and give to them for free. They respect me a lot for that."

"I like your guts," Giwa remarked.

"Thank you, and I'm flattered." KC said and they laughed as they reached KC's house. They fell on the bed as they entered the room, almost at the same time. Giwa needed that rest. Lecture would continue later in the evening at Shark's Bar. The way he saw it, it was going to be a long evening.

* * * * *

For the first time in his life, Solomon wished he was a priest. The presence of Father Gyang paved way for them as they underwent every registration process. In fact, the cassock was like a ticket for express services. Whenever they were spotted at the tail of any queue, the person in charge would beckon Father Gyang to come closer, and when he did, they attended immediately to him, or to Solomon for Father Gyang's sake. Almost every staff venerated the priest, or maybe the cassock. When he got the clue, Father Gyang would pose as the Jambite, when called upon, he would then drag Solomon along. The whole process that could take days or weeks took Solomon just one day. They were also able to secure him accommodation in room 5 of Abacha Hostel. Exhaustion was written on their faces by the time they finished. Father Gyang couldn't spare some minutes for valediction, he simply said "bye bye" and got into his car.

"Read hard, *biko*! The Lord will be with you, he will strengthen and guide you. Remember what I told you last night; forget all forms of distractions, including Adaku, because it seems to me that you children are not completely off each other yet. Focus on your books and attend the morning and evening mass. Don't forget that the spirit of Father Brown is watching you o!" Papa Adaku held his right ear as if he was sounding his warning to himself. "You must try to please him. You will do very well as a psychologist." Mr. Obi tapped Solomon on the shoulders "Do you need anything?"

"No, I am okay, Sir. Thank you very much for your words of advice." *As for Adaku, only the winds of destiny would decide our course.*

"But if..." Mr. Obi's words were caught in the loud hooting of Father Gyang's Benz; an indication that his time was up. "*Nna*...bye bye o!" He ran into the car and they zoomed off. Solomon imagined the dozens of apologies Father Gyang would be receiving from Papa Adaku for wasting his time. He returned to his room and was all by himself throughout the night.

For the next three days. Solomon took time to walk around the school. He took note of roads, names, places and faces. At the end of his first three days, he had a mental map of the university's structures. Lectures were scheduled to commence the following week. He had purchased quite a number of the relevant textbooks and had begun reading them but found them hard to comprehend.

Another occupant of the room, John Ambi, arrived from Taraba State. Solomon found out that they were in the same department and also in the same level. An instant friendship sparked off between them. Their thoughts, values and experiences were similar in many ways. John and Solomon went everywhere together except to church. John was a member of ECWA Students' Ministry (ESM) while Solomon was a member of Nigeria Fellowship of Catholic Students (NFCS). Sometimes they visited each other's fellowship; at other times, they had mild arguments pertaining to their churchs' doctrines but their friendship was not ruptured in any way. They made more friends in the course of the session but they stuck to each other closely.

Solomon showed John the places he needed to visit in the course of the registration. A month into resumption, John was at his last point of registration. Solomon excused himself to submit his registered course form at the Faculty. As he went down, he saw a face that looked very much like him, and who could pass for his twin. Later on, he met the boy's friend in front of Economics department, and through a brief chat, Solomon found out the boy's friend was called KC. He discovered that he had nothing in common with his replica except that they were students of the same university.

* * * * *

"Rule 10: Always keep your market far away from your abode."

"What does that mean?" Giwa was rubbing Vaseline on his skin as he got prepared to go out with KC.

"We are leaving for Abuja this morning." KC said.

"What! Why? I thought we were going to town.

"I just told you to get prepared too. I never mentioned where we would be going to but now you know. We are visiting General Hamza this afternoon at his home. He is due for another supply." KC was casually dressed with the merchandize safely tucked into different pockets of his jacket.

"I just hope something good comes out from there."

"Are you joking? That is my most valued and esteemed customer; just come along and you will be glad you did. No one has ever had the privilege of coming with me to see General Hamza. By now you should be on your knees thanking me for such an opportunity."

"Mtcheew! Go away joor! You must be really mad." That journey marked Giwa's first visit to the city of Abuja. Although he had seen parts of it on TV and in newspapers, the sights he saw physically were breathtaking and he gawked at almost every magnificent building. KC became satisfied that Giwa was pleased with the sights of the city. "

"This is what I call a city where we ought to live the good life I am talking about. Do you see why we have to make it at all costs?" KC was giving parts of his usual sermon.

"Yes! I see... Wow... This is amazing..." Giwa responded without looking at KC. By the time they reached General Hamza's House in Maitama, Giwa was speechless.

*   *   *   *   *

"I want to see the General," KC said without answering any of the soldier's questions. He obviously intimidated the young soldier by insinuating a level of familiarity with his boss.

The soldier pressed a button and spoke through an intercom. "Morning Sir, two bloody civilians at the gate waiting for your permission, Sir!"

General Hamza's voice came through. It was clear, "Where are they from?" The young soldier came closer to KC who whispered in his ear.

"They said they are from the jungle, Sir!" the corporal responded.

"Ok, let ...What do they have from the jungle?"

KC whispered again. "Pawpaw leaves, Sir!" said the soldier.

"Ok, let them in immediately," General Hamza dropped the receiver. KC and Giwa were ushered in by another soldier inside who recognized KC. He apologized that the other soldier was deployed recently. KC was not bothered. At the second gate to the entrance, they saw a young boy, effeminate in many ways. He eyed them in the manner of a disgruntled woman as he went out. KC whispered to Giwa, "That is Oga's unofficial wife," he used his right thumb to point backwards.

"You mean...I don't really get it." Giwa was getting confused.

"What you think is what it is. Don't you see the way that boy spends money in school?" KC said in a low tone.

"Aha! I have been thinking of where I have seen him before. He was at the Shark's Bar the day before yesterday too."

"That is correct," KC affirmed.

"So this is where he gets all that money... I can't believe that guy is a..."

"Shh! Enough! Let's focus on what brought us to this place. Remember it's business first."

Giwa had never seen nor entered a mansion like that in his life. His eyes swung from the height of the building to the decorated walls, to the fleet of expensive cars, the well-trimmed flowers, lined-up trees and everything. The interior of the guests' sitting room, as Giwa learnt, was also mind-blowing. He fixed his gaze on an aquarium that hosted seven gold fishes. KC sat down while they waited for the General. In the meantime, a woman appeared and greeted them. She looked very shabby in expensive materials, she was disorganized, but her scruffiness could not hide her underlying beauty. KC introduced her as the General's wife. She called, "Giwa!" Giwa was startled. He looked at her again and could not believe his eyes.

Eleven

The last time Giwa saw Amina was a day after Amina's graduation in 1996. He vividly recalled how she wept as he walked her to an elegant SUV, with it were two other new Army-green Peugeot 504 saloon cars that had very long antennas at their backs. Four soldiers well dressed in their khakis closely guarded two other men in mufty. Giwa came to know, later, that the shorter of the two was Amina's father, Col. Zubairu, and the other man that was also in a long Kaftan was her father's friend. The two men shared a few jokes and laughed wildly as Amina came closer to the car, Giwa was trailing behind in slow steps. Both of them were crying. When she was about three meters away from the car, her father's friend stopped laughing. His eyes went over intently at Amina. He licked his lips as he ran his eyes over the curves. Giwa didn't like the manner in which the man was looking at his school mother. He wanted to walk her until she sat in the car but the man asked who the boy was and what he wanted, he barely finished speaking when Giwa felt his arm being pulled violently. He staggered a little. Col. Zubairu asked the soldier to leave the poor boy alone. He urged Giwa to go back to school and continue his studies. Zainab, Amina's sister, was also there, her mood was very indifferent but Giwa saw her smiling sheepishly when her father's friend thrusted a wad of notes into her hands. Giwa turned for one last look at his mother, he caught her watching him go, then he stood there and was waving until the convoy of three cars sped through the gates of Plateau High school, she was waving him too. That was the last time he saw the once angelic Amina, the once beautiful and brilliant queen of PHS, the wanna-be medical doctor.

Giwa couldn't believe that the young shabbily dressed lady standing before him was Amina. "Amina! Oh my God!" Giwa exclaimed. "Amina Zubairu!"

"Giwa Bako!" She stood smiling as though she had known he

was coming. They embraced each other but Amina was quick to let go of him. Her fingers went through her hair, scratching the scalp and arms, intermittently, looking around. Giwa sensed Amina was not alright. He couldn't imagine that he would ever see Amina again but fate had brought them together, Giwa was exceedingly happy. She asked Giwa if he had a phone, stayed in Abuja and whether he would spend the night. All her questions were met with an emphatic "no".

They heard heavy footsteps coming from the stairwell, it got louder and by the time the General appeared, Amina had disappeared from the scene.

"Hey, young men, KC how are you?" the well built General wore a pair of basketball shorts under a large T-shirt. His legs were heavy but they looked very clean. He shook hands with them and walked towards a mini bar. The General returned with three glasses in his left hand and a bottle of Andre on his right hand. The three of them held their glasses as the General uncorked and poured them a glassful each of the wine.

He motioned them to sit after he had sat down on the three seater sofa.

"I thought you would be coming tomorrow but I am more grateful that you came today. You know sometimes I expect you like my salary; the earlier, the better, hahaha," the General laughed, alone. "So who is this young gentleman?" He quizzed as if he was just seeing Giwa. "I thought we had a 'no third party...'"

"... agreement!" KC completed the General's statement. "Correct Sir, but this very smart boy is the closest pal I have right now. He is fully into the swing. We are expanding now so you should please accept him as you accepted me the first time I came with Donald."

"Very well!" the General declared, "but not him alone on any visit."

"Fine, if I am not here with him, then I am dead," KC smiled. The General smiled, he raised his glass.

At the General's office, KC brought out the consignment he had; thirty grammes of Daddy's Cocoa, thirty grammes of henny and ten wraps of Mary-J. He laid them on the massive mahogany in front of General Hamza who quickly poured a little of the white powder — Daddy's Cocoa — and sniffed it.

"Aaah! Oooo! That's it... KC, you are a good fella." He laughed for a long time then he unlocked a drawer and brought out a large envelope which he pushed to KC. "Here, two hundred thousand naira in cash."

KC split the money into equal halves and stuffed both halves into large inner breast pockets of his jacket.

"The General, General of all Generals," KC hailed and the threesome laughed.

"Once a General, always a General," General Hamza remarked proudly.

At this moment, Giwa was able to match the face of the General with the man that came with Amina's father to take her home after her graduation. He remembered the rumour they heard that Col. Zubairu gave his first, and most beautiful, daughter in exchange for the post of a military administrator of a state. Amina got married to the General five months after her graduation and her father died in a plane crash along with some colonels seven months later.

Giwa found a sheet of paper and quickly scribbled his school address on it. He clutched it tightly while KC and the General said goodbye to each other. Amina met them on their way out. Giwa dropped the small piece of paper on her palm. Amina mumbled something which he interpreted as 'goodbye' and went straight to the General's office.

"He uses the henny to control her, whenever she sees me around, she knows a fresh supply has arrived. That is the sad part of it, she is already addicted but who cares, let the rich sniff themselves to death..."

"Oh, cut that crap!" Giwa blurted, "If I had a gun, I would have shot you in the head five times already. Do you know who Amina is? I cursed myself a thousand times since I found out that the Henny was meant for her." Giwa's eyes were red and filled with tears. "She had a bright future, she was a priceless jewel! Now look at her," he pointed at the mansion they had just left, "look at the rags you have turned a pretty woman into." Giwa sobbed a bit as he scolded his friend. His teardrops were dried by the back of his palms.

They reached a hotel in the mutual silence that accompanied them since Giwa's outburst. KC booked a room for two. Each took a cold bath, ate and rested. Much was not said afterwards, each of them was saddled with a burden of guilt in his heart.

Dinner was sumptuous, followed by two bottles of their favourite stout, they began talking mirthfully again.

"Have you ever heard of the Knight's Club?" KC asked.

"Nope, a club is a club, isn't it?"

"No way, the Knight's Club is currently the best in Abuja and it runs for twenty-four hours but it gets quite kinky at night. It's quite a bad place to be and it's really good for our kinda business."

"So, in other words, you want us to visit, right?"

"On point!" KC had already lighted a cigarette and had taken his first puff. "We will have a couple more drinks, stay off those money-eating Abuja girls and sell four packs of 5g Cocoa to any four of my regulars and 3 packs of 5g Henny.

"And after that?"

"Back to our room of course, or do you expect us to pass the whole night there?"

"Then how do we get there?" Giwa was becoming nervous.

"That shouldn't be a problem when you are with KC." He crushed the short end of his cigarette on an ash tray. At the receptionist's corner, he made a few inquiries. Within minutes, a taxi driver was at their table. He was ready to go.

The Knight's Club was something else, it beat Giwa's wildest imagination. It was a large hall with several compartments at the extremes. Snooker tables vastly occupied the centre of some cabins, there were other cabins with tennis tables, and some were makeshift rooms. KC said those ones were actually made for quickies. In the hall, people were partying licentiously.

KC walked over to a table where a group of boys were seated sipping assorted wines. He shook hands with them then he walked to a corner, a guy from that table excused himself to see KC. In a few seconds, Giwa saw them exchanging cash and the stuff. KC was back with Giwa.

"One down, three more to go."

"That was a fast one," Giwa replied.

Another guy from the same table came over and pulled KC by the hand to a corner. They transacted theirs too. KC was back again, suggesting that they change their standing position and take seats later. A beautiful girl came to the centre, she held a pole and danced wildly around it as the tempo of the music increased. She took off her clothes in bits until she was left with her pant and bra. Men came close to her and forced some cash into her pant and bra. Her right hand was used to fetch the money while she danced. The music was terminated abruptly, and the young girl walked away, the DJ announced the arrival of another stripper.

"They are paid by the manager to give you those sexy moves that would swing you to action. I hear they double as the manager's sex toys." KC spoke as the other girl took her turn to grab the pole. She looked like someone Giwa knew albeit a grown version; she swung her hips unabashedly and gathered more accolades and cash than the former. "Now that is one of my recent Henny customers."

"Do you know her name?" Giwa suddenly be came very curious.

"I don't think so but she goes by the stage name Latifah, I could hook you up if you really want to meet her."

"Please do."

Latifah had finished her round. She changed into something else, equally seductive, and was sipping from a small bottle of Smirnoff Ice while waiting for a good man with a fat pocket to take her home. KC spotted her and drew Giwa to her table.

"What's up Latifah?"

"The sky is up and the ceiling is above my head but God pass dem. Mr. Henny, where have you been? And don't tell me that stuff is finished again." She counted six thousand naira and handed it to him, immediately, he gave her a pack of 5g Henny. She slurped the liquid in her bottle.

"Oh by the way, I came by with a friend, or should I say a fan of yours, and he wants to say hi."

"Thanks but don't need fans now," she checked her purse, more like to ensure its contents were intact. "Right now all I need is money..." Latifah lifted her head to take a quick glance at KC's friend, the fan she didn't need, but the guy's face held her attention for a few seconds. Her lower jaw dropped by itself.

It's not possible! Giwa! What are you doing here? She tried to speak but the words wouldn't come out, she regained herself. Giwa opened his arms and she instinctively hugged him. KC was speechless. Giwa's first visit, and they had two mutual friends already.

She pulled Giwa to sit beside her. Giwa now sat between Latifah and KC.

"This is the Jemima that I once told you about, you know, back in secondary school."

"Jemima, Jemima..." KC's temple wrinkled as he tried to match the name and the event.

"KC, please stop pretending like I have never mentioned her name before, remember the letter?"

"Oh yes, I remember now," KC laughed. "Funny story, but

seriously …" KC made funny gestures with his face asking if Giwa was really certain. Giwa nodded in the affirmative. Jemima followed every move but ignored them. KC smiled. He excused himself to get the three of them drinks. It was simply going to be an order for another round of what everyone of them had drunk.

Jemima watched KC melt into the crowd, then she turned back to Giwa.

"So what brought my former darling to Abuja?"

"Same thing that brought you to Abuja," he looked into her eyes with a mischievous smile.

"You no dey serious my friend! Are you a dancer like me?"

"No, I am not a stripper." She frowned her face. "I see you prefer to be called dancer, okay I am not a dancer but I am also a hustler, and that should make us even." He leaned back on his chair.

She spontaneously wore a sober mood. Her eyes fixed on the table, "I had to make ends meet all right? What do you expect? I came here to pursue a diploma in Theatre Arts at the University of Abuja. I lost my dad in the year we finished secondary school. Mum got married to a nincompoop who swindles her of her money. She cares less about us. My younger sister has just completed secondary school too so I brought her to stay with me because she complained that my mother's husband was throwing some passes at her. I was affaid that he was going to rape her too, then I brought her here with me. She knows that I work at the Knight's but doesn't know that this is what I do."

KC arrived with three chilled bottles. He dropped two and went for a dance with some bimbo he had just met. The girl was laughing hysterically as if she had just won a lottery. She had hooked up with the wrong person. KC just wanted to dance, nothing more than that. He would definitely leave her at the club, where he met her.

Giwa produced a bottle opener which was also a key holder from his pocket and uncorked their drinks. He drank a quarter of his bottle thirstily.

Jemima reached her hands into her purse and brought out a box of cigarette and a lighter. She lifted them up like a surrenderee. "May I? Hope you are not surprised?"

"Go ahead, smoke anything you want but I won't sell anything to you."

"But it's business! Faces should not be considered," she pleaded.

"Not when your life is at stake."

She lit a cigarette and released a thick cloud of smoke, though she blew it at the opposite direction, the smoke still fell on Giwa. He coughed while she sipped her drink.

"You know, your friend's stuff, the henny, keeps us going. That's what enables me to perform those stunning steps. It keeps me from seeing faces, I just do my thing and off I go in the morning. Some men are downright ugly that you can't stand them in a sober mood."

Giwa let out a loud laugh. "So when will you stop this business?"

"I don't know, just as far it goes but I do hope to settle down some day with a real man, not a drug peddler."

"Well, I know you are not talking about me because I have less than five years to quit."

"Whatever!" She sighed.

KC reappeared, this time touching his wristwatch with his right hand. Giwa decoded and nodded. He checked his own watch. It was quarter past two in the morning.

"Nice meeting you again Jemima, or should I say Lati-fah?' Giwa got up to leave.

"Anything," she winked. "Same here, I hope to see you again soon," she smiled. Giwa admired her, the old feeling was subtly returning, and he couldn't lie to himself about it.

KC led the way in the same manner they came in. He knocked on the driver's window of the taxi that conveyed them. The driver woke up and started the engine. Abuja roads were free of vehicles at that hour of the morning so they arrived their hotel room in less than thirty minutes.

"Did you sell the other packs of cocoa and henny?"

"Are you asking me now that we are back? Yes I did, and your boy is now loaded with extra thirty grand. We leave Abuja first thing at dawn, we will catch some more sleep when we get to Jos."

"That is fine by me. I am already tired of seeing how bad some good people have turned into," Giwa lamented.

"Welcome to Abuja," KC said, and switched off the light.

* * * * *

As they ascended the Plateau from Riyom Local Government, the cool breeze welcomed them. The passengers of the 504 wagon started talking again. Giwa and KC were seated at the back. They too were silent for the better part of the journey.

"We are stopping at Platinum Bank on Ahmadu Bello way," KC said without looking at Giwa.

"Okay." Giwa decided not to prolong the conversation by asking further questions.

KC read his mind and explained that they were going to deposit the cash in the bank.

At 9:30am on the dot, KC and Giwa were in front of the gate. The hangover of the previous evening dizzied them as they shuffled to enter.

"Lucky us! Here he comes," KC said.

A man was seen between the thin bars of the gate. He was obviously a banker walking a pretty customer out. Giwa sensed the man was booking an appointment for a date. KC suggested that they wait outside the gate for him.

The man's face glittered when he saw KC, he didn't waste time to politely dismiss the girl. He gave her a white paper which she grapped quickly, said "thank you" and dissolved in to the moving crowd on the busy street.

"That's a good one, isn't she?" he said, turning to face KC and Giwa.

"You know me now, what lies between me and you is strictly business," KC didn't want to comment.

"Gosh! I miss Donald. You know, he would always spare some time and talk about them girls, girls, girls!" He smiled and revealed his stained teeth and lips. "Benson Jimoh, pleased to meet you, man." He offered Giwa a handshake.

"Yeah, it's my pleasure too," Giwa warmly replied. He noticed a mysterious charm around Benson that attracted him to every customer. The banker was decorously dressed in a black suit and a dotted blue tie. "KC told me you are his good banker friend."

"Yes I am. Did you guys take part in yesterday's demonstration by the students, you really look like..."

They looked at each other. "No, we didn't," KC answered him. Somehow, they had just been informed about what took place in their absence.

KC told Benson to feel free to transact any deal with Giwa on his behalf in the event that he was unavoidably absent. Benson advised that they scout for a more legitimate business soon because the Central Bank was about to come up with new guidelines for banking reforms, part of which would question the source of money for customers who have up to a million naira in their accounts.

They were ushered into the banking hall and to his mini cabin. He scribbled some figures on a small sheet of paper.

"Here, your account balance including the two hundred thousand you have just deposited." He handed over the note to KC.

Giwa peeped and was amazed. His eyes almost doubled in size. *KC has a mind-blowing 5.7 million naira holed up in the bank.*

Giwa was shown the figures on paper, with the intention to intimidate him rather than try to convince him that there was money in the business. Giwa smiled. He vainly tried to act like he had seen such a figure before.

As soon as they got out of Platinum bank, Giwa couldn't suppress his excitement. "KC the wonder boy, KC the millionaire, KC the Smart big boy..."

"Abeg o! Make people no hear you o!" KC looked around them. "Now you have an idea of what I am talking about. Real millionaires don't talk, they allow their money to speak for them. My target was ten million but with you by my side now, at double momentum, we will definitely hit a target of twenty million in three years."

"What? Tell me you are joking! How do you expect us to raise 14.3 million in three years?

"It's simple, stick to the plan," KC replied bossily.

"What plan?"

"The plan is: Follow me!"

"Oooh you sick Smart boy," Giwa poked him. "Of course, I will follow you."

They flagged down two motorcycles. KC described Hajo's Kitchen in Angwan Rogo to them. "I know the place," the other *okada* man stated before KC finished.

"Very good. Take us there," KC said as he climed the *okada*. Giwa had already climbed his and was waiting for a 'go'.

At Hajo's Kitchen, the mood was tense. Everyone looked sad or disturbed. KC ordered for eba and egusi soup, Giwa ordered for the same. Hajo's twin daughters were rather too excited, they laughed and chased each other around the kitchen. Very few customers patronized Hajo's Kitchen on that Friday. One of the twin girls stood before KC and pointed at his forehead, "Kill you!" The other twin appeared in front of them and did the same thing and the mother warned them to stay away from her customers. KC was feeling uneasy. Giwa was just confused. They paid their money and left.

Angwan Rogo was unusually calm on that Friday.

"Something is wrong somewhere," KC said.

"Perhaps it has to do with yesterday's students' demonstration."

"I don't think so," KC opened the door and Giwa fell flat on the bed. "What's that? Go and freshen up in the bathroom first. After a good bath, then I will smoke and sleep too."

Giwa didn't argue, they bathed and sleep aggressively cajoled him to its bosom. KC couldn't sleep, his mind travelled to several places. He remembered the words of his Jewish friend, Shimmon Jacob, an underground agent of the Mossad who fronted as an agricultural engineer. Shimmon had always preached about 'alertness' and never took signs for granted. KC turned restlessly on the bed until sleep snatched his senses away.

In a dense forest, KC was wearing the Biafran soldier's uniform and was fighting along with his juvenile father against the Nigerians. Suddenly, the Nigerian soldiers outnumbered them. All other Biafran soldiers were dead except KC and his father. The soldiers wore masks and were shouting '*Allahu Akbar*! *Allahu Akbar*!' They shot at his father and were coming for him when he set his AK 47 on auto mode and sprayed some of them but they still closed in on him.

* * * * *

"Greatest Nigerian students!"

"Great!"

Solomon was woken up by the noise he heard. John was already looking through the window with the curtain behind him. Nanjwan, the notorious Aluta progenitor, popularly known as Fidel Castro, or simply Castro, was delivering a warm-up speech to a group of students that were not more than two hundred.

"What is happening out there, John?"

"Didn't you hear about the secret meeting that was held yesterday by some students concerning the persistent lack of water and electricity on campus for the past two weeks?"

"No, I have not heard of it."

"Well, this is the outcome of the meeting; there is going to be a protest, the demonstration starts from here," John spoke and didn't know when Solomon joined him at the window.

"So where are all our other room-mates?"

"In the mob I guess."

"And why are you here?" Solomon yawned.

"Same reason you are standing here by the window." They laughed mildly. On the Throne of Declaration, Castro vituperated ceaselessly for over twenty minutes, charging the students to fight for their right and never give up the struggle. He was resplendent in a T-shirt, a fat combat short and trainers. Sweat trickled from his face as he berated the SUG and the school's management. The weather was cold but Castro was sweating. He swept sweat off his temple with his palms and rubbed it on his shirt.

"Great Josites, the denial of a right—!"

"Is an invitation to fight for it!"

"The denial of a right—!"

"Is an invitation to fight for it!"

"Aluta—!"

"Continua!"

"Victoria—!"

"Acerta!"

He came down from the Throne of Declaration and led the way chanting.

"So-li-darity for-ever! So-li-darity for-ever! So-li-darity for-ever, we shall always fight for our right!"

Many more students came from different rooms to join the crowd. Solomon and John were contented as mere spectators, or passive supporters.

"But do you think they will succeed with their *aluta*? I have an ill feeling about this o!" Solomon was perplexed.

"Haba! Why not? This isn't their first time. My cousin told me that Castro has led three successful demonstrations. He was supposed to have graduated a year ago but he got, or was given two mysterious carry-overs. I learnt that he contested for SUG president twice and was disqualified consecutively. My cousin jokingly refers to him as the 'Lincoln of our time'. I like the guy, and his pronounced biceps, although he is short and very dark, but I still like him. He is indeed charismatic."

"So what happens to our breakfast and lectures?" Solomon tried to change the line of discourse.

"Breakfast… yes! Lectures… mnmn!" John shook his head. "You don't want to try going to school today."

"Why? I thought the *aluta* is voluntary."

"Yes, but my cousin said any time they come back from a

demonstration, they would pass through the lecture halls on their way back and beat up students who refused to join the struggle and chose to go to class instead. The point is, if you are not joining the movement, stay back in the hostel or your home."

At noon, voices of students became very audible from a long distance. There was long traffic along Bauchi road. The students burnt tyres at Jones junction and forced every driver to attach a small branch with green leaves on his car as a mark of solidarity for the students.

They came back marching triumphantly with Castro leading the protest. Behind him was the Vice Chancellor in black suit and tie. He wore a pair of white transparent glasses. The VC was also in the company of the Registrar, and Dean of Students' Affairs, all of them were soaked in their own sweat. There was a water tanker which had 'Water Board' boldly written on it. It was slowly following behind. The student-driver added the honk to the noisy music that the students were chanting.

A sympathetic woman appeared with a bottle of coke and attempted to give the VC but it was intercepted by Castro. He smashed the bottle on the ground. The woman was quickly chased out of the crowd. Castro was on the Throne of Declaration again, this time with a megaphone, wet in his sweat yet resilient as ever.

"Greatest Nigerian students!"

"Great!"

"I want to talk!"

"Talk!"

"I want to yarn!"

"Yarn!"

"I want to declare!" He was looking at the VC and the others.

"Declare!"

"First of all I want to give a big *gbosa* to all of us for being part of this rally. I assure you, our sweat has not gone in vain. With us here are some of the villain and nefarious rogues; people that have dared to stand in the way of the over thirty thousand Josites. An injury to one of us is an injury to all. Our demands are very plain; give us light and water, we have suffered enough. The university has been informed three times already, yet no meaningful action was taken. Nigerian students! Shall we continue to watch this academic oligarchy and self imposed technocrats trample on our inalienable rights?"

"No!"

"The denial of a right—?"

"Is an invitation to fight for it!" By this time, there were thousands of students watching. Every other student wanted to identify with the success of the protest.

"Posterity will never forgive us if we fail to make a decision. Nigerian students are united, powerful, eloquent, unconquerable, resilient, courageous and *gidigba* for ground!"

"Yes o!"

"We will call the VC, NEPA Manager, SUG president and the Ministry of Water Resources tanker driver that was hijacked with his water tanker, to tell us why they neglected us and allowed us to suffer for two weeks."

The VC was helped to stand on the Throne of Declaration. "Good afternoon students..."

"Nooo... nooo... woo" The students became rowdy again. The VC had just violated their protocol. Castro ascended the Throne of Declaration, the crowd was mute when he waved his hands motioning them to calm down. He snatched the megaphone from the VC.

"We want to be addressed as the Greatest Nigerian Students or Great Josites!" Castro handed back the megaphone to him.

"Okay. Great Josites!"

"Great!"

"Great Josites!"

"Great!"

"I sincerely apologize for what you went through. Frankly, until now, I have never been aware of your travails. Since I have seen your predicament with my own eyes, I promise you, I will get to the bottom of this as soon as I leave this place." He overtly denied being told and heaped all the blame on the helpless Dean of Students' Affairs who had earlier told the students that the matter was on the VC's table.

Next was the NEPA Manager, his bald head glowed ostensibly under the sun. He used the students' code of greeting and assured them of 24 hours light as compensation before the regularization of the usual intermitent supply, or 'rationing', as he put it.

Clifford Gyang, the SUG president, could not go beyond the usual "Great Josites!" in his salutation. The students shouted him down calling him "an irresponsible coward". The students began to stone him with empty tins and plastic containers. Clifford Gyang was irrepressibly abashed. Castro came to his aid. The students shouted as he ascended on the throne again.

"Castro! Castro! Castro! Castro! Castro!..."

Clifford Gyang came down and sneaked out of the crowd amidst frequent knocks and insults. The crowd deified Castro for the moment. Castro signalled the miserable lanky tanker driver to come up.

"Greatest Nigerian students! All staff of the Ministry of Water Resources ran away from their office before we came. This man came and met us at their premises so we brought him, the tanker and plenty water to clean ourselves up before water flows from our tap. Meanwhile, allow him to just greet us."

"*Sannu ku yan makaranta, sannu ku*," the poor man greeted in Hausa. He couldn't speak English. The students booed him. Castro whispered into his ears and gave him the megaphone again. "Great Jwassites, Great Jwassites!" The crowd suddenly hailed him. Drenched in his sweat, the poor man was smiling sheepishly.

"Yeaah! Baba!" The students were laughing at the old man. He felt like an entertainer on stage.

Castro took the megaphone for the last time. "Greatest Josites, I want you to give seven *gbosa* to all of us for this rally!"

"Gbosa! Gbosa! Gbosa .... Gbosaaa!"

A student collected the megaphone from him, another hefty student lifted him on his neck. The students shouted as he was transported to his room, "Castro! Castro! Castro!..."

Twelve

There was a sudden rapid outflow of clean water from the taps outside before the crowd had dispersed completely. Electric bulbs came aglow too. Loud music could be heard from different rooms and almost every student seemed to be beaming with a wide smile.

"Wow! This is the most fruitful aluta movement I have ever seen. Our demands have been met within the shortest space of time," John remarked as they grabbed their buckets to join the queue for water behind the hostel.

"I agree with you," Solomon affirmed, "but why did they have to wait for an uprising before doing what they were employed to do? What happened today has informed me to partake in every worthy aluta struggle."

"Na so bros, dem no dey hear word, na only action dem like and na so we go dey give dem the action." Another student who just joined the queue also keyed into their conversation. The circle of the conversation widened as more students gave their opinions about the demonstration. The more they spoke, the more their opinions revolved around Castro. Castro took the day. Their new god then appeared with a plastic bucket in his hand. All the students at the tap site began to shout his name even before he reached the end of queue. He dropped his bucket and shook hands with the many students he didn't even know by name. A student in front of the line took his bucket to the end of the queue and attempted to replace it with Castro's but Castro declined.

"... but we got this water because of what you did. You deserve to use the water before us." The student tried to convince him.

"No! No! No!" Castro humbly refused. "Not what I did, it was because of what we all did. We struggled together and we shall all fetch this water. I will rather remain here with my bucket on the line." The students were calm; they absorbed every bit of Castro's words. When he finished speaking, the locale resembled a graveyard. The students revered him in their hearts.

The bucket-space donor spoke again, "Castro, I have a beautiful sister to give you in case you don't have a girlfriend." The crowd burst into laughter, Castro laughed too, and the cheer returned.

* * * * *

The University was returned to normalcy. John and Solomon found themselves in class on Friday morning; the mob action of the previous day dominated the discourse of every three or more students in a group. Solomon saw some students pointing towards his direction, unsure of being the one in focus, he turned and beheld Castro metres away from him. Many students hailed him while some girls moved closer and dazed him with warm bear hugs. Castro suddenly became more popular than the VC. Before noon, Solomon heard that Castro was seen walking into the Vice Chancellor's office and coming out with a more triumphant smile.

Solomon and John went under a mango tree to get some kunu and chin-chin for lunch. They were running out of money and couldn't afford to eat at a restaurant. Boiled groundnuts accompanied lunch and they popped the pods as they went for their last lecture of the day which was scheduled for 3:00pm.

Chaos suddenly took over the whole school environment; students were running helter skelter, around, and meaninglessly. The kunu seller began to pack her empty plastic bottles; a strapped baby on her back let out an ominious cry. Solomon and John stood up and caught the sight of a thick cloud of smoke from afar; it was Angwan Rogo. Some houses were being burnt; they couldn't understand what was happening. The school gates were locked intermitently but more students were trooping in helplessly, more were crying, some were numb. A lot was going on in very little time as people flooded the campus. One student was ferried by two others; he was soaked in his own blood. Patches of red flesh pleaded for urgent stitches, or amputation.

"My God, my God! My mother! Oh I am finished, I can't make it, I'm dead... oh..." He was rushed to the University clinic.

A few students followed him to the clinic shouting, "You must make it! You must survive!"

Another student was brought in hanging lifelessly on another student' shoulder, he too was moved to the clinic. More injured, dying, and dead students were transported to the clinic. In a matter of minutes, it was reported that some Muslims were killing Christians and destroying their houses. Soldiers appeared in two large trucks and took positions round the school. They had mean faces and looked rather anxious to use their magazines. Smoke flooded the area; the air smelt of toxic smoke, blood and roasted meat. The kunu seller was already rolling on the floor and weeping uncontrollably; she broke into tears when, through the fence, she saw her house in Angwan Rogo dressed in red flames and a cap of thick black smoke. She told Solomon and a few students who tried to console her that her sick husband was at home with two other children and that she didn't know what had become of them.

Solomon raised his head again and saw a mob of students with sticks and stones around an object. The sight made him throw up the kunu and chin-chin he ate at lunch. It was a young Muslim boy, he was beaten and butchered beyond recognition. The students had become wild. More lifeless bodies were brought into the school. Another tall student identified and dragged a young Muslim student, and pushed him to the centre of the arena. Another round of butchering would have started but someone in black suit dived on the helpless lad, he covered him,

"You will have to kill me first before you kill him." He held the boy tightly. When he raised his head to look at the mob, they discovered the guy in black suit was Castro. They became still; none of them could lift their weapons again.

"Greatest Nigerian students!"

"Great," came a weak response.

"Greatest Josites!" Castro shouted again.

"Great!" A stronger response.

"Remember, an injury to one Nigerian student is an injury to all Nigerian students!" He spoke with courage, charisma, and authority. "A Josite is a Jossite, regardless of his colour or tribe or religion. His lips were dry though his dark skin glittered in his sweat. "I plead with you all as united Josites to respect the sanctity of life of very student, and fight in defence of the lives of students. Great Jossites! I suggest we move to the fence to defend josites who are escaping from Angwan Rogo."

"Great Josites!"

"Great!"

"Let's go there!" Castro pulled off his suit and gave it to the young Muslim student who was already shivering in his wet Kaftan. The soldiers didn't shoot at all. They said they had not been given the orders to shoot yet. As the crisis became intense, the soldiers started shooting in the air to scare students from jumping the fence in order to attack Angwan Rogo settlement and also to scare off the raging fighters in Angwan Rogo from reaching the university's fence. With each passing second, the crowd became wilder, from only-God-knows-where, some students appeared with bottles of dry gin and wraps of Indian hemp, cigarettes too, and were smoking and drinking amidst the crisis. They acted like wild lions that had been starved for weeks; throwing stones blindly, and at long range over the fence, hoping to kill someone. More students stood by the fence watching Angwan Rogo and other parts of Jos rise in a thick smoke. Those who came from Angwan Rukuba also said that Christians in that neighbourhood were killing Muslims in a reprisal attack. The city of Jos was on fire.

* * * * *

KC's eyes popped open, he found himself on the bed drenched in his own sweat. *It was just a dream after all.* He still heard voices chanting "*Allahu Akbar*! *Allahu Akbar*!" The voices grew louder and clearer. He drew his window curtain aside and saw a crowd coming with clubs and machetes, among them were the ones KC used to sell or dole marijuana to. He pushed back the curtain and woke Giwa:

"Giwa, Giwa get up!"

"What is it KC? What is happening?" He woke up in a cauldron of confusion.

"We are finished," KC was trying to light a wrap of his Mary–J and Giwa had no idea where he got it from. "Grab your credentials, drop them in this bag, we are leaving now." KC took a long puff and shook his head. The puff must have triggered the redness in his eyes.

"KC, what is going on?"

"Just shut up and listen!"

Giwa was mute, then he heard loud shouts. His credentials had always been in a separate bag, he just needed to strap it on his back. Giwa pushed KC's into the small bag and tried to have a glance through the window. A stone smashed the glass in front of his face.

Impulsively, he flinched, sprang backwards and fell on the floor. KC was hitting the ceiling. Giwa got up, made for the door, and moved on to the fence of his compound but before he could jump, he saw a mob lynching a young student. Cold blood coursed his veins; in another flash, he was back into the room, kneeling.

"Father, please forgive me all of my sins, protect my family from..."

"What are you doing?" KC kicked Giwa's buttocks while trying to load a revolver and smoking at the same time.

"KC, we are dead. You know what I just saw?" Giwa was sweating and crying. A warm liquid spread around his thighs and downwards. It was his urine. He was so confused that the sight of KC with a pistol looked familiar to him. He had never been that close to a gun before, and he wasn't scared either. It was rather a strange feeling that would baffle him later.

"Get up and let us go. Prayers are for survivors and people who are a day away from death, not men like us who are only inches away from it." KC hung his rosary on his neck as he spoke. "Holy mother, help us to survive." He kissed the tiny lady embodied on the rosary.

More stones smashed their louvres, they were obviously surrounded. KC led the way out through the door. He fired a bullet into the sky once, the crowd dispersed. He aimed and fired an aggressor that was approaching him with a dagger and scored a bull's eye on his forehead. Two more shots were fired and the crowd dispersed further. He pulled Giwa along as they ran on the main road. Their attackers were following them, they were hit by stones but they wouldn't stop. KC allowed Giwa to move in front him, he turned back and shot two of the attackers who would have brought them down, the others ran backwards.

"Giwa! Don't stop, don't worry about me, just run for your life," KC shouted as he tried to maintain a gap between Giwa and the mob. They stopped fleeing and they were at the fore front, coming towards KC again. He noticed two boys with long rifles, dane guns, in the crowd and they were leading the mob which had retreated seconds ago. KC turned and saw Giwa very close to the fence. He fired three more times before he ran out of bullets. He flung the gun away and ran like a cheetah. The men with long rifles were running after him, shooting sporadically. It was a miracle that none of their bullets hit KC, and then their shots died as he neared the university's fence. A soldier took them out with just two bullets to enable KC survive. Students cheered as KC and Giwa were hauled across the fence into the campus.

KC felt like an action film hero with wounds all over his body but was happy to be alive. He hugged Giwa tightly for a few seconds and whispered into his ears, "We made it brother, God is on our side... You can say your prayer now." He released Giwa and they were given two sachets of water, 'pure water', to quench their thirst. Giwa gulped his water in no time. He was numb, confused, and calm.

* * * * *

Solomon witnessed the narrow escape of the last two students who joined them. He thought KC would not make it but he was happy when he saw KC coming up across the fence. At a closer look, he realized KC and the other guy that looked like him were the boys he saw a few days ago. He focused his gaze on them even when they were locked in a tight embrace. He studied the wet map on Giwa's trousers which turned out like an eccentric design. His guess; Giwa must have been a few millimetres close to death seeing the blank expression that stuck to his face.

John kept shifting his gaze between Solomon and the boy in semi-wet trousers. His friend caught him looking at them, he didn't need to guess what John was thinking about, and even his intended question.

"Shhh...I have seen him before, and no! We are not related in any way: He is from Kaduna and I am from Plateau." Solomon wished he had a brother; he thought with deep longing in his heart.

"But did you confirm..."

"Yes I did, and there is no possible link. Can we just let this matter rest?"

A student at the fence screamed and fell down. Other onlookers came around him, he was shot in the neck. They were later told by a soldier that it was a bullet from a long range rifle. All the students were advised to stay in the classrooms except for some few stubborn ones who insisted on dying as 'heroes' if they had to. Solomon was only pleased be back inside, under a roof. The gory sight was already making him feel sick. He saw KC again. KC must have recognized him immediately, "Solomon right?"

"Yes! I am glad you escaped, I saw a few others that couldn't make it."

"My brother, make we go now! My body still hurts but I'm grateful that I'm alive."

Solomon agreed and moved on. He remembered seeing KC use a gun. At that moment, Solomon feared that KC was into something, he was more afraid for his look-alike who was following too.

* * * * *

Giwa sat on a decking of cement, between two ceramic sinks; there were several other ceramic sinks in the room. A few students were also seated there, bored, frightened and sad. He didn't know it was Zoology lab 2 until he heard someone saying it, it then occurred to him that he was in a lab upstairs. Most of the lab equipments and specimens were either dilapidated or in a state of disrepair.

"Aha! There you are Smart boy! Lost you in the crowd." KC came walking majestically, more from the pain in his body than from a wish to assume a gangster's walking posture. He held his left thumb and index finger closely in a way that almost spelt an 'O'. "We were this close to death, but thanks to Jesus and the Holy Virgin, we made it." He pointed upwards and kissed the Virgin on his rosary.

Giwa was still, but was fully conscious, "Why don't you start by telling me about the gun you had in your possession all along." Giwa replied without looking at KC who had just taken a seat beside him.

"What you should have asked is whether the gun saved your life or not, that is what matters. And yes! It did." KC flared up in a loud whisper.

"Ok thank you Mr Gunman for sparing my life and your credentials too…" Giwa held the bag out to KC. "I am just mad at you for not telling me about it."

"Sorry, I should have told you about the 'untold rule': Don't say everything, and no one will hear everything."

"And which number is that, I am beginning to lose count of your damn rules!" His lips curved inwards to show a portion of his frontal teeth that conveyed his fury.

"Just give it a number and place it under the miscellaneous portion of the rules."

"KC, look at me!" Giwa hit his chest. His pupils dilated as he stared at KC. "Right now, I don't give a damn about any rotten SBC,

Smart Boys or whatever it is. I think the gun could have been used on me since I knew nothing about it…"

"What you know nothing about will not kill you or get you killed."

"That's a lie, many people have died in that way. What about victims of bomb explosions? Did they know about it? Please don't tell me that nonsense."

"Be calm, stop nagging like a pregnant woman and allow me to explain." KC tapped Giwa gently. "Ok, I met this Jewish guy, Shimmon Jacob, about one and half years ago at the Knights club in Abuja. Actually, one of my cocoa buyers introduced me to him. I sold Cocoa to him twice on two different occassions. The third time he asked me for it, I was out of supply, however, I had 5g of the diamond fleece so I persuaded him to try it. He was reluctant at first but when he tried it, I became his friend. He told me that he stayed in Jos and worked as a consultant agricultural engineer. He had a two year contract with the state. Shimmon was overly scrupulous; he was always mindful of the positions of objects, the people he interacted with, and people walking or driving behind him. He would always lurk somewhere around our rendezvous for at least an hour before the actual meeting hour each time he set an appointment with me. Daddy's Cocoa must have cast a spell on him; he came to trust me more than any other person that resided in Jos, asides his Israeli friends in other parts of the country. He visited my place once. I used to think Shimmon was too cautious or unnecessarily fearful until one day he opened up and told me everything about himself and his family. He had a wife and two beautiful daughters back home in Tel-Aviv. It was from his lips that I first heard of the word 'Mossad'. He told me that there was an imminent crisis that was about to break out in Jos and would likely spread around some state, even to most northern parts of the country." KC paused. He stared into space, his back rested on the wall. KC spoke as though he was taking cues from an invisible teleprompter.

"So what's the connection between your Shimmon and the revolver?" Giwa became more curious.

"Shimmon showed me some documents and pictures of guns and ammunitions that were bought and kept in readiness for a massacre. Were it not for today's event, I would have still held onto my doubts. He had warned me particularly about my neighbourhood as the hub and a launching battle field. I asked him if the government and our own State Security operatives are aware of it and he said 'yes'. They knew about some top government functionaries that were involved in it so most of the files were concealed or shoved aside. Any officer who attempted to make a fuss about it was taken out. He told me that the police and all the forces had been compromised. Then I asked him if he or his country could do anything about it. Shimmon told me bluntly that his mandate was to gather intelligence report, especially as it affected his own country, and, perhaps, the U.S. His second function was to be a consultant agricultural engineer to the state. Those guys are so loyal to their country and concerned about their citizens. Giwa, can you believe that Shimmon told me all these things only three days before he left the country? As at the time he told me, he had only a week to leave Jos but he disappeared three days later. He left me a note saying he was sorry he had to go and left no forwarding address. Shimmon said I shouldn't try to find him, he said he would look for me. I had goose pimples all over me when he mentioned at the end of his note that Shimmon Jacob was just a pseudonym. However, he reiterated that all he told me about the security threat was true and that I should move out ASAP, As Soon As possible, another term I learnt from him."

"I can't believe this?" Giwa was scared.

"Better believe it, it's very true."

"Okay, but I still don't get the gun connection."

"Shimmon left the note with a big parcel which was wrapped like a birthday gift with my name on it. In his note, he gave me a strict instruction not to open the parcel until I was home and my door firmly shut. The gateman was too naïve to believe Shimmon would return after some days. He kept watch over an empty house. When I got home, I had to open seven layers of carton paper before I saw the gift. It was a stainless revolver with just ten bullets. Another note was contained in the box which carried step-by-step instructions on how to use the revolver and everything else I needed to know about the gun. In the note, I was warned never to use it or carry it about. It was he who suggested that I should hide it in the ceiling and lodge the bullets only when I want to use it. He advised that I leave because the blood-thirsty miscreants were scheduled to strike at any moment. But I doubted him." He paused again for seconds that almost passed as an hour of silence to Giwa whose ears were itching to soak up every detail. "I messed up! I shouldn't have trusted my instincts. I thought that if I gave those rascals and touts some Mary-J for free, they would give me a leak. If something was about to happen then I would move out even before they start but I was almost killed today. God! I saw two of my pals among the mob. Would they have killed me?"

"Why didn't you wait to ask them that question?"

"Oh don't be silly Giwa," they laughed quickly as if they were in a hurry. KC buried his head in his palms, he raised it in an instant. "We saw the signs but we ignored them, the tension in the hood since we came, the restaurant... My goodness! I should have read the signs."

"No *wahala*, we are alive now and that is what matters. Think about it, your money is in the bank and your merchandize at the warehouse, what else have you got to lose?"

KC patted Giwa on the back, "I must tell you that I have never had even a brother that cares and understands my feelings like you do. Your words make a lot of sense to me. I am sorry I didn't tell you anything about Shimmon or the gun earlier. I swore never to tell anyone all that he told me but here I am, letting the cat out of the bag, and I don't regret it."

Darkness was creeping in, wails had turned to sobs; the night was getting darker as clouds gathered together. Flashes of lightning from the sky gave a little colour to the night. Tiny twinkle of stars were enshrouded by thick clouds. Rumbling sounds of thunder accompanied gun shots that were heard in the distance.

A dusk-till-dawn curfew had been announced by the State Governor on all radio stations. All people were asked to remain where they were. The tension that engulfed the city hung in the air like electric cables.

A heavy rain fell at midnight, it swept pools of blood, and flushed bodies into the streams. Almost every living being kept vigil throughout the night; hunger registered on the faces of most students. When they couldn't endure it, they burgled shops within the campus and made away with every edible substance. Rumours continued to hover like helicopters searching for landing grounds; there were stories of people who resisted gunshots with their bare skins because of the charms they carried, rumours of ruthless boys dressed in army uniforms and wearing unmatching trainers. The rumour had it that the fake soldiers killed people in their homes during the curfew periods; it amplified the tension in the whole city.

After two whole days, the roads were opened and people were allowed to search for their relatives, their children, dead bodies of family members and visit the remains of their burnt houses to see if anything could be carried out. KC and Giwa held their breaths as they feebly trekked to the quarters, to KC's warehouse.

* * * * *

A dark green Toyota Hilux pick-up truck pulled over in front of Giwa and KC, then a young soldier alighted from the vehicle and ordered the duo to come to the vehicle. Giwa was skeptical but KC warned him to obey, he pulled Giwa and they got to the car. They watched as the back door was opened. A man who looked very familiar to Giwa stepped out of the car and a young girl also came out.

"Giwa! I am glad you survived," she said plainly as she smiled while he froze, as though he was seeing her for the very first time. Hannah looked more different to him this time. She was more beautiful, more mature, and less friendly. Back then, his Hanny would give him a bear hug even in the presence of her father. Then he realized the man was Hanny's father whom he had met about a year ago.

"Sorry I couldn't recognize you immediately, Sir."

"No problem at all young man, I would have passed by you like that without remembering your face too, were it not for Hannah who sighted you from afar, so I asked the driver to pull over for her to greet you."

"I really appreciate, Sir," Giwa said, slightly abashed, he turned to face Hannah who screened him from head to foot in a somewhat different manner. Giwa would have put up a confident attitude had he not remembered the contours that still marked his trousers. He wasn't sure whether she had seen it but the consciousness muzzled his gallantry.

She introduced Capt. Dogo to Giwa. Giwa greeted the young captain who posed in the car and simply raised his hands to acknowledge Giwa's greeting.

Her father seemed very excited. "Actually, Capt. Dogo is a son to my bosom friend. We were classmates in secondary school and even in the university. He was the one I called first when I heard Jos was on fire, and I gave him Hannah's address, I asked him to take her to the barracks. Unfortunately, he reported that Hannah was not in and she couldn't be found or traced. I panicked while her mother wept. At midnight, we got a call from an unknown person, he told us that Hannah was safe and was in Angwan Rogo. I couldn't believe him until I spoke to her myself. Then I called Capt. Dogo to locate the man and keep my daughter at his place until the curfew was over..." Hannah's father twittered excitedly, "... and can you believe it, Hannah was rescued by a young Muslim man named Harisu, he is an *okada* rider. She was going to Terminus on this very Bauchi road on his bike. He saw a roadblock ahead of them then he turned back and headed for his own house in Angwan Rogo" Engr. Musa spoke like an eye witness to the miraculous escape, more than the okada rider himself would testify, "In Angwan Rogo, Harisu locked her in his mother's room and gave her his mum's clothes to wear and as luck would have it, it fitted her perfectly." He laughed. "Hannah is such a lucky girl. She was fed and cared for by Harisu's family until Capt. Dogo went for her. We are just coming from Harisu's house where we went to say thank you to them. I couldn't come to Jos until this morning because of the curfew." He paused for a short moment looking at his beloved daughter. He turned back to a pale Giwa and a bored KC. "You know, there are many good Muslims out there, even better than some Christians, and it's not even about Christians or Muslims, indigenes or settlers, it's about humanity. Some people are just downright callous and inhumane."

"Sir! I have a meeting by 10:00am and it's already 9:30am," the impatient Capt. Dogo finally spoke. He tried to be polite, but his face showed traits of impertinence.

"Thank God for your daughter's life, we have to go now." KC spoke up too.

"I hope that nothing like this will ever happen to any of us again," Giwa said as Engr. Musa went back into the car.

Hannah didn't say much, it seemed she was still recovering from the shock of narrowly escaping death.

"Please manage this, I hope it helps." He produced a wad of cash from his pocket and handed it to Giwa. "Please stay safe." Giwa received the money and bowed his head thankfully. He raised it to see the tail of the speeding Hilux pickup truck.

"If that man knew how we escaped, he would have made an epic movie out of it and saved his daughter's miraculous tale for a testimony on Sunday. Oh my! It's even Sunday already. Why didn't the old man just head to church and save us a boring..."

Giwa barked at KC before he finished talking, "... why don't you get a daughter and feel what it is like to have her alive after a bloody crisis like this? You are not grateful that we have gotten more cash and if you don't know, I still have a soft spot in my heart for Hanny, seeing her alone was worth all the time and even more…"

"What's the use of money in a time like this when all businesses are halted? You have money yet you can't buy what you want, you know how we have struggled over loaves of bread burgled from campus shops," KC tried to put up a defence.

"So what are we up to?"

"Still heading for the warehouse of course, I mean our new house."

Giwa stopped, he wasn't listening anymore, something strange had caught his attention. KC was astonished; he didn't understand how one burnt car caught Giwa's attention amidst hundreds of cars charred almost beyond identification. The burnt car looked like a Mercedez Benz. Giwa read out the embossed aluminium plate number which had fallen off along with a large piece of the front bumper of the car. Hes stood still, stunned.

"KC what is the plate number of this car," he asked, in case he had not read it properly.

"What? What is interesting about the car?"

"Just tell me what your eyes can see!"

"AE 884 JJN. That is what I can see."

"Oh! My God! My uncle." Giwa's eyes reddened, filled with moisture. He stood stiff at the University Staff Quarters junction, in front of the car.

Giwa sobbed. "I wish it were not, my God!"

"Hey, hey! Is he not alive? Maybe we should just go to the house and check him there. Giwa please be a man. Your uncle cannot die in this manner..."

Giwa cleared his eyes. "Let's go to Uncle Harry's house, I want to see him or at least be sure he is alive whether the witch is there or not."

"That is the spirit, you have to be optimistic." KC patted him on the back.

The road was filled with people who had the word 'worry' on their faces; a few were seen expressing joy seeing their loved ones again. Giwa was quiet; he walked quickly and was oblivious of everything else. He would sometimes forget KC was beside him and would not nod or shake his head whenever KC spoke, many alternatives to being dead sped across his mind. He had hoped to reconcile with Uncle Harry someday but his biggest fear informed the urgency for a reconciliation. He contemplated Aunty Mercy's horrible face and what she would likely say or do when she set her eyes on him. The way he felt, he was ready to face anything or anybody. Pictures of Uncle Harry flew through his mind; smiling, in a hospital bed, or burnt.

KC finally kept mute when Giwa would not face him. The boys walked in silence until they reached Uncle Harry's house in Dogon Dutse.

Thirteen

The Obis came back from Mass to meet Solomon and a stranger standing comfortably in front of their gate. Adaku was the first to note two people in front of their gate from about a hundred metres away, and also identified Solomon among the two of them. Mr. Obi was more than glad to see Solomon, he hugged him twice. The rest of the family took turns to embrace Solomon and shake hands with his friend. Adaku grinned, she hugged him last and lasted longer in Solomon's embrace. Mrs. Obi smiled, and the children also watched Solomon and their sister admiringly while Mr. Obi's smile transformed into a frown. He cleared his throat and Adaku understood, then she released herself and fought back a flood of tears from her eyes.

"Young man, I believe you must be Solomon's friend," Mr. Obi remarked curiously.

"Yes, I am, Sir."

"What is your name?"

"John Ambi, Sir!" he humbly replied, partially bending respectfully each time he spoke to Mr. Obi.

"Actually, John is from Taraba and lives in Jalingo, he didn't want to travel far because the school authorities said that students could be called back at any time, I'm sure that will be in about two weeks. John is my roommate and coursemate and we attend NFCS together." Mr. Obi nodded his head approvingly as he heard Solomon mention 'roommate' and 'coursemate' but his face glowed when he heard 'NFCS'. Apparently, he had concluded in his mind that John has a positive influence on Solomon. "I was wondering if..."

"That will be no problem at all provided my little queens are safe." Mr. Obi looked at his daughters. He told Solomon before he asked, as if he read his mind.

John bowed more respectfully. "I am very grateful, Sir! May the

Lord bless you."

"May the Lord bless you too," Papa Adaku was obviously elated. "By the way, how did you survive the crisis?"

"Hmmn Papa! I only have God to thank o!" Solomon raised his hands in the air. "I would have been a dead man by now," he shook his head.

"Ewoo... Chimmoo... Nwammoo... Chai!" Mama Adaku raised her voice as though she wanted to adjust to her crying mode then she switched on to her prayer mode. "*Tufiakwa*! No weapon fashioned against you, or any of us in this family will prosper, we are covered by the blood of Jesus! You are the apple of God's eye. Jesus and Mother Mary are interceding on your behalf. They don't know our God is a living God." She began to rant in an unknown language which her husband suspected was speaking in tongues, a language he abhorred largely because he believed it was uncatholic.

Mr. Obi interrupted a pious preliminary prayer session which could have metamorphosed into a long public prayer. Business was the only thing Mr. Obi preferred to do publicly. He opened the gates and ushered everyone in. Sensing the absence of the family, Mrs. Obi opened her eyes and found out she was left alone.

As they ate lunch, affectionate glaces were exchanged between Solomon and Adaku, they stole glances and smiled delightfully. John noticed what transpired but turned a blind eye. He was in the full picture of the blossoming romance between Solomon and Ada. Mrs. Obi caught Solomon's gaze and pretended she was blind too.

"Ankul, what d'you buy for me?" little Nnenna abrupty demanded of Solomon.

"Oh, baby Nnenna, I'm sorry I couldn't buy you anything, all the shops in Jos were locked up because of the crisis but next time I will buy something for you"

"Then what d'you buy for Ada?" Nnenna was heading somewhere, unintentionally throwing a rope around Solomon's neck.

"Nnenna, it is not good for children to talk while eating, if they do, they will not grow up. *Biko* just eat your food o!" Mama Adaku came to Solomon's rescue knowing that Nnenna's question was likely to re-ignite embers of suspicion in her husband's mind.

"But Ankul you have not..."

"Will you stop asking and finish your food? If you don't shut up, I will finish it for you." Mr. Obi shouted at Nnenna. She shrinked like a snail would into its shell. Solomon was glad for the relief.

After lunch, Papa Adaku left the house for their annual thanksgiving and bazaar committee meeting and Mrs. Obi went for their Igbo women meeting but not before Solomon and John had narrated their ordeal. By the time they finished, Adaku and her mother were already in tears.

Solomon took advantage of the parents' absence to show John around. Adaku went along with them. They first climbed the famous mountain on which the Hilltop Hotel was situated. The hotel was old and in a state of disrepair. The view from the top of the hill was awesome; almost all areas of Pankshin town could be viewed from the top of the hill. Solomon held Ada's hands as he described all the areas and some of their basic features. They descended the hill and went into the scenic Wulmi Rocks which appeared like they were arranged by man. John was amazed at the rare beauty that was capable of satisfying the eyes of the most jaded aesthete. Adaku was overjoyed in the arms of her charming prince, she lauged at anything that Solomon said even when he coughed. John could tell that Ada was having a taste of paradise. Their last stop was at the Pankshin mini dam. It was a huge reservoir of water. Solomon said he was told that it was capable of supplying up to three surrounding local government areas with water but as it was, only Pankshin town alone was supplied with treated water once a week and sometimes they lacked it for a whole two weeks.

"People have learnt to dig their wells and power their houses too," Solomon added.

"It's not only peculiar to Pankshin, my brother; it's the whole of Nigeria. Things don't just seem to go right," John remarked.

"It's getting late, we had better hurry before Papa comes back, or before one of you two becomes this year's annual sacrifice to the goddess of the dam." Adaku pointed at them teasingly.

"If it's about your father, fine! But if it's about the superstitious annual sacrifice, I can bet you that I will remain here until dawn and nothing will happen," Solomon boasted fearlessly.

"At least one person dies here in the dam every year," Ada tried to defend herself.

"It's not true!" Solomon argued.

"It is true," she said and dipped her index finger into her tongue. She wanted to swear that it was true.

"Okay, did anybody die last year?"

"No, but someone died the year before last."

"And does that mean that the dam will take two people this year?"

"I don't know," she shrugged. "Maybe! And if it should, then I would prefer it to take John so that I won't lose my sweetheart," she stuck her tongue out jokingly.

The boys burst into laughter and she joined them. They began to walk back the way they came.

"I think we should hurry home before I become the sacrificial lamb for you people." John increased his pace ahead of them.

Ada could not but feel on top of the world with her arms locked in Solomon's arms. "Did you miss me?" She looked into his eyes and inquired.

"Of course I did, honey. I missed you more than anything in the whole wide world."

"Really?"

"Yes!"

"Oh Solo, I wish you would just stay with me forever, I love you very much. I will like to come and visit you in school." She did most of the talking until they neared Mr Obi's house.

They held hands until they saw Mr. Obi's car approaching the house from the opposite direction. It was too late. He had seen them already. The frown on his face said it all. Another check was the cold response he gave them when they greeted him.

* * * * *

In the days that followed, Mr. Obi observed Adaku's reluctance to leave for school early and noticed she always came home early. She would finish her chores early and would be seen in the company of Solomon and John. For most of the time, John would be at a far end. The love affair between Solomon and Mr. Obi's daughter was becoming too glaring. Tongues began to wag in the neighbourhood about the latest Romeo and Juliet. All of Adaku's siblings became aware of the growing intimacy between their sister and supposed brother. Nevertheless, they were indifferent to it. Mama Adaku didn't mind, she subtly approved it. The relationship strained another relationship; Solomon and Papa Adaku's, especially when he saw Solomon with his daughter.

"This nonsense has got to stop, I cannot continue to tolerate it under my roof!" Mr. Obi spoke to his wife a week after Solomon and John arrived.

"Papa Adaku, I know you want her to marry an Igbo man, preferably after acquiring her degree, but times have changed."

"Are you trying to support your daughter now or what?"

"My daughter ke! I'm just trying to be fair regarding this matter o! You and I know how Adaku has improved since Solomon had been helping her with her school work. You know that she feels happier whenever he is around and we want her to be happy too or don't you?" She asked him.

"So what do you suggest we do? Wait until she becomes pregnant in our own house? We have to do something and we have to do it fast before we are left with a burden of shame on our heads. I need you to support me on the plan I'm about to hatch now else I become the villain."

"And what could that plan be?"

* * * * *

At dawn, before 6:00am, Papa Adaku had left the house, he came back when Adaku and her siblings had gone to school. Solomon and John were helping the other apprentices to display the building materials in front of the shop.

"Solomon please come, I will like to see you."

"Oh! Good morning sir," Solomon greeted in spite of the fact he knew Mr. Obi was calling him for something grave. Mr. Obi grunted in response to Solomon's salutation. He led the way to the master bedroom. Any verdict that was passed in that room could hardly be withdrawn. Any invitation to that room implied a serious offence committed, series of beatings, a pronouncement of punishment, or an irrepealable verdict. Once they were called into their father's room, Mr. Obi's children would tremble and try to recall their recent misdeeds that their father had not known but was likely informed about. It was in that very room that Ada was beaten when she was caught in Solomon's arms; in the same room, Sochukwu, Ada's immediate younger sister, was flogged for stealing money from his shop. The children always looked sober and remorseful each time they came out of their father's room, usually, a sibling or two would wait in the sitting room to condole with the other who was punished or reprimanded. Only little Nnenna and Solomon had never been invited. Unexpectedly, Solomon's turn had come.

Clothes, mostly wrappers, were left carelessly. There were several other large boxes and a giant-sized bed. The room was quite stuffy and dark. Mr. Obi motioned Solomon to sit on a small stool while he sat on the giant bed. Solomon hoped his encounter in the room would pass away with the speed of a flying bullet, since there was no sign of Mr. Obi's *koboko* in the room. Papa Adaku cleared his throat.

"I have made arrangements with Mr. Okafor for you to occupy his boys' quarters at G.R.A. You will work at his filling station whenever you are on break." Mr. Obi's words landed like hot balls of burning sulfur on Solomon's ears. He didn't want to believe that he was not imagining things. Solomon sat stiff like a wooden idol. "Considering your plight, I have paid your rent for two years upfront; it will be your own business to secure accommodation after that. In addition, I will give you an extra thirty thousand naira to purchase foodstuff for yourself and cooking utensils. Henceforth, you are permitted to visit this house only on Sundays from 10:00am to 12:00pm. Don't forget that I am doing all these for the sake of Late Father Thomas Brown, may his soul rest in peace."

"Sir! Are you doing this because of the relationship between me and Adaku?" Solomon demanded looking into Mr. Obi's eyes.

Solomon received a ferocious slap from Mr. Obi. The slap barred more words from finding their way out of the young boy's mouth. Papa Adaku's face boiled with rage. Solomon held his left cheek. "Shut up! How dare you question my authority in my own house! I brought you here and I can send you out at will." He rose to his feet and pointed a warning finger at Solomon. "You have until noon, before Ada comes back, to pack out of my compound. Thank God you brought your friend to help you pack out. Now get out." He was pointing at the door. Solomon rose up quietly with his left hand still smootching his cheek. "One more thing ..." Solomon paused as he held the door knob. "Ada must never know your new apartment. Your new landlord said he will send you packing anytime a girl visits you. Do you hear me? Now leave my room!"

Mrs. Obi was heading for her room when Solomon came out, their eyes met, she felt bad knowing what must have transpired and was moved to tears. She quietly took away her face and made a detour. Little Nnenna was getting used to seeing her siblings step out in a sorry mood from her father's bedroom.

"Sorry Ankul Solo..." She held his hands as he walked into his room. It was like she unleashed a torrent of tears from his eyes. He sent her back and shut the door behind him.

Inside his room, Solomon wept like a baby. He regretted that his parents were not alive and pitied himself. Then he cleaned his face and made for Father Chollom Gyang's house.

"I knew it would come to this!"

"How do you mean Father?" Solomon said soberly after he had narrated his morning's ordeal with Papa Adaku.

"There is nothing I can tell Mr. Obi to make him allow you to stay in his house now. He would have kicked you out a few days ago had I not restrained him. I think the best option for you is to pack out and leave his house. Don't worry about your love. What is yours will always come back to you Solomon. Remain the good boy you have always been. Personally, I don't blame you for falling in love and I don't blame him too for being protective of his daughter. Besides, you violated the main rule that allowed you to stay in the house."

"So Father, does that mean that you are on Papa Adaku's side?"

"I am on the Lord's side son, and if it is the Lord's will that you leave, so be it. Jesus and the Holy Spirit are not unaware of the problem you are facing, what you don't know is that they are right beside you. I have gone ahead of you to talk to Mr. Okafor to treat you like his own son. I pray he does so. As he walked back to the place he used to call home, Solomon felt like he was walking in the middle of the desert. He became totally oblivious of the people, surroundings, and noise around him. On learning the sad news, John didn't waste time to help him pack out. By noon, the duo had settled partially in Solomon's new house. Solomon recounted more episodes of his life to John as they sat in their new room. He cursed his parents wherever they were.

* * * * *

A few cars were parked outside under a huge tree in Harry's compound, there were some cars also parked inside the compound. Giwa identified many of their neighbours amongst some few strangers. Almost every one of them wore a sober mood. KC sensed that the inevitable had happened but he held Giwa's arm in a way which said "it's all right." A million questions raced through Giwa's mind as he hurriedly walked to the door.

Mr. Zakary quietly broke out from a small group of sympathizers and stopped Giwa by the door. He shook Giwa's hand and held it.

"He was on his way to pick you up from school, he thought you might get hurt but he..." Mr. Zakary swallowed a lump. He placed his hand on Giwa's shoulder but Giwa shook himself free of KC and Mr. Zakary's hands.

A last ember of doubt stuck to his mind, Giwa dashed into the sitting room to confirm his fear, or doubt. It was filled with women, mostly from around the neighbourhood. They wore dull wrappers while some of them had black blouses. A portrait of Uncle Harry was poised on a stool with a condolence register in front of it. Giwa travelled to the past in a dozen flashes seeing Uncle Harry's laughter and anger. However, a motionless picture stood before him with a sombre face that said, *it is true, I am dead.* A rapid sequence of mental photographic slides of the burnt car with an imagined charred body in it swiped across his face in seconds. The gentle touch of a young girl brought him back again to reality; it was Kauna. Giwa grabbed her and hugged her for a minute while he sobbed in her arms. More women came and said some consoling words which Giwa could not hear as he was engulfed in tears and the heavy burden that burned corrosively in his heart. Two women separated Giwa from Kauna; one of the women guided him to a chair, while the other pulled Kauna to the kitchen. He began to dry his tears then he recognized some of the women in the sitting room.

Giwa saw the outline of two big breasts sagging within a loose blouse and permed hair that was scattered in all directions accompanying the dangling breasts in the blouse above a loosely tied wrapper; the face was that of Aunty Mercy and she was coming towards him. The expression on her face told him she would love to dilacerate him into a thousand pieces. *Only if I give her the chance.*

"And what on earth are you doing in my husband's house. Isn't it enough that you killed him? Now you want to kill me too? Let me tell you something, you will not succeed! My blood is bitter! I am covered by the blood of Jesus Christ...!"

So much for consolation or even a welcome address, I was mistaken to think she will ever change. Aunty Mercy continued ranting in front of Giwa, stiffening her fists like she was ready to crush him but she was better informed about touching him. Something deep inside her heart told her that touching him may cause her some disgrace that she was not ready to bear, yet she was self-propelled by the imperative to dramatize even what she wouldn't actually do

"Leave me to tear this piece of evil into rags. This filthy animal that has tormented my family ..." She was held back by some women who pleaded with her to calm down and go back to the kitchen. She showered abuses on Giwa but it didn't mean more than the whirring sound of a mosquito to him. He felt she needed to wear a bra.

Kauna reappeared and called him to the back of the house, and she tried to explain what happened. "... he was trapped in a roadblock formed by a mob and..."

"I know what happened, I saw the car this morning." She was amazed. "You did? How did you recognize it?"

"The plate number was not burnt." They talked, then he came out and remembered he had left KC outside at the front door of the house.

"I am sorry about your loss man, it's so sad. I knew he would hardly be alive the moment you told me it was Uncle Harry's car. Be strong man. I know you are left with the lioness but you have to be strong..."

"Hold it right there KC! That woman is left with herself. The only link that held us together is dead. From now on, she is on her own and I am on my own. I wished a thousand times she was the dead person, we probably would have been sipping champagne tonight." Giwa stared into the ground with his arms folded across his chest. "It's time we left, I can't stand this house any longer."

"Before you go, I will like to inform you that your uncle's burial has been slated for Saturday, just in case you have a tribute for Harry which should be included in the booklet for the funeral programme," Mr. Zakary appeared from behind Giwa. "I am sorry about your loss, it's our pathway, all of us. Harry told me you weren't in good terms with his family before his death and he wanted to make things right, then came the swift cruel hands of death and they ferried him across to the great beyond."

"I had a longing to reconcile with him too but his death came too soon." Tears fell from Giwa's eyes as he spoke. "Uncle Harry was my father for a long time before that witch came into our lives..."

"Now watch your tongue son, that woman could pass for your mother."

"Or maybe your own wife; I can safely say she is already your concubine." Giwa braced himself as he addressed Mr. Zakary.

"I now know why Mercy and Harry couldn't put up with you.

You are just as disgusting as faeces on a plate."

"Tell me more, do you want me to open your can of worms now or later?"

"I would rather not mind you. Forget about the tribute, it wouldn't make sense for the cause of the death of the deceased to appear with a glowing tribute in the funeral programme."

"Oh! Good riddance... Who wants to be seen in a booklet with a witch anyway?" He spoke to Mr. Zakary's back.

"Giwa, it's enough," KC found his mouth. He was stunned when Giwa was confronting Mr. Zakary, he was more surprised because he had never seen Giwa muster so much guts. KC. dragged him gently towards the gate.

It was a long walk back to the university staff quarters. By the time they got to KC's warehouse, they were famished. Thankfully, KC had bought some biscuits and two bottles of coke from a lone shop that was opened, it seemed the man was in a hurry to dispose his goods. They sat on their door step and devoured their meal silently.

Between the noisy nibbling of their biscuits and whistling trees, another distinct sound was picked by KC's ears. He motioned Giwa to be still then he traced the sobs to his neighbour's room, he went into the room. Their conversation was so audible that Giwa picked almost every word from outside. She was crying because of her boyfriend, Azi, who had been missing since Friday afternoon. Giwa felt she should be grateful, at least for the break in the constant fights they usually had. After all, he was only missing: *what if he was dead like Uncle Harry*. Giwa felt zero need to go in and console her, he had lost all his property and his uncle. He thought he deserved more condolence than Aunty Mercy, Azi's girlfriend, anyone that was affected by the crisis.

KC came back to continue his meal. He looked worried in a way, "It's about Azi..."

"I heard everything, she is lucky he is only missing. Perhaps he will be found somewhere," Giwa mentioned unperturbed.

"Don't be mean, that girl needs some sympathy."

"Tell me about it... Please open the door. The way I feel now, I could make good use of your bed which has been idle for years."

"Phew! I would need the bed too. This has been the longest weekend of our lives." KC rose to open the door.

The adjustment period seemed rather shorter than the weekend in which Giwa and KC, among thousands of students spent in the classrooms of the school. Hunger alone made the weekend seem like two whole years and other factors combined to stretch e weekend to the length of a decade.

Giwa was becoming used to a new place of abode, new clothes and new feeling of being the Smart boy with a hidden gangster attitude. He showed up at Uncle Harry's burial and left like any other distant mourner, although throughout the week, before the funeral, he would think of Uncle Harry before he went to sleep and after he woke up. And each time wishing he had made things right with Harry before he passed on. At the funeral, Aunty Mercy made a show which drew sympathy from people who didn't know her well; she attempted to dive into the grave while the casket was being lowered into it. She was prevented but she gave two more overt attempts and was dragged back into the house. All along, Giwa stood at a distance, KC stood by him. Many other people acquainted with the family wouldn't go beyond a superficial greeting to Giwa when they spotted him at the burial. He felt a bit ostracized and blamed it all on Aunty Mercy's slanderous tongue. Kauna appeared with two plates of food and a couple of drinks for Giwa and his friend. They had seen each other a few minutes before and signalled a pleasant greeting. He didn't know that she was marking his position in the crowd, she later brought food for them. The food was quite timely. Kauna stole some time to chat with Giwa and at the same time take a break from the ceaseless directives of Aunty Mercy and her friends.

"Bring this, bring me that, cook this, grind that, wash this, serve him, do everything; Giwa I am so tired. This past week, there has been so many activities for me to do. The day before yesterday, I went to bed wishing I would die in my sleep."

"I still wonder what you are doing in this house," Giwa said as he munched a piece of meat.

"I asked myself the same question yesterday but I will make up my mind about something now that the burial is over." Kauna quickly changed the line of discourse. "You know, it occurred to me recently that Uncle Harry had been the main reason why I remained in this house, he played with me sometimes and that made me happy. Sometimes I feel like the blood relationship was between me and him. He talked about you sometimes but not in the presence of Aunty Mercy."

"Seriously?" Giwa was pleased to learn that.

"Eh hen!" she nodded "He was ..." Kauna snapped her fingers "it seems your name was used by Uncle Harry as his next something..."

"Next what? Next of kin?"

"Yes! I think so. I think that will make you become the beneficiary of his money, at least that was what I overheard his banker telling the lioness about. He even asked if you were around but Aunt Mercy cooked some story that you were lost somewhere."

Giwa squeezed his face. *She could as well say that I am dead too.*

"Never mind, they will definitely find you when the time comes. He said the bank has a strict lawyer who will insist on seeing you first, dead or alive, before they start processing the money."

KC only said "thank you" to Kauna. He tried to be invisible in the course of the conversation. He handed Kauna his empty plate and added another "thank you." Kauna gathered the plates and made for the house then Giwa called her back.

"This will help you in case you make up your mind to leave," he handed her ten thousand naira. "You deserve a better life, don't wait in this house until you wake up in the world of the dead."

Kauna allowed tears to roll down on her cheeks freely. She hesitated for a moment then she surreptitiously grabbed the wad, split it into two halves and tucked it into her small bra. Her eyes were dry as she went into the house.

"Come on man, I know a place where you can relax and deplete your sobriety."

"It had better be the Shark's Bar."

"Where else? My brother, where else?" KC shrugged with an extended smile on his face as he spoke.

Things happened to be somewhat normal at the Shark's Bar. It was as lively as ever and Innocent was more than excited to see KC and Giwa. He cleared a table for them to sit. Some boys were smoking and laughing as if nothing had ever happened in Jos. Giwa saw a young boy covered with POP on his neck, he was drinking and closing his eyes as he gulped.

Duff, Gasko and some other fellows trooped in with lighted cigarettes in their hands, Duff was obviously cracking a joke as they walked in and he was already laughing about the joke before his audience joined in. Giwa was happy to see his friends alive. He beckoned them to come. Gasko had a POP on his left arm and a bandage held his left wrist and his neck together. As they came close, he noticed Gasko was also limping and he had some open wounds on his head. The POP was designed with nicknames and some symbolic drawings.

"I see you were involved in a desperate struggle to remain alive," Giwa remarked as he stared at Gasko's face using the remaining light of the setting sun.

"My brother no be small thing o! It takes a real man to survive like me..." Gasko shook his head.

"Mamba! Mamba!" Duff shouted. "Can you believe that Gasko made use of a kitchen knife to fight his way back to life? He is the only brother that almost got killed. The guy went home when he calculated everyone's absence, in order to help himself from his father's safe, and then the mob arrived. Lucky bro! he was not burnt down with the building" Duff spoke more than Gasko would ordinarily say. "If to say na me eh! Dem for hear ram with wetin I get." He put his hands under his shirt at the waist. "I would have cleared them with my gangster bitch."

"Gangster bitch? What in the world is that?" Giwa inquired.

Duff lifted his shirt high enough for Giwa to see the handle and the trigger of a 9mm gun.

Giwa was shocked. Duff tapped him on the back and told his guys to secure a table.

Innocent came with two cold bottles of Guiness and laid them gently on the table. Before he opened the bottles, KC had lighted his first stick of cigarette for the evening. "Innocent, how did you survive the crisis?"

"Hmm... Sir, we were locked up here throughout last weekend and we survived on beer which the soldiers helped us with, until finally, the ocean dried up, except for soda."

"That is funny, we will talk more about that later."

KC puffed his cigarette then he took a sip. "It is high time we hustled enough to move out of this city, the security is damn too porous but first, we have to change location. The room we are occupying is a warehouse and if we are ever traced to the house then we are doomed."

"So what do you suggest we do?"

"Some new flats are being built along Bauchi Ring Road, I guess it will be a good idea if we occupy one or two of those rooms before the place gets crowded."

"Seems you still have other unexposed skeletons in your closet."

"Maybe, but time will tell the rest."

Fourteen

Rooms 101 and 102 were considered sacred rooms at La Modillo Hotel. Room service did not apply to those rooms and the occupants were not known to the workers of the hotel. Accommodation fee of those rooms were paid directly to the owner of the hotel. Only electricians and plumbers were allowed into the rooms once in a blue moon to fix faults.

SBC members converged in room 101 again, KC and Giwa were the last to arrive at about 8:00pm. Da Don complained about their lateness for the meeting but they made no excuses nor offered apology. They all sat quietly watching some boring documentary until the TV was switched off by Nosky at 8:00pm on the dot.

"Smart Boys!"

"Struggling for the good life!" Giwa was not familiar with this greeting method but he joined in the second time since it was easy to follow.

"Smart Boys!"

"Struggling for the good life!" they all answered in unison.

"First of all, I must commend all of you for using your Smart Boys' ingenuity to escape from the claws of death during the crisis that occured a few days back. By now I guess you have seen the advantage of having a warehouse." He looked at KC and Nosky who nodded simultaneously. "In case one of you is still using his room as a warehouse then he should know that he is liable to suffer great loss in the event of any crisis." Da Don paused as if he anticipated any reaction, then he continued, "Secondly, I wish to inform you that we have received fresh supplies of our merchandise and we can get as much as we want with only half of its wholesale price on the condition that we pay back all outstanding amounts before we place an order for a fresh supply. Boys, I don't want you to forget that we are a well organized and focused group. As such, I will be greatly appalled if any of you is found guilty of excessive drug abuse, womanizing, or being open to people. In short, you all know the rules, don't just violate them. I assure you, you can't stand the dire consequences."

KC checked his wristwatch and Da Don understood the need to hasten up. It had been agreed that except on initiation days, no meeting would exceed thirty minutes. It was all part of playing smart.

"Thirdly, each one of us should acquire a GSM handset, we are just getting used to the era of mobile phones in this country, especially in this city that a mobile network was lauched a few months ago. The good news is that the prices seem to be going down. We all ought to make sacrifices to ease our communication." Da Don brought out a Nokia phone and waved it for all to see; "I acquired mine a day before the crisis broke out. Here's my number, 080..."

"Oh please! Da Don, can't we take down the number after the meeting?" KC cut in before Da Don could finish calling out the number.

"Fair enough..." Da Don coughed lightly. He pretended not to be embarrassed.

"Lastly, I think it's high time we located Daddy's Cocoa store, they said it is in high demand in the market and..."

"Da Don, I don't suppose this is part of what we were to talk about; we can't possibly involve too many hands in this project."

"Black Mamba folks will give us a hand."

"What if it's not true, what if it's a mere speculation? Da Don, please this is not the right time for such discussion. Maybe we should give it more time. Besides, you and I agreed that it was going to be our last major hit." KC had never been more grave in his speech.

"Okay. All right guys, we are done for today, see you next month or when you come for your supplies. He clapped his hands and squeezed his fingers, one into another, "Smart Boys!"

"Struggling for the good life!"

"Goodnight fellas. KC, can you wait behind?"

The Smart boys were eager to leave the room seeing how tense the meeting became at the end. There were so many things they had no idea about. Apart from KC and Da Don, none of the other boys knew what Daddy's Cocoa was, except Giwa, but he was still at sea concerning Daddy's Cocoa store. He didn't know what it was. He waited at the lobby for a minute and KC came out fuming.

"Let's go home."

"What about..."

"Let's get the hell out of here," KC barked.

Getting back to their new place along Bauchi Ring Road was a lot more difficult than it was when they resided at Angwan Rogo. Fewer vehicles plied the road and most of them were private vehicles. KC's silence made the trek seem longer. Giwa was mute.

KC woke up with a smile on his face. Giwa was up and was perusing an old magazine, he saw KC's smile but was unsure of reciprocating it.

"Sorry about last night, I shouldn't have transferred the aggression on you." KC sat on the bed as he spoke.

"It's okay, as long as I am not the cause. I guess it is one of those things I am yet to learn about."

"True. Giwa, I don't think we will have to wait for those three long years before we retire and go into something legit."

"Did you have a dream about retiring or what? Who did you see in your dream?"

"Oh, don't be ridiculous, far from it. But I saw my father in the dream, he asked me to come back home and fight the Biafra war alongside him."

Giwa let out a long and almost uncontrollable laugh. KC joined in for a brief moment and asked why Giwa thought his dream was very funny, "Who on earth still talks about a dead republic? Honestly, you just reminded me of a word I almost completely forgot about," Giwa said. "Abeg make I hear word joor!"

"I am surprised I have not told you about my father. Giwa, to my father, Captain Osita Chidibere, the Biafra revolution is still a stone throw away. He detests any human being that originates from Benue and the North. He calls them Hausa *ewu*! When I told him I was coming to school in Jos, he cursed and called me a 'never do well'. Each time I think of it, it gears me to be determined and work hard to earn some money so that I can prove him wrong. That man is a brave soldier but a stark illiterate; however, he is a genius when it comes to operating guns and artillery. He still has the recipe for the locally manufactured *ogbunigwe*. He is popularly known as OC and he still hides a small cache of ammunition that is known only to him. Who wants to know anyway! Right now he is just a village mechanic. I don't want to be brave and end up as a pauper in the village like my father. He basks in his glory of the past. He would always tell people of the moment he used his last round of the rocket launcher to fire on an oil tanker that led a convoy of Nigerian soldiers thereby destroying the oil tanker and five other trucks in the convoy, at least eighty-five people were said to have been killed in the blast. When the story got to Ojukwu's ears, Private OC was immediately catapulted to the rank of 'Captain', and most importantly for him was the handshake he got from Ojukwu. You may not believe it but his photograph with Ojukwu remains his priceless treasure."

"Wow, but he is inconspicuous in the pages of the civil war history, a brave soldier like him should have been celebrated."

"But you must know that history only favours its writers or those close to them."

"Even at that, he ought to be honoured somehow."

"Perhaps so, my friend. He was offered a position to serve in the Nigerian Army after the war but he declined, he thought Ojukwu would come back from exile to lead the Igbos into another battle of freedom but his hopes were dashed when Ojukwu returned in 1983 as a Nigerian. Capt. OC still believes that one day, Nigeria will plunge into another civil war, and that is mainly why he wants his children to remain in the East." KC pictured his father as he spoke.

"Now you want to retire because of what your father told you in the dream or what?"

"*Tufiakwa*!" KC rose from the bed. Capt. OC has lived his war life, I don't want to be dragged into all that stale story of the war. I want us to retire early because Don may soon play a fast one on us or even use us as his pawns to get to where he wants to get. I suspect he is acting on directives given to him by our major wholesale supplier, the one whom I suspect was behind Donald's death. I am sure he is out of stock now."

"What on earth are you talking about? I'm lost here." Giwa could not hide his confusion. He had meant to ask numerous questions since the previous night."

"Never mind."

* * * * *

Giwa had reached his second year as a non-academic student and his fourth year, supposedly his final year in the university. It was a year and few months after Uncle Harry had died. In the past year, Giwa and KC visited Abuja a dozen more times and had established markets in Bauchi, Kano and Kaduna cities, where they sold their merchandise in each city. He was able to visit Kyauta twice at Zonkwa and kept her in the care of his childhood friend, Samson. By the time Giwa was visiting for the second time, Samson was already a father and a full time commercial farmer. Occasionally, he rode his motorcyle for commercial benefits.

Giwa had become a Smart boy to the core, he went to different states alone and sold cocoa and henny. At some places, the people were unaware of his other products apart from the Mary-J. Gradually, he introduced them to the others except for Daddy's Cocoa which was exclusively reserved for General Hamza. In a few months, they would be out of stock for Daddy's Cocoa and Giwa had no idea were they could get more but he guessed KC was cooking up a 'plan B'. Things went pretty smoothly in the business. At a point, Giwa contemplated buying a car but KC warned him against it. They starved themselves of luxury to fatten their account. Other members of the SBC had bought cars, Don had changed his own twice. He owned a Honda CRV.

"We are sure to hit more than a hundred thousand to reach the ten million naira line by the time we get back," KC said as he searched for clothes and other accessories they would need for their two-day trip to Abuja. Giwa had set his own stuff in a shuttle bag while KC took his bath. He was sitting and watching KC get prepared for the journey.

"Ten million naira will just be half of the target amount, and we are set to sell just the last round of the diamond fleece. Where and how do you expect us to get another ten million and retire this year as you proposed?"

"Have I ever led you astray?"

"Nope!"

"Good! Getting the remaining ten million is my headache, so allow me to drink my panadol *ko*!" He stared at Giwa with a look that said *it's my business.*

Giwa had mixed feelings of perplexity, anger and discombobulation. "I thought we were partners," he fidgeted. "Apparently, you like to keep secrets from me; every day I learn something new from you, something you knew all along but you say them in bits."

"You know I can't possibly tell you everything in one day." KC drew the zip of his bag.

"And ten years wouldn't be enough time for you either, why can't you just fill me in here and now!" Giwa spoke with intensity. He wanted to swallow KC.

KC remained calm, he knew better than letting out a closely guarded secret even under duress. "And you know I can't tell you anything right now."

"Then I quit, I don't wanna be your partner anymore."

"Cool! Should I give you papers and a pen to sign?"

"How about a knife on your bare back?"

"Why don't you just calm down, very soon, I promise." It was as if KC had poured cold water on a rising flame. "Just stick to the plan bro!"

"Which *yeye* plan again now?"

"Follow my lead." KC strapped his bag to his back grudgingly. They boarded a cab and they arrived Abuja much earlier than they had expected to arrive.

At the General's house, Amina appeared calm and sober, she engaged herself in a gradual transformation. From the moment they started mixing her henny with powder gotten from the baobab fruit, Amina had continued to exhibit some signs of change. With KC's consent, Giwa would mix henny in lesser proportions for Amina's supply. Amina and her school son exchanged letters secretly after their first meeting until it became as frequent as every week. He monitored her changes and was much more satisfied when he saw her again. The General's house had become a normal sight to Giwa. They sipped wine while they waited for the General. KC's eyes were glued to the TV while Giwa and Amina chatted about everything.

"I hope he doesn't know that we have known each other for a long time?"

"If you don't tell him, he wouldn't know, not from me. How is school going?"

Giwa was caught unawares; he couldn't bear to tell her that he had dropped out of school more than a year ago. *School?* "Yeah! School is fine. I should be rounding up by next semester."

"That will be fine. *Insha Allahu,* you will stop this dirty business after school *ko*?" she demanded, drilling her eyes into his. "It is very risky, I guess circumstances have forced us into this mess that we are in but we have to get out of it."

"Sure! You are right, Mummy."

"Don't be ludicrous," she hit him gently on the chest. Instantly, she rose up and assumed a sober face. Giwa turned and saw that the General had entered. KC was up on his feet. They all greeted General Hamza separately but he responded only once for all of them. He shifted his gaze to KC.

"Ah! my good friend, you are welcome. Giwa, *Sannu da zuwa*, you are welcome my good friends." He spoke with a cheerful smile on his face. The smile changed into a frown when he faced his wife. "And what are you still doing here?"

She was shivering and biting her finger, "Nothing."

"Will you disappear from this place and appear in your room now?" Only a whiff of her perfume remained in the sitting room when he finished speaking. "Gentlemen, straight to business if you please." He ushered them towards his office.

"There is one more thing General," KC said while he tucked the wads carefully into his jacket.

General Hamza had just taken his first sniff. He sneezed and inhaled air copiously with his mouth and nostrils at the same time. A small patch of white powder stuck to his nose. He had a sudden need to be left alone, from the look on his face. "And what could that be?"

"We are out of stock for Daddy's Cocoa."

"Then place an order for it."

Giwa chipped in, "Exactly the problem sir, we can't place an order for it because it is no longer found in the market."

"And sourcing it may take months or even years," KC added.

General Hamza frowned. He slammed his fist on the table. "Nonsense, go and find my cocoa wherever it is. If you want me to add to your pay, I will, but just bring me my cocoa. I don't want to hear any more excuses."

"We just felt it is better we inform you in case you don't see us again," KC politely remarked.

"I have your phone numbers, I will call you if I don't see you, and if I do, you won't like it. Get out of my office!" General Hamza had lost his temper. He barked at everyone whenever he lost his temper.

KC and Giwa left the office and his house. KC gave the soldiers at the gate a wrap each of Mary-J and they hailed him like they had just been given bars of gold.

"We just have to look for it wherever we can find it. I guess we have now come to the end of the road."

"I thought you had a plan."

"Yes I do and we may have to execute it sooner than I thought."

It became a routine that the first day of their trip to Abuja, KC and Giwa would first transact business with General Hamza at his home office, then they would check into a hotel, have their bath, sleep, eat, drink and wait for the club to reach its peak at midnight. At the club, they would distribute their merchandize and dash back to their hotel. They followed every bit of the routine but they stayed longer at the club. It took a while before Latifah's turn came for the strippers' dance at the Knight's club and when she eventually did, she didn't excite the crowd as she usually did, holding them spellbound. She gave an average performance and disappeared like any other stripper. KC found her and brought her to Giwa, she looked pale and worried. Jemima held a bottle of dry gin in her right hand and smoked cigarette with the left.

"Here he is," KC released her arm from his grip. He spoke to Giwa amidst the loud blare of music in the hall. "She wants to know if you have more henny." KC left instantly.

"Is it true Latifah?" he spoke into her ears. He gasped, a terrible odour emanated from her armpit, and mouth along with a disproportionately combined smell of gin and tobacco. Impetuously, he maintained some distance away from her. It was a grotesque figure of Jemima he was staring at. Her weavon hung loosely to her natural hair and it was guaranteed to fall off at any moment; her hair needed to be combed and treated. Giwa dragged her outside the club to a corner where they could feel a soft fresh breeze of the night. He kept her at a safe distance so that his nose would not be too offended. She leaned on the wall.

"Jemima, what is the meaning of this?" He ran his hands up and down like he was measuring her from a distance.

"The name is Latifah boo...L-A-T-I-F-A-H." She puffed the cigarette until it reached the filter, she threw it on the ground and blew the smoke at Giwa's face. "I said Latifah, that is my name." she staggered a bit then she regained her posture.

"Okay Latima... Hmm Lati...whatever. What has happened to you? Gosh! You look terrible, you really need help."

Jemima said so many things that Giwa could not comprehend. She kept mentioning the "damned doctor" even when Giwa had seized her bottle of gin and poured a bottle of cold water on her head. KC found them and tried to persuade Giwa to leave her but Giwa wouldn't leave her there by herself.

"Will you please give me a hand or will you just stand there looking at me?" Giwa shouted at KC when he insisted that they left immediately. KC gave up and joined his friend to lift the drunken Jemima to the taxi they hired.

"Oga una go add money for dis extra luggage wey una carry o!" The driver said as they took the backseat.

"How much? Abeg just drive reach the hotel first na?" KC replied.

"Me I don tell una my own o!" the driver murmured, cursed, and spat intermittedly as he chauffeured them back to their hotel.

KC checked her into a different room and asked Giwa to stay with her till she was sober. Jemima belched more and more until she started vomitting in the toilet. Giwa brought her out and cleaned the toilet, he made a sugar solution and gave her to drink. She drank and dozed off on the carpet, then he lifted her up and placed her on the bed.

The night stretched longer before Giwa fell asleep in the coolness of the air conditioner and the loud snore of Jemima.

"Room service," said a voice at the door after a loud knock, "Room service," the knock persisted. Giwa woke up to find Jemima's right hand on his chest and her right leg across his legs. She was breathing heavily and her breath stank.

He carefully got out of the bed and answered "yes" as he reached the door. He unlocked it and ordered for toileteries before a breakfast of coffee.

"What happened last night?" Jemima posed with a sleepy voice and eyes half-open.

"You were drunk and you were acting strange so I brought you here." Giwa replied sternly as he sat on the bed.

"Yes, and we ..." she sat up on the bed and began to caress Giwa. "And we..."

He pulled himself away from her and stood up. "If that is what you are thinking, then you will be disappointed to know that we didn't do any thing. We couldn't have done anything while you vomited everywhere like a pregnant woman."

Jemima bent her head; she saw some vomit stains on her satin spaghetti top. The stains were ignored, her hands went into her bag, brought out a stick of cigarette and lighted it. She puffed it and inhaled deeply. "So what do you want me to do now? Thank you for saving me? Get out!"

"I don't need you to thank me, I just need you to be more responsible, that's all."

"Is that so? Tell me more about it? Tell me more about responsibility, does it involve selling drugs to people like me?"

"Listen, I am doing what I have to do in order to survive."

"That doesn't make me any different," she shouted back at him and reached for the ashtray beside the bed.

The hotel maid came back with the toiletries and a towel. Giwa received them and handed them over to Jemima, "Here! You might want to use these." She snatched them and shuffled to the bathroom. Jemima came out after three quarters of an hour; looking beautiful, clean and nicely scented. She tied the towel above her breast but it showed a generous part of her laps. She became sober and humble. Giwa felt a frisson growing in him. He stood up to grab her but she moved backwards.

"Don't! Please don't do it Giwa," she shivered.

"Why? Am I not better than your customers?"

"That is the point. You don't deserve to be infected." Tears rolled down her face.

Giwa pretended as though he didn't hear her well even though the desire in him had died instantly. "Infected? With what?"

"Stop acting like you have never heard about HIV!" She sat down and let a stream of tears flow down her face. Giwa's blood ran cold, he sat on the chair in disbelief.

"What?"

"It is just a week now since the damned doctor told me that I have been infected and that I should start coming for anti-retroviral drugs, ARVs - immediately. I hate it that I have become a walking corpse. I don't have a future anymore," she sobbed.

"Hey now! That is not the end of this life, perhaps you need to do what the doctor says you should do in order to live longer."

"But I will still die anyway!"

"Yes! But tell me who will not die, infected or not."

"I blame it all on those nights I used the damned henny and passed out without knowing how I was used, and whether with condoms or not. God! I feel so stupid."

"Hey, don't cry, let me just take a bath. I will be right back then we'll have coffee together and you can tell me more about what happened before you were diagnosed with HIV." She nodded and he went into the bathroom.

Giwa came out and found no trace of Jemima; the coffee had become cold and was still on the table, untouched. Her clothes and her bag had disappeared. He was shocked but had an idea of what happened when he saw his wallet on the bed with the contents displayed except for some money which was not up to ten thousand naira. *The bitch made away with my money and she wonders how she got the virus?* He sighed and smiled to himself.

"Well, I am not surprised that she ran away with your money, I figured she could be that naughty, precisely why I checked her into another room. That could have been our big money o!"

"You are right."

"I need not ask whether she left with the two packs of henny you said you hadn't sold last night."

"I hope she makes good use of the money, that girl is stupid." Giwa fumed.

"I say we go to the bank and deposit the larger part of the cash before some *ashawo* comes our way again, what do you say?"

"Aye, aye, Sir!"

Benson Jimoh called from Jos to confirm that the money had reached KC's account. KC's money in the bank stood at ten million and one hundred thousand naira. He hung up the phone immediately and turned to Giwa.

"We made it, we are a hundred thousand above ten million naira." They hugged each other. The boys entered a bar and bought every one and extra bottle of what they were drinking. They were amused by every word. The day gave in to the night and they were now sitting at the bar of their hotel, sipping malt and water having drank enough beer for the day. KC's left hand was lighted at the other end. He became unusually quiet.

"Ever heard of Dr. Idoko in the University of Jos?"

"Sure! Faculty of Pharmaceutical Sciences; a very strict man with the fear of God in him. Why asking?"

"Hahaha, how are you sure that he is godfearing? *Abegi*!"

"Well, at least, that is what everybody says."

"A God-fearing person can only be determined by God himself."

"So what is it about Dr. Idoko?"

"That man could be the very key to our store of Daddy's Cocoa." KC puffed his cigarette and blew rings of smoke above his head.

"Wait a minute," Giwa looked around, "are you not talking about the man that says prayers for his class before and after every lecture?"

"That's correct; the one who is the secretary of the chapel on campus. Are you still doubting me?"

"From what I know about that man, I cannot possibly believe you." Giwa gulped his water hurriedly.

"Dr. Idoko was the first student to graduate with First Class honours in Pharmacy from the University of Jos. He was sent to study for his Masters' degree and Ph.D in India and U.S.A respectively. He came back to Nigeria and took his position as a lecturer in the University of Jos. He also became a consultant for the NDLEA and he was sent to join some pharmacists to work on a drug using coca leaves in Bolivia, along the line he got greedy and worked for a drug cartel in Bolivia. The Bolivian authorities discovered; and they sent him back to Nigeria. Here again, he was seduced to work for a druglord who was part of a bigger cartel in the global market. Dr. Idoko produced an unprecedented drug in the world of narcotics. He called it the 'Super Coca', otherwise known to us as Daddy's Cocoa." KC maintained his calmness.

"That is unbelieveable; you mean Dr. Idoko is behind the invention of Daddy's Cocoa?"

"Absolutely, and Super Coca gives you five times the feeling of regular coca. The product was used to trace the druglord back to this country and he was assassinated, his workers were arrested and jailed while most of the drug was destroyed by fire. Dr. Idoko was also arrested but his lawyer did a very good job, keeping him out of jail in exchange for the formulae, millions in the bank and an oath that compelled him never to disclose the formule to anyone, or be caught in any drug peddling scheme. He accepted the terms and became a born again Christian lecturer at the University. He was closely monitored for the first five years, the NDLEA authorities took their eyes off him seeing that he could no longer be connected to any illicit drug peddler."

"Interesting!" Giwa remarked. "What evidence do you have to prove that he has not destroyed all the Super Coca in his possession?"

"Good question, Dr. Idoko's gateman was bribed by Donald to search the house for a substance Donald described to him. Donald got three million naira from Chief Femi Otunba, his *oga* in Lagos, to secure a bag of 50kg worth of Daddy's Cocoa. That was five years ago."

"That quantity must be worth ten million naira now," Giwa remarked.

"Even more than that. Donald took 10kg for himself and gave the rest to Chief Femi, Donald never received supplies of Daddy's Cocoa from Chief Femi until his demise. I deliberately sold the last 5kg in bits to the General alone seeing that it is very scarce and if I sold to other people, it could be traced to me."

"And now you have sold your last bit yesterday."

"That informs the search for the remaining two hundred kilogrammes of Daddy's Cocoa, and that alone will make us millionaires."

"Why don't you just search the house?"

"It's not there!" KC had finished smoking and looked drunk.

"How do you know?"

"Because Donald informed me alone that the bags are not there. When Dr. Idoko found out that one of the five bags of 50kg each was missing, he inquired from the security man, and of cours,e he denied knowledge of it; he was fired anyway. The security man was only happy to have his job terminated instead of being imprisoned. Donald said that he knew Dr. Idoko would not be dumb enough to leave those bags in their hiding place after one of them was discovered missing. He probably moved them to a safer location which is likely known to him alone."

"Maybe Da Don was referring to the same store when he mentioned Daddy's Cocoa store the other time."

"Definitely, he also knows about the remaining 200kg, Donald confided in both of us. It was meant to be a secret and Da Don said it out in front of everyone. Fortunately, it didn't make much sense to the rest of the crew. If everyone knows what is involved, lives will be lost here."

"What if Da Don plays a fast one on you?"

"He can only succeed by killing me first, he can't succeed without involving me. I advised him against invading the man's house but to find a more diplomatic way; he bought the idea and got acquainted with Dr. Idoko's first son, Tobi. For many months now, Tobi has been engaged in a fruitless search for a possible location of the hidden golden fleece."

"I don't understand, why are you telling me all this now?"

"Because I have a plan and I know Da Don is up to something fishy, I can't tell but my instincts are so loud about it. I want us to move in fast, ahead of him. I wanna take one last shot and back out, maybe start a new life somewhere."

They talked until midnight; KC slept and left Giwa in his thoughts, staring into space. He could hardly believe he was coming close to retirement and facing the good life, becoming a millionaire in his twenties.

* * * * *

The duo boarded the first taxi leaving Abuja for Jos in the morning. KC was unusually perplexed. He spoke little, laughed little and thought more on their way. His talk mainly centred on his family and his community in Imerienwe village of Ngor-Okpala Local Government of Imo state. The bond between the two friends became stronger each time KC revealed more of himself to Giwa.

"I have used your name as my next of kin at the bank; Benson is aware of it. If anything happens, make sure some money gets to my family," KC said after some minutes of silence.

"Please don't talk like that. Are you scared of the money coming your way?"

"Don't be silly."

"Then you better cheer up and think of a flawless plan that will take us to the top of the world."

* * * * *

KC dropped his bag and freshened up, Giwa took his bath too, and was getting ready to catch some more sleep.

"Get up, you have to accompany me to La Modillo. I want to see Da Don. My mind tells me he is up to something."

"Can't it wait till evening?"

"No it can't," KC barked.

Giwa found a convenient space outside room 101. He heard KC exchanging words with Da Don, a loud bang was heard and Giwa saw KC walking furiously out of room 101. Chiefo opened his door and watched KC walk out of the corridor. He dashed into Don's room then he came out immediately. His eyes locked with Giwa's eyes, just when KC reached him and they descended the stairs.

"Would you please stop and explain everything to me? Talking to yourself will yield nothing."

KC slowed down, Giwa's words pulled him back to his senses. He turned to face his friend.

"You know, two heads are better than one; a problem shared is a problem solved," KC said philosophically.

"Two good heads; problem shared is half solved, get it right!" Giwa corrected.

"Ok," KC shrugged defeatedly. "Da Don wants to do something stupid and I disagreed with him, but if he insists on it then he will do as he pleases whether I like it or not."

"Maybe you should explain what the stupid something is, then we will know whether it is actually stupid, and the degree of the stupidity," Giwa responded like some consultant waiting to hear his client.

"Da Don wants us to kidnap his acquaintance, Dr. Idoko's son, and then ask for the presumedly hidden drugs as ransom for the life of his son. Now, isn't that stupid?"

"Very stupid, he is crazy... I mean, that is the dumbest thought the dullest Smart boy could ever conceive."

KC fumed and panted and collected himself. An innocuous smile played on his lips. "And suprisingly, yet annoyingly, the dumbest boy turns out to be the head of the Smart boys, life has certainly improved upon her ironies."

"What if he tries that? No, he can't. When does he intend to carry out this plan?"

"I bet he will want to execute his plan next week which leaves us with very little time to stop him. He swore to eliminate me if I dare stand in the way of his plan and the nincompoop says he wants to make use of the Black Mamba boys for that operation. The whole plan is a failure even before they start executing it. My pain is that if we allow them to do it, they will ultimately ruin our chances of ever laying our hands on the diamond fleece, or ever becoming millionaires at all. I guess it's time we turned some friends into enemies; follow me to the warehouse, there is something I want you to see."

KC opened the box and carefully removed its contents until it was almost empty, he lifted a red piece of cloth and underneath it was a small envelope without a label on it. He brought out a red powdery substance that looked like pepper. It was in a transparent polythene bag.

"This should be the last secret I will ever hide from you Giwa."

"Are you talking about this pepper?"
"This is not pepper."
"Okay, correct me if I am wrong."
"It is nicknamed, 'hell sender'. It's a lethal type of pepper developed from inorganic substances and coated with elements of real pepper, don't even sniff it. You can guess where I got it from."
"Shimmon Jacob?"
"Absolutely." KC beamed and a wide grin to reveal all his teeth.
"Hell sender is usually applied as spice in one's victim's food, and after a maximum of forty-eight hours, the victim will be in hell." He gave this to me too, he said I may find use for it someday, I suppose the time has come."
Giwa shook his head. "KC, don't do what I am thinking."
"But if he pushes me to the wall I will end up with no choice." His eyes were ablaze. "In any case," KC locked back the contents including the lethal pepper, "if you want to use it, you know where to find it. I am terribly hungry."
"Did you just read my mind?"
At lunch, Da Don called KC on phone. He apologized that he overreacted. KC reserved no doubts about the apology. The conversation ended. Da Don hung up and called back after some minutes, KC was asked to deliver cocoa at Ibrahim Taiwo Close; he was further instructed to wait in front of No. 36. He said a red car would meet him and transact the deal with him.
"One more thing! This client prefers to deal with one person at a time so it means you have to go alone. KC, you are the smartest dude I could trust on this job. No fall my hand abeg."
"I'll do my best, you will hear from me when I am done." He hung up and hissed. He swallowed a mouthful gulp of water, paid the bill and lighted a cigarette. "It's Da Don, he wants me to deliver some merchandize by 5:30pm, says he has just gone out of town."
"Then what? You give him his kickback as usual?"
"That has always been the tradition."
"KC, don't you think Da Don is about to set you up, the fight, the spontaneous apology, abrupt mission, think about it!"
"Hahaha, na today? E don tey na! I'm not doing this for the first time and this should be my umpteenth quarrel with Don. But if you insist on being cautious, then I will allow you to follow me at a safe distance just in case it gets messy."
"What about impeding Da Don's plan for next week?"

"We'll figure that out by the time I get back."

No. 36, Ibrahim Taiwo Close was just as quiet as the other houses on that street. The whole street was calm as usual. Birds made more noise than human beings and vehicles combined, Giwa guessed it was a neighbourhood of big shots in Jos judging from the rooftops and the fences which were unusually higher than normal fences. Occasionally, a gate of one of the houses would be opened by a tattered or average looking gateman and a sleek car would find its way in, or out of a mansion. On Ibrahim Taiwo Close, every car was posh, every home was opulent, the children looked beautiful and healthy, even their dogs too. The air was fresher and the young girls defined 'aje butter'. Still, it was on the same close that some of the biggest deals of the SBC were carried out.

KC stood in front of No. 36, an old green building; he had been standing since 5:30pm and listening to music through his headphone to ease his nervousness and allow the time to pass away, he swore to leave the location at 6:00pm if no one appeared.

Giwa was about fifty metres adjacent him. His job was to ensure that everything was smooth and that it was not a set up. *Perhaps I should have just stayed back and caught some sleep*, Giwa thought.

A red Honda with tinted glasses pulled up opposite KC, the glass was rolled down automatically. A big headed guy in dark specs observed KC for split seconds, the dreadlocks on the guy's head made him look more like a modern juju priest. There were other people in the car but the guy wound up too fast. Tuface's voice was the only other thing that was heard as it wafted from the car as if he was playing live in the car. Observing from the shade of his cap, Giwa picked many details that KC ignored. The same car reappeared after some minutes; it came and passed by Giwa. He noticed the brake light when the car pulled over a few metres away from KC.

Another guy popped out his head from the passenger's side and signalled KC to come. KC dipped his hands into his pocket and seemed to bring out the merchandize after a flash salutation. In lightning speed, the glass of the back door was wound down and KC displayed a great surprise on his face. Giwa only saw a silver wristwatch on the hand that came out of the back seat with a pistol in its grip. It fired four shots in quick succession into KC's chest and stomach. The shots came faster than Giwa could shout "KC!" and were loud enough to bury his voice. The car roared and zoomed off with a loud screech in an instant. Giwa was stunned for a moment. It seemed like he was watching a scene in an action film. KC was in a pool of his own blood. His eyes were open and when he tried to speak, blood oozed out of his mouth. Beads of sweat had formed on his forehead as his body vibrated, for the last time. He looked at Giwa and smiled.

"KC, please talk to me! Please talk to me KC! Don't leave me alone, I'm dead, I am finished." Giwa was weeping when he heard the siren, he knew that someone had called the police, everyone around the scene had fled for fear of being arrested as suspects.

He ran to the main road where he boarded an *okada* and finally made up his mind on where he was going when he reached Terminus. The onus was on him to make smart and expedient decisions. He needed somewhere to think, somewhere to mourn, some place to strategize his revenge.

Fifteen

When school fully resumed after the crisis, it was ascertained that Solomon and John had lost three of their classmates in the crisis and the death toll of both students and staff of the university was estimated at seventy-six, many others were injured. The peace process had begun and many non-governmental organizations were at the forefront of mending the broken wall of peace using funds acquired from government and diplomatic communities. Many of the organizations held community parleys and some even staged rallies in an effort to quell the tangible tension existing mostly in the slums and suburbs of the city.

"Prof. Ganiyu Pwajok said until the core issues that caused the crisis are addressed, there is a high probability that the gory scenario will replay itself again."

"Are you saying what Prof. said is true, or is it true because Prof. said so?" John queried.

"Both; I am saying it is true and because Prof. Ganiyu Pwajok said so, weren't you at the lecture the other day? He said issues relating to religion were left as sacred, implicated clerics and politicians who were indicted in the white paper report were left untouched. The white paper report was not even implemented." Solomon panted as he spoke passionately about Prof. Ganiyu's views as though he was the Prof. himself. "You see, Prof is an intelligent man, the most senior lecturer in our department and a man of high moral standard."

"In other words, Prof is always right?" John asked sarcastically.

"Yes! Prof. Ganiyu is always right!" Solomon stamped his right foot like an aggressive counsel to an innocent man. Solomon's chest heaved with emotion.

"Everything is becoming normal again, people walk about freely as if the crisis happened in the civil war era." John spoke as they came toward a shade cast by a huge mango tree. He tried to digress from their discussion seeing that Solomon stiffly held to his belief.

Solomon did not respond and the boys settled down on a wooden bench under the mango tree. The woman who sold kunu and chin-chin was warming up each day as the days rolled further away from the day her sick husband was burnt in their house. He couldn't move from his sick bed but ordered the children to run out of the house. They were reunited with their mother four days after that fateful Friday her husband was turned into ashes. She had since relocated to a one-room apartment around Tina junction. Mamman Boyo was rapidly adjusting to the life of a widow. Since resumption after the crisis, Mamman Boyo's place had become a hub for dispensing crisis tales and rumours. It was at that place that Solomon heard of a pregnant Igala woman who was killed in Angwan Rogo, her stomach was ripped apart and the foetus was killed too. In the same place, he learnt about three boys in Angwan Rukuba who killed, roasted and ate a Muslim man, Maman Boyo doggedly swore that boys ate human flesh in order to fortify their charms. He was also told of an Alhaji who offered bags of cash for his life but the boys refused and burnt him in his cash, and an ex-soldier who shot a bullet that went through three boys, Solomon laughed about the story because he felt it was unbelievable. Each day, her customers came with new stories and theories about the crisis; some came with different versions of older stories. As the days went by, people talked about different issues away from the crisis. The release of the exam timetable also helped.

"Mamman Boyo!" Solomon and John greeted almost at the same time.

Mamman Boyo had her back facing them but turned around when she heard their voices, "Ehen! Una welcome o! How school na? How lectures? I hear say una go soon start exams abi?" Solomon left John to do all the "fine" and "yes" responses. John made an order for a bottle of kunu and two chin-chins for each of them. She quickly served them and returned to the young female student who appeared to be consumed with pity. Solomon assumed Maman Boyo was narrating her unforgettable ordeal of the crisis to a customer for the millionth time.

While John was partially eavesdropping, Solomon's mind flew away from the school; it dwelled on his strained relationship with Papa Adaku, his new house in GRA with a monstrous landlord, and then on Adaku. His heart was growing fonder for her. They exchanged letters secretly and through one of the letters, Adaku informed him that she had finished writing her WAEC and NECO O'level exams. In another letter, she told him of her mother's approval of him as her boyfriend but that her mother would not wish to disobey her husband. Her performance in school impressed Solomon, and he thought of how she was growing into a beautiful lady with her curves well spelt out. He sucked the kunu from its bottle with a straw until he reached the bottom of the bottle, the slurp caught John and Mamman Boyo's attention.

"What is it? Is it Adaku or her father?" John asked mischievously, knowing what Solomon would mostly likely be thinking about.

"It is you!" Solomon ran his eyes sardonically at John.

"Me! Why?"

"Because you don't stick to your own business, that's why!"

"And is it a crime for me to help my friend? At least I have a duty to prevent him from deep thoughts that could lead him to scavenging rubbish heaps like that man there." John pointed at a mad man dressed in rags and scraping the crest of a heap of refuse.

Solomon alternated his gaze thrice between John and the mad man. He smiled, "Na your papa go mad like that man there." He spread the five fingers of his right hand on John's face. They burst into laughter.

"How much be your money sef Mamman Boyo?" Solomon asked as he dipped his hands into his pockets.

"You know wetin una chop na," she gave them a smile.

Solomon paid for their lunch and they made for their class.

"But John, you know, on a serious note, I can't stop myself from thinking about Adaku. The feeling is so strong, could this be love?"

"You will have to pay your consultation fee first before I answer your question."

"And what are you? Mr. Sigmund Freud, or Pavlov?" Solomon hissed and increased his pace.

"Okay, okay, to tell you the truth, you are in love and considering the beauty of your Adaku, personally, I would not blame you because if I were in your position, I would change my name to Romeo."

* * * * *

Solomon and John Ambi held on to each other even to their

third year in school, they shared the same room in Abacha hostel, their distant but faithful involvement in campus politics earned them an allocation of a special room on the third storey of the hostel with just the two of them as roommates. Both of them were at the top of their class. The two were contiguous; if they were not in Pankshin during short breaks, they would be in Jalingo. If there would be any reason they would be away from each other for hours, it would be because of Ada. Whenever they found themselves in Pankshin, they would meet with Ada at their secret rendezvous in the Wulmi rocks. At such moments, John would excuse them. Doubling as their chaperon and watchman, John would climb a rock and pretend as if he was looking out for trespassers, occasionally he would sneak a peek in case they got too close for comfort. On their last visit, he caught Adaku with the corner of his left eye as she planted a kiss on Solomon's cheek.

At Mr. Obi's house on Sundays, Solomon would be formal with the family. He addressed Mr. Obi as 'Sir' and his wife 'Ma', Baby Nnenna was simply referred to as 'Baby girl,' while Adaku and her other sisters were just called, 'Sister'. Mr. Obi hoped the use of iron hands was producing the desired result and nursed the thought of being more amicable towards Solomon someday when Adaku's heart was far away from Solomon's. He was wrong.

On a hot Saturday afternoon, it was John's turn to cook lunch while Solomon lay, reading on his bed. They heard a knock on the door. Their eyes met, without a word, they both thought, *who could that be?* Solomon motioned John to get the door and when John opened it he was frozen; John's mouth was agape, he couldn't utter a word for a few seconds, and then he called Solomon.

At the door, Solomon rubbed his face twice in order to be sure that he was not dreaming.

"Why don't you guys let me in first before you begin your inquiry?" Adaku said as she pushed her way between the boys and sat on the only available chair in the room. She heaved a sigh of relief after she sat down seeing that the purpose of her visit had been achieved. The boys were too surprised to welcome her, they closed the door. John kept calling her name, Solomon was dumb.

"Sweetheart, I know you have a truckload of questions about my visit but I will like to have a cup of water before you bring them on."

Solomon spread his arms. "Welcome, my angel," he said, with a bright smile on his face. Ada rose to her feet, attracted by a force greater than a magnet, and they were locked in a tight embrace, a typical ideal moment which Ada wished could last forever. John suddenly concentrated on the food he was cooking. They released themselves after a prolonged hug.

John brought her the cup of water she requested for. She spoke after a drink. She lost her grandmother, and her father and mother had gone to attend the burial in the village. She told him about the lie she concocted about going to see a friend, where she boarded a taxi, up to the point where she stood by their door.

"I'm sure you never knew that I would ever make use of your hostel address," she winked her left eye.

"Yes now! If I had known, I would not have given you my address but now you are here, I can't lie that I am not happy." He winked too.

John went out and returned with three bottles of drink in time as the food was done. He served his jollof rice with spinach. His food was hurriedly finished and claimed he was going to see someone — in case Solomon needed some privacy. "Ada, I hope I'll see you when I come back," he asked, although certain that he would not come back until she was gone.

"Well, I don't know." She looked at Giwa, "It all depends on how soon you come back." She was happy that John was going out, she wished he had gone an hour earlier.

Lunch was over, and there was more talk. They listened to updates about each other. Solomon stretched himself on the bed, before he knew it, Ada was lying down beside him. He closed his eyes, his heart was beating more than a hundred times in a minute, he perceived her body spray, it was nice. Solomon was scared; he closed his eyes more tightly. He felt his lips twitching, and then yielded to passion. Her tongue slid though his mouth, and his in hers, then their lips touched. Solomon opened his eyes and beheld Ada with her eyes shut and kissing him. Ada moaned pleasurably and was going beyond her bounds when Solomon moved her away. She frowned.

"Ada, what do you thinking you are doing?" he demanded angrily.

"Showing my love of course!"

"With a kiss?" He pretended not to be part of it.

"What could be better than expressing my love for you with a kiss?"

"That is a lie; you weren't hoping for just a kiss, you wanted more than that."

"And what is wrong with my boyfriend making love to me?" she yelled rebelliously.

Solomon looked at her scornfully, weighing her action and the consequences oblivious to her. "Ada, I see your friendship with your neighbour, Blessing, is beginning to have a negative influence on you."

"You always critize Blessing, you probably hate her or you don't love me. You always reject any idea that comes from Blessing. And for goodness sake, what has Blessing got to do with us? How is she part of this conversation?" Ada mumbled some words and went into tears.

It has to be Blessing, who else could teach Ada the techniques of arousing a man? Solomon was enraged, but looking at his fragile girl again, he was moved. He drew her head to his chest and she sobbed. "Sweetheart, I didn't mean to make you cry, please dry those tears. It's not like I hate your friend Blessing, but she has a bad reputation in that neighbourhood, and I fear she may influence you. I have tried to keep it away from you but it's time I let you know that she is loose. You need to hear what the boys in your neighbourhood call her..."

Ada dried her tears and lifted her face up from Solomon chest. "What do they call her?"

"Food For Boys, or FFB for short."

"Are you serious?" she raised her eyebrows quizzically.

"John can confirm it to you if you wish. It appears you are the only one, aside from Blessing herself, that doesn't know she is called that name. Sweetheart, you see, having sex, or making love, as you wish to call it is not a proof of love. And it is just an instinct that ought to be satisfied at the appropriate time. Perhaps that is why human beings are different from animals and that is likely why marriage is sacred. Ada, if we have promised ourselves that this love will lead us to the altar, why can't we just wait?"

"I think you are right, but Blessing told me that if I don't make love to you, you will be having sex with other girls apart from me."

"Does that give you the license to give away your virginity so cheaply?"

"But Baby, I don't want to lose you now!"

"Oh yes you can, just give me what you are offering and I'll call it quit the moment you walk out this door," he said sternly as he pointed at the door.

"No…no! I'll keep my thing o! I will also wait." She giggled and smiled sheepishly.

"You have to go back home, Baby Nnenna should be crying by now."

"Hmm Nnenna is a big girl now o! She doesn't cry anyhow any longer. Solo, close your eyes…"

"I hope you don't want to mess up again this time."

"Please, trust me!" She blindfolded him with her handkerchief, then she brought out something from her handbag. She held out his hands and dropped a box in it. Solomon was very eager to see what he was holding.

She removed the blindfold from his face. "What is it?" he asked without looking at the object in his hands.

"Look at it honey, it is all yours."

"My goodness! This is unbelievable, a Nokia 3310 for me?" he shouted.

"Sshh..." she crossed her index finger vertically on her lips. "It is just a phone."

"How did you get it? This phone is expensive. Did you steal money from your father's shop?"

"Please hold it there Mr. Interrogator. First, you must promise to accept the phone if I tell you about its source?"

"Cross my heart!"

"This phone was given to me by your landlord."

Solomon nearly jumped out of his skin, "My what? Mr. Okafor?"

Adaku nodded as she stared into his bewildered face. "He has been offering me money whenever my dad isn't looking but I wouldn't collect it. Yesterday, he came and gave me this phone, then he tried to touch me but I refused to allow him have his way then I gave him back his phone. Mr. Okafor insisted that I should keep it. Sweetheart, you know I can't use it at home because if my parents find out about the source, they will kill me."

Solomon inspected the phone again, he was impressed with the features he saw. "You should be going now."

"I'm glad I was able to see you." She handed him another small pack, "here is the sim pack, and my mother has also acquired a phone with an MTN sim. I wrote her number at the back of the pack. Just text me only, and instantly, whenever I send you a text with her phone."

Solomon held her handbag as she combed her hair in front of the mirror. "Your phone… when do you hope to own one?"

"Papa Nnenna said he will buy me a phone when I gain admission into a university."

"And where did you apply to?"

"Unijos and Nsukka."

"Which would you prefer to attend?"

"Is that a rhetorical question? Unijos of course, I don't want to be far away from my love." She hugged him and they moved out. John appeared from a neighbour's room to tell her goodbye but Solomon dragged him to accompany her to get a taxi.

* * * * *

Giwa checked into the Bond hotel, at the outskirts of Bukuru town. A fictitious name was needed; it had to be used. He could not think lucidly as quick scenes of the gruesome murder kept replaying in his mind. *Those bastards!* He was smart enough to immediately remove the remainder of the merchandise, wallet and phone from KC's pockets before he left the lifeless body with an expired student ID card. His next stop was the warehouse which he emptied of its most valuable contents and stacked them into his duffel bag. In their room, he also fetched all necessary items. Giwa wept alone in the hotel room with no one to console him. He thought about his father, mother, Uncle Harry, and then his best friend and companion, KC. Giwa's phone was ringing, he checked his wristwatch and saw it was a quarter to midnight, Da Don was the one calling. Giwa picked the call.

"Hello, Da Don."

"G, what's up?"

"Am okay." Giwa tried to sound calm.

"Are you with KC? I will like to speak with him, I have been trying his number for some hours now."

Liar, murderer, Giwa wanted to say but he controlled the impulse. "Da Don, KC is dead." Giwa tried to swallow lump in his throat. He imagined Da Don screaming at the other end of the line.

"Are you sure about that? I was with him just this morning o! This can't be true." Giwa knew Da Don had merely called to: verify that KC was actually dead, find out if Giwa knew he was responsible for the murder, and find out his location and probably fashion out a means for his elimination too. Giwa confirmed the first but could not confirm the other two hypotheses so he played along.

"Da Don, I am scared, the killer could be coming after me too."

"Don't worry, just calm down, I promise you, I'll get to the root of this matter." Da Don assumed his assurance had an effect on Giwa. "Where is your location at the moment?"

Giwa had anticipated the question much earlier, "I am in a safe location but I am fine."

"Then try and come to my place at La Modillo, we need to find out this killer and plan our vengeance immediately, time to show the world that no killer of a Smart boy will get away with it."

Like you avenged the death of Donald. "I agree with you Da Don," he replied. "I'll see you tomorrow night, I can't walk freely on the highway, the police might be looking for me."

"That is true. I will see you tomorrow evening then. Take heart bro, SBC is a family, we have lost a pivot. It is well."

"Thank you Da Don, I don't know what I would do without you," Giwa made use of his latent dramatic skills.

* * * * *

"We should have smoked the two of them at a go." Chiefo remarked when Da Don hung up the phone.

"Naah...slow and steady wins the race," Da Don rubbed his palms. "With one target at a time, you won't miss a single shot."

"The earlier the better Da Don."

Da Don calmly replied, "Gaining G's trust is more important, he will be walking into this room by tomorrow night, after that he will be all yours. You may do as you please but don't leave a single trace." Da Don lighted a stick of cigarette.

"Trust me, I always flush my shit and leave the toilet clean, no dirt, no stain, no trace." He took a mouthful gulp of a palm-sized bottle of Alomo Bitters.

* * * * *

The night stretched longer than a year to Giwa, he turned around frequently on the bed. The thought of using some of their merchandize came, but he did not want to arouse any suspicion.

Besides, he needed a sound mind to plan his revenge. He thought about Benson Jimoh and the 10.1 million naira snoring in KC's account, he smiled at the prospect of Capt. OC becoming an overnight millionaire; contemplated whether news of the money would cheer him or scare him. Giwa was thankful that the crew had no intimate relationship with girls, otherwise the whole crew would have been compromised.

Giwa phoned Benson Jimoh at dawn, Benson answered with a sleepy voice but it came through, clearer, when he was informed that KC had been shot to death the previous evening.

"If you are sure of what you are telling me, then, I'll call you later in the morning, say around ten... Maybe... At the bank?" Benson stammered as he spoke.

"Of course, but I am not sure meeting you at the bank will be a good idea."

"Oh yes, you may be identified or be called as a suspect since you were a witness. Why don't we meet at Crest Lounge in Rayfield at that same time?"

"That will be fine." Giwa hung up. Benson Jimoh was a smart banker and was thinking ahead already.

In a baggy jeans trouser, under a heavy jacket with a face cap and thick dark glasses, Giwa felt naked on the street; he felt like there was a bold writing behind his jacket that said, 'here's the runaway witness.' Occasionally, he would turn and look around but everyone seemed to be minding their own business. The weight of the world which he carried on his shoulders seemed to be entirely his business. He reached a newspaper stand by the Central Post Office along Ahmadu Bello way. He scanned the many captions from different dailies but none contained the news of KC's death: 'THREE POLICEMEN KILLED IN MAKURDI', 'ANOTHER GOVERNOR'S WIFE CAUGHT LAUNDERING MONEY IN LONDON', 'UNKNOWN GUNMEN ATTACK VILLAGE IN BARKIN LADI LGA OF PLATEAU STATE'; Giwa kept hissing as he read the captions of the papers. None of them caught his interest. He finally found what he was looking for in the *Daily Star* newspaper. It appeared as a rider at the top right corner of the newspaper. It had KC's picture with a line of blood rolling across his cheek.

"CULTISM: VARSITY STUDENT KILLED BY RIVAL GANG MEMBERS"

Giwa was shocked when he read the completely distorted story.

He figured that the reporter added his own spice to the story. The police however gave a report that theorized KC as a cultist who was possibly killed by his rival gang members, a security man at one of the houses near the incident said he saw a friend of the deceased robbing him of valuables before the police came. The report stated that the friend must have set him up. In a maze of inept hypothesis and vague analysis of the crime, they cooked a story in order to close the file of the homicide. Tears gathered in Giwas eyes as he read the story over and over again. He bought the paper, folded it and tucked it into the pocket of his jacket. His phone rang, General Hamza was calling for the first time.

"Good morning, General."

"I have a paper in my hand now with the picture of your friend," his voice was deep and husky.

"Oh yes, so you have seen it already?"

"I just bought it." Giwa knew the General was not a man one could mince words with.

"Did you have a hand in his death?"

"No sir."

"Good. If you ever get caught, call me. If you know who the killer is, call me, and if you have a dose of my cocoa, call me. I'm sorry about the death of your partner."

"Thank you sir." The line went dead from the other end.

Giwa checked his watch, it was twenty minutes to ten. He boarded an *okada* and headed for his appointment with Benson.

At five minutes to ten, Giwa found his banker friend already seated at a corner with a half-empty bottle of stout on his table. He came closer, Benson stood up and gave him a warm hug. "I am deeply sorry about your friend," he said softly in a mild whisper.

"It's okay, thank you." Giwa replied still hugging Benson and looking at the copy of the *Daily Star* newspaper sitting right next to the bottle of stout on Benson's table. They freed themselves and settled down. A waiter appeared to take Giwa's order. Giwa pointed at the bottle and raised a finger. The waiter understood and went away.

"So, straight to business." Benson adjusted himself on his seat. He folded the newspaper and kept it aside, on another empty chair, away from Giwa.

Business? Giwa screamed in his mind but managed to say "Okay!"

"I am sure you are aware that KC had named you his next of

kin." He looked into Giwa's eyes. Giwa agreed without uttering a word. "This means that, aside all those legal and bureaucratic jargons, you are now a millionaire, being the sole inheritor of KC's fat account."

"Well, uh, technically, yes! But KC used my name because he trusted me to deliver a large amount to his family in the event that something happened to him."

"Family? Who is talking about family here? I invited you here to strike a deal between the two of us." Benson paused and allowed the waiter to open the cold bottle in front of Giwa.

"But..."

"No buts! KC is dead, nobody cares if he has a family, I suggest we strike this deal, clean our mouths and go our separate ways, unless, of course, you wish to retain me as your banker."

"Go ahead, tell me what the deal is."

"It's fifty-fifty, but I'll leave you with the hundred grand on top of the rounded figure."

"What?" Giwa realized he had shouted when a few other customers turned towards their table. He lowered his voice into a whisper. "Are you this mean? I am expected to give his family members something substantial, what do you want me to end up with? I am not down with your proposition at all."

"Look Giwa, I have to settle my head and some people at the legal unit too, I just may end up with something little." Benson shrugged as if he had just conjured a harmless plan. "Listen, the dead is gone, life is for the living. Just take it or leave it."

"What if I don't?" Giwa asked sternly. He emptied his first glass and poured himself another.

"You don't have a choice my friend," Benson opened page 39 of the *Daily Star* newspaper and pushed it towards Giwa.

I have read it a dozen times already, Giwa wanted to say, he saw a portion of the story underlined in black pen by Benson.

... Daily Star gathered from an eyewitness that a friend of the deceased, who was spotted with the boy before the murder, appeared immediately after he was shot and robbed him of valuables in his pocket before the police arrived. According to the area inspector in charge of 'B' division of the police command, the unidentified friend is at large and is wanted by the police...

"You sick sleazy bastard!" Giwa cursed Benson to his face.

"Call me whatever but I am sure the police will be thrilled to have me drag you into their net. I am quite reluctant to do so because there is no bounty over your head." Benson smiled mischievously. "It's checkmate man, just take your share and leave!"

"Blackmail huh! Are you trying to blackmail me?"

"No... Just call it 'backup espionage,' and take my advice, leave that shoddy business you are into and try something legal." He rubbed his palms against each other.

"And what makes you think I would want to receive lectures on legal business from a fraudster posing as a banker?"

"It's a quarter to eleven." Benson glanced his wristwatch, "I should be at work by eleven o'clock."

Giwa was mute, he prayed silently in his heart for the first time in years. He asked for divine guidance. He then included Benson in his mental checklist of enemies, Da Don was still occupying the top spot. "When do I get my 5.1 million?" he reiterated the exact amount incase Benson's 'fifty' meant something else.

"Here and now." Benson produced a transaction slip of Giwa's personal account in Platinum bank which hitherto had just ten thousand naira. "Five million, one hundred and ten thousand, two hundred naira, and thirty kobo."

"You had this in mind a long time ago didn't you?" Giwa probed Benson looking at the slip in his hand.

"It was expedient!" Benson stood up and buttoned his black suit. He stretched his right hand to Giwa. "Till I see you again."

Giwa shook Benson's hand. "It's goodbye from me because I don't hope to see you again."

"Fine, you can use your bank book to..."

"I know, I will just need you to arrange 2.5 million in cash for me by tomorrow, after that, we will say goodbye for good."

"From your account?"

"Where else?" Giwa sipped from his last glass. "Your boss must be waiting for you right now."

"Tomorrow then."

* * * * *

Giwa did not call Da Don until he was at the premises of La Modillo Hotel. He stood quietly in front of room 101 and heard two voices which he recognized.

"Abeg, allow me to waste this guy tonight."

"E no go work my guy, if him die for dis place, wetin you go talk? We have to find out what he knows tonight then tomorrow he will be yours, as I promised."

"No dull me for dis 3 million o!"

"Relax my guy, please leave, he will be here at any moment."

Giwa heard footsteps coming towards the door so he quickly knocked on the door which flouted the coded knocking system of the SBC. Chiefo opened the door and a pusillanimous countenance hung on his face when he saw Giwa. "Good evening!" Giwa said, wishing he had the revolver which KC used to save their lives during the previous year's crisis strapped to his waist. He would have dug a hole into Chiefo's forehead. At that moment, his only weapons were a switchblade and a spoonful of lethal pepper.

"Bros, how you dey?"

"Tight!" Giwa shook his hand for the first time. Da Don waited inside with a warm hug.

"I'm sorry about KC's death," Da Don said after Giwa found a seat.

"I still find it hard to believe, I am so worried and scared."

"Relax, this is a safe house. Do you have any idea who may be behind KC's death? You know… any cheated customer or something of that sort?" Da Don quizzed hoping the crime would not be linked to him.

"I don't know, honestly… I don't have the slightest clue."

"Perhaps it was the customer who ordered for the merchandize yesterday. If he is the one, then, you, Chiefo and myself will track him down tomorrow at Zaria road, he has another house there."

"I will help you identify him when we get there," Giwa played along.

"I was just about to get us suya across the road, will you come with us?"

Perfect! "No, I'll be fine right here, it really feels like a safe house." Giwa switched on the TV as if it were his own.

"I see you are at home already." Da Don walked out.

He came back with Chiefo holding a small polythene bag filled with suya and wrapped in an old newspaper.

"Bros, Da Don told me about your friend. Take heart o!" Chiefo consoled him, saying something he obviously didn't mean. He stretched out his hand again, this time Giwa took note of the silver wristwatch he saw on the hand that held the gun that killed KC.

Chiefo quickly withdrew his hand from Giwa's, afraid his watch could signal something. Chiefo excused himself to get liquor to "push down the suya". Da Don had spread the meat on the table in the room and went to ease himself in the bathroom.

"You can start eating if you want." Da Don urged Giwa as he entered the bathroom.

Giwa seized his ideal moment and didn't waste a second in sprinking his 'hell sender' on the suya. He sat on his seat and fixed his gaze on the TV while inhaling the aroma of the suya and hoping it would have no effect on him too.

Chiefo came back with a bottle of dry gin and without his wristwatch. They landed at the same time on the suya. Seeing that Giwa would not eat, they devoured it hungrily and it pleased Giwa that they bought their one-way to hell, as he hoped.

They talked some more after eating, Giwa chipped in at intervals. Much later, Giwa was unable to sleep even when he heard Da Don snoring loudly. Before dawn, Don was gasping for air, then he became comatose, his breathing was stabilized but he was unconscious and perspired waveringly. Giwa had to double-check by pinching him repeatedly.

At 5:30 in the morning, Giwa left La Modilllo Hotel and the only thing witnesses could later tell the police was that they saw a fat guy leaving their lobby in the morning and he was the last person that was with both Da Don and Chiefo.

Giwa smiled as he read the official version of Chiefo and Da Don's death in the *Daily Star* newspaper a day after their death. He smiled and leaned back on his seat in the bus. For the first time in three days, he was able to catch some sleep. The bus was heading to Imo state.

Sixteen

Adaku arrived in the company of Father Gyang and Mr. Obi on her first day in the University of Jos as a student. The school was in full swing, she had never been to the admin block or visited any of the lecture halls, but knew where the boys' hostel was located; shehad visited Solomon two more times since her first visit. It was after her third visit that some neighbour reported to Mr. Obi that he saw someone like Adaku within the hostel area. Mr. Obi confronted her mildly; seeing he had no strong evidence, he didn't push any further. He had been advised by different people that at eighteen, Adaku was no longer a small girl and she ought to be treated differently.

The last time Mr. Obi accompanied a student to the university, it was Solomon, and since his cold battle for the heart of Ada with Solomon began, he never had a reason to visit the university as the walls would only remind him that he was a school dropout. "I will give my last kobo for my children to be educated," he would often say, as if his parents should take the blame for not educating him. Mr. Obi had quit school voluntarily.

It was on their last visit that Father Chollom used his white cassock to work wonders and they were able to complete a week long registration process in one day. He hoped Father Gyang would work out the miracle again hence his insistence for the Reverend to come along with them. Mr. Obi wished Adaku was admitted to the University of Nigeria, Nsukka. His main reason, as he told his wife, was for Adaku to be close to her people — Igbo people. But Mama Adaku knew better; it was an attempt to take Adaku far away from Solomon. Mama Adaku joined her daughter in thanking God that Adaku could not secure admission in Nsukka and they were more grateful when they saw Adaku's name on the admission list of University of Jos published by the *Vanguard* newspaper. Mr. Obi was equally excited about the news but the thought of Adaku and

Solomon in the same school gave him the feeling of a fish bone stuck in the throat.

The University had begun an online registration process for new students, it was quite hectic and the queues of students were longer than those of the previous years. Some students were lucky to complete their registration before noon but the unlucky ones were asked to return the following day owing to poor internet connectivity and inefficiency of the computer operators themselves. Adaku was among the lucky ones, thanks to Father Gyang who used his usual magic, and was highly impressed at the new online registration processes which enabled one to pay school fees, download course forms and even secure space in the hostels online. With that development, many corners had been cut. At noon, Adaku was done with her registration and was heading to be checked into the hostel by the porters. Solomon had hinted her on the hostel to choose and even the particular room he wanted her to have. They spoke on phone a day before she arrived.

"Daddy, we just passed Solomon and John."

"Is that what brought you to school?" Mr. Obi barked without turning to see his daughter in the back seat, Father Gyang pulled over the car.

"Adaku, go and call them, I hope they are not too far behind." Father Gyang said as the engine came to a stop. Mr. Obi wanted to protest but he couldn't offend the man of God. Ada jumped out even before her father could protest, if he could.

"Igwe," Father Gyang often addressed Papa Adaku as that whenever he was in high spirits, the moment was however inappropriate. "Igwe, I have followed your fight with that poor innocent boy and I think it's high time you let things be," he spoke solemnly as if he was delivering a sermon, "remember, *que sera...*"

"*Sera*," Mr Obi completed. Father Gyang was already used to saying '*que sera sera*' in most of his sermons. "But Father, it is not about that my son o! It is about my daughter ..."

"That is why I said you should leave it to fate, time will sort things out. Believe me, Igwe, this is not a fight you can fight alone. Love is a strong bond; if you are not careful you will soon become their mutual enemy. If you have not found something worth dying for, then you are probably unfit to live. Now they are in the same school and you cannot afford to hire adequate spies to report to you their movements. What these young people need is trust, a few words of caution, and who knows?" He shrugged, "Solomon may just turn out to be a good son-in-law."

Father Gyang's last sentence incensed Mr. Obi but, again, he repressed the feeling of daring to oppose a man of God. "I have heard you, Father."

"Welcome Father," Solomon and John appeared at the side of Father Gyang and greeted him through the half open glass window. Mr. Obi opened the passenger's door and stood outside. He stretched his hand for both boys to shake. They exchanged pleasantries and in a short while, the five of them were cracking jokes as if they were all peers. It pleased Adaku to see her father laughing so hard in the presence of Solomon. Her father hoped Father Gyang would be impressed at that sight.

Ada became the first occupant of her hostel room on the ground floor. Solomon helped her to select the choicest space and they all helped to clean up the room while Father Gyang stood outside and gave directives. By 5:00pm Papa Adaku and Mr. Obi were set to leave for Pankshin. Before then, Mr. Obi pleaded with Father Gyang to sanctify Ada's new room and then follow it up with a prayer for all the children. Had Ada's mother been around, the prayer would have taken longer than usual but Father Gyang was not an eloquent prayer leader.

As if he suddenly remembered something, Mr. Obi stepped out of the car and called Solomon aside, out of the earshot of others. "Look, I know you still like my daughter, and I have been harsh on you. I am sorry we could not really understand each other. Now she is in your hands, please take care of her as your own sister. I am not God so I can't see what will happen after I have gone." He pointed to the sky, "Remember, God is watching you, Jesus is watching, the angels are watching, and even the spirit of Father Brown is also watching." At the mention of Father Brown, Solomon felt cold currents running through his nerves.

"Papa Adaku, I promise to take care of her and do everything necessary for Adaku to excel academically and in all spheres. I can only guarantee you that just as long as I am in this school." Solomon put on his most sincere face as he spoke.

"Ehen! One more thing, your rent at Okafor's place will be expiring by next month, he has asked me to tell you to renew it but I won't do that. I am packing your belongings back to your room in my house." He went into the car leaving Solomon dumbfounded.

Solomon was unable to say goodbye; tears filled his eyes as he waved them. He could hardly tell if he was dreaming.

* * * * *

Under Solomon's tutelage and guardianship, Ada became a focused and determined student, his jealous eyes shot at every young guy who had the intention of wooing Ada. At first, she was bored with Solomon and John's triangular life in school, they didn't spare much time for sports. Ada somehow adjusted; Solomon and her books competed for her loyalty. She also got used to attending two different fellowships, skipping one of them each week. Solomon was soon nicknamed Ada's bodyguard but he cared less.

By the end of their second semester examinations, Ada was reluctant to go home; she became Solomon's research assistant instead. Solomon and John needed an extra month to complete their undergraduate projects. Ada stayed with them during that month and she proved to be useful after all. She helped them with cooking and washing of plates, and was also there to help them gather academic materials, and any other thing they needed. When they finally went home, Ada's father couldn't hide his exasperation with Ada. Solomon narrowly convinced him that Ada was of immense help to them. Astoundingly, Mr Obi simmered down.

They enjoyed another happy month in Pankshin and then John said he was going back home to Jalingo, and that he would be gone for good except for short visits. Solomon also informed them that he would be going along with John. John's uncle had offered them a temporary job in a private school which he established in Jalingo. Mr. Obi was not pleased with the development. He was not happy to let John go, but letting Solomon go with him was like releasing his left kidney. Solomon had become his personal assistant. Mr. Obi trusted him to be his eyes whenever he was away. He became satisfied with every task completed by Solomon.

* * * * *

KC had informed Giwa on the dress code in the East especially when one was carrying a huge amount of cash; one just had to look shabby. You would dress like a pauper and carry the cash like it was some cheap thing in a cheap sack. Giwa had been told of a woman whose gold necklace was snatched off her neck and it injured her; a man who almost lost his life pursuing the bag of cash that was ripped off his shoulder; and a poor fellow who lost his middle finger before a diamond ring was removed from it. KC had told Giwa about numerous cases of street theft especially in Aba and Onitsha. When Giwa arrived Owerri, he assumed every young person was at least a potential thief; much to his dismay, he seemed to be invisible on the streets. Everyone seemed to focus on something. Giwa felt lonely amidst the crowd around him. *Here I am with over two million naira in cash and no one seems to be looking at me,* he thought as he walked along Douglas road until he reached Ahiazu junction. He was worn out completely when he reached Imerienwe village. There, he inquired about Capt. OC and he was told that Capt. OC resided at Amafor autonomous community of Imerienwe village. *KC never told me that,* he pondered as the *okada* rider gave details about Capt. OC.

"Are you sure about the Capt. OC I am talking about?"

"Yes now, the one wey dem talk say him pikin die for Jos na, dem bury di pikin yesterday na, wetin be di nem sef?" The motorcylist hit his temple, "ehm…ehm…ehen! Kelechi!"

Giwa confirmed that the *okada* rider was talking about KC's father then he climbed the bike and they hit the road. The wings of the night were closing in on Imerienwe village, gates were being shut and provision stores too were closing for the day. Giwa was glad he was safe.

The *okada* rider spoke Igbo so much that Giwa had to confess that he was coming from Jos, and was not familiar with Igbo language.

"*Onye Hauwusa,* na una dey kill our people for Jos abi?"

"No…We don't kill, people that kill do not love peace." It dawned on Giwa that he had killed too. He sought for peace in his heart.

" Nnaa, all Hauwusa people, na killers dem be."

I am not Hausa, I only understand Hausa, Giwa almost said. It occurred to him that an average Igbo man residing in the South-east presumes all northerners to be Hausas. He felt the needless point to argue with the *okada* man who held on to his belief.

"Na dis wan be di house," the *okada* rider stepped on the brakes. "Captain OC no like Hauwusa people o!"

"Na so I hear." Giwa paid the okada rider.

"Nnaa see him broda for dia dey come. Chukwudi!" the man

called. "Chukwudi! Una get visitor." The *okada* rider sped away.

"Hello, good evening, brother," Chukwudi greeted, he walked up to Giwa and shook his hand. Giwa was quite impressed with his salutation. He heard him pronounce the 'th' in 'brother' properly, and the final 'r' in the same word was also picked by Giwa's ears; this made him to assume Chukwudi might be as smart, or even more educated, than KC.

"Good evening," Giwa held his hand warmly, he took note of Chukwudi's resemblance to KC which was glaring even in the enveloping night. I suppose you are KC's younger brother," Giwa asked without needing an answer.

"Yes, that is true, I am his brother from the same father and mother." He tried to speak English impeccably, perhaps to make a statement.

"I heard what happened to your brother, please accept my sympathy." He couldn't say he saw what happened and he knew the killers too, he might just be lynched if the truth gets out on the soil on which he stood.

"My brother, the Lord giveth and the Lord taketh, who are we to complain? Our prayer is that KC has found rest." Chukwudi tried to change the line of conversation, "What is your name please? I know you are definitely not from this part of the country because you do not have an Igbo or Yoruba accent."

"David, my name is David." Giwa realized he had just used the name which had been dormant for more than a decade. "I am from Kaduna but I reside in Jos, Plateau state. KC was my classmate. I was his class rep, actually, the class representative. I am here on behalf of the class to condole with you and your family." Giwa saw himself picking paces in the lying art he was becoming familiar with.

"Nice to meet you David," Chukwudi shook his hand again. "May the lord bless you brother."

"Thank you."

Chukwudi, like his older brother, was a school dropout. He started a diploma programme at the Federal Polytechnic in Nekede but left after his second year. He said he was born again and suddenly stopped drinking and smoking. He joined the Loveworld Ministries and was very active to the point that he was appointed, or rather anointed, as the third pastor of the Loveworld Ministry, the campus branch of the Ministry. Since his appointment as the pastor in charge of the campus branch, Chukwudi had transformed the contents of his wardrobe; it only contained suits of different colours and matching ties. Chukwudi became a smart dresser; he once told his two hundred member congregation that he would never stoop so low as to wear any African wrapper or lace. He used relaxer on his long hair and would always comb it backwards. Chukuwdi would never eat eba or pounded yam without a spoon. He acted with what he called 'prestige'. He was conscious of his steps, his sitting and even sleeping posture. Chukwudi once remarked that he was going to be a millionaire, which spelt the imperative for him to start acting like one before the actualization of his vision.

"My parents named me Chukuwdi but you can call me Chuks. Better still, call me Pastor Chuks like my members do call me."

"Your members?" Giwa was puzzled.

"Are you surprised? You see, the difference between my late brother, KC, and I, though many people say we have a lot in common, is that I have a vision and he doesn't." Chukuwdi was boosting his ego. "Not that I am boasting but where is Kelechi today?" He continued without waiting for an answer. "He is six feet below, and who am I? The President and General Overseer of Overcomers' World Ministries. Praise the Lord!" At that point, Giwa wished he had reserved a portion of his lethal pepper for Pastor Chuks who inflated himself to the size of a whale. Giwa was tired, hungry and angry.

"Can I see the captain and other family members?" Giwa cut in, obviously tired of Pastor Chuks' gibberish.

"Oh my! Pardon my lengthy words of wisdom, sometimes I get so overwhelmed by the Spirit and before you know it," he snapped his fingers, "I begin to preach and prophesy. You are welcome, Brother David." Chuks shook his hand again. He led them to the front door of the compound. "Captain is in the sitting room with my mother."

KC's mother was very fair in complexion; she could pass for an albino if one didn't look well. Captain OC sat with a keg of palm wine in front of him and was drinking the palmwine. He spoke Igbo to the boys, and Pastor Chuks responded in English. Captain OC flared up and suddenly, Chuks spoke Igbo language with noticeable reluctance. Giwa was clueless as to what they were discussing but he knew Captain wanted Pastor Chuks to speak in Igbo when he flared up.

"*Hauwusa ewu,*" Captain OC remarked scornfully.

Giwa knew that the captain was referring to him but he smiled, he went before the old man and squatted. "Please accept my sympathy sir," Captain OC hissed, KC's mother came and raised Giwa up.

"You are welcome my son," KC's mother said, sympathetically. "All the way from Jos! *Eiyaa! Nwamoo biko nnu,* sit down!" Pastor Chuks introduced his two aunties who were also in the sitting room while Mrs. Chidebere went to the kitchen to find something edible for Giwa.

The silence in the sitting room grew so loud; Captain OC broke it. "I blame all these on Ojukwu." Captain OC brought Giwa's attention to the heroic picture of himself and Ojukwu. "If he had not given up, Kelechi would have been living in Biafra, he wouldn't have died." He turned to Giwa, "From the day Kelechi told me he was going to Jos, I had disowned him. He became a *Hauwusa ewu* like you, now he is gone. *Tufiakwa*!" The veteran soldier spat tiny drops of palm wine and saliva on the floor.

"Don't mind the captain my son, I hope you can manage this eba and oha soup, we don't have anything but the pride of an ex Captain in this house." KC's mother appeared with a tray in her hands as she walked towards Giwa, and laid it on a stool in front of him as she spoke.

Captain OC brought out a box of snuff and inhaled it. He drank another cup of palm wine. He stood up and cleared his throat, "*Hauwusa ewu,* you should leave this house by tomorrow morning or else..." he belched, "if I come back by tomorrow evening and find you in this house, I swear I will kill you like those eighty-five *Hauwusa ewus* I shot with my rocket launcher. Ask Emeka Ojukwu, he knows me. Eighty-five!" He raised five fingers in the air as though the five fingers represent eighty-five. "*Una kachifo.*" He told the others and staggered to his bedroom. He sang a song that became very faint and was replaced with a distant snore. Captain Osita had gone to bed.

Giwa licked his hands after the meal, a clear sign that he relished it; he washed his hands and drank water. One of KC's aunties offered him palm wine but he declined.

"My son I hope you fit manage the eba," KC's mother asked as she packed the dishes away from the table.

"Mama, KC did not lie when he told me his mum is an expert

cook."

"Eiyaa... Kelechi is very funny o! It's a pity." Tears filled her eyes; she shook her head and made for the kitchen.

"What of your mother, is she not an expert cook too?" KC's mother asked when she returned.

"Yes, she was before she passed away three years ago."

"Eiyaa!" the three women chorused sympathetically.

"Your papa *nko*?" the other woman posed.

"He died when I was small like this," Giwa arbitralily chose a height that was little above thirty centimetres. At that point, Giwa observed tears rolling down from one of the women's cheeks under the brightness of the kerosine lamp hanging on the mud wall in the house.

"KC was a very fine gentleman," they nodded in agreement. They gave him the liberty to paint their son white. "KC was hardworking, industrious, obedient, loyal, trustworthy, dependable, cheerful, generous and highly intelligent." The women nodded at every modifying word ascribed to Kelechi. At a corner, Pastor Chuks was indifferent, he knew his brother better. Giwa continued. "The day I heard that he was shot, I concluded that it was a mistaken identity because KC was very innocent, he was among the best students in our class. He talked about coming home someday as a National Youth Corps member but the cold hands of death snatched him away. By the time Giwa finished, the women were sobbing and asking "why" as if death was part of the conversation.

"Let me show you your bed, you will sleep in my room tonight." Pastor Chuks stood up and yawned.

"All right then, goodnight Mama and my aunties. Please pray for the repose of the soul of KC, he was a friend indeed." The only honest statement that Giwa could utter.

"Brother David..." Pastor Chuks beckoned Giwa to follow him.

"Goodnight everyone." Giwa said again as he trailed behind Chukwudi.

"All those things you said about Kelechi, are you sure your Kelechi, or KC is my brother? God-fearing?" Pastor Chuks shook his head as he lay on the bed. "It is either you are talking about another Kelechi, his clone, or you don't know my brother at all."

"Alright, you want to know the truth?"

"Yes! And the truth shall set you free."

"You shall know the truth then." Giwa quickly fathomed a way of telling a modified truth that would actually set him free and not get him killed instead.

"KC was my business partner, we sold goods together and had one account. He had once told me about you and his home. I was his next-of-kin and long before his death, he had instructed me to give his family his share if anything ever happened."

"What kind of business were you into with my brother?"

"I am afraid I can't tell, just leave it at that," Giwa pleaded.

"It must be cultism then, *branaka ka shama la,* I shall not possess any illegal and ungodly wealth, *ya sinke yamala lesoto, carica papaya.*"

Giwa could not really comprehend the strange language Pastor Chuks mixed with his speech. It didn't sound like Igbo in his ears so he concluded that Chuks was probably speaking in tongues. He had heard something like that before.

"KC was not a cultist!"

"But that is what the newspaper said, I read it, no one else read it in this house. That was why I was quiet when you were saying all that unholy trash." Pastor Chuks whispered angrily.

"Are you going to accept the money or not?" Giwa retorted.

"How much is it?"

"2.3 million naira." Giwa said it casually as if it was not a fortune.

"Jesus Christ of Nazareth!" Pastor Chuks sprang up and sat on the bed. "Two point *gini*?"

"I didn't know how to tell your family, that is why I decided that I will give you and maybe you people will find a way of sharing it."

"Does any other person know about it?"

"No."

"Where is the money?"

"Right here, in this house and in this room."

"Cash?"

"Of course!"

Pastor Chuks chanted another round of the heavenly language. "My God is never asleep, surely at the end of the tunnel, there is always light. My sweet Brother Kelechi, may your soul rest in perfect peace at the bosom of our Lord," he raised his hand to the ceiling as he offered his prayer. "Brother David," Chuks tried to face Giwa, "you are a friend indeed. If not, who would care to come this far to deliver the message of a dead friend? You know, your friendship reminds me of the story of David and Jonathan in the Bible, 2nd

Samuel and 1st Kings. David was kind even to the relatives of his dead friend Jonathan. Halleluyah!" Pastor Chuks burst into an explosive sermon. "Bro David, you are a blessed child, you are the second version of the real David..." Pastor Chuks sermonized until he heard Brother David snoring. He searched the small Ghana-must-go bag and found the 2.3 million naira in cash after seven layers of polythene bags were torn. Pastor Chuks had just received a testimony which none of his family members would ever know. Three months ago, he changed the name of 'Loveword Ministries' to 'Overcomers Ministries', a third of the congregation left his ministry even after he told them that he was instructed by God to maintain that very flock under a different shepherd. Since then, Chuks had been thinking of ways of maintaining his fleeing flock and two million naira was brought right into his bedroom. Chukwudi would never lie to himself, he knew he was running a business; at least 'man must chop', since he knew was not going to be able to cope academically having obtained his O'level certificate from a 'miracle center'. Running a ministry was a job without sweat for Chukwudi. As long as problems occured, people would attend his ministry. Somehow, he prayed for more problems to befall his members.

At dawn, Giwa received the treatment of a king, Pastor Chuks ran helter skelter to have all of Giwa's needs met. He fetched two buckets of water and kept them in the bathroom for Giwa. Before Giwa finished bathing, a steaming cup of tea was kept on the table with a large loaf of bread. Eggs were a rare delicacy at the captain's house, rarer were the fried ones, and Brother David didn't seem to understand the privilege he was given; maybe because Chuks said it was a normal breakfast. Pastor Chuks insisted that Giwa wore a black suit in the scorching heat of Imerienwe. He said that Giwa looked better in it. Captain OC had gone out before daybreak to check his traps in the bush. Giwa was relieved, at least he would not have anyone address him as 'Hauwusa ewu', before he left. Pastor Chuks cajoled him to visit his Overcomers' Ministry before he left but Giwa declined. Finally, he persuaded him to spend the night at Owerri and Giwa agreed.

Mama Kelechi became a proud owner of ten thousand naira and her sisters had five thousand naira each, every other person in the compound got a thousand naira, they showered blessings on him and urged him to visit again. Giwa added another ten thousand naira in an envelope and gave Mrs. Chidebere to give her husband when he returned; he wondered whether the old man would reject it or whether he would accept it with a curse —- "Hauwusa ewu!"

Pastor Chuks showed Giwa around Owerri city; he took him to the few tourist sites and later they settled down at an exotic restaurant for a sumptuous meal. Chuks handled the bills. He felt like he was the boss, like it was his own sweat that generated the money. Giwa wondered how KC would feel if he was viewing Chuks from another realm. He denied himself of extravagance and saved money aggressively in order to become a millionaire, but here was Pastor Chuks spending like he knew how to make one million naira in a day.

"Have you ever been to Concord hotel?" Pastor Chuks asked as if he had been there a dozen times before.

"No, I don't even know where it is."

"Don't worry, I will take you there, we shall have dinner there, and then I will check us into two different rooms. In case you like any of those 'yellow pawpaw' sisters, they will be arranged for you."

"Pastor Chuks!" Giwa smiled sacarstically.

"Brother David, it is not always o! Just once in a while."

"I hear you, your brother taught me to stay off women."

"You believed him?"

"Of course!"

It felt good to be blown by the cool air emanating from the gigantic air conditioner at the bar of Concord hotel. Giwa sipped on his bottle of Guiness while Pastor Chuks kept phoning one Blessing that he said was a wonderful musician. She finally arrived when Giwa was on his second bottle. Blessing was shy but extremely pretty. To Giwa's surprise, Pastor Chuks who had been drinking a bottle of juice ordered for a bottle of Moet and two glasses.

"A bottle of Moet costs ten thousand naira sir," the waiter said, in case Pastor Chuks was unsure of the price.

"Even if it is fifteen thousand, just bring it!"

"Okay sir," the waiter disappeared.

"Please meet my late brother's closest friend and business associate, Brother David."

Giwa bowed slightly. Blessing smiled shyly and stretched her tiny hand. "I am Blessing Madueke, a 300 level student of the department of Mass Communications, Imo State University (IMSU)." Giwa found her introduction rather too elaborate; he wanted just a name without a surname.

"Blessing is the lead vocalist in my choir," Pastor Chuks said boastfully and Giwa nodded. Another waiter arrived with grilled chicken on a small tray. Blessing's eyes had already devoured the meat before her hands touched it.

Giwa was ready to go to bed after his second bottle, he said goodnight to Pastor Chuks and his lead-vocalist girlfriend. The next morning, Giwa slipped a note under Chukwudi's door, he knew they were still asleep. He boarded a bus that was going to Jos. An urge to run away from Jos engulfed him. He couldn't take any chances of living longer in Jos else he might get shot someday, like his friend KC.

Seventeen

At the outskirts of Zonkwa town, near a large textile factory, Giwa sold cigarettes, small bottles of dry gin and kola nuts on a large cart. Covertly, he sold Mary-J but only to clandestine buyers. Four years was enough to transform him from a single digit millionaire into a street hawker. He chose to come back to his childhood village which had become a town, where he was not known any longer. Far from the eyes of the police, from General Hamza, or any of the SBC boys, though he doubted they would be looking for him; or even the Black Mamba boys who may want to avenge the death of their Chiefo —- if they had a clue of who the murderer was.

No matter how much he tried to save, Giwa's finances kept plummeting, he had to cater for his needs and Kyauta's needs. Kyauta was out of school when he came back as a fugitive. He sent her back to school and she was later transferred to his alma mata. Giwa could not come out of his hiding so Samson did all the running around for him. With no land to farm, Giwa resorted to hawking. He had sourced local farmers who secretly cultivated cannabis in the bushes and they supplied him. Not even Samson or Kyauta knew Giwa was selling something else apart from the cigarettes and kola nuts which they loathed and villified him for.

After Kyauta completed her secondary school education at PHS, feeding became a problem for them. Samson would often supply them with sweet potatoes from his garden. At the height of his financial agony, Giwa was robbed by a mob of local thugs. They stole his money and his 'merchandize'. He mourned his loss, his tears increased as he watched Kyauta go to bed on a hungry stomach. Giwa wished any of his parents, Uncle Harry or even KC was alive. His whole world crumbled. A last option was to sell the old house which his father had inherited from the missionaries. The fugitive became tired of his miserable life.

The next morning, Giwa thought of committing suicide. While he contemplated, two men visited him. They were strangers. *The end has come*, Giwa thought as Kyauta came up behind them.

"Yaya, these men said they are looking for you, they said they are from Jos," Kyauta spoke as she passed between the men into the house. Giwa was more worried when he heard that they were looking for him and they were from 'Jos'. He suddenly felt an instant urge to visit the toilet.

"We just want to be sure that you are Giwa David Bako," one of the men spoke. The other one wore a pair of small transparent glasses on his face.

"May we come in?" The strange fellow with the glasses asked. "We have something very important to talk about."

The final whistle is blown, either ways I am toast. "Come in," he replied, ushering them into the shabby house as he led the way. *I may not have to commit suicide after all, let the law handle me.*

Kyauta appeared with two plastic cups of water and placed them carefully in front of the men who were seated on the threadbare cushions of the house. Giwa found himself a wooden chair, he signalled Kyauta to go to her room. The man with the pair of eye glasses gazed at her behind admiringly as she disappeared; he turned and caught Giwa's disapproving frown. He didn't need to be told, business was paramount.

"I am Barrister Terseer Ugba from the Legal Services Department of Platinum Bank Nigeria Plc. With me is Mr. Victor Ayuba of the Security and Verification Unit of the bank."

Terseer gulped some water, Giwa was relieved that the men were from the bank, he feared it might just be a delusion. "I'm here in respect of the will of your late uncle, Haruna Bako."

It sounded more real to Giwa, he relaxed. "Yes," he nodded, "Haruna Bako was my uncle."

"What was the relationship between you two?" Mr. Victor asked.

"I just said he was my uncle." Giwa was puzzled.

"Yes we know, but how were you related?" he asked again.

"Okay, Uncle Harry was my father's younger brother, and he was a medical doctor before he died. Married to Aunty Mercy but they had no children. He schooled at PHS, University of..."

"Thank you, that should be enough," Mr. Victor cut in. "We just wanted to be sure that the information we have is correct and up to date." He whispered something into Barrister Terseer's ears, the barrister nodded. "Do you have any means of identification like National ID, school ID, results or anything?" All that was procedure, as far as Victor was concerned, Giwa was the person they were looking for.

Giwa went inside and came out with three different ID cards. "Do you need anything else?" he asked, wishing they would just leave.

The barrister cleared his throat, "Your aunt, Mercy, got an injunction from the court restraining the bank from locating you and handing over your uncle's estate. Her claim was that you were involved in his murder but the loopholes in her story were many, in view of the place, and event that surrounded his death. Be that as it may, our bank was obliged to honour the injunction. We were, however, allowed to hand over the estate to you last month."

"Why? Did Aunty Mercy change her mind?"

"No, she didn't until she died last month in an auto crash," Mr. Victor answered.

Barrister Terseer continued, "We will like you to sign these documents after reading the clause and we will also require three recent passport photographs and three photocopies of your identity cards.

"Is that all?"

"Yes Sir," they answered in unison.

"How much are we talking about?"

"Roughly 3.2 million naira sir, aside from tax and other charges," Barrister Terseer replied. Giwa jumped and touched the ceiling of his mind. On his face was a coy smile.

"What about Uncle Harry's house?"

"Well, Sir, I am from the bank representing our esteemed customer, Haruna Bako, who made you his next of kin. I wouldn't know about the house but the last time I spoke to your aunt's lawyer, he said the title deeds to the house were in her name," he said as he watched Giwa studying the documents before signing them.

"Did you say you are from Jos branch of Platinum Bank?" Giwa realized he had asked a stupid question. "Sorry, I meant to ask if you know one Benson Jimoh, whether he still works there," he asked without lifting his head from the papers.

"Oh! Benson, he died last year." Victor replied.

Giwa raised his head, he wore a sad face "What a pity." Inwardly, he was glad that Benson would not be around to cheat him again.

"What killed him?" He merely asked to show concern, news of Benson's death thrilled him in some way.

"Nobody knows for sure, his dead body was found in a brothel in Abuja on a Sunday morning," Victor replied again. Giwa wasn't surprised.

The men left after an hour. Giwa had asked them to make the cash available to him the following day and they would be rewarded with a hundred thousand naira each. The deal was sealed. He no longer was afraid of going back to Jos, half of 3 million naira was enough to strike a deal with any policeman he could think of, and should there be any assassin, he would use the same amount to buy him off the job. He swore to himself that he was never going to be poor again. At night he did not sleep. Giwa weaved a plan.

* * * * *

"Get your things ready, we are leaving Zonkwa for good tomorrow," Giwa told Kyauta.

"Why?" She cleared the table and made for the kitchen. "Yaya why?" She asked again when she returned.

"Because I want us to start living in Jos."

Kyauta was elated with the news; she was worried at the same time. "How will you get the money?"

"We will sell this house and everything in it, and then we will go to Jos and start over, you will go to the university and I will search for a job. He spoke as though he had an 'A' level certificate. Kyauta hugged Giwa. She was excited. He watched her like an eagle over its nest. He always drove away the boys that came around her. Samson often told him that when no man comes to seek for Kyauta's hand in marriage, Giwa should marry her since he chased the boys away. Giwa always insisted that Kyauta was too young and naive. Kyauta hated him for that, but the news of the possibility of her school endeared him to her. She was cautioned about saying farewell to the entire neighbourhood.

Samson's family was the only family that was informed about Giwa's departure. Samson bought the house from Giwa at a giveaway price of a hundred and twenty thousand naira; an amount which swept Samson's savings in addition to the extra fifteen thousand which he borrowed. The two families ate supper together at Samson's house on the eve of Giwa's departure. With the money acquired, Giwa was able to buy himself a phone and another one for Kyauta too.

"Always remember that you have a home in my house," Samson told Giwa before they boarded a taxi. Kyauta and Zhaitun, Samson's wife, were drying their tears as they bade each other goodbye.

A lump formed in Giwa's throat when the vehicle moved away from Zonkwa, from the diminishing figures of Samson and his wife waving at them. He wondered whether Samson had a lump in his throat too, and how he would react if he found the forty thousand he kept for him with a note back in the house.

* * * * *

Giwa checked himself and his sister into the same room he once lodged in for two weeks at the Bond hotel in Bukuru town. He took her out around the town and showed her some few places he was familiar with. Giwa walked around town carefully; afraid he might be known by someone, but the town had become more populous and no one cared about him. The next day, he was at Platinum bank on Ahmadu Bellow Way in Jos, his cash was ready as both Terseer and Victor waited for him with anxious smiles. They had deducted their share. Giwa examined the amount with his eyes. Kyauta was waiting outside, he handed over the money to her with a strict directive to move straight to the hotel and have the door locked until he arrived. He held another bag and meandered around different shops in case he was being followed.

Giwa strolled out in the evening again, this time he was alone and headed for a bar. Kyauta was at the hotel room eating, drinking and watching films till her eyes were blurry.

Sitting in a nameless bar, on a table, alone, Giwa was drinking and calculating his proposed expenditures.

"Who is this? The elephant! King of the jungle?"

"Hey! I can't believe my eyes," the other boy wiped his face with his dirty face towel. Gasko and Duff appeared.

Giwa was surprised that his old friends were not dead yet. He rose to his feet and hugged both of them. Duff's teeth were stained, obviously from tobacco smoke. Giwa was excited to see the boys alive; they looked rougher so he guessed they must be tougher. He ordered drinks and a packet of cigarette for both of them. They caught up on old times, reminisced about the good old days at PHS and their brief stay around the university campus. Giwa was pleased to learn that both Gasko and Duff were expelled from the university on accounts of examination malpractice and cultism; at least three of them could be called 'dropouts'. The latter was not really confirmed by the university's security, but the boys were at the university's exit door anyway.

"So who is now heading the Black Mamba?" Duff and Gasko looked around, surprised that Giwa had known of their membership of the cult group.

"How did you know about it?" Duff asked almost in a whisper.

"I was with you on the day you were initiated, matric day, remember?" Giwa winked at them. "You thought I was too dumb to know that your 'after matriculation party' was actually an initiation, right?" The credit was actually KC's but Giwa portrayed himself as a smart boy, like he was smart from the outset.

"An elephant never forgets," Duff remarked. He recounted the story of the mysterious death of Chiefo and that of SBC's Da Don, how members of the Black Mamba split afterwards, how the police raided La Modillo hotel and how they were expelled from the university. Duff said the Black Mamba was nothing powerful, only the members believed they had powers, but they were susceptible to any trouble common human beings could face. They renounced their loyalty to the group since they found out. They now operated as a two-man gang; watching each other's back.

Giwa drank his third bottle, he ordered for more drinks for his friends and he left. The three boys agreed to meet at the same place, the same time and on the same table the next day. The idea of Duff and Gasko fit into Giwa's calculation neatly like knights on a chessboard.

Before noon, Giwa was able to rent a four-bedroom flat in a developing area in Bukuru. With less than four hundred thousand naira, he was able to pay the landlord for two years upfront. Before dusk, he had bought a Peugeaut 504 Saloon car and had it parked in the house and then went back to the hotel. Kyauta was bored with all the luxury, she wanted to go back to Zonkwa, having nothing else to do apart from sleeping, reading, eating, and watching. One more night wasn't a bad idea to her.

"So where do in you reside in Bukuru?" Duff lighted his stick, he exhaled bubbles of smoke above his head."

"Rwan Chugwai, it's a new settlement behind BEE

Comprehensive High School." Giwa sipped his stout. "You guys will be my guests tomorrow evening. We have come a long way, I think it will be good if we stick together." They agreed. Duff slapped Giwa's palm, a sign that he was pleased with his words.

"Guys, how would you like to make two million each?" Giwa asked.

"Who do you want me to kill?" Duff revealed the tail of his 9mm to Giwa, "I still got my gangster bitch."

*   *   *   *   *

The National Drug and Law Enforcement Agency (NDLEA) recruited Solomon T. Bakka a year after he completed his mandatory National Youth Corps Service. For one year, Solomon roamed office buildings of different companies and agencies, dropping application letters. He surfed the Internet daily, looking for vacant positions he could apply for. With the help of John Ambi's uncle, Solomon was invited along with John for an interview in Abuja, it was their first visit to the city. John's uncle's driver chauffeured them to the venue of the interview and they were suprised to see thousands of prospective interviewees scattered under the sun, waiting for their names to be called through a megaphone, and there and then, they would queue up to be interviewed. The process was hectic. No sooner had they arrived than their names called upon for the interview, the interviewers only needed to be sure that Solomon Bakka and John Ambi were present. They were asked to leave as soon as they mentioned their names. They were not bombarded with questions like the others. John's uncle had become a Senator representing Taraba North Senatorial Zone, he was also the House Committee Chairman on Federal Character. Senator Ambi was rumoured to be a close ally of the Senate President. John called him to inform him that the interview was done. Senator Ambi then asked him where they would like to be posted to and John didn't hesitate to say Jos. The boys were persuaded to stay two more days in Abuja; it was an offer they couldn't resist. By the end of the two days, John and Solomon happily left Abuja with their employment letters in their hands and twenty thousand naira each as transport money even when they were being transported to Jos by the Senator's driver. Solomon had never been treated to such luxury as they had experienced in the Senator's house. He now understood why people kill for power.

The two boys reported at the NDLEA training school after a week. Solomon passed out of the training school after six months and was posted to an outstation in Lamingo, a residential building in Haske estate. The entire building was the investigations department of the NDLEA, it was a covert office, no name, no sign, nothing drugs law about it. Only staff of the agency were allowed into the building, all other people were attended to outside the building.

At 8:00am, Inspector Solomon T. Bakka reported at the Investigations Department of NDLEA on Monday 9th of November, 2008. The commanding officer arrived work at 8:15am and was not surprised to see a new face in his office. He inspected every officer of the department with a mean look.

"You must be Solomon T. Bakka."

"Yes Sir!" he straightened himself.

"You are taller than I thought you'd be." Solomon smiled at the compliment, he considered it so. "Have you taken a tour around the offices?"

"No Sir," Solomon replied, still at attention. He realized the Commanding Officer was tall, huge and very dark with red eyes and red lips. Solomon did not expect he would be Yoruba. The name above his left breast pocket was C. Kolade.

"Relax," the C.O told him. Solomon was at ease. The man held out his hand to Solomon, "I am Christopher Kolade."

"An honour to meet you Sir," Solomon reciprocated.

"What part of the country are you from?"

"Plateau, Sir!"

"I see you are a son of the soil."

"Yes Sir."

"Now let's begin." They walked through the brief corridor, the door of the first room was labelled I.P. "I.P stands for..."

"Immediate Priority." Mr Kolade stared at Solomon, somewhat impressed. "I read it in the NDLEA handbook," Solomon confessed stutteringly, seeing that Mr. Kolade was amazed. There were four officers in that office, each of them had a telephone and a computer on his desk.

"George Adamu is in charge of this unit. George, this is Solomon Bakka, a fresh fox from the training school." George acknowledged him with a slight bow, Solomon did same. "You will get to know the others before the end of the day." Kolade slammed the door, and they moved to the next. "CD & R, what is that?"

"Criminal Data and Record Unit."

"Bravo!" Kolade remarked "I could not remember any of the acronyms when I got out of training school myself. Well, that's probably due to the fatigue we passed through, you foxes didn't experience fatigue, did you?"

"Yes, we did, Sir."

"But not as much as ours." He opened the door, two female officers and one male officer stood up. "Where is Caroline? Aha, there she is, Caro meet Solo, hope you don't' mind if I call you that?" He turned his gaze to the pretty Caroline before Solomon could respond, not like his response mattered to Kolade. "Solo is a fresh fox here, you will know the others before the week runs out. You will be working closely with Caro and her team." He slammed the door. "Now to the next office, it has the fewest number of staff in the building, DT & V" he turned and faced Solomon who was trailing behind him.

"Drug Typology and Verification Unit," Solomon said as his boss opened the door. There were only two officers in the room when Kolade opened the door."

"Hello Maggie, meet Solomon Bakka, a fresh fox." Solomon suddenly became tired of being referred to as a 'fresh fox'. "Maggie's job is to ascertain and classify any contraband or abused drug in any guise. Whenever drugs are seized, samples are sent to Maggie who makes the analysis and gives me the report on the substance. There's her assistant, he is also called Solo. "

"Perhaps we should call your Solomon, 'Solo 1' and my Solomon 'Solo 2' for easy identification Sir," Maggie chipped in.

"As you wish," Kolade smiled. Giwa smiled too. The door was shut from inside. "And this is the C.O's office, my office." The Commanding Officer opened the empty office for Solomon to see his well furnished office. "Ordinarily, this should be the last office but we have created another unit and you will be the pioneer head of that unit, it's actually a store but we have converted it into an office for you. It is quite small but you will like it." Kolade led him to the empty kitchen, then to the store. The door was labelled 'C & U' "Do you know what it stands for?"

"No sir."

"I bet you wouldn't, it is not in any handbook. It is my initiative." He bragged. "C & U stands for 'Closed and Unsolved'; it is a local extension of the Criminal Data and Records Unit. I presume there are a lot of closed files handed over to us by the police and some of the ones treated by our staff were closed prematurely. Your job is to exhume the corpse of the buried files, look out for the missing links and try to solve some of the cases. Should you need any other thing, Caro will be there to put you through." He called Caroline, who came with about three dozens of closed and unsolved cases in old files.

Caroline smiled generously as she dropped the files on Solomon's table. She catwalked out of the kitchen. "You have to investigate these closed cases," he leaned closer to Solomon, "I am sure we will be able to nail some freaking bastards walking freely on the streets, those barons who think themselves above the law. The success of this unit depends on you Solo." He tapped Solomon on the shoulder, "if it works out great as I expect, the C & U unit will be replicated in all Investigations departments of the NDLEA." He walked out of the office. Solomon heard his footsteps approaching his office again. "One more thing," Solomon looked up from his chair. "I will need a weekly report from you every Friday, it's a tradition in this office. Good luck fox." Kolade disappeared.

"Good luck fox" Solomon mimicked his superior mockingly, in a low tone, after the footsteps of the C.O had died down. He scanned the dusty files with his eyes, looked around the empty cubicle, a cockroach was strolling majestically on the wall. The first file was used by Solomon to smash the cockroach on the wall, and it fell with its back to the ground. The file acquired a wet stain on it. Irritated, he put it aside. The second file was labelled SBC. Solomon blew the dust on it. It was a file transferred to the agency from the 'B' division of the Nigeria Police Command, Plateau State. The first page had briefs on the case and that was why it was closed and transferred to the NDLEA. The grammar was very flawed but Solomon managed to understand what it meant to say.

When it was reported to the police that two men were found dead at La Modillo, the police ransacked the rooms of the victims and found a file which was attached to the one which Solomon read. The attached file contained names of the Smart Boys' Crew members and their code names. Some were just code names. A photo of Da Don was included in the file with a dead person on the floor. There was another photo of a dead person who looked familiar to Solomon. Behind the picture was written 'KC'. The bell rang louder in Solomon's memory but he could not remember the place, or the event. According to the report, KC died two days before Da Don and Chiefo. As was deduced, KC and Da Don were both members of the SBC, its reference was the list of members contained in the SBC file. On the other hand, Da Don and Chiefo were neigbours and top dogs of their fraternities. It was likely that they were friends, or at least acquaintances. The report speculated that the two were killed by the same person or substance. A post mortem report, however, could not ascertain the actual cause of death but the doctors said it was related to a malfunction of the heart and it was highly improbable for two friends, or neighbours, to develop a heart failure on the same night.

Before Solomon read further, his first hypothesis was that the killer of KC was possibly the killer of both Chiefo and Da Don. The killer was likely a customer who paid for drugs and did not receive it, or it was their wholesale supplier who supplied and was not paid on time. His second guess was that KC and the other guys were killed differently for different reasons, and it was merely coincidental that they were murdered in the same week. His third supposition was that a fellow member of the SBC sought vengeance for KC's death.

There were so many questions, yet very few answers. There were many missing links and the information on the victims was very scanty. Solomon scratched his head as if it would produce answers. *This is just one of the over thirty cases and they expect me to solve this grandiose puzzle?* Solomon asked himself. He closed the file and kept it aside. He took another unsolved file and read its briefs. The contents were vague, he closed it immediately, shoved it aside and picked another one, its contents were more vague; the missing details were so enormous, Solomon doubted if it could ever be solved.

"Do people eat lunch where you come from?" Solomon turned and saw Caroline leaning on his door. Caroline was the prettiest woman in the building, and she was conscious of it.

"No we don't, we just stare at the lunch eaters as they eat." Solomon stood up and checked his watch; it was ten minutes to one o'clock. He understood the call.

"You dey craze!" Caroline yelled sarcastically and they both laughed mildly. "Studying those files without a break may scatter one's mind." Solomon agreed with several nods as they walked out of the building.

When they came back from lunch, Solomon returned to the SBC file which he studied halfway before it was pushed aside. He went through the incomplete names of the gang members as they had filled it in on small forms stamped with their own blood. The sheets stank and he held his breath as he flipped through the names. The last sheet had the name 'Giwa Bako' with code name 'G?' "Giwa Bako, Giwa Bako, Giwa Bako, Giwa...." he called the name as if he learnt it by rote. A striking sense of familiarity surrounded the name. He dashed out of his office, into Caroline's office. "Please, I need some information."

"About?" Caroline raised her head immediately as if she was expecting his visit.

"One Giwa Bako, I saw the name on the list of the defunct SBC cult members."

"You heard him Audu, now get on it, see whatever information you can get on the name and print it."

"Yes ma, Audu replied." He punched the keyboard of his desktop.

"Stella, call the SSS office and let me know whatever you can find about him."

"Yes ma," Stella replied casually, she was upset that Caroline interrupted the computer game she was playing. Both Stella and Audu were subordinates of Miss Caroline. Rankwise, Solomon was above them, but Caroline was above Solomon.

"You may go back to your office, I'll see you in fifteen minutes with the details I get on that Giwa Bako." She buried her face on the screen in her front. "One more thing," Solomon halted. "Those boys were all students of University of Jos, right?" Solomon agreed, "Audu, email the Director of University of Jos MIS now!"

In ten minutes, Caroline arrived with three sheets of paper. "It appears you are looking for your clone or twin brother." She dropped the sheets of paper on his table. "If you need anything else, anything, my office is always open." Solomon's jaw dropped when she stressed the word 'anything'. "You will have your desktop, telephone and intercom by next week here in your office so that it will ease your work." Solomon followed her with his eyes until she disappeared.

He looked at the sheet of paper and saw a passport of himself staring at his face. He thought it was his form until he saw the name. *Ehen! No wonder...* His mental web connected the faces and all the events instantly and he was surprised. *KC is dead, Da Don too is dead but what about Giwa?* He went through the MIS form and the short notes. Giwa was from Kaduna, schooled in Zonkwa and PHS and was in UniJos for only a year, his status showed he voluntarily withdrew himself from school in his second year. The other note from the SSS which Stella jotted down indicated that the address he gave was currently uninhabited. His uncle was killed in the 2002 crisis while his wife died two months ago in an auto crash. Giwa's current location was unknown.

Eighteen

"We don't do overtime here," Solomon heard Caroline's voice. He nearly hissed. A quick look at his wristwatch told him it was was ten minutes past four o'clock. He had been thinking and studying hard. Caroline waited a few seconds for Solomon to tidy up his table. The security man was ready to close the door when they came out. "Where are you headed?"

"To meet my prospective landlord, we agreed to meet at the house by 5:00pm," he replied. "The house is about two killometres away from this place," he said before she could ask "where?"

"How big is the apartment?"

"It's a two-bedroom flat."

"Do you have a family?"

"Not yet." Solomon spotted a benign smile on her face. "But I should be getting married soon, I have a fiancée." He watched her smile metamorphose into a frown that was directed at no one but himself. He almost felt sorry for not wanting to flirt with his pretty colleague.

They got into her Honda Accord that was nicknamed 'end of discussion', it was cleaner on the inside and it smelt of cinnamon and lime. The car's air conditioner was automatically turned on as soon as she switched on the ignition. A few seconds later, Celine Dion's voice came through the speakers. He directed her to the house and was reluctant to alight from the car when they got to the house. He wished the ride would last at least for an hour. Caroline zoomed off without saying goodbye. It was in that instant that Solomon remembered that he had not phoned or exchanged text messages with Adaku throughout the day.

November 9th was Adaku's birthday and he was conscious of it throughout the weekend until the morning of that day. In the last four years, Solomon had made it a duty to be her first and her last caller on her birthday. In between the first and last calls, he would send text messages. In his tradition, they would go on a date, he would buy her gifts according to the size of his pocket which she usually cherished, and would read a love poem composed just for her. This time it was different, Solomon was one hundred percent preoccupied with satisfying his new boss and establishing his prowess on his first day at work. He was eventually consumed by the work he was given that it only occurred to him when he was away from the office, and away from Caroline, but he turned it into a plan. The meeting with his new landlord didn't last more than thirty minutes. Solomon was lucky, the man didn't have a list of dos and don'ts, they only negotiated on the rent and Solomon promised to pay immediately.

A text message alert appeared on the screen of Solomon's phone as soon as he was through with the landlord. It was from Ada:

> *On the first day of your job you chose to ignore me and forget about my birthday. Hmmn!*

The brief message conveyed tons of worries to Solomon. The 'hmmn' in the text alone was weightier than all the other words combined in the text message. Ordinarily, Ada would have called but it was her birthday, it was her right to be called on that day. *I'm in deep shit.* Should he put up any form of defence, it was going to lead to an argument that would end up in a quarrel that would lead to a temporary break up and then making up a few days later. Solomon was not ready for that, he wanted to appease her in a single shot.

Solomon was able to reach the fourth floor, in spite of the blackout in Abacha hostel, with the help of the torchlight of his phone. The whole hostel was dark save for some glimpse of candlelight from windows, which from afar looked like white boxes of a chessboard. Solomon stood in front of room 76, it took him two minutes to decide whether to enter or not to enter, but he knocked anyway. He opened the door without waiting for a response, and walked into the room with a small box of cake on his right hand and a small polythene bag with a loosely wrapped rose flower on his left. His countenance suggested an artificial seriousness.

Nandi, Adaku's roommate who had been reading with the candlelight raised her head and smiled. *Talk about the devil.* Ada was already sobbing under her blanket but dried her eyes when

Solomon appeared.

"Welcome Sir," Nandi greeted. Ada didn't utter a word; she got out of her bed and went to the wardrobe.

Solomon understood that a volcano was about erupting. "I am so sorry honey."

"Abeg, abeg!" she turned and saw a kneeling Solomon, "don't even start!" She drew her breath and it sent back mucus from her nose into her throat. She swallowed it and fixed her gaze into the wardrobe again, looking at nothing. "If I was yours, you wouldn't come at this time of the night to wish me a happy birthday. A simple text message sent twelve hours ago would have made a world of difference to me. I don't need your cake and all your candies. That flower in your hand would also find a space in the waste bin. Solomon," she called him by name, a strong indication that she was furious; all other endearing names of Solomon were lost in her anger. "I am a woman, not a piece of trash that you will come to appease with your cheap gifts. I am worth more than all these. All I need is love, respect, and attention, but it seems your new job has deprived me of all that."

Solomon absorbed all the fiery pangs she could inflict. "Baby, I said I am sorry."

"You should be sorry for yourself by the time I get another boyfriend." She knew exactly the words he detested.

"Honey, I will not stand up until you say 'yes'." He reached his hand into his pocket and brought out a small box which he popped open.

"Jesus Christ!" Nandi shouted.

Adaku turned to see what the cause was, and the glitter of the gold ring caught her eyes, she was too shocked to believe her eyes.

"Will you marry me?" Solomon asked while still on his knees. Adaku forgot about the anger she felt towards him, it was not something she had expected, it came too soon. She walked towards him and lifted him up. Solomon anticipated something else but not a soft and brief passionate kiss on his lips. She removed the ring from its box and slid her left middle finger into it. It fit perfectly.

"Does this answer your question, my prince?" She looked into his eyes with her arms around his neck, she was not even shy of Nandi's presence; Adaku was intentionally oblivious of it. Nandi was amazed.

Solomon was pleased; he felt like someone who had crossed seven rivers and seven seas with just a leap. He thought about work the next day and the assignment he was preoccupied with. Finding Giwa was his major concern, not for the sake of the job. It became his personal mission.

* * * * *

The next morning, Solomon arrived at work feeling fresher than a bathed new born baby. At 8:15am almost all the staff of Investigations Department of the NDLEA were seated in their offices. Caroline came to Solomon's office, they exchanged pleasantries. He walked with her to her office door and then turned back to enter his office. The C.O's door was half-open; Solomon opened it wider and saluted. The C.O invited him to enter.

"How did your first day at work go yesterday?"

"Hectic, Sir."

"That means you have started work in earnest, right?"

"Yes, Sir."

"Good," Kolade scribbled on a plain paper. "If you want to work efficiently then you must keep your eyes off women." He spoke as though he was reading it from his table. "Okay, you may leave now."

"Thank you, Sir." Without being told, Solomon figured the warning was about Caroline, he pledged within himself never to extend his friendship with her beyond the confines of their office.

He browsed through the SBC file for the umpteenth time and saw something written in pencil on an old sugar paper. Though the writing was faint, Solomon was able to read its contents, he rewrote it on a sheet of paper.

TO SUPPLY

Mary – J	- - -	200kg	
Henny	- - -	60kg	
Cocoa	- - -	75kg	
Diamond	- - -	xx x	(operation Idoko)

Immediately, Solomon decoded 'Mary-J' was another name for cannabis or weed. Aside that, he didn't know what the other items were but he knew they were drugs. He needed to indentify the types of drugs, he hoped they would link him to the distributors or producers. It was a very thin ray, a one-over-one-hundred chance of helping to solve the case, but he explored it anyway. Margaret was the best person to be of help at this point, being in the DT & V unit but he chose to go to Caroline's place instead.

"Can I have a minute with you?"

"Here or outside?" Caroline asked, wishing to give him all the attention he needed. Stella didn't look happy, Solomon assumed it was for reasons best known to her. He went on to occupy the visitor's chair in front of Caroline's table.

"Who am I to take you out of your chair?" he smiled and handed her the paper which he wrote on. "I was wondering if you would have some ideas about it." Without waiting for her response he continued; "I suppose Mary-J is another name for Indian hemp or marijuana."

"That is correct," she said as she studied the paper. "That is a good one," she thumbed her fingertips on her table. "How come it was overlooked by the police? Are you sure it was in the file?"

"Yes ma!" Caroline frowned, she didn't like the idea of the young guys calling her 'ma'; It made her feel old.

"I didn't see it before o!"

"It was faintly written with a pencil on an old paper, the paper is still in my office."

"Now, these are the kinds of things we should look out for, once you are able to establish who supplied the drugs, it will become the job of IP unit to track him down. The problem here is that the main guys involved in this deal are dead so we can't tell whether the drugs were actually supplied or not, maybe that's why it was marked 'unsolved' and closed. "

"Looks like trying to find a needle in a haysack."

"It's worse than that Solo." She suddenly remembered henny as a short form for a liquor but could be used for heroin." I would rather we stopped assuming and go to Maggie's place now." Caroline could have referred him to Maggie but she chose to go with him, she was also interested in the case.

It took Margaret, head of DT & V unit less than ten minutes to decipher the code names of the drugs and place them appropriately. She was part of an online network that shared most recent information and discoveries on illicit drugs, their types and nomenclature. 'Henny' was actually 'heroin' as Caroline speculated. 'Cocoa' was 'cocaine', Maggie guessed and confirmed it after punching a few keys on her computer. The threesome racked their brains in order to identify the 'Diamond Fleece' but to no success.

"Then what's with the 'Operation Idoko'?" Solomon asked after a long pause. "The way I see it, Diamond Fleece was not quantified, could it be that Idoko is the 'Diamond fleece' himself or he has the key?"

"That is just a name without a surname, of course we can infer that Idoko is an Idoma from Benue state." Solomon nodded as Margaret spoke. "But finding this Idoko without a surname is like looking for a Chinese guy in Beijing." The three officers burst into laughter.

"Okay then, Caroline should help us out," Solomon remarked after the laughter had died down.

"Me? How?"

Solomon cleared his voice. "We will go through the criminal records of all the Idokos including nicknames that have ever been involved in one drug scandal or the other."

"That is a good idea," Margaret said. "I will like to know the outcome of your search."

Audu and Stella were asked to suspend whatever they were doing and search for any Idoko that has ever been involved in any illicit drug scandal since record keeping in NDLEA began. Stella's growing chagrin had reached its climax.

"Madam Caro, why is it that this new officer is always making you to interrupt our work? I don't like losing concentration..."

"Will you shut up and obey my order before I query you?" Caroline shouted her down. "I shall not tolerate any indignation from my subordinates. Is that clear? And that applies to you too," she pointed at Audu who was trying to mind his own business. They all busied themselves.

At the end of the 25 minutes search, seven Idokos were identified as from 1980. Solomon was quick to strike Dr. John Idoko out of of the seven, he said he was the secretary of their chapel in the University. Two of the other Idokos were dead. The third one was serving a jail term in Kikikiri maximum prison in Lagos, the fourth one was a petty drug peddler and was in an unknown location. The fifth Idoko was confirmed to be roaming about the streets of Makurdi having lost his senses while the sixth Idoko, who was formerly a petty peddler, became a professional farmer in Otukpo of Benue State.

"Is there any possibility that the third Idoko could be brokering sales of drugs from prison?" Solomon asked. It was directed at Stella who instantly got on the phone with the office of Nigeria Prisons Service at Kirikiri."

"Negative. They said, he has had no visitors since his mother died 8 years ago. He sits alone in his tiny cell and speaks to no one else aside from the oldest prisoner of Kirikiri." Stella maintained a straight face as she spoke. It seemed it was a dead end.

Solomon returned to his office and dropped his head on his table, trying to think but all ideas eluded him, he couldn't sleep either. He studied Giwa Bako's MIS form again.

STATE OF ORIGIN:	Kaduna
LGA:	Zangon Kataf

He dashed into Caroline's office again, Stella looked mad. Solomon had anticipated her reaction but risked it if it meant getting his work done. Audu was quite indifferent though he knew Giwa's appearance might interrupt his work temporarily.

At Caroline's directive, Audu and Stella were engaged in another round of activities. Audu reported that Zangon Kataf LGA had no online database of its indigenes and no files of indigenes either, the only information about its indigenes was an estimated number. Stella made a few calls to the Kaduna state police command; she was later linked to the Zonkwa station. A random search was arranged in Zonkwa town and the effort yielded positive. Thirty minutes later, Stella was informed that Giwa Bako had left Kaduna with his sister two weeks ago. He was gone for good. Both parents were dead and they had no history of ancestors as they were confirmed to be immigrants. Another *cul-de-sac.*

"Maybe you would like to see this," Audu printed seven pages of report about Dr. John Idoko. Solomon didn't remember that he was a pharmacist; that he may have had something to do with drugs.

"Where did you get this?"

"From the web, some American drugs agency."

"Good job Audu, good job!" Solomon raised his right thumb to Audu. He thanked them all and excused himself to study the material he had just acquired.

Solomon was surprised to learn that the saintly Dr. John Idoko had a horrible past too. The most remarkable thing about Dr. Idoko was that he invented the 'Super Coca'. Super Coca was introduced to the global cartel and was widely accepted. However, with the help of foreign agents, the product was used to track its producer who was raking in millions of naira as of the late 80s. Dr. Idoko was apprehended by the NDLEA. With the help of a wise counsel, Dr. Idoko was able to strike a deal listing all his marketers, forfeiting his enormous wealth, and giving them the formulae for the Super Coca. His Super Coca factory which was a house he built in Kuru village was destroyed. Dr. Idoko agreed to live a clean life since then. Until the combined agents of NDLEA and SSS took their eyes off him, Dr. Idoko was a different man. Solomon was intrigued. He headed for Margaret's office.

"Found anything yet?" she lifted her eyes from the magazine which she was reading.

"Nothing much... What do you know about Super Coca?" Her eyebrows moved upwards. She dropped the magazine and asked Solomon to sit.

Caroline barged into Margaret's office. She didn't mention a word, she obviously didn't want to be left out of the loop.

"That drug is on the 'A' list of global cartels and agencies alike." She dropped the magazine and began to punch the keys of her system. "Super Coca has been out of the global, and even local markets, for more than a decade. No one in possession of Super Coca has been arrested in the last eighteen years. New forms of illicit drugs are being formed or refined but none has matched up to the strength of Super Coca." She read from her screen, "The drug was invented by Dr. John Idoko, a prominent Nigerian pharmacist working in the University of Jos..."

"The report I have with me says he traded the formulae too for his life," Solomon mentioned, looking keenly at his paper.

Maggie returned to her computer screen. "Yes, this material also confirms it and that it was replicated without success. The conclusion was that Dr. Idoko gave the formulae and left some elements out, or the combining proportions of the substances were not balanced. He was not pushed; however, part of the condition for his release was that if the quantity of Super Coca increases in the global market, it would be linked to him. Slowly and gradually, the product found its way out."

"That man is a genius!" Caroline remarked having swung her gaze intermittently between Maggie and Solomon. "He deserved a Nobel prize for that feat but its necessity lacked credibility, and the intention behind it too was just like that of Alexander Kalashnikov."

"AK 47," Solomon added, "could it be that the Super Coca is also what Da Don referred to as the Diamond fleece?"

"Probably," Maggie shrugged.

"Maybe those guys believed he had some of the Super Coca remaining or likely, they thought they could get him to produce the drug again."

"The boys are dead anyway, we might end up flogging a dead horse." Maggie had given up.

Solomon left the office quietly; he didn't know what to look for or how to solve the puzzle on his desk. The only thing he wanted to do, even more that finding the nonexistent Super Coca was to find Giwa. He was the only person in the building who knew that Giwa was KC'S closest friend. He had seen KC handle a gun before and knew those guys were tough. Finding Giwa was his key. He thought about engaging Dr. Idoko in an informal interrogation, but the chances were that he might lose his job if his boss ever found out.

"At work, you can only do your best and leave the rest," Caroline's voice drifted into his ears. He knew it was an indirect call for a late lunch. It was already past two o'clock when she reached his office.

"Yes ma," he stood up and followed her. They talked about other things far away from the SBC case and it helped to decongest his thoughts. He sent Ada a text message with a promise to call after work. He told her the work was stressing him out and hoped she would understand.

Solomon bought a newspaper on their way back. He wanted to think about something else; something to reduce his weariness of the case. He didn't blame the Police and CD & R unit for closing the file prematurely. He then understood why Caroline brought those files cheerfully to his office when Kolade asked her to. The newspaper entertained him for half of an hour, and he was done for the day. Caroline didn't offer to drop him and he wasn't eager to follow her either. He hoped to maintain things that way — strictly office friends.

Solomon was fully prepared to close the SBC file having exhausted almost all channels for its solution. His second day at work, the clock was already ticking against him, a report would be required from him on Friday. Solomon busied himself with moving into his new apartment after working hours, the work was faster with Ada's help. Ada went back to the hostel and Solomon put finishing touches on the arrangement of the items in the apartment.

Preparing for work the next morning, he heard the news of Dr. Idoko's disappearance. Intuitively, Solomon decided to keep the SBC file open. He hurried but didn't forget to grab a copy of the *Daily Star* newspaper which had the news as its caption.

'VARSITY LECTURER DISAPPEARS'

For breakfast, he bought akara, he barely greeted the security man when he walked into the building descending on the newspaper and akara at the same time. His left hand was engaged with the akara while his right held the newspaper, and he consumed both simultaneously. In the newspaper report, Dr. John Idoko was supposedly kidnapped by some unknown persons. The police said it was too early for them to come up with a statement as the matter was being investigated. Solomon guessed that the kidnappers were part of the Smart Boys Crew who had knowledge of the Super Coca and were about to force him to cough out the formulae or hand over the hidden product, if there was any. His second guess was that the kidnappers were motivated by the money they would get as ransom, *and if so, why didn't they kidnap the Vice Chancellor?* His third guess was that the kidnappers were cultists who sought revenge for one of their victimized members, but it was highly unlikely because Pharmacy students were the least involved in cult activities on campus.

Caroline barged in with a copy of the Wednesday Pilot newspaper. She dropped it on Solomon's table. "I thought you would like to see this, good morning."

"Of course I would, morning ma." Caroline squeezed her face while Solomon perused the cover of the newspaper.

'UNIJOS LECTURER KIDNAPPED'

Solomon devoured the details of the caption but wasn't surprised not to find anything new contained in the newspaper.

"What's your take on it?" Caroline posed.

"The guys we are looking for are at work."

"Or?"

"The kidnappers are just doing their business, but how much does he have?" Solomon was puzzled, he thought deeply.

"If those boys wanted money, then Dr. Idoko is the wrong person. Two decades ago, they would have hit a goldmine with Dr. Idoko in their net." Caroline agreed with Solomon.

"What if they kidnapped him for some ritual purpose?"

"Naah!" Caroline snapped. "Don't even think that far, Dr. Idoko is too old for any ritual purpose. Their victims are mostly young girls, children and mad people."

"It seems you know a lot about it, were you once in the business?" He grinned.

"Shut up joor! Na your head I go first comot, for say I dey do dat kind business ." They laughed for a short moment. "Seriously, I think you should follow up this development, it may lead us to the gangsters and you'll have your name crested on the agency." Solomon was silent. "You'll have to brief the Commanding Officer about the case, see if you can be allowed to join the police on the case. You should pull out as soon as it is categorically clear that the kidnap had nothing to do with the Super Coca or any narcotic drug."

"Working within my bounds..."

"That's right."

Commanding Officer Kolade was enthused with Solomon's summary of the SBC case, particularly with the additional report he was able to gather on Giwa, and Solomon's demystification of 'Operation Idoko' as well as the 'Diamond Fleece'. He was more intrigued with Solomon's assumption of a likely connection between the Diamond Fleece deal and Dr. Idoko's sudden disappearance.

"But why didn't the boys carry out the operation four years ago, why now?" Kolade looked into Solomon's eyes.

"Honestly, I wouldn't know sir. All the other members could not be indentified by the university apart from Giwa Bako. Apparently, he is our only lead and the most recent report we heard about him was that he left the town of his birth, Zonkwa, in Kaduna state a few weeks ago. My guess is that he is somewhere around Jos and had been planning the operation until it was executed yesterday." Kolade listened patiently, with rapt attention, to the newest officer in the building.

"You will follow this case through to the end, I want that Giwa boy alive. Meanwhile, I will like you to keep this information between only the three of us, and that includes Caro." He pointed a finger at an imaginary Caroline, not even at the direction of her office. He drank a glass of water. "I don't quite trust some officers in the agency, that is why I want to limit the report to the three of us." He got on the phone with the state commander and was linked with Superintendent Joel Okonkwo who was in charge of the Idoko kidnap investigation. He dropped the phone after some minutes.

“Solo, you are going to join the investigation team on the Idoko case, they must not know what you have aside from the fact that Dr. Idoko once dealt in narcotics. Reserve all other information to yourself. There are so many moles in the Police force. I want to nail that boy, don’t mess it up please. Let me know if there is any other thing you will require.”

“Alright sir.”

“I also want a daily briefing on the progress of the case.”

* * * * *

Superintendent Okonkwo did not express any delight in seeing Solomon, he looked at Solomon despicably as if he had leprosy. Solomon, somehow felt relegated but he was not intimidated. So far, Okonkwo’s preliminary report had it that the kidnappers dragged Dr. Idoko on foot into the bush. But after combing through the bush with no success, they speculated that he was transported in another vehicle and they made it out through the main gate since the back gate was riskier for them. The security men who were on duty at the main gate on the previous right were therefore arrested and termed as suspects without evidence.

Judging from superintendent Okonkwo’s preliminary investigation, Solomon was sure that the case was going to end as ‘closed and unsolved’. He didn’t want it to end that way. He requested for an officer to assist him interrogate the security men on duty at the back gate on the previous night. Okonkwo was happy to release him along with the least officer. He considered Solomon a nuisance already. Solomon found out that the last car that left the premises on the previous night was a blue Peugeot 504 saloon car. Two other elders of the chapel who passed through the back gate attested that the purported blue car was parked about 250 yards away from the chapel, the same spot on which Dr. Idoko’s car was found before dawn the next morning.

Superintendent Okonkwo advised the family to keep their fingers crossed and wait for the kidnappers’ request for a ransom at which point they would track the boys down and rescue their father. Later on, he was seen on TV telling journalists that the kidnap was a wave of crime that was reaching the northern part of the country from the South-south. He maintained that the kidnappers would soon ask for money, meanwhile he said they had suspects in their custody and that investigation was still ongoing. Solomon wished he was in position to fire Superintendent Okonkwo. Grounds of gross incompetence and ineptitude were enough reasons.

Thursday was worse, Superintendent Okonkwo and his team indulged in idle questions and a vain search. Towards evening, he was found in a beer parlour, drinking and calling members of Dr. Idoko's family to ask if the kidnappers had named their price already. Solomon felt sorry for anyone who would be contacted, if they would; because he knew Superintendent Okonkwo would turn that person into another suspect. Pressure was on the Police to find the criminals and rescue Dr. Idoko.

Solomon reported the fruitlessness of the team he was assigned to under the asininity of Superintendent Okonkwo to C.O Kolade. He was then allowed to go home. He had vowed to make his last appearance on Friday if the obstinacy of Okonkwo continued. Ada visited his new abode. She had completed her project, and that cheering news, to Solomon, made up for the futile hours he spent all day with Superintendent Okonkwo. He told her all about it, and by the time Ada left his house, he felt somewhat better. He had an overwhelming desire to have her permanently in his home soon. He needed a wife.

Nineteen

Tuesday the 10th of November was the day set by Giwa and his two friends, Duff and Gasko, for the kidnap of Dr. John Idoko. They had spent a week watching Dr. Idoko's routine before deciding on the fateful Tuesday. Giwa ensured that the plan was watertight. He didn't want to leave a strand of hair behind. He ordered that none of them should drink or smoke before the operation but Duff claimed that they would need to see "more clearly" and Giwa obliged.

Giwa had an ill feeling Kyauta may compromise things, besides, she wasn't part of the plan from the outset. She had no inkling what her brother and his friends were up to, and he didn't want her to get involved in case it got messy. Kyauta was abruptly sent to Zonkwa. He told her to stay with Samson's family for at least a week before coming back. Giwa's instructions were clear; he stated that she must return alone.

The trio sat in the Peugeot 504 saloon car which Giwa had newly purchased. Being the most experienced driver among them, though without a license, Duff took control of the wheel. Gasko was in the passenger's seat and Giwa was right behind him. At the start of the operation, Giwa offered a silent prayer for success.

"You are sure there won't be any need for my gangster bitch?" Duff inspected his well polished 9mm which sparkled under the moonlight.

"No, you won't have to use it, not today. I don't want any bloodshed." The neat boss replied calmly.

"Abeg, no com cause any gbege for hia o! Na clean runs we wan do." Gasko smoked his last stick; he was the hit man.

* * * * *

The weekly meeting of the chapel's elders ended at 9:00pm. For some reasons, or as a tradition, Dr. Idoko was always the last man to leave the building. On that Tuesday night, his last-man-out tradition worked in Giwa's favour.

Except on rare occassions, Dr. Idoko always used the campus' back gate at any time. It was closer for him to access the road to his house on Zaria Road. The road to the back gate was not patronized by many motorists because of the potholes that dotted it. Dr. Idoko preferred it that way; he didn't like clashing with motorist at night on narrow roads or even highways. The boys knew this.

Giwa stepped out of the car which was parked about two hundred and fifty metres away from the chapel building, he walked to the church and waited until 9:33pm when Dr. Idoko's car emerged from the chapel's gate. The driver's window was wound down.

"Good evening sir. Please, I need your help," Giwa greeted politely. Dr. Idoko halted the car.

"Yes, what is it?"

"Sir, I am a member of this chapel."

"Do you expect me to know the thousands of students who worship in that building?"

"Certainly not sir. The problem is that I need you to help me with your wheel spanner. I had a flat tyre down the road, my jack was in the boot quite alright but the spanner had disappeared. I will return it back to you as soon as I am through." Dr. Idoko paused for a moment.

"Where did you say your car is?"

"Down the road towards the back gate sir." Giwa felt some apprehension. He hoped it was convincing enough. Dr Idoko decided to help since the poor boy was already on his way.

"Hop into my car and we will go down to yours." Giwa didn't delay a moment. It went smoothly as he planned, his unctuous voice didn't betray him. Gasko disappeared and Duff started a fake lifting of the jack as soon as the light rays from Dr. Idoko's headlamp hit their car. The car came to a stop.

"The flat tyre is at the front left wheel," Giwa directed; Dr. Idoko was following him. Behind Dr. Idoko, Gasko appeared quietly. Before he could turn his back, a strong hand grabbed him and a handkerchief that had been soaked in chloroform was placed on his nose. Within seconds, Dr. Idoko's body looked lifeless. They threw him into their boot. Dr. Idoko's car was locked and they headed for the small gate. The security men at the second gate had a habit of inspecting cars coming into the campus but not the ones going out. Duff was fully aware of it before their operation but he tipped the security man at the gate who was too excited to let them out without asking them to put on the 'inner light' for a fast inspection.

Giwa held his breath until they were on the express road heading for Bukuru.

Duff was the first to talk. "We made it! Woo hoo hoo!" he shouted.

"How long do you think the man would be asleep?" Gasko asked, feeling that Dr. Idoko inhaled an overdose of the chloroform which could lead to his death.

"We will have to keep our fingers crossed until the man wakes up." Giwa said from the back. It was his operation, he was the captain. Giwa had sworn to himself not to celebrate the victory until he found himself in a plane flying out of the country or in some distant state and starting life afresh. He hoped it would be his last hit. Enough drinks, cigarettes and weed were already stored for Duff and Gasko in his room. He wanted them to stay in the house for the whole week, Giwa would not take any chance of Duff getting drunk in a bar and boasting about his bravery and abducting a university icon.

"What about his phone?" Giwa asked.

"I dropped it in his car with his shoes, wristwatch and Bible."

Dr. Idoko was dragged into a dark room with heavy and dark curtains, they gagged him and went to drink while watching TV. They listened to the radio too, the boys were unable to sleep. They were nervous. It was their first kidnap operation. Duff said he'd have preferred to smoke the man with his gun if that would get him the needed cash.

On Wednesday, the news of Dr. Idoko's disappearance was on the headline of almost every local TV station. The boys watched and listened to different versions of the same story of the kidnap, none of the stories pointed towards them. The operation was so clean that the Police PRO confessed that they were equally confused; they couldn't speculate who the kidnappers were neither did they know the purpose of the kidnap. The media concluded that the kidnappers would contact the family or the authorities of the university to ask for a ransom as it was usually done in the Niger Delta.

At noon, Duff came out to the sitting room to announce that Dr. Idoko was conscious and was struggling vainly on the chair. Dr. Idoko was blindfolded as well. The three boys entered the room.

Duff and Gasko were commanded not to talk and to use their masks at his directive. Dr. Idoko heard their footsteps. Giwa motioned Gasko to remove the gag.

"Who are you bastards and what the hell do you want?" he ranted without seeing who his kidnappers were.

"We want your life, we want to make use of your heart, eyes, and liver for a ritual." Giwa understood the rules of bargain, starting from the worst to the acceptable terms.

"No, no please, I beg you in the name of God, please don't kill me, please, I swear I will give you all I have but please spare my life," Dr. Idoko cried helplessly while pleading for mercy. Duff was laughing behind the university don. Giwa was thrilled.

"Shhh, don't cry old man, we have listened to your plea, and we have decided to be merciful on one condition."

"Just tell me whatever it is, I swear I will do it."

"Are you sure?"

"What can be more precious than my life? I need to get back to my family please," Dr. Idoko was more humble than the earth.

"Alright, I'll make it very simple for you," Giwa declared. "In 1991, you struck a deal with the government through NDLEA, you gave them your Super Coca formulae, your wealth and the remainder of your Super Coca, all in exchange for a normal life. In other words, for a life out of prison. Now I want you to do the same thing." Giwa snapped his fingers at Dr. Idoko's ears.

"Sir, isn't there another option? I have done all that already."

"Not quite, I have the privilege of being informed that you have 200kg of Super Coca hidden somewhere here in Jos. I want the location, and when I have it then you will be at home with your wife and children, one big happy family again. I'll be chilling with my friends too; one rich happy family. No one will get hurt if you cooperate with us."

"Everything was destroyed by the authorities, there's nothing left."

Giwa was perplexed. "If everything was truly destroyed, why did you fire your gateman when you discovered 50kg of your Super Coca was missing about eight years ago?"

Dr. Idoko turned his head around as if he was looking at them with his lips and cursed himself. For a moment, he felt he was hearing God's voice because he thought it was a secret he shared with God only. "Who are you?"

"Hush! Calm down. The game is over. We did not wait for years to get you in our net for nothing. Seven million naira can change our lives for good." Giwa said it to his friends' hearing so that they could grasp the money at stake and possibly begin a mental calculation. Within himself, he knew the money would reach the shores of thirty million naira if sold at wholesale price.

Three hours later, Giwa and his friends returned to the dark room with masks on their faces. They brought a TV with them. At 1:00pm, a repeat broadcast of NTA news would come on air, they didn't want John Idoko to miss it. At the appointed hour, the blindfold was removed from his face while they wore their masks. It took a while for him to recognize a TV in front of him. Dr. Idoko was gagged again from the time they left the room earlier till they came back. He saw different pictures of himself on TV and the car as it was left. He also watched his wife pleading with the kidnappers to spare her husband's life. She spoke in tears, Dr. Idoko was moved to tears when he saw his last son crying too. "Daddy... I want my daddy..."

Abigail Akinwumi had finally found herself under the spotlight as the reporter on the case. Giwa contemplated her possible reaction if she knew he was behind the kidnap, and whether she would make the report with that indifference on her face. He chose an emotional point to switch off the television. "That is just how popular you have become in the last six hours. Fortunately for you, the media isn't talking about the Super Coca. It appears it's our mutual little secret. Why don't we keep it that way?" He used the mean tone of a terrorist willing to negotiate.

Duff pulled his gun and pointed it at Dr. Idoko's forehead in an instant. "Boss, let me blow his brains out since he won't talk."

"No, D, don't do it."

"Mmmm!" Dr. Idoko indicated that he wanted to talk. He perspired profusely.

"Do you want to talk now?" Idoko nodded his head. "Are you sure?" He nodded again. Giwa pushed Duff's gun aside, Duff's threat had worked too. Giwa ungagged him. Dr. Idoko begged for a cup of water. Gasko was quick to get a glass of water for him. The man breathed heavily while looking at the unknown faces behind the masks, he was ready to divulge a secret he had kept only to himself.

"Sometime in October 1999, I discovered 50kg was missing from the stock I had hidden in my garage. At that time the garage was forbidden for my children. Only my wife, myself and the gateman had access to the garage. Naturally, I suspected the third person, although he denied outrightly. I was sure he took it. I couldn't have had him arrested — because it would boomerang on me — so I fired him, and he didn't hesitate to leave my house. Shortly afterwards, I heard the story of two innocent children who were run over by a vehicle. According to the news then, no one came up to identify them so I offered to give them a decent burial at St. Peter's Anglican Church's cemetry in Tudun Wada. Before the burial, I made the caskets and kept them in my garage. The children were buried with the powder. The powder is beneath the cloth on which the dead children lie upon. Their graves are marked with the names Cyprain and Cyril. I had to register with the cemetery guard before burying them."

"Are you sure about all these?"

"Shoot me dead if you find out I'm lying but please let me go if you discover it is the truth."

"Fair enough!" Giwa was convinced. "Nevertheless, you will be tied here until we have the merchandise." Dr. Idoko was asked what he would like to eat and he was served. After each meal, his mouth was shut and he was allowed to watch the television until they decide on the next line of action. It was hard, but they eventually came out with a plan on how best to make a heist in a cemetery without attracting much attention.

Giwa hoped to carry out a flawless operation as his eyes were on the prize. Duff was already thinking of a second-hand car and throwing a big party. Gasko was eager to start up a legitimate business; something like running a beer palour. They craved for success.

* * * * *

The cemetery guard did not buy their idea at first; he said it was ridiculous to have two corpses transferred to another graveyard. Eighty thousand naira was used to persuade him to cooperate with them. It was his annual salary given to him in an instant; an amount he wished he could resist. The man opened a book which confirmed that Dr. Idoko was actually the buyer of the spaces and also the location of the graves of Cyril and Cyprain. They spotted the location and made an agreement with the cemetery guard to stage a drama when they returned at night.

Reverend Francis was a late night sleeper, he heard thuds from the far end of his backyard. Assuming the sound was coming from the cemetery, he crept to the location and beamed his torchlight on the sons of darkness. He became stunned when he got there. Giwa and Gasko had been too busy digging the second grave that they didn't notice when Duff sneaked away and when Reverend Francis arrived.

"Demons, sons of the night, who are you? And why are you digging up graves at this time?" He shouted, flashing his torchlight at the two of them. The boys were covered with dust. The sweat on their skins reflected rays from the torchlight even under the enshrouded dust.

"Sir, we just want to..."

"Do what? At this ungodly hour? You must be insane." He spoke with the authority of a priest, as if the robbers were part of his congregation, the penitent ones. He took out his phone and started punching some numbers.

"You don't want to try that," Duff cocked his pistol behind the priest's head. Instantly, his phone fell to the ground and Reverend Francis raised his hands up in total surrender. "If you say one more word, you will find yourself a space in between those graves, I swear."

"I am sorry, I didn't mean to scare you people," Reverend Francis said. Giwa and Gasko continued digging the second grave while Rev. Francis joined the cemetery guard in his cubicle, tied, gagged and blindfolded. When Rev. Francis and the cemetery guard were freed at dawn, the three robbers were long gone. The skeletons of the corpses were intact as well as the caskets too. Nobody knew what was actually stolen.

As soon as they reached home, Giwa ran a quick test for Daddy's Cocoa on the substance and it proved to be genuine. He pleaded with Duff and Gasko to try the stuff only when they had received their share of the money.

* * * * *

Barde, Solomon's police partner in the team, welcomed Solomon with fresh information on a heist that was carried out at St. Peter's Anglican cemetery on Thursday night. He knew about it because it was not far from his neighbourhood. He told Solomon that he noticed a white powdery substance around the casket. Solomon was excused by the team's assistant leader. They were fortunate, Superintendent

Okonkwo, in the course of the investigation, made it a duty to arrive last. At 8:30am, Barde and Solomon were at the scene, they waded through a crowd of people to get to the fore front. Solomon was able to get a sample of the powder which was mixed with dust before it was completely trampled upon. With Barde's help, he was able to get information on the owners of the graves and the depositor of the caskets. Solomon was utterly shocked to find out that Dr. Idoko bought the spaces for the burial of the unknown brothers, Cyprain and Cyril. Barde was returned to his boring team at the police station while Solomon dashed to his office with the sample he got.

"Morning, Maggie. Quick, can you run a drug typology test for this sample?" Solomon was panting.

"Morning, why not?" she produced some glassware and masked her nose and mouth. Ten minutes was enough time for Maggie to produce a result.

"It's a narc, where did you get it from?"

"It's a long story but can you run a test for Super Coca?"

"Mmm…yes, but I am not familiar with the procedure. Give me a minute to check it online."

"Solomon, have you found anything?" Caroline breezed in without greeting.

"Maybe."

"What do mean by 'maybe'?"

"Maggie's verification will confirm what we have found."

The C.O's footsteps and paces were calculated and heavy. They heard him coming towards Maggie's door.

"Good morning officers."

"Morning sir!" they responded in unison.

"Can somebody tell me the cause of the third world war?" he looked at Solomon, implying that the question was addressed to him.

"Sir, he has found the Super Coca," Maggie replied from another corner. "I have just run a test and a verification test for the sample he gave me."

Kolade raised a quizzical eyebrow, "What the hell is going on?" he was visibly angry, he felt he had been kept out of the loop. "Solomon, you were supposed to report to my office, and you are supposed to be with Superintendent Okonkwo's team at this moment."

Maggie became the fourth person in the inner caucus of the SBC case. Kolade was determined to handle the case discreetly. The members were all updated by Solomon to the last detail, including his meeting with Giwa Bako and KC twice on campus a few years ago. Caroline said that Giwa was a carbon copy of Solomon. In other words, they were looking for Solomon's other face. The four had ascertained that the kidnap of Dr. Idoko was related to the Super Coca which previously, no known agency had any intel on.

"What if the person we are looking for is not Giwa but a member of the SBC?" Caroline asked.

"Since my instincts have led me, I mean us, this far, I doubt if it will let us down at this moment. I strongly believe that Giwa is the key to solving the SBC case," Solomon replied.

"Are we depending on reason or your instincts?" Kolade wanted to know.

"Both, Sir — reason and instincts."

"Well, if Solomon's reasoning and insticts are our best bet for now, why don't we just hold on to them?" Maggie concurred and the others tacitly agreed in silence.

"What do you suppose should be our next line of action?" Caroline threw the question into the air. The de-facto leader grabbed it.

"We wait patiently for Dr. Idoko to be released, maybe by next week at most. In the meantime, I suggest we reproduce Giwa's picture and send to all our outstations while softcopies will be mailed to the headquarters to be broadcasted among branches of the NDLEA only."

"We'll be doomed if it reaches the police, the case will remain 'unsolved', once again," Kolade cautioned.

"What if the kidnappers ask for ransom?"

Solomon answered Caroline before she finished her question, "They won't, these guys are not professional kidnappers or robbers, they will not risk giving clues. They are after the drug and later, the money. And I'm afraid they are very close to it."

At the end of the briefing, Kolade stuck to Solomon with a tacit pledge to follow him until, at least, the SBC case was solved.

* * * * *

Superitendent Okonkwo was more apoplectic when Solomon arrived with Kolade. He could not conceal his anger.

"Where the hell have you been? You absconded without my permission," he was enraged.

"Has the team found anything new?" Solomon demanded, emboldened by the company of his boss.

"What do you mean, you narcotic bastard, who are you to talk to an officer of the law like that? This is my team," he said, facing Kolade and hitting his own chest, "On this team we kick your ass out if you don't work hard," he shifted his stare to Solomon.

"He is my staff and he reports directly to me," Kolade roared and stood in front of Superintendent Okonkwo like a Goliath challenging him to a duel. "For your information, he has been at the office with me since morning while you were wearing your asses out waiting for a ransom call."

"Well, I want him out of my team this very minute!" Okonkwo thundered as he moved closer to Kolade. He dared Kolade, who was standing on police turf. Ordinarily, Okonkwo would be pleading on bended knees for mercy if Kolade had confronted him elsewhere, but his ego ordered him to show himself as a tough person, at least while his surbordinates were watching. "I never recommended him anyway!"

"Fine, I was out of the team from the first day I came, I don't know how you get your rank anyway. It will be my pleasure to leave your team," Solomon mustered guts and spoke behind the intimidating live statue of his boss.

"Thank you, and the next time I see your dirty faces here, I'll have you spend a month in a stinking cell," Okonkwo yelled at the two figures in dark green uniform already leaving his office.

"Wait until we find the substance you are abusing that gives you this much foolhardiness, then you will know who we truly are." Kolade spoke without turning his back as they walked out of 'B' Division.

For the third day in a row, Superintendent Okonkwo was unable to gather any useful information aside from establishing the fact that Dr. Idoko was kidnapped. Okonkwo's problem was that he didn't even know where to look, and he was not humble enough to admit it.

* * * * *

Dr. Idoko came around on Saturday morning, he found himself in a hospital with his wife and children by his bedside. A teeming mob of journalists gathered outside the hospital to interview him. It seemed like a dream to him. A portion of his buried past had been resurrected and he didn't know for how long it would stay alive. He resolved to keep the details of the ordeal away from the police, while hoping the NDLEA would not nab him again if they got wind of what transpired.

"Thank God I am okay, that is all I can say for now." Dr. Idoko was shoved into a friend's car while the journalists scrambled like a swarm of bees for more photo shots of Dr. Idoko. The car sped off with other vehicles of friends trailing behind to his residence. It was a joyous moment for family and friends, some friends were grateful that the kidnappers didn't ask for a ransom, others thought their prayers had caused the kidnappers to free him out of confusion.

* * * * *

The good Samaritan farmer who found Dr. Idoko's unconscious body and reported to the police station along Zaria road was later incriminated by Superintendent Okonkwo as a prime suspect. Solomon pitied the poor man when he heard about it from Barde. He also informed Solomon about the hospital in which Dr. Idoko was being treated and his response to the treatment so far. Solomon dialled Kolade's number and in less than an hour, they were cruising in Kolade's car and headed for the Jos University Teaching Hospital, JUTH.

The duo arrived as Dr. Idoko was being led out of the hospital to his friends's car. The sight of Solomon's face urged him to stop. He pointed an accusing finger at him but didn't say a word, his wife pulled him gently and they sped away amidst the waiting convoy.

"It is Giwa who was behind the operation," Solomon remarked.

"He assumed you were the person," Kolade chuckled.

"With the way Dr. Idoko pointed his finger at you, I'm inclined to assume you are a suspect," Superintendent Okonkwo appeared in front of them.

Solomon joined his fists together and he pulled them up. "Where are your handcuffs?" Okonkwo felt embarrassed.

"Go ahead and show us how ridiculous a policeman you can be," Kolade urged him.

Okonkwo shook his head and went away with his boys. Solomon wondered what their report would look like. He thought about the poor farmer who found Dr. Idoko on his piece of land along Zaria road. The man would eventually be released but not until he spends a few nights with the mosquitoes in the police cell. Kolade suggested that they should interrogate Dr. Idoko at home. Monday afternoon was agreed upon, just in case they might get a lead. Solomon's first week had been fruitful. He needed the rest of the weekend to set his plans straight.

* * * * *

Only one media house reported the news of the attempt to steal corpses at St. Peter's Anglican Cemetery; no string could connect it with the kidnap of Dr. Idoko. The stories died down and Giwa was ready to trade.

Giwa had securely locked 200kg of the Diamond Fleece in his room and was trusting Gasko and Duff to guard it. They had enough to drink and smoke. Giwa was careful not to drop plenty cash for them else Duff would hire some bimbo who could squash their plan at the eleventh hour. *I'll find myself a good girl to settle down with when the whole deal is over,* he thought, as he walked towards the General's gate.

"Hold it there!" A soldier barked. Giwa guessed he was a Private so he paid little attention.

"I am here to see the General," he said confidently.

"Who are you?"

Giwa removed the dark spectacles from his face, "Tell him I am from the jungle." The private got on the intercom.

"He says what do you have?" The soldier's voice was softer.

"Tell him I have pawpaw leaves."

The gate was opened for Giwa, he marched in reminiscing those days when KC was beside him. Now he was his own boss and was about to become a millionaire. He waited in the sitting room. A chubby woman appeared from the kitchen. She recognized him instantly but he could hardly believe it was Amina Zubairu. Amina looked more beautiful and elegant. "Look what those years of zero supply have done for you." He was happy to see her in her sane mind. She was mad at Giwa for not replying her letters and was sorry for him when she heard about KC's death. She took down

Giwa's phone number and went back to the kitchen when the door to the General's office was opened. A young boy walked out of the office. He ignored Giwa who didn't give a damn about him or his sore ass too.

General Hamza came out tying the string of his basketball shorts properly. "Who do we have here? The elephant himself, king of the jungle!" He laughed. There were tiny drops of sweat on his face. He hugged Giwa, something he had never done before. The smell of his sweat repelled Giwa and the hug didn't last more than two seconds.

A bottle of Pink Lady was shared between them and they caught up on the last four years. His wife prepared fish pepper soup. Giwa enjoyed the delicious meal and drinks in the luxury of the General's home.

"Is there anything for me?" the General asked standing up, and belching irritatingly.

"Who am I to come before the General without a gift?"

"Hahaha, the elephant! King of the jungle! Shall we?" General Hamza pointed towards the door to his office, where all dirty and shoddy deals were executed. In the office, Giwa removed a 50g pack of Daddy's Cocoa which he fetched from the freshly stolen lot.

"Consider this as a propitiary gift from me to you for starving you of your favourite in the past few years." Giwa pushed it to the General's front.

The general smiled. "You can imagine what it feels like; it's like fasting for four long years without a reward." He poured a little on the well polished table and gave a generous sniff, "This is home, hoo!" General Hamza was obviously excited.

"The General!"

"Yes! What is it my king?" the General bowed sardonically to Giwa.

"I need help."

"Anything at all, and I will do it, just keep my cocoa coming."

That won't be a problem, there is already enough quantity to kill you, Giwa wanted to say. "I have over 150kg of your cocoa, Daddy's Cocoa, and I am willing to part with it for just thirty million naira, can you arrange a buyer for me? You'll have your cut when the deal is done." Giwa reserved the remaining cocoa for himself, he would sell it in smaller packs much later.

"What! That is a ridiculous offer, I can get fifteen people with thirty million naira each to buy your merchandise. How soon do you want it sold?" General Hamza indicated strong interest in the business, "and what is my percentage?"

"I want to sell it very soon, say, by Monday. You will take the tithe of the amount, that is three million naira."

"Let's make it four million."

"Deal." Giwa stretched his right hand to the General.

"I'll give you a call on Monday or Tuesday," the General said.

Giwa left the General's house on the same Saturday, he went to the hotel he used to patronize with KC, and then he was at the Knights club. Jemima was dead.

"Latifah passed on two years ago." That was all he got from the only stripper who knew her, others had changed their line of business, died, disappeared, or had totally forgotten about his Jemima; their Latifah. Giwa felt sorry for her. He left the club and on Sunday morning, he was on the first bus leaving Abuja for Jos.

* * * * *

"You are sure he is not one of the guys that kidnapped me?" Dr. Idoko asked when the three of them were left alone in his son's room. The agents asked for a private moment, Dr. Idoko's son's room happened to be the closest to the sitting room.

"I assure you he is not," Kolade clarified to him. "However, the person we are looking for looks just like him." He produced a picture of Giwa from his pocket. This is the guy.

"The boy asked me to help him with my wheel spanner, we got to their car, from there I saw myself in a dark room, I was strapped to a chair and gagged for four days, then I met myself in JUTH." He shook his head, "It was a terrible experience."

Solomon pried. "What did they ask you for and did you tell them anything?"

Dr. Idoko shook his head, "Nothing, I told them nothing, then they asked me for money and I said I was broke, maybe that was why they let me go." Solomon sensed Dr. Idoko was making up the story.

"I am sorry Dr. Idoko, maybe we should help you out. Those boys have been tracking you for the past, at least, five years. They are drug peddlers and they wanted your Super Coca," Dr. Idoko's eyes widened as he was haunted by his secret once more. "Those boys probably acted upon the information you gave them on where you buried those siblings. How did we know?" Solomon answered the question he asked by himself. "After the robbers made away with the substance at St. Peters cemetery, we picked a sample of the powder we found there and the quality matched your Super Coca. We also found your name as the depositor of those corpses at the cemetery." Solomon kept a straight face as he informed the man.

"I'm finished," Dr. Idoko said under his breath.

"You are not finished yet. Fortunately for you, you have a lifeline because we are the only ones that know about it."

"That is the same thing those rogues told me."

"Okay then, that makes three parties." Kolade stated.

"So what do you want from me?"

"Good question." Solomon observed the changes on his face. "First, we want to know if that was all the Super Coca you had in your possession; secondly, the quantity you hid which was stolen; and thirdly if there is any useful clue you might give us that will lead to the arrest of those criminals."

"I swear that was all the coca I had, I was afraid to sell it or destroy it. It was just a hundred kilogrammes. I know nothing about the boys or where it was kept after my abduction."

"Does that mean that we can arrest you if we find the quantity of the Super Coca to be more than that? Need I remind you that you are the only producer of Super Coca in the whole of this country?" Solomon threatened him.

"Hmm, actually, the quantity is more like 200kg of the drug," Dr. Idoko heaved a sigh. "That's the much I can say."

"It will be enough for now." Kolade motioned Solomon to stand up too. Dr. Idoko pleaded not to be invited should they apprehend the kidnappers. The deal was sealed. The officers got into Kolade's car. He paused before he started the engine.

"How and where do we find Giwa?"

"I have been asking myself the same question all weekend even up to this very moment," Solomon said.

"Why don't we spread some agents in disguise to bring in samples of the cocoa which we will use to get the Super Coca, and when we do, we shall trace the product to the supplier."

"Sounds like sailing round the world on a canoe, by the time we'll get the supplier, the Super Coca might have been down to 2kg. Remember, it is very much in high demand, its sale would spread like wildfire." They drove straight to the office and they reconvened at the end of working hours. Caroline and Maggie didn't go home. They waited to be updated.

* * * * *

At the end of Monday's meeting, Kolade gave a directive to all staff of the Investigations Department of NDLEA in Jos to appear in mufti the following day and comb all joints, hotels, and anywhere possible for Giwa. His photo was distributed to each of them. The search was to commence from Tuesday morning to Wednesday after working hours. They were advised to carry their pistols and pair themselves if necessary. Solomon was anxious to pair himself with Caroline; he thought the search would make more sense in the comfort of her car. Local taxi drivers and *okada* riders were potentially troublesome, the thought of that alone compelled him to stick with Caro as he needed to think clearly.

Monday evening was a vain search and so was Tuesday morning. Caroline drove them through many nooks and crannies. At noon, Solomon decided to take a break and visit his fiancee in school. He alighted from Caroline's car and stopped a commercial motorcycle. He employed his usual strategy of negotiating the price when the rider was already in motion; at such moments *okada* riders were reluctant to drop off their passengers if the passengers can't agree to their terms.

"Yaya! Yaya! Wait, wait..." Kyauta shouted as the *okada* zoomed off. She picked her phone and started dialling Giwa's number. She had just returned to Jos.

Caroline saw her calling Solomon 'Yaya'. She noticed a faint resemblance between them so she pulled over and walked up to the young girl who was busy on the phone. She patiently waited for her to hang up the call.

"It seems I saw you calling that guy that just left on *okada* 'Yaya', do you know him?" Solomon had told her that he had no siblings, an opportunity had provided itself for her to confirm that.

"Oh! That guy? No o, he just looks like my older brother, I almost mistook him for my brother, thank God he didn't respond. I would have embarrassed myself."

"What is your brother's name then?"

"Giwa, Giwa Bako." Kyauta was getting irritated with the way the woman was looking at her.

Bingo! "Wow!"

"Why... Why did you ask?"

Caroline was short of the right answer. "Nothing ... I just used to know one Giwa Bako at the University of Jos" Caroline fibbed. "That was way back in the early 2000s. "Just tell him Carol says hi, just in case we are talking about the same person."

Duff and Gasko came to pick her at the location she described to Giwa. Caroline had to back away when she noticed the boys waiting for Kyauta.

"Who's that woman?" Gasko asked without looking back. Notorious B.I.G's voice was heard in a rap, booming from the car stereo.

"Mtcheew! Don't mind her, we just met and she was asking me about something." Kyauta was cautious to leave out the real answer because she knew it would attract scolding from them, and perhaps some punishment from her brother.

"In any case, you should not be talking to strangers like that, if you do, you may lose your life someday, you know Giwa would not approve of it," Duff advised.

* * * * *

General Hamza was true to his words, he called on Tuesday morning. The buyer would be at his house with the cash. Giwa was advised to make the 150kg merchandise available. All his plans were tidied up; Kyauta was expected to return from Zonkwa. Duff checked the car's engine and said it was fit to cover the distance to Abuja.

"So what happens when we reach Abuja tomorrow?"

"You will be rewarded for your labour," Giwa replied Gasko bossily.

"Tomorrow is pay day, right?" Duff asked.

"Of course, you will be paid to the last dime in cash. You guys should decide whether you want to be paid here or in Abuja..." Duff didn't wait for him to complete the sentence.

"Abuja of course, I no come dis world to count people o! Man must flex too na. I want to spend my money in Abuja with the president." They laughed at Duff's joke. Giwa was ready, even eager, to let them go.

"After tomorrow, we are all going to split, we must not meet for a minimum of a year except you want us to be behind bars for some long years." They all agreed. Gasko was counting down in minutes for their Abuja trip. Duff was developing a tall tale he would tell and retell in joints he finds himself in far away from Jos.

* * * * *

Caroline was close to the target, she knew that calling Solomon or any other person at that moment would amount to a waste of time, and could make her lose her target. She allowed two cars in between the blue Peugeot 504 saloon and hers. She might lose them if they got a clue that they were being followed. A traffic hold up provided her an opportunity to dial Solomon's number, twice, but he wasn't picking. Kolade's number was another option but the poor network impeded her call. They got out of the hold up and she followed them as they took the quiet road of Rwan Chugwei. At that point, she knew they could be conscious of the possibility that they were being followed. She pulled over and resumed following from afar, a safe distance, and she was able to take note of the compound which they drove into. Maggie's number was switched off. *How could she stupidly take a phone with a low battery on a serious mission like this?* Caroline fumed. She couldn't risk calling any other person that could jeopardize the mission. Solomon's call finally came through.

"Where on earth are you? I have a strong lead on our guy, I don't want to leave the place. I am alone here; Kolade's phone isn't going through and Maggie's phone is switched off. I want you here now!" She ended the call when she saw the blue 504 coming out of the house again. Caroline opened her bonnet before the car got to her position.

Twenty

Adaku and a few other girls still occupied their rooms in the hostel. Most of the students had gone home for the break. Nandi had also gone home and Adaku was left alone in the room. She cooked Solomon's favourite — spaghetti and beans, and was reading a novel while she waited for him.

"You look famished honey," Adaku commented when she opened the door for Solomon.

"Famished is the word. In fact, I'm worn out." Solomon fell with a thud on her mattress like a bag of maize. He removed his wristwatch and phone from his pocket, dropped them on a short stool, then he lay supinely on her bed. His legs rested on her rug. "Nothing to show after all the work..."

"Honey you shouldn't be overworking yourself like that, you need a lot of rest."

"Can I, at least, get a glass of water? Your admonishment won't quench my thirst." Solomon's phone was ringing, he ignored it; he wished it was switched off. Ada handed him the glass of water. She peeped and saw the caller was Caroline so she ignored it too. The phone rang a second time. "Who's calling me?"

"I think it is Caroline."

"Caroline?" Solomon jerked up and sat on the bed. "You think?" He was angry. "Give me the phone," he ordered. Ada gave him the phone, reluctantly, with a hiss. She went to serve him from her pot. "Hello Caroline." He listened for a few seconds. "Are you sure about that?" Solomon took his watch and strapped it to his wrist as he held the phone with his shoulder raised on one side towards his head. The phone was wedged between his right shoulder and head slightly bent towards the shoulder. "Rwan Chugwei...Bukuru, yes, I'll be right there. Give me thirty minutes. He ended the call as he reached her door. Adaku dropped the steaming plate of food on the table and held her arms akimbo. She watched him with rapt amazement. A mild feeling of betrayal hit him. "Sweetheart, I have to go now, we are close to catching a big fish."

Adaku slid the engagement ring off her finger. She dropped it on the table. "If you leave this room, your ring will follow you outside. You and your ring will not just stay outside my room, but you will also stay outside my heart. I can't take this any longer. Must you be there? Are you the only one working?" Her voice was rising higher with each word. Solomon felt a wave of guilt spreading through his nerves. "Solomon, you know what? I am even confused. I don't even know whom you love but today, you must choose between me and your job!" Tears were running down her cheeks. Solomon was moved, he made to hug her but she shoved him away.

"Sweetheart, I love you and I love my job too. Honey, please..." He pleaded, yet indecisive. A part of him wanted to stay back with Adaku, but a larger part wanted to end the manhunt.

"I am not your sweetheart, your NDLEA is your sweetheart, or maybe that Caroline is your sweetheart." She sat on her bed and wept. She thought he would throw his arm around her shoulders to console her.

"I'll make it up to you when I come back, I promise. Love you!" Solomon went out in a flash and descended the staircase quickly. A text message appeared on his phone. It was from Caroline.

> *I don't know how you are going to do it, but I want you to appear as a roadside mechanic. I am pretending that my car is faulty here.*

Solomon then saw that he missed her call earlier. Reaching Caroline's place at Rwan Chugwai wasn't going to be a problem; but appearing as a roadside mechanic was definitely going to be a big problem. It implied risking himself to look like a madman. He hoped Adaku would never find out. Getting an amiable mechanic wasn't easy but he got one who was about closing, the same mechanic rented his tool box to Solomon but the box was filled with scrap metals and just two useful flat spanners. A dirty jungle hat covered a good portion of his face. Caroline couldn't help her laughter when she saw Solomon emerge from a bend.

"It's not funny Caroline, let's get to work." He felt different components of the car's engine with his hands, doing nothing on the car but bent on it while she updated him on the recent happenings.

Solomon tried to loosen some knots with his amateur dexterity. Notorious B.I.G's voice blasted again as the blue Peugeot 504 passed, the boys in the car looked hard at Solomon while he pretended to concentrate on his work, not minding passers-by. He noticed his replica's absence in the car. Caroline looked at her watch as if she was late for some appointment.

"I believe those guys suspected I was following them, that is why they came back through this road. I made a quick move and opened my bonnet as if something was wrong, so I had to ask you to appear in your Christmas clothes." She grinned. "Thank God you came on time sha! They may have known what I was up to."

"Christmas clothes eh! Thunder faya you." Solomon grined too. Finally, Caroline was able to reach Kolade who, fortunately, was still with Maggie. Kolade's suggestion was for a meeting at the office by nine o'clock of the same evening. Solomon was to remain in or around the car and feed them with any occurence from the target's house within his sight. So far, from what Dr. Idoko had said, and what Reverend Francis corroborated, Giwa was part of the three-man team that organized the operations. It was based on that finding that Kolade felt six officers were enough to bring the criminals down.

The night seemed much longer than Solomon thought it would be. He was called almost every thirty minutes up until the early hours of the morning. At 5:30am, Kolade ordered his men to surround the building. At his command, they all climbed the fence simultaneously at 6:00am on the dot. Giwa and his boys were already set to leave. Duff was about to switch on the ignition.

Six officers appeared in mufti, and each of them held a pistol. Duff made to pull out his 'gangster bitch.' "Don't Duff, if you shoot, we will all be dead. We are already outnumbered," Giwa mentioned.

"But we are already dead anyway, why don't we just shoot the bastards?"

"Come out now guys, slowly and carefully with your hands up, time is up! The game is over," Solomon shouted, seeing that they were contemplating their options in the car.

"Okay boys, come out!" Kolade's thunderous voice compelled them to surrender instantly.

"If I had known, I would have shot you since yesterday," Duff shouted. He looked at Caroline as she approached. Maggie had seized his 9mm.

"Am sorry, it's too late now brother," she locked his wrists in a handcuff and the others followed.

Solomon's team found three bags in the boot of the Peugeot 504. Three other officers went in and came out with the fourth bag of the Super Coca, and a young girl. Each bag was labelled 50kg, and only the seal on the fourth bag was broken. About 200kg of Super Coca in all.

"We will not need the girl. She just came in yesterday," Kolade remarked.

Giwa stared at his replica. He knew the face from a long time ago, he didn't know it would someday come back to hunt him. "Can I make one call before you take us away?"

"Yes, you are entitled to it but only when we get to the office," Caroline responded.

In three different cars, Giwa's team were separated and moved in a convoy along with the officers. The third car was Giwa's car. Kolade directed that they be driven straight to the state headquarters of the NDLEA, a facililty with over forty cells for criminals. Each of the boys was booked into a cell. Giwa was given his phone and sixty seconds to call one person, preferably his lawyer.

"The General," Giwa paused. "Fine, but we are in trouble, the NDLEA intercepted our merchandise on our way out." Giwa listened to the speaker at the other end. "Okay, thank you. Bye." He handed over the phone to Caroline. Their shirts and accessories were handed over to the cell guards. Kolade transported the drugs and his team to their office building. The whole team was tired after the successful raid. Kolade excused them to nap, clean up, and reconvene at the office by 4:00pm.

* * * * *

"I just got off the phone with your supplier." Chief Femi Otunba looked anxiously at General Hamza. "The stupid boy has been caught by the NDLEA." General Hamza shook his head.

"Are you saying he won't be coming over for the deal?"

"Yes, I am saying the deal has flopped. Lucky you, but those guys may come knocking on my door and if I am not careful, my face will be splashed all over newspapers, no one can tell how far it might go. They don't even have the guts to arrest me but my name shouldn't be seen again in those useless tabloids on account of something which I can handle."

"Then you have to find a way of letting the boy go, you are a man of influence General Hamza," Femi advised. Femi Otunba had been supplying drug peddlers on wholesale. He once sold the Super Coca. When the General advertised the merchandise to him, he liquidated one of his properties to purchase it. Femi was desperate for the Super Coca. It was a deal in which he stood to gain over two hundred percent profit.

"Look Femi, I know you are more concerned about the stuff that the poor boy in that cell wants to sell." Femi nodded. "I can find a way of getting it over to you but it will definitely take some time. I have loyal moles in that agency. The problem is that if I don't get that boy out, he may implicate me."

"That shouldn't be a problem."

"How so?"

"You must find a way of neutralizing him." General Hamza was confused. "If you don't want to get implicated, you must eliminate him." Femi said, more clearly.

"Hmm Femi, Femi, correct man!" Hamza looked at the floor, "It won't be a bad idea after all."

Amina was listening to the conversation. She feared her Giwa would be silenced forever. It was hard to imagine. She went back to the kitchen, cleaned her unused knife and kept praying for the right opportunity to use it on the monster that she was forced to live with.

*   *   *   *   *

General Hamza had promised him that he was going to get them out in an hour. Even though Giwa had no phone or watch on him, he was certain that more than five hours had passed since they spoke. The sun was beginning to set and it was going down with Giwa's hopes of being released. *I swear I'm going to implicate that useless General if he doesn't get me out of this cell by tomorrow*. The feeling of being betrayed overpowered him. Giwa had no one to live for aside from Kyauta and he was prepared to die if she would live.

He held the bars when he heard a familiar female voice; the space between the iron bars was too narrow to allow his head penetrate and peep. Desperately, he tried to mentally assign a face to the serene voice he was hearing but he was too hungry to think clearly. Footsteps were now approaching his cell. A young man offered him doughnut and a plastic bottle of coke. A lady appeared also in uniform. Giwa was unable to eat his doughnut any further than a mouthful bite. He held his breath for a long time, surprised, and ashamed of himself. Hannah was the lady in uniform.

"Giwa Bako?" He dropped his head and would not look at her. "It's a pity I am meeting you at the wrong place but I must say I am pleased to see you again." Hannah was also an officer in the Bursary department of the NDLEA. She belonged to a group of Christian officers who called themselves Second Chance Officers. They often met weekly for prayer meetings within the office, and as a routine, they would reach out to poor souls who were held in detention in their facility. Usually, they would preach to them starting with food — man's first need. "Giwa, this is another Hannah, not the one you used to know. I don't care what you did or attempted doing that got you here in this cell but I want to tell you that the keeper of your soul is anxious to forgive you. That person is Jesus Christ. He is willing to give you a second chance if only you will give him your heart. Yes, you may have been betrayed by friends but Jesus will never let you down." She spoke solemnly to Giwa. By the time she was through, Giwa was already sobbing.

"It's too late Hanny," he cried. "I am already on the road to perdition. Here, I am getting just what I deserve."

"That is why he loves you. The Bible says he loved us even while we were yet sinners, and that he came to set the captives free. Giwa, if we set you free here, then you are not free. But if your soul is free, then you are free indeed. Jesus came for the sick and not the physicians. You are the very person Jesus is looking for."

Hannah prayed with him after he declared that he had surrendered for Christ. She left him with a promise to return the following morning. Activities of the Second Chance Officers were encouraged because most of the repented souls freely confessed and volunteered useful information to the NDLEA. Many of the criminals were unbreakable, less than three of every ten detainees compromise.

For the very first time in his entire life, Giwa felt a strong wave of peace in his heart. He wondered if Gasko and Duff heeded the other two Second Chance Officers, and how they felt if they did. Amidst sobs, he recollected his past and wasted years, wishing the hands of time would move backwards so he could share the good news with KC and other members of the SBC. He wished it would take him back to Duff and Gasko so he could share it with them too before they were initiated into the Black Mamba. If Hanny was right about the second chance, then he stood a good chance of sharing his story with Kyauta. He would find Samson and tell him too, and Amina, perhaps the General too, Giwa thought. He had never felt cleaner in his mind than after his brief interaction with Hannah.

* * * * *

The half a dozen officers that were involved in the raid convened at Kolade's office. The Golden Fleece was safely hidden in a large metal box with two large padlocks and the door of Maggie's office too was firmly locked.

"Officers, if our operation was a football match, Solo here would have been the man of the match, or MVP, as some would say," Kolade looked at Solomon admiringly. "I must confess that I have never had an officer of your intellect, dedication and commitment to duty." He took his gaze away from Solomon. "However, that is not to say that we didn't do a superb teamwork. I am proud of you all but the work is not over yet. Solomon, Caroline, and George will debrief our suspects at the state office, in their cells, and then we will give a comprehensive report by tomorrow."

"Sir, what happens to the drugs?" Caroline asked.

"We are not taking them to any store; I have heard stories of cocaine being replaced with cassava flour or cannabis with dried and crushed maligna leaves before they are destroyed in front of the camera. I will not take that chance. I am suspicious of those sleazy bastards at the headquarters, and I won't place food on their table. The drugs will remain in this office until the national commandant of the agency comes to see it for himself. Then we will burn it all in his presence." Kolade responded clenching his fist as if Caroline was one of the "sleazy bastards" he was referring to.

Solomon thought about Adaku but he wanted to do his work first then he would spend more time with her during the weekend. He was lost in his thought when the team was dismissed. He stood up to go but Kolade sat him down. He brought out a small video camera from his cabinet.

"I want you to use this camera during your debriefing, anything can happen but this camera will give us solid evidence in case your clone changes his statement in court. I want everything recorded from the first minute to the last second."

* * * * *

Debriefing Duff was a huge waste of time, he wouldn't utter any word. Caroline was bored to death. Thankfully, she was not given any camcorder to record the two hours of silence, wild stares and minutes of dozing off while on duty. George and Gasko would have engaged themselves in a fist fight but for the iron bars between them. In the end, George couldn't provide more than half a page of notes he had taken from the aggressive and futile interview with Gasko.

"What did you say your name is again?" Giwa asked.

"Solomon."

"Solomon who?"

"Bakka."

Giwa shrugged. "So Mr. Solomon where are you from?"

"Listen Giwa, I should be asking you all that." He set the camera and began his inquiry, starting with the Super Coca. Giwa told him about his first meeting with KC, about Donald and the formation of SBC, Giwa told him about KC's death, how he killed Chiefo of the Black Mamba, and Da Don. He talked about the drugs they sold, General Hamza, Duff and Gasko, who bought what and where drugs were sold. It was like filling the dotted lines and missing links of the SBC file Solomon was given a week ago. *Giwa was truly the key*. Giwa spoke at length until midnight when Solomon's video camera had run out of battery.

"Why are you this honest, why tell me all these? This is uncommon with criminals." Solomon was perplexed.

"Because I am no longer a criminal."

"Since when?"

"This evening, when I met Jesus Christ." Solomon was humbled by Giwa's confession. He dropped his pen and pushed his file aside. Solomon went off record.

"Tell me about your childhood, where were you born?"

Giwa cleared his throat, "According to my late mother, I was born in a village called Tambes, somewhere on the Plateau. My father had advised that they kept the secret from me but she told me the truth a few years before her death. I was asked to keep it a secret too, and I did until this moment. My mother said my father was actually banished from the village for having an illicit affair with the chief's favourite wife who my mother said was attracted to my father. We had to leave immediately and go as far away as we could. They decided that Zonkwa was far enough. My uncle, Haruna, was also with them and I was an infant, not even up to a year old. She told me my father's actual name but I cannot recall it at the moment. He changed it to Bako and it applied to the children, including Harry." Giwa chuckled.

"Wait a minute, you mentioned Tambes. It is a village in Pankshin, and coincidentally, it is the village of my birth. I was born in the house of the village head but later on, I was told that my biological father had been banished from the land. Before my mother died, she warned me never to step on the land again. She used to visit me at the parish where I grew up but she stopped abruptly. After a long period, I learnt she had died." Solomon was silent. They suddenly picked the common events in their past. Giwa was thinking fast too.

"I think my father's real name was Bakka."

"You are my blood, my brother?" Solomon had finally found something more interesting than the case itself. The boys held hands and cried. They were separated by the bars but held together by a transcendental bond. "From the first time I saw you, I had an inexplicable feeling. Oh my God!" He spoke almost in a whisper as tears rolled down his cheeks.

"I felt the same way too. KC helped but the odds were far apart then." Too many things had happened to Giwa in the little space of a day. He had finally talked with his brother after many years of not knowing he had a brother.

At 3:00am, Solomon left with a promise to return at 8:00am. Giwa needed some rest too. He asked Solomon to bring their sister along with him. The cell felt warmer to Giwa, he was ready to face the punishment for all his crimes. He drifted into sleep. The night had to be short because the day was far too long.

* * * * *

"I'm sorry sir, we cannot release him until Officer Kolade tells us to do so, and he said these boys are high profile criminals," the cell guard maintained.

"Nonsense, I don't give a damn! As far as I'm concerned, I am the state commander and I want to carry up the case. Kolade is under my command."

"But the case is currently under his department sir, let him handle it or at least, let him give me the go-ahead to release him to you for transfer to Abuja headquarters."

"If that boy is not given to me in five minutes, I will have you fired," Lohsur threatened. Lohsur was the state commander; a short arrogant man whom Kolade believed was the biggest mole in the agency. Lohsur would have been sacked years earlier but he had the backing of a higher authority, even in the presidency. By merit, Lohsur was not supposed to rise above the rank of an inspector but concessions and politics in the agency worked out in his favour. It took just a phone call from General Hamza, a friend of his godfather, who was once in the army, to get Lohsur to become wild. His job was to get Giwa out of the gates by 8:30am to a place where a bunch of thugs would snatch him and escape with him. At least, that was what Hamza told him. He grabbed the keys and fished out Giwa himself. He dragged him out and walked towards the gate. The cell guard phoned Kolade.

"Where are you taking me to?"

"Just shut up and keep following me." Giwa was handcuffed so Lohsur dragged him by the arm.

Across the road, opposite the gate, Solomon held Kyauta's hand. A combination of surprise and annoyance showed on his face. He was madder because the much despised Lohsur was violating the procedures of the agency. Hannah was walking up to the gate, she was rushing to stop Lohsur if need be. A bus pulled over, Amina alighted from the bus and was running towards them, shouting "Giwa! Giwa!!" She got Giwa and Lohsur's attention but they were so distracted that they did not notice when a car in tinted glasses and no plate number, slammed its brakes in front of them. Giwa and Lohsur shared four bullets equally on their chests. They were shot in the same manner in which KC was killed.

As Giwa struggled to breathe, red, foamy bubbles escaped from his bloodied chest. His punctured lungs could no longer support his laboured attempts at respiration.

Eyes at half mast, he saw Solomon, Kyauta, Hannah and Amina. They seemed to be floating above him. He smiled at the most important people in his life, and then their faces gave way to that of his mother, his father, Uncle Harry and KC. Finally asphyxiated, with thick rivulets of blood running down both sides of his mouth, his lips stretched themselves in the semblance of a grimace as his frozen gaze fixed itself permanently on the cloudless blue sky.

Epilogue

Amina's mouth yearned to curse, but she wouldn't let it out yet, probably not at all. The curses welled from her heart; a cumulative grievance, hatred, even dissatisfaction with the man who happened to be her husband. She strode steadily through the gates of the mansion that housed her sorrows for more than a decade. The sight of junior soldiers in their khakis irked her much but not as much as their retired superior. A wish for an earthquake, or perhaps a volcanic eruption right in the centre of the house choked her mind. *And the stupid bastard will never be missed.* Tears had finally eluded her. Exhausted, she had poured it all over her blouse all the way from Jos. A fresh burst of energy ran through her when she set her eyes on General Hamza's gate; a firm resolve to settle a prolonged score.

She walked through the sitting room, noting the aquarium — her object of amusement in the house, wishing she was just one of the golden fishes, without emotions, just eating, breathing, swimming and waiting to die. In the kitchen, she pulled a drawer, unlabelled like all others whose contents confused her. Some of the drawers were empty but she was never at a loss for the one drawer which contained her most cherished unused knife. It came with a set of cutlery from Aunt Fatimah, being her wedding gift. For some bizarre reason, the unused knife was set apart, and while its peers were used, overused, broken, or thrown away, it remained stain-free. It would be fresh if it were a fruit. She caressed the sides of the blade — a habit she had formed since her first week in the house — the knife felt warm. The kitchen was her home in the house, and the knife her son. It knew about her agonies of miscarriages, the punches she got, the frustration of not living her dreams, everything bad she felt. When the effects of her drugs ebbed, it was always there, faithfully lying in the drawer, to provide an odd succour. The more she withdrew from the henny, the fonder she grew of her knife.

Cleaning it had become a daily routine for her, a ritual.

Tears clouded her eyes again, probably from some reservoir ducts. Two drops, one from each eye, escaped when her eyelids came together for a split second and sprang back to their place. A tear fell on a side of the blade while the other touched the floor. She wiped her tears and she cleaned the moisture on the unused knife. Heavy footsteps reached the door of her kitchen and she couldn't mistake it for anyone else's. It had to be the one man she loathed.

"Where on earth have you been?"

Silence.

The question graduated into a command, "I said, where on earth have you been?"

Another deafening silence followed. She stared through the window, at the garden, not even minding the turkeys with their red heads. She was staring into a picture she created in her mental faculty twelve years ago. The time seemed ripe for its actualization.

"Will you not answer me you rotten woman, you cheated on me, didn't you?"

Ha! Look who is talking about cheating, you must be mad. Amina was still mute. The kitchen door was slammed furiously. The loud bang hit her like the pangs of pain he had inflicted on her over the years. Without looking, she knew his fists were tightly held together. His slow steps informed her that he was reaching for his punching bag. She could tell, in less than three guesses, the exact clothes he was wearing, and even the meanness that now clung to his face. He was her first husband, and she was his second wife. She didn't know how his first wife died but she wasn't prepared to give up in the jaws of his fury. His footsteps drew closer, faster, and he didn't see the object that was clenched in her right hand. She anticipated the killing blow, even calculated its velocity and momentum as it swung past her head while she ducked under his arm. She had practiced the act mentally, a thousand times, but never, for once, physically, yet she was determined never to miss her single chance.

In one move, she reached for his chest. Finally, her knife was used for its conceived purpose. She drove it through his T-shirt, under his left breast. The blade was completely swallowed by his flesh and she felt his last pulse on the handle of the knife before she released it.

Author's Note

People who are familiar with the geography of Plateau and some other parts of Nigeria mentioned in this fiction will notice distortions in the settings of a few places. I suppose it is all part of the liberty enjoyed from poetic license.

Since September 2001, Plateau has continually witnessed bouts of ethno-religious violence, though stemmed at some period. Now, Nigeria suffers from the escalation of violence mostly in the North, evolving in manner and dichotomy. Drug abuse among youths seems to be on the increase, somehow infused into the spate of violence. I hope someday we will find peace.

You can reach the author via kotjyadok@gmail.com

Kraftgriots

Also in the series (FICTION) (*continued*)

Vincent Egbuson: *Zhero* (2011)
Ibrahim Buhari: *A Quiet Revolutionary* (2012)
Onyekachi Peter Onuoha: *Idara* (2012)
Akeem Adebiyi: *The Negative Courage* (2012)
Onyekachi Peter Onuoha: *Moonlight Lady* (2012)
Onyekachi Peter Onuoha: *Idara* (2012)
Akeem Adebiyi: *The Negative Courage* (2012)
Onyekachi Peter Onuoha: *Moonlight Lady* (2012)
Temitope Obasa: *Strokes of Life* (2012)
Chigbo Nnoli: *Save the Dream* (2012)
Florence Attamah-Abenemi: *A Bouquet of Regrets* (2013)
Ikechukwu Emmanuel Asika: *Tamara* (2013)
Aire Oboh: *Branded Fugitives* (2013)
Emmanuel Esemedafe: *The Schooldays of Edore* (2013)
Abubakar Gimba: *Footprints* (2013)
Emmanuel C.S. Ojukwu: *Sunset for Mr Dobromir* (2013)
Million John: *Amongst the Survivors* (2013)
Onyekachi Peter Onuoha: *My Father Lied* (2013)
Razinat T. Mohammed: *Habiba* (2013)
Onyekachi Peter Onuoha: *The Scream of Ola* (2013)
Oluwakemi Omowaire: *Dead Roses* (2014)
Chidubem Iweka: *So Bright a Darkness* (2014)
Asabe K. Usman: *Destinies of Life* (2014)
Stan-Collins Ubaka: *A Cry of Innocence* (2014)
Data Osa Don-Pedro: *Behind the Mask* (2014)
Stanley Ekwugha: *Your Heart My Home* (2014)
'Yemi Omolola Ajagbe: *The Triumph of Childhood Trials* (2014)
Ndubisi George: *Woes of Ikenga* (2014)
Nwanneka Obioma Nwala: *Wives on the Cross* (2014)

Printed in the United States
By Bookmasters